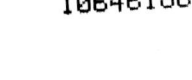

Cover design: C.S. Fritz
Formatting: Albatross Book Co.

For further information, contact:

Thousand Acres Press
825 Wildlife
Estes Park, CO 80517

Library of Congress Number: 2021945162
ISBN: 978-1-7372762-9-6

Tim Rayborn

"Qwyrk and Jilly are back, on a new crusade to save a boy named Lluck who is having some rather bad luck in Leeds. Once more evil forces are on the move, and an unlikely alliance of Otherworldly beings and mortals are the only defense. The worldview is wacky, the plot line is twisty, the dialogue is a demented fruitcake of British humor, and you won't be able to stop turning the pages…"

~Diana L. Paxson, author of *Sword of Avalon*

"Qwyrk is back along with Jilly, Blip (pardon me, Mr. Blippingstone) and friends for another adventure! In this tale, we get a deeper glimpse into Qwyrk's world, discover a boy of unusual circumstance and talent, learn more about Jilly's background, and there's even a fabulous queer love interest, all tied into a race against the clock to save the world from a nefarious being. Tim serves up another fun romp through a well-built world, full of wit, mystery, and magic!"

~ Laura Tempest Zakroff, author of *Anatomy of a Witch*

"Tim Rayborn does an outstanding job of expanding this magical world and the challenges posed by changing friendships and adversity alike. His ability to explore both outer and inner battles and bring to life a realm of magic that overlays reality and involves a number of characters in life-changing events will attract all ages, from advanced elementary children through adults. Tim Rayborn's series is fun, lively, unexpected, engrossing reading. *Lluck* is just as highly recommended as its predecessor, adding another series of encounters to an involving fantasy series."

~ Donovan's Literary Services / *Midwest Book Review*

CHAPTER ONE

"I'll be dead in a few seconds... or worse."

Still, he kept running, plowing through snowy lanes, stumbling more than once on wet cobblestones blanketed in a thin sheet of slippery ice and powder. His breathing was furious, his heart pounded, and he knew he was running out of time. He sprinted back out to a main street and worked his way through thronging crowds of holiday shoppers, trying to hide in their numbers.

"Blend in, shake them off!" But he knew his pursuers weren't interested in these people; they were only after him. He ducked into another alleyway, sped for the exit on the other side, and almost crashed into a padlocked gate.

"No!" He slammed the bars with his fists.

They were near; he could smell them, like bad fast food and garbage, with a hint of cheap cologne. But he tried pulling on the lock, and sure enough, it came loose. He laughed and opened the gate. Dashing through, he shut it behind him and relocked it.

"Have fun with that, you knobs!"

He turned around and there they were: grotesque, lumpy goblin creatures with mottled grey skin, bulbous noses, and large, pointy ears. They were mostly bald, except for some wiry black curls under said ears. Their snarling grins revealed bared, off-white crooked teeth. Beady yellow eyes completed the horrific ensemble.

"Well, well, what 'ave we got 'ere?" the larger one grumbled.

"Looks like a lost waif in need of some assistance to get to where he's goin'," the other replied.

"I'm not going with you, you tossers!" he shouted, defiant. He raised his fists in front of him. They just laughed.

"You gonna take us on in a fist fight, little boy?" the big one mocked. "That oughta be entertaining. Maybe I'll even let you get in a blow or two in before I mash your pretty face into the pavement!"

"Oh, I won't fight you, you miserable troll! I'm just getting ready."

"Ready for what, lambkin?" the smaller one sneered.

"For this!" He threw his open hands forward in one jerking motion, and at once, both fell on their behinds, slid on the ice, and smacked their heads on the stones. They groaned, but didn't get back up. He stepped over them (well, on them really, just to make a point; he might have even dug his boot heels in a bit) and made his way back to the crowds.

Once on the main street, he looked around and saw the town hall in the distance, with its multitudes packed in to celebrate the holiday festivities.

"All those people milling about; you can lose them there. Then get the hell out of here and head south."

He paused, took a deep breath, and ran again.

ONE

* * *

"I do love a good festive celebration!" Blip announced. Resembling a bipedal frog sporting a handlebar moustache and a proper Victorian-style mutton chop beard, he strolled along the pavement in his Regency riding boots, while swinging an ornate walking stick, every so often accidentally hitting a passerby and eliciting an astonished yelp. A red, woolen scarf wrapped snugly around his short, froggy neck completed the ensemble."

"I love it too! It's so much grander than the one in Knettles," Jilly Pleeth said in a hushed voice. She looked down at him, quite grateful that a magical two-foot creature who liked to expound on nineteenth-century philosophy couldn't be seen or heard by anyone over the age of thirteen, give or take a bit. Of course, there were plenty of children about, a few of whom gasped and stared; but most ignored him, being far more fascinated by the lights of the Leeds Christmas market, the aromas of cinnamon, nutmeg, and chocolate, the sounds of carols and stall hawkers, and the general merriment of the season. It was all rather like one of those displays in a department store window, but larger, louder, and less garish.

"We'll have to keep an eye on the time, though," she continued. "I need to meet mum and dad back at the train station in about an hour. They'll be done with their stupid real estate meeting and keen to get back home before it gets too dark."

"Come, come, my dear, no need to be so reserved, at least not in this instance! It's the holidays, and the day of your birth is also upon us—twelve years!—so just this once, it is entirely satisfactory that we kick up our proverbial heels and live a bit. The holiday market is splendidly arrayed in front of us, a fine old tradition that I am glad to see being kept alive. So, throw caution to the wind, and embrace the revelry!"

"Oh, it's not that," she whispered. "It's just, since most people can't see you, I look like I'm talking to myself, like I'm a bit mad."

"Hm, well yes, I do suppose that could cause some to think that you are a suitable candidate for admission to Bedlam, but again, this is the time for inversions of the social order in a controlled way, don't you know? The Feast of Fools! The Boy Bishop! Saturnalian silliness! So I say, let them think that you are singularly odd and be done with it! And other children can see me, so what does it matter?"

"Yeah, but they probably just think you're one of Father Christmas's elves, anyway," she said with an impish grin.

"Do not mention that reprobate in my company!" Blip admonished. "You know very well that the Father Christmas affair is a bone of contention with me!"

"Are you ever going to tell me what happened between you two?" she asked.

"A gentleman does not duel and tell, I'm afraid."

"You fought a duel with Father Christmas? Like, with pistols, or swords?"

"Twilziwop, actually."

"Twilziwhat?"

"Twilziwop. The opponents stand on a slightly raised beam and attempt to gain advantage by engaging one another with feather-stuffed cloth sacks, knocking the opponent completely off, if a good blow is struck."

"Hang on... you had a pillow fight with Father Christmas?" Jilly stopped in her tracks.

"If you want to put it in such vulgar terms, yes, I suppose."

"I don't believe this! Well? Out with it! What happened?"

"I shall say no more. My lips are sealed, save that I hope never to encounter the scoundrel again."

Jilly sighed. "Fine, but just remember, it's his season, so there will be reminders of him everywhere. And various blokes dressed up as him, too."

"A sorry state of affairs for which I can offer no remedy at the moment. However, when I am seated in the Lords..."

"Mr. Blip, look!" Jilly pointed.

"It's Mr. Blippingstone."

"I know, but look! They're about to light the main tree in front of the town hall."

"Excellent, splendid even! Nothing like decking the halls with greenery, good lighting, fa-la-la's, and general conviviality! It makes me want to burst into song!"

"It's really crowded here, though," Jilly answered, hoping to change the subject away from Blip launching into some horrid rendition of whatever carol came to his mind. "We might get a better view from over there." She pointed to a side alley across the main street and perpendicular to the hall, where no one was standing.

"A fine suggestion. Let's be off, then!"

They made their way to said alleyway and sure enough, it afforded a perfect view of the tree, an impressively tall—if slightly scraggly—pine arrayed with a multitude of shiny ornaments. Standing at a podium next to it was a man dressed in a dapper long, grey coat, and sporting a charcoal scarf, his salt-and-pepper hair neatly groomed. He smiled at the crowd and waved, his hand poised over a switch that would no doubt bring the whole thing to illuminated life.

"Good people of Leeds! It's my pleasure to light this lovely tree and inaugurate this festival with a splendid spectacle of color," he said. "But as we remember the joys of the season, let us not forget our obligations to those who are less fortunate. I urge you all to donate whatever you can to my organization, Greylocke Charities, where your Sterling will be put to good use for projects in Britain and abroad. Let's help everyone to have the happiest of holidays!" The crowd applauded.

"Who is that gentleman?" Blip mused. "He seems to be of very good stock."

"Don't know; Mr. Greylocke, I presume?"

"I never quite know with you if you are being magnificently perceptive or anarchically petulant."

"True," Jilly said with a smirk.

The man in grey flipped a switch, and the tree was at once aglow in a wash of sparkling and dazzling colors. Some in the crowd gasped, and another round of applause erupted.

"Ah, that's quite lovely, isn't it?" Jilly exclaimed.

"It is indeed, child. A fine reminder that even in the dark time of the year, hope can be rekindled, that even when the sun sets early, we know it shall rise again on the morrow, that even..."

Blip's musings were interrupted when both of them were hit from behind and went sprawling on the pavement.

"Ow! Hey, watch where you're going, you..." Jilly looked up to see a youth, probably no more than thirteen, standing there over them. Lanky and tall for his age, he had dark hair, brown eyes, and a tanned complexion. He was breathing hard and looked scared.

"Sorry," he whispered, turning to look behind him. "I didn't see you there, I just, look, I can't explain, I have to go, all right? Sorry again."

"Wait a moment, young gentleman!" Blip commanded as he pulled himself up and recovered his walking stick. He pointed it at the boy. "Don't move."

Jilly was surprised by how authoritative Blip sounded, and even more so by the fact that the boy obeyed him. He even looked a bit cowed.

"I'm not the first of my kind that you've seen, I take it," Blip continued.

The boy shook his head. "No, no, I think I've seen you lot before."

"And there is something about you, young man. Something special, I daresay."

"I... I don't know what you're talking about. Look, I can't stay here, all right, they're after me!"

"Who?" Jilly asked. "Who's after you?"

"You wouldn't believe me if I told you," he answered.

"Um, hello? Standing right here next to him." She pointed at Blip. "Quite sure I don't get too shocked these days! I know all about the magic world. It came crashing into my life last summer."

"Look, I don't want to get anyone else involved. This is my problem, all right? My fight, not yours. Just go out there and forget you ever saw me. It's better for you and me."

"Listen, young gentleman, if you are in some kind of trouble or danger, we can help. It's what we do. We're damned good at it, if I do say so. So, what is the problem?"

"Sorry, I have to go," he said, shaking his head and backing away from them. He turned and ran back down the alley he'd presumably just come from.

"Wait!" Jilly shouted, but he'd already run back out to the street on the other side. "Blip! We have to go after him!" Jilly started down the lane in pursuit.

"I'm not sure that is such a good idea!" Blip called after her.

"Why not?" She looked back to him, just as she ran into

something big and immovable, sending her tumbling to the pavement again. "Oof!"

"Because of them!" Blip answered, starting toward her, his oversized boots hindering his progress.

Jilly roused herself, looked up, and gasped.

"Well that's a very unpleasant sight," Blip said behind her. "Very unpleasant, indeed. About as unpleasant as an upset stomach on a fairground ride, or perhaps a hangnail immersed in salted lemon juice."

She looked up at two grey monsters, one larger, one smaller, both with skin like an elephant's, pointy ears, big noses, and horrid yellow eyes.

"Well, well, well. What do we find 'ere, Master Sneezewort?" the smaller of the two enquired in a shrill and raspy voice.

"Why, it would seem to be a human girl, Master Silktassel; a tiny mortal and her obnoxious little pet," the larger one replied, his voice deep and gravelly.

"Pet!" Blip shouted, stomping toward them. He gripped the end of his cane and pulled, revealing it to be a sword in a scabbard. "How dare you, sirs! I know what you are and what you indulge in, you abnormous ruffians. But I assure you that you have threatened the wrong folk! We have friends, very powerful friends who will not take kindly to your harassment and implied threats!"

"Do you see anyone else here, Silktassel?" The bigger one scratched his head and then picked his nose. Jilly winced.

"I do not, Sneezewort. I'm thinking that this 'ere little jirry-jirry is all talk and bluster and that he might therefore make a fine afternoon snack."

"Oh yeah, with some tea and cucumber sandwiches? Oy, do you remember? Are we supposed to extend the pinkie when drinking our tea, or is that just something we do when we're drinking their blood straight out of their necks?"

"I think it's a personal choice. I mean, if you're drinking the blood of royalty, you'd probably want to extend your little finger as a sign of respect, but for common mediocre morsels like these, it ain't worth your time."

"Common mediocre morsels?" Blip fumed.

Jilly had never seen Blip so livid.

"I'll have you know that I am a candidate in contention for a seat in the House of Lords," he said, shaking his fist, "and when I am so seated, you pug-nozzled pustule, you will be in for, as the young ones say, a world of hurt!"

"Ooh, I do like when they're down for a bit of a fight! What say you, Silktassel, should we divide 'im up between us? Split 'im right down the middle? Then maybe we can wash 'im down with the little girl?"

"All right, you tossers!" Jilly yelled, standing up and shaking her finger at them. "I've had just about enough of your crap." She stomped toward them, fist raised. "If you don't get out of here right now..."

Silktassel and Sneezewort looked momentarily surprised.

"Is she threatening us, Silktassel?"

"I believe so, Sneezewort."

"All right little girl, what ya got, eh? Gonna scream and burst our eardrums, eh?"

"Oh, just you wait!" Jilly sneered.

"Hey, you pillocks, over here!"

Jilly glanced past them to the far end of the alley. The boy was there again, waving his arms in the air.

"Come on, you lumpy arse-faces," he taunted. "I'm right here. Leave them alone; I'm the one you want!"

Silktassel looked at him, then back at Jilly and Blip, and bowed in a mocking manner. "Some other time, perhaps?"

He and his larger companion turned and lumbered down the lane in pursuit of their original quarry. But as they got closer, something odd happened. The boy stood there, just waiting for them, not looking especially frightened of the hundreds of pounds of fanged, blobby goblin-flesh bearing down on him. He flicked both hands toward them. They slipped on some ice, crashed into each other, careened into the side of the wall, and lay motionless, knocked out cold.

The boy laughed and clapped his hands together in triumph, before nodding to Jilly and Blip and running off again.

"Wait!" Jilly called out.

"Jilly, let him go," Blip cautioned, putting his hand on her arm. "We've been given a gift, so I suggest we make our exit and be away from these foul creatures."

"What are they?"

"Darkfae of a sort. Misshapen, grotesque, goblin monstrosities. They come in many forms and are not terribly bright or talented, but in groups, they can be quite dangerous. If they are looking for this lad, we can be sure that they are doing it at the behest of someone else, and that could spell trouble. I vote that we wander back through the market and head toward the station. These brutes won't pursue us there; they dislike large crowds even more than Shadows do."

"Shadows," Jilly mused and then her eyes widened. "We need to tell Qwyrk, I mean, if we could contact her. She might know what's going on. What if it's something to do with the whole de Soulis thing, you know, some supporter of his?"

"Yes, she has been frustratingly out of touch for some time," Blip agreed. "And you may be right. It's damned irritating, I know. I don't normally wish for her help, but I concede that it might be of use in this instance. Come, let's be off."

"But what happens if someone else sees them, or they wake up?"

"Oh, rather like me, they cannot be observed by most mortals. The fact that you can see them is probably due to being in my presence for some time now. You could be inadvertently imbibing a bit of the old jirry-jirry magic, you lucky girl!"

"Wait, does that mean that I might be able to see Qwyrk, too?"

"I honestly don't know, though Shadows are of a different order than these cretinous villains. I suppose we shall find out when you see her next. Now then, let's be on our way."

Jilly gave one last look down the alley. The creatures sprawled there in blissful unconscious slumber and the boy was nowhere to be seen.

"I want to find out who he is," she said. "We have to see if we can help him."

"First things first, my dear," Blip replied as he took her hand and dragged her back out into the main street.

A slightly out-of-tune brass band had struck up the refrain of a familiar carol, and a nearby chestnut vendor stood ready to supply chilled patrons with roasted, toasted, nutty delights. Blip inhaled deeply and smiled. "You know, thinking about it, we're in no immediate danger. I suppose we could take a few more moments to enjoy the festivities before making our exit."

"Yeah, I guess that'd be all right," Jilly answered, looking around at how "normal" everything seemed. "It still amazes me how this crazy magic just happens right under everyone's noses and nobody even sees it."

"That is the whole point, child, to be inconspicuous and let the mortal world progress on its own."

"Well, I'm just glad that I can see some of it, even if it's things like those two ghastly blokes." She pointed at the chestnut vendor. "You want some of those nuts?"

"I would not say no to such an offer."

Jilly bought a bag and handed it to Blip, who eagerly unwrapped them and devoured them like a boy digging into his favorite candy.

"I've never seen you do that before!" she commented with a laugh.

"There are a few mortal delicacies that I enjoy greatly, these being one of them. I am happily suffonsified," he answered through a full mouth of half-chomped nuts.

Jilly giggled to see him acting in such an "uncouth" manner. If only Qwyrk were here...

* * *

Their ordeal momentarily set to one side, they failed to notice a face in the crowd watching them emerge from the alley with great interest as they talked and wandered off toward the station.

* * *

In a small inn on the outskirts of northern Leeds, they waited to meet with her. It was a still night, but it was biting cold outside, and there was little activity in the establishment, certainly no sign of their special guest. They wore charcoal bowler hats, matching black trench coats over impeccable black suits, and sunglasses, even though it was already late. Each also sported a walking cane.

"This is the appointed place and the right time," one said to the other. "She will be here; I have no doubt that she is a woman of her word."

"Perhaps," said his companion. "I would hate to think that the work we've done so far might go to waste, even though we have received remuneration for it."

"Um, excuse me," the pub manager said to them. He was an older fellow, with a generous build, a receding hairline, and a thick northern accent. His shirt was permanently stained with numerous reminders of beers served in the past. "I was told to come see you? There's someone waitin' for you over in the dart room. She asked to be left alone in there; wouldn't let anyone else come in. She says she's ready to see you now."

"Thank you, sir. That is the best news I've heard all evening." He turned to his companion, "You see, Mr. Chives? I knew our efforts would not be in vain."

"I do hope you are correct, Mr. Dill."

Excusing themselves, they walked to the back of the pub and into a smaller, dimly lit room. She waited there for them, seated behind a small pub table. She wore a long, woolen purple cloak with a hood drawn over her head that obscured most of her face. A faint aroma of rose and amber wafted through the air. She exuded magic.

"I'm glad that you could make it, gentlemen. Please come in and sit down." Her voice was soothing, melodious, like a posh news-reader, but with something more esoteric than one might normally find on said nightly news.

"Thank you for agreeing to meet with us, ma'am," Dill said. "I think you will find that our discoveries are of interest to you." He and his associate pulled up nearby chairs.

"What have you learned?"

"He was definitely in Leeds as of yesterday. There have been no less than three reports of strange happenings in the presence of a boy matching his description. Events that were, shall we say, out of the ordinary and very clearly in his favor. He was spotted going to a cashpoint and randomly punching in numbers on the keypad. He did not even have a card for the bank, but apparently, the machine spat out several hundred pounds for him. Later, he was seen running across a street when a bus came around the corner, traveling too fast. It nearly struck him, but at the last moment, it swerved and missed him completely. He was not hurt, and the bus itself was undamaged, when it could very well have flipped over." She took in a sharp breath. "So, he's all right?"

"At least in regards to that incident, yes. I cannot confirm his status at the moment, but given his unusual nature, it would not surprise me if he has so far eluded any bad fortune and has providence on his side. It *is* what he does, ma'am."

"I am well aware of his abilities. So where is he now?"

"That, I am afraid to say, is not known to us at this precise moment, but we have learned that something odd happened today near the town hall, which means he is still likely within the city limits. We found two goblin Darkfae lying unconscious in an alleyway; that is no mean feat, as I'm sure you are aware. Whoever did it must have had considerable power, and probably more than a little luck, if you'll excuse the play on words. When they came to, they babbled to us something about a young lad tripping them up before they ran off. These kinds of incidents can only occur so often before we will be able to pinpoint his location. Magic leaves a trail, just like fingerprints."

"Are these Darkfae still after him?"

"Unknown at the moment, ma'am. It might have just been an unfortunate random encounter; unfortunate for them, that is. But if they are indeed pursuing him, we can safely say that someone knows about his abilities and likely wants him for some purpose."

She sighed. "Please work fast, and find out where he is. I fear that if he slips away from the city, the trail may go cold and we'll never find him."

"We will do everything in our power to prevent that from happening, ma'am."

"Thank you," she answered. "Let me know what you discover as soon as you do. You know how to contact me." She stood up, her cloak billowing about her almost in slow motion and went to leave the room.

"I do indeed," Dill answered, looking at the thin gold ring set with a green stone that he wore on his right ring finger. "Pardon, ma'am," Dill started, "before you leave, may we ask who it is that we have the pleasure of doing business with? Your down payment was most generous, and we feel that such knowledge could further enhance our working relationship."

"I would prefer not to say at the moment." She didn't turn to face them. "However, I can assure you that you have my gratitude, and I will see to it that you are paid in full, regardless of the outcome."

"I understand, ma'am, and that is very generous of you. Thank you, ma'am."

Without saying another word, she exited the room with an almost impossibly graceful motion.

"There is something about her, Mr. Dill, something very special indeed."

"I don't doubt it, Mr. Chives. Do you think she's dangerous?"

"I do not know yet. She is clearly very interested in this boy, but as to why? That remains a mystery for now. We shall take her payment, but if she proves to be troublesome, there are ways of dealing with her."

"Agreed, Mr. Dill."

"Now then, shall we indulge in a pint of the local refreshment? I so enjoy discovering what these out-of-the-way places have on offer."

"I like that idea very much, Mr. Dill."

"Peculiar times we live in, Mr. Chives. First, William de Soulis returns, and now this. Things are happening, my esteemed colleague. They are, indeed."

CHAPTER TWO

Jilly looked out her bedroom window at an impressive snow fall; thick, white flakes contrasted with the darkness beyond and created a soft carpet across the backyard. "I'm glad we made it home in time, it's really coming down now!"

"Yes, one wouldn't want to be caught out in it," Blip replied, lounging on her bed and polishing his monocle. "Lovely weather, but best viewed from inside a snug and warm home. A glass of brandy and Johann Sebastian Bach's *Brandenburg Concertos* would not be amiss at the moment, it must be said."

Jilly ignored his thinly-veiled request, given that she didn't know if her parents had that recording, and trying to explain what she was doing retrieving a bottle of brandy and a glass from their liquor cabinet would take a fair bit of effort. They did notice *some* of the things she did, after all.

"I really wish we knew more about that lad in Leeds, and why those things were after him," she said, changing the subject.

"Those goblins? Well, they're stupid louts to begin with, usually insufferable porridge-brained imbeciles like those two. They do others' dirty work like the good little pawns that they are, and they don't ask questions."

"Are they all like that? Big, nasty, and dumb, I mean?"

"No, not all. Some are quite clever and use that to their advantage in dominating and coercing the foolish among them to do their bidding. They make promises they can't or won't keep, stir up the resentment of other magical creatures, and try to harm the weak and vulnerable, while claiming to represent them, that sort of thing."

"Huh. Sounds a lot like some politicians."

Blip nodded. "It does indeed, my dear, it does indeed. But I promise that when I am seated in the Lords..."

"So, why would they be chasing him?" Jilly interjected, heading off that discussion for at least the fiftieth time. "I mean, is it because he has some kind of power?"

"Yes, I would hazard a guess that he can somehow bend the laws of probability when he concentrates on doing so."

"Do what?"

"It seems he can, quite literally, make his own luck; that is, cause events to go in his favor."

"That's amazing!"

"Indeed! And a rare gift."

"What kind of creature can do that?"

"None, specifically. Though there have been stories in the past about beings, mortals and otherwise, who possessed such a talent, it seems to be one of those anomalies that occasionally just pops up. He appeared human to me, it must be said, which makes him all the more odd, since he exuded fairly strong magic. In any case, such an ability would make him quite valuable."

TWO

"Right, if someone could control him, they could change luck to work out for them, by forcing him to do it."

"Precisely, which is why I suggested that those two ridiculous goblins were acting at the bidding of someone else, someone who knows of the existence of this boy and wants to capture him, probably for dark and nefarious purposes."

"Blip, we have to do something!"

"It's Mr. Blippingstone. And I agree. Is there anything that this new toplap contraption of yours can tell us?" He looked at Jilly's computer—resting on the bed nearby—with a mixture of confusion and revulsion.

"Laptop," Jilly chuckled. "I don't know, maybe? I'm so happy mum and dad gave it to me as a birthday present! It's much faster than their old computer, and now I don't have to work in the office downstairs."

She sat down next to him and opened it up. "What would I search for, though?"

"I don't know. Someone who knows a thing or two about our world and this rare phenomenon may have deemed it worthy to put into cyborg space."

"Cyber."

"Eh?"

"Cyberspace. That's not quite the right term, anyway."

"Hm, whatever. It's all abominable, if you ask me."

Jilly smiled. "I'm very glad you're here, Mr. Blip."

"Mr. Blippingstone. And I am as well, child, I am as well."

* * *

The next morning, after her parents had left, Jilly and Blip sat in the living room. Jilly was finishing a mug of tea, while Blip expounded on the intricacies of Kant's *New Elucidation of the First Principles of Metaphysical Cognition*. She tried her best to ignore him and looked out the window; after six months of his company as her "official" childhood companion, she was getting quite good at it. The snow had stopped, but the skies showed no signs of clearing.

"We should go to the *Swapping Shop* this morning and see if we can find any information on this whole business," she suggested. "I mean, maybe there's an old book about people from the past who could make themselves lucky, or something. It might give us a few clues about who that lad is, and what he might do next."

"It's possible," Blip conceded, "but my dear, do we really want to trudge through the snow on a hunch? It is dreadfully cold out, and I don't have the same immunity to the elements that some other magical beings do."

"Oh come on, where's your sense of adventure? We're on a mission, a quest to unravel a mystery! What's a little chilly weather compared to that? Where's your sense of fun?"

"I am quite fun, thank you very much! No one likes a good jest more than I do. For example: I once tried to teach my horse philosophy, but sadly, it did not work. After all, you cannot put Descartes before the horse. Ha! That's a real knee-slapper!"

Jilly considered leaving him at home. Or even better, just running away altogether.

A short time later, they were bundled up, despite Blip's objections, and ready to sojourn on up to the shop near the town center. The *Aloe Plant Swapping Shop* prided itself on holding all of the esoteric mysteries of the universe in one convenient three-story location, along with an assortment of candles, incense, and quality organic chocolates for after one's meditation.

TWO

"I still think this is a fool's errand," Blip complained, once again bedecked in his scarf and Regency boots. "There are better uses of our time."

"Don't worry," Jilly said in a reassuring voice as they left the cozy warmth of her house and waded out through the fresh snow that had fallen in the wee hours of the morning. "I'm sure we'll find exactly what we're looking for!"

* * *

"Well, that was a complete waste of time!" Jilly cursed.

She stomped out of the store, Blip following close behind, and turned left to make the rather-too-long-in-this-weather trudge back home.

"Indeed," Blip concurred, "one would think that in an establishment like this, there would be at least one tome on the effects of paranormal probability enhancement and the likelihood of genetic transference of such anomalous abilities down family lines. But nothing at all? A pathetic and useless vendor, not worthy of the prime location on the high street that it has been gifted."

"Come on then," Jilly sighed with resignation. "You were right; let's head on back home."

"What was that? I'm not quite sure I heard you correctly."

"I said let's go home."

"No, no. The other part, before that." Blip grinned in triumph.

Jilly rolled her eyes. "Fine, you were right. It was a waste of time!"

"Ha!" Blip clapped his hands together and strode ahead with insufferable smugness.

"Pssst! Jilly!" A voice came from the alley on the side of the store.

"Eh? Who's there?" she asked, squinting into the alleyway but seeing nothing. She noticed that Blip had assumed his karate kid crane pose, and she was very grateful that no one else could see him.

"Down here, come on! To the castle!" A faint shadow moved across her line of sight and faded into the distance at the far side of the old lane.

"No, it can't be!" she said, her hope and excitement mingling. She ran off down the alley in a flash, her smile growing bigger with each step.

"Jilly!" Blip called out. "Wait! Don't go chasing after phantom voices, it could be dangerous! We don't know who it is!"

But Jilly was already halfway down the lane and out of ear-shot, or rather, she pretended to be. After making a few twists and turns through the maze of old lanes, she emerged onto the town's overlook, which rested on a high cliff above the river, and was dom-inated by the majestic (if crumbling) ruin of a medieval castle. A light covering of snow dusted the ground, and the place was com-pletely abandoned, which was perfect. She saw another flicker of a shadow that seemed to beckon her to enter into the ground floor of the castle's dilapidated tower, and she bolted over to it without a moment's hesitation. She heard Blip panting along far behind, but paid no heed.

"Wait for me!" he puffed. "Don't make the same mistake that Hannibal did when..."

But Jilly paid no attention to him.

It took a moment for her eyes to adjust to the darkness inside the tower. But soon, she saw a shadowy shape with two red, glowing eyes standing at the far end. Now, normally this would terrify a young girl, even one as brave and adventurous as Jilly, but this was no ordinary phantom, and instead she just shouted, "It *is* you!" and ran to it.

Before she could say a word, it reached out to her. In its wraith-like hand was a dull silver amulet inscribed with archaic-looking symbols, hanging on a length of cord. "Here, put this on."

Jilly looked at it for a fraction of a second before taking it and slipping it over her head. All at once, the shadow took form and sure enough, there she was: a slender, elfin being with short, blonde, pixie-cut hair, pointed ears, and blue-green eyes, dressed in a stylish black leather jacket, form-fitting blue jeans, short black boots, and a wool scarf (that matched her eyes) wrapped around her neck. She smiled the warmest of smiles and held out her arms. "Hello Jilly!"

"Qwyrk!" Jilly yelled and ran to those open arms. The two nearly collapsed to the ground in a heap of laughter, teary eyes, and more laughter.

"Oh, Qwyrk! It's you, it's really you! I've missed you *so* much!"

"And I've missed you too, my dear, so much that it was painful to be away. I hate that I was gone for so long!"

"Really! It's been six months!" Jilly stood back and wiped tears from her eyes, while Qwyrk did the same. "I worried that you were never coming back, or that maybe something horrible had happened."

"Now that's highly unlikely." Qwyrk grinned. "Do you think after all the crap we went through last summer that I'd just let myself go and get killed or something stupid like that? Not likely! You're stuck with me, I'm afraid!"

Jilly laughed. "But where have you been? Have you discovered anything new? Did you find out who else tried to bring back de Soulis?"

"Not really," Qwyrk sighed in frustration. "I mean, we've uncovered a few things—some Shadows that might have helped him—but whatever they've done, they've managed to cover their tracks really well. I wanted to come here and see you, so often, but I just kept getting called back to search in other places. I've been all over Europe and Symphinity investigating, questioning, threatening—all right, that last part was kind of fun when it came to Nighttime Nasties. So far, I haven't found a whole lot."

Her irritated expression softened.

"But I remembered your birthday was coming up, and I knew I couldn't miss it. So I had a chat with my old mentor, Qwyzz, about what he might be able to do to help you see me properly again, and he came up with this nifty little magical contraption." She pointed to the amulet. "When you wear it, you'll be able to see me as I am. No need to be around evil sorcerers and their murdering, psycho Shadow bodies from now on! So, happy birthday, dear one!"

Jilly hugged her again. "Thank you! This is the best gift I could ever have. It's perfect, and I can see you and that's everything to me!"

"Ahem," Blip announced from the entrance to the tower. "Seeing as you've decided to return and grace us with your presence, Ms. Qwyrk—and this, I must reluctantly admit, is not entirely unwelcome—might I presume to partake of the demonstrations of affection that are appropriate during such reunion moments?"

"Blip, you sentimental old bastard, come here!" she laughed.

He ambled up to her and, surprising them all (probably Blip included), jumped into her arms and embraced her. "Damn good to see you my dear, damn good indeed, and I confess I never thought I would say that. However..." he said as he jumped back down to the ground after a moment, "there is only so much uninhibited joyful expression that one should engage in at any given time, even in this most festive of seasons. Anything beyond that is improper, indecorous, and frankly, a bit jejune."

Qwyrk smiled down at him. "Never change, Blip."

"I wouldn't dream of it. Now then, it is in fact fortuitous that you have returned, as we find ourselves investigating something of a mystery."

"Oh?" Qwyrk raised an eyebrow. "Do tell."

"How about we tell you back home?" Jilly said. "It's quite cold out, even though I know it doesn't really bother you. Um, why are you wearing a scarf and a jacket, anyway?"

"Well I like the look, and since it's the right time of year, there's no reason to go about flouting the fashion of the season. I mean, I could walk around naked if I really wanted to, but I doubt that would sit well with those who can actually see me."

"Not to mention being most uncouth," Blip interjected.

"But yes, of course, I'd love to chat and catch up back at your house! You can fill me in on all of the details of your new mystery. I could do with a bit of a break from all the tedious work I've been stuck into."

"I'm not so sure that this is something to welcome," Blip said in a darker tone.

"All right, now you have me worried." Qwyrk furrowed her brow.

"Come on, "Jilly said, "let's get back to my place and we can fill you in."

* * *

They elected to walk back, since Blip steadfastly refused to allow Qwyrk to hold on to both him and Jilly and make the journey in a series of long and high jumps, something she was quite good at doing. "That will never happen again, I can assure you," he'd said with a conviction that made both of them realize it was better to drop it and do things the old-fashioned way. An uneventful, if cold, stroll found them back at Jilly's home a half hour later.

"I suppose we could've teleported," Qwyrk said as they entered Jilly's house. "Qwyzz cooked up a special potion for me that lets me do it much more easily now. None of that needing to go home first and wearing myself out. I can basically go anywhere I like, as long as I know where I'm going."

"And the fact that you failed to mention this before we walked back in the cold was purely an accident, I take it," Blip said with a sour tone.

"No, I just thought it would be funny to see you shiver a bit!" She grinned.

Blip scowled.

"My parents are gone, as usual, which is actually a good thing," Jilly said, as they wandered into the living room. Odin, the squinty-eyed family dog, slept peacefully in the corner of the living room in his new heated dog bed, while a pretty, lighted tree adorned one corner and gave the whole place a festive air.

"I'm beginning to wonder if they're ever here," Qwyrk quipped as she flopped herself down on the familiar living room sofa and memories—good and bad—of last summer's adventures came back to her.

"Yeah, I feel that way a lot of the time," Jilly answered, a bit of sadness in her voice.

"Oh, my dear," Qwyrk said, standing right back up and going to comfort her with another hug. "I'm so sorry; I didn't mean anything by it. Please forgive me. I wasn't trying to make light of it, not at all."

Jilly just smiled and took her hand. "I know; it's all right, really. They're annoying as parents go, but I do wish they were a bit more interested in me, that's all."

"And you deserve that, every bit of it," Qwyrk answered. "They have an amazing daughter, and they're robbing themselves of precious time with you. I hope they come to their senses some day!"

"But you're back!" Jilly brightened up. "And that makes everything wonderful again."

"Well, I think you're giving me too much credit," Qwyrk said, flattered that Jilly held her in such high esteem. She and Jilly sat down on the sofa, and Blip hopped up to join them.

"So, why did you come back now?" Jilly asked. "Not that I'm complaining, or anything! That and the amulet," she said as she held it up, "are all I could want, really."

"Like I said, I knew it was your birthday, and it also gave me a chance to check in on Simon down in Leeds."

"Oh right, how's he doing? Taking care of the Ecklesons' garden and all that?"

Qwyrk grinned. "It actually looks quite nice now, if you can believe that! He still hasn't convinced them to get rid of the plastic flamingos and the garden gnome, though. And the rosebush is just a rosebush, thankfully; the dragon egg underneath it won't be stirring again for quite some time."

"Well, start slow and work from there, I suppose," Jilly said. "Jimmy's all right then?"

"I don't know; I figure I traumatized the poor boy enough last summer, so I left him alone this time!"

They shared a laugh and even Blip grinned. "The look on the lad's face when I smashed into his window was a bright moment in an otherwise horrific encounter, I must say."

"Yeah, that was classic!" Jilly grinned.

"So, tell me what's happening," Qwyrk said, taking a turn for the serious.

Jilly looked at Blip, "Do you want to tell her?"

He nodded. "We were in Leeds, partaking of the holiday festivities: chestnuts, hot cocoa, convivial atmosphere, fa la la's, and all those sort of things. Thank goodness that charlatan Father Christmas was nowhere to be found, just his feeble imposters who never seem to go away, no matter..."

Qwyrk gave him the "get on with it" look.

"Fine!" he grumbled. He relayed the events, while Qwyrk listened, increasingly uneasy and agitated. There was a moment of silence after he'd finished.

"Well, crap!" she said, breaking the quiet tension.

"This isn't good, is it?" Jilly asked.

"Not likely, no," Qwyrk answered. "Bollocks! Why is it that every time we meet up, some supernatural nonsense happens?"

"There is something special about that lad," Blip noted. "He may be human, but he's also more. His talent for bending probability is quite unique. I've seen nothing like it in some time"

"Yeah." Qwyrk nodded. "There are a whole lot of evil buggers out there that would like to have that kind of power in their arsenal. Thank Goddess that de Soulis never knew about him."

"What can we do for him, Qwyrk?" Jilly asked. "He was obviously scared and running for his life. I mean, the way he took out those two goblins was brilliant, but I'm worried that whoever sent them after him will just send more."

"A sound concern, my dear," Blip added, and Qwyrk nodded in agreement.

"Oh yeah, you can bet they're not done yet," Qwyrk said, "but at least he has some pretty impressive power going for him. If he could knock them out cold, he'll probably be all right, at least for the moment."

"We should try to find him," Jilly offered. "We were looking for some clues about who he might be up at the *Swapping Shop* right before we ran into you. This town's so odd; we figured there must have been something about people like him already written down."

"Any luck? So to speak."

"Not a thing, I'm afraid," Blip offered. "Not so much as a minuscule morsel of information, an infinitesimal drop of insight, a smattering of..."

"Blip?" Qwyrk interrupted, already having had enough. Actually, she was rather enjoying it all again, though she'd never admit that out loud. "Have you tried talking with Agnes—Granny—across the street? She might know something."

"I thought about it, but she's away a lot lately," Jilly answered. "I've no idea where she might be now."

"Crap," Qwyrk swore, her hopes for an easy solution dashed.

"Do you think he ran away from somewhere? The boy we saw?" Jilly asked.

"Probably," Qwyrk said. "He may have parents looking for him, or he may have been on his own for a while. With his abilities, he wouldn't want for food and money; he can probably just manifest both whenever he needs to."

"Gosh, I wouldn't mind being able to do that!"

But Qwyrk didn't share Jilly's enthusiasm. "That kind of power takes a lot of responsibility and training to wield properly. Right now, he's not much more than a time bomb. He needs guidance, or one of his probability manipulations is going to end up hurting someone, maybe even getting someone killed."

"So what can we do?"

"I think I'll take a jaunt down to Leeds this afternoon and sniff around a bit, see if any magical trails got dropped behind. Magic that potent must have left some residue."

"Exactly what I said!" Blip announced, looking pleased with himself.

"We could come with you," Jilly suggested.

"No, I should do this on my own, and it's *not* because you can't take care of yourself. You more than proved that when you buggered up de Soulis' plans right good. But I can cover ground more quickly than you can, and I won't be seen. And if I do run into him, I can talk with him and find out what's going on. If he saw Blip, then he can probably see me, too. But I promise I won't leave you out of the loop. Actually..." She paused for a moment. "I know how you can help. Can you sketch him for me? I mean, it'll be from memory and won't be perfect, but if you can approximate what he looks like, that would help."

"Yeah, I think so. Let me get my sketchpad." She jumped off the sofa and ran upstairs to her bedroom.

"Is it serious?" Blip asked.

"I doubt it's good news," Qwyrk answered. "These kinds of things usually aren't."

"Agreed. Given the unfortunate brouhaha over the last crisis, should we keep silent and try to solve this on our own for the moment? Especially if there are any stragglers from the de Soulis camp milling about in the shadows... no offense intended."

"None taken. Probably a good idea," Qwyrk said, realizing that bad news was once again making her agree with him, which rather irritated her.

Jilly came bounding down the stairs a minute later, sat down again between them, and began sketching. "Right, I'll have a go," she said. "He was maybe thirteen, with really dark hair that was a bit of a mess. He looked kind of Indian, South Asian, but different, somehow. He had dark eyes and was wearing a brown coat and blue jeans with black trainers, or hiking boots, or something. I didn't pay too much attention."

Blip nodded in agreement. "That's what I remember, as well. The boy looked like he hadn't had a proper bed, bath, or grooming in at least a few days."

Jilly drew as fast as she could and then held up her sketch. "This is him, more or less. It's not much to go on, but maybe it will help."

"I concur," Blip added, looking it over. "It's a reasonable likeness."

"It's better than nothing, thanks." Qwyrk folded it up and put it in her jacket pocket.

"So, you'll come back, right?" Jilly sounded a bit nervous.

Qwyrk gave her a reassuring pat on the shoulder. "Darling, I only just got here. I promise I won't disappear on you. This brief little reunion is the best thing I've done in months. I'll be back in a bit, and I'll let you know what I've found, if anything. And if nothing, we'll think of something else to try tomorrow."

"That's all right, then! I'll check online and see if I can find anything useful. Mum and Dad may be gone most of the time, but they did get me a nice new laptop for my birthday, so now I don't have to use their ancient computer in the office."

"See? I think they care about you more than they seem to; they just have a hard time showing it."

"Yeah, probably. But I can still be annoyed with them, can't I?"

"Of course! What else are parents for?"

Jilly laughed.

"Right," Qwyrk said as she stood up. "You get cracking on that snazzy new computer of yours, and maybe we'll get some answers."

"Yeah," Jilly glanced at Blip, "this new 'toplap' is brilliant."

"Petulant poppet," Blip grumbled.

Qwyrk looked back and forth between them. "Are you irritating him?"

Jilly nodded with a mischievous grin.

"Nice one! Keep up the good work!"

"If you're quite done being stroppy, Miss Pleeth," Blip admonished, "perhaps we could examine any pertinent information that you can retrieve on that blasted 'laptop' of yours."

"You see, sir?" Jilly said. "Technology can be a beautiful thing!"

"You'll come around to the modern world one of these days, Blip," Qwyrk added, "hopefully by the time you take up that seat in the House of Lords." And with that, she winked at them and disappeared in a flash of violet light.

CHAPTER THREE

Qwyrk knelt in the alleyway across from the Leeds town hall. She sniffed the air and her nostrils filled with the scent of sulfur and a hint of burnt coal, with a touch of grilled but rotten meat and cheap men's cologne? She exhaled and could see her breath in the winter cold.

"Well that's disgusting," she mused. "But yeah, definitely magic here." She could see traces of a glowing substance—almost like chalk dust—on the alley wall, presumably where the big goblins fell. It was something no mortal would be able to see.

"They've left their marks all over the place. Question is: where'd they go? And where did the boy go?"

She wandered down to the far end of the alley and sniffed again. A different scent lingered here, like sandalwood and patchouli incense.

"Bollocks! I hope it's not some woo-woo hippie wizard! That's all I need!" Her mind briefly flashed to the other hippie-ish fellow she'd met last summer, and she shuddered. "Can't be him, at least. He's off gallivanting around Goddess-know-where with one of my best friends." She shuddered again.

Shoving those unsettling thoughts from her mind, she tried to focus on which magical "scent" could point her in the right direction. She saw something, a kind of ripple resembling a mirage, floating in the air. Like a trail of breadcrumbs, it led away down the street to her right. Checking that there weren't too many mortals about who might be startled to see a shadow with glowing red eyes wandering casually down the pavement, she headed in that direction.

"The sun's setting, anyway," she decided. "I won't attract much attention."

After a good fifteen minutes and many twists and turns down a maze of streets, past solicitors' offices, corner shops, and an organic juice bar (there's always at least one), she found herself at a dead end. The magic ripple ended in a close, just some old office buildings and the like that seemed to be shut for good. She looked around in frustration; there were no signs that any of them had been disturbed in quite a while.

"I can see you, you know," an adolescent's defiant voice sounded out from a first-floor window of the building in front of her. "I know what you are; well, at least that you're not human."

"You're right. I'm not," Qwyrk answered, still not catching sight of him. "You ran into some friends of mine yesterday, you know."

"What, those stupid goblin things?"

"Good Goddess, no! I mean the girl and the jirry-jirry, over by the town hall. They said those creeps were chasing you, and they tried to help you, but you ran away."

"Of course I did! They couldn't help me, and they would've just gotten themselves killed if I hadn't stopped those creeps."

"That's an amazing thing you can do, by the way, make things turn out well for yourself."

"Yeah it's all right. But everyone thinks I'm a freak. I don't even know what I am. Just that I have these abilities, right, and I'm the only one who does. So I have to hide them, not talk about them."

"You can talk to me."

"Why should I?"

"Well, you said you know what I am. And one of my jobs is helping people, especially young folks like yourself."

"All I know is that regular people see you like a shadow, but to me you look more like an elf, or something."

Qwyrk rolled her yes. "Bloody hell, I'm *not* an elf, all right? Elves are just... silly. Yeah, I'm a Shadow, and I really can help you, if you'll let me. Those things after you yesterday, do you know what they wanted?"

"I reckon they wanted me to help them do something, probably something bad. That's all anyone seems to care about: what they can get out of me."

"Do you know who sent them? I'm sure they weren't acting on their own."

"No, no idea."

"Look, if you do know something," she said, not believing him, "you need to tell me. Those creatures might be incompetent, but they're dangerous, and they'll likely come for you again."

"I know. That's why I'm getting out of here. I have enough money to get a train to London, and it'll be a long time before they can find me there!"

"But what about your parents? They must be worried sick."

He didn't answer.

"Look," Qwyrk tried again. "If you come out and chat with me, maybe I can help, honestly. I won't hurt you. You can trust me."

There was a pause and then the ground floor door opened, and a young lad of about thirteen stepped out of the building. He looked very much like Jilly's drawing and description; Qwyrk was impressed with her friend's skills, yet again.

"How do you get in and out of a locked building?" she asked.

"Come on, you know what I can do."

"Right, never mind. My name is Qwyrk," she said holding out her hand to him. He edged toward her and finally took it, shaking it gently.

"I'm Lluck," he answered.

"Well, that's an appropriate name," she smiled.

"I think my mum gave it to me. Don't know why she added the extra 'L' to it though."

"Two 'L's at the beginning?"

"Yeah, like it's Welsh, or something. I don't even know how it's supposed to be pronounced, so I just say it like the regular old word."

"Where is she now, your mum?"

"No idea. I've never met her. She got rid of me right after I was born, apparently. Guess she didn't want to be around a freak."

"No, that can't be it; I think there's more to it. What about your dad?"

"Again, no clue. Never met him, and I don't know who he is or where he is."

"I'm so sorry. What happened?"

"I've bounced around the foster system my whole life. None of my foster families have been horrible or anything, they're just, I don't know, so different that we don't connect at all. They always seem to know there's something odd about me, but they just try to avoid me as much as possible. We never talk about it and they hardly even notice when I'm gone. When I left my latest hosts a couple days ago, I told them I was staying at a friend's house for a few days, and they just shrugged. They don't know that I don't have any real friends. No one ever does." He looked away.

Qwyrk began to feel sorry for him.

"So, why are you here?" she asked.

"It's like, all my life, I've known I was different, right? And sometimes, it's like others know, too. I feel like I'm being watched. Sometimes it's really creepy but sometimes, it's kind of nice. When I was little, I'd tell myself that the nice times were my mum—my *real* mum—checking in on me, making sure I was all right. But the creepy stuff, I don't know what that was. I figured it was all just in my head, at least until those things found me a few days ago. That's why I bolted; to get away from them."

"It's not all in your head," she said. "Look, this is going to sound strange, but I think that one of your parents might be different, like me, and the other is probably human. That would explain why you have these abilities. See, people like you are rare, and it's not safe for you to be in our world for too long. So, your real parents probably thought it was best to hide you with humans, and hope that you could have a normal life."

"Don't know. But even if that's true, I'm not normal."

"But what's 'normal' anyway? And you're not a freak, either. You have a very special gift, and if you can learn to control it, you could be amazing."

"I do well enough on my own," he said with a degree of adolescent defiance in his voice that Qwyrk found irritating.

"Well enough up till now," she said, "but what happens if those dumb monsters come back again? What if they bring more of them?"

"Don't know. I'll think of something. Like I said, I'm getting a train to London tonight, so unless they want to run alongside it all the way there, they'll be left looking dead stupid."

"I have a better idea. Why don't you let me help? Come back with me to Knettles. My friends are there, the ones you crashed into yesterday. They're brilliant—well, one of them is—and we have a bit of a knack for solving weird mysteries. Maybe we can find your real parents. Those creatures won't be able to get to you. It'll be a nicer, warmer place than here. Maybe even some food. What do you say?"

Lluck stared off into space for a moment and sighed. "Fine, for now. But if I don't like it, tomorrow I'm getting on a train for London, or Manchester, or wherever, and you're not stopping me."

Qwyrk nodded. "Fair enough."

He motioned behind him. "I'm just gonna get my things."

"You will come back, right?"

He gave her a look that said, "Of course I will," and dashed back into the building. She was relieved when he emerged a few minutes later with a large rucksack over his shoulder.

"So, how are we getting to Knettles?" he asked.

"I have more than one way, actually, but the best is just to pop right into town from here. It'll only take a few moments."

He looked at her in wonder. "You mean like, teleportation or something?"

"Yeah, it's cool!" She put an arm around him. "Hang on!"

*   *   *

"Do you think she's found anything?" Jilly asked Blip. She stared out her bedroom window at the darkening sky over the snow-blanketed backyard.

"Well, she is quite resourceful, I am pained to concede. If she has discovered anything, it will no doubt be of some interest." Blip sat on the edge of her bed, this time polishing the blade of his sword cane with a white cloth.

"Who do you think he is?"

"I'm not sure. I believe that the lad is both human and more than that, which suggests a mixed parentage."

"So, he might have like a faerie mother and a human father, or something?"

"It's entirely possible. His sort of talent is not normally found among, as you say, Fae, to say nothing of humans, but the mingling of their essences may have resulted in just such a unique magical mutation. It's quite rare, in any case. Because of the magical intricacies involved, children are rarely born of such unions. Oh, um... your parents have spoken to you about such biological things, I presume?"

Jilly rolled her eyes. "Yes, I'm fully aware that babies don't come from storks, thank you. Not so sure about faerie babies, though..."

"It's essentially the same process."

"Fair enough. Anyway, I hope he's all right, whoever he is."

"As do I. Come," he sheathed his sword and set the cane aside. "Shall we begin with a discussion of Husserl's Phenomenology in its early days? It's quite delicious, if I do say myself, a veritable Yorkshire Pudding of consciousness studies with a healthy dollop of epoché gravy!"

"Um, it sounds fascinating, but can we put it off for a bit? I'd rather wait until Qwyrk gets back; then maybe we can start on it tomorrow, all right?" Jilly was proud that in recent months, she'd become adept at stalling and avoiding his painful philosophical lectures.

"Very well, but I'm just offering up thrilling ways to pass the time that will be both enlightening and amusing. We could both use a hearty serving of ataraxia."

"Pssst! Jilly! Blip!" Qwyrk's head (and just her head) appeared in the middle of Jilly's room, surrounded by purple light.

Blip fell off the bed, and his cane hit him on the head. "Great horned owls of Minerva, woman! Are you trying to given me an apoplectic attack?"

"Sorry!" Qwyrk said in a not-convincing voice; actually she seemed to suppress a laugh. "I just wanted to make sure it was safe to come in here before I..."

"Before what?" Jilly asked, more than a little unnerved at seeing only Qwyrk's head.

"Um, I'll just have to show you. Hang on, be right back." She vanished in a flash of purple sparks.

"Did you know she could do that?" Jilly pointed to where Qwyrk's face had been and looked at Blip, who was picking himself up off the floor.

"No, and I'd be quite happy if she never did it again! Uncouth, undisciplined..."

In another flash, Qwyrk was back, with her full body this time, and she wasn't alone. The lad who had bumped into them yesterday was with her.

"Right," she said. "Jilly, Blip? This is Lluck. You've already met, sort of."

Lluck smiled a little and waved. "All right? Sorry about yesterday. It all happened so fast. I just needed to get out of there, and you were sort of in my way."

"Yeah, hi," Jilly said, looking him up and down.

Blip nodded. "Greetings, young man. Despite the chaos of the situation, you handled yourself most admirably against those repulsive creatures."

"Um, thanks, I guess."

"Qwyrk," Jilly said looking at her, "how did you find him so fast? I thought maybe you'd come back with a bit of information or something, but not, well... him!"

"I've been doing this sort of thing for a while, you know. That little alley tussle left quite the imprint for those of us that can see it. All I had to do was follow the magical trail, like ethereal breadcrumbs."

Jilly wondered for a moment why food metaphors were all the rage this evening.

Qwyrk recounted what had happened, and why they'd decided to return here.

"So, um... Jilly," Qwyrk hesitated. "Would it be all right if he stayed here for a day or two? I know it's not convenient, but it's the best solution I've got at the moment."

"What, you mean like sleep here, in my room? Qwyrk, that's a really bad idea." She looked at Lluck. "No offense, mate."

Lluck just shrugged.

"Can't he stay somewhere in town, like at a B&B, or wherever?" she asked.

"I'd really rather he didn't, Jilly. He's special, and that makes it a bad idea to leave him unattended. If those goblins found him before, they'll do it again. I need him safe so I can keep an eye on what's happening."

"She's quite right," Blip offered. "Plus we have no mortal coinage to set him up in such an establishment, and even if we did, I doubt they would accept a girl of your age going in and paying for an evening's lodging on his behalf; and it would have to be you. I must agree with Qwyrk that it's better for the boy to remain here for the time being."

"But how am I going to explain that to my parents, eh? 'Oh, mum, dad? I have a boy staying in my room now, at least for a few days. I hope that's all right with you?' Even *they* aren't going to be good with that. Also... boy. In my room. What the hell, Qwyrk?"

"If it makes you feel any better," Lluck said, "I don't really want to be staying in a girl's room, either."

Jilly pointed to him. "There! See? We both think it's a rubbish idea. So, can we just come up with a better plan?"

"Fine, how about just for tonight?" Qwyrk implored. "One night, Jilly, that's all. I'll try to sort out something else in the morning. I just really don't want to let him out of my sight right now."

Jilly let out a heavy sigh of exasperation that was maybe a little bit too dramatic to make her point. "Fine, all right, one night only. And he sleeps on the floor, over there, as far away as possible."

"You know, I *am* standing right here," Lluck pointed to his feet.

"Sorry," Jilly grumped again. "I just don't like having my personal space invaded out of the blue, you know?"

"No, I get it," he said. "I don't, either."

"One other thing," Qwyrk said with hesitation.

Jilly gave her a raised eyebrow with a half-squint.

"Do you mind inviting him down for dinner tonight?"

"Oh, come on, Qwyrk!"

"Sorry! It just seems cruel to leave him up here with us while you go and eat. Just tell your parents he's a friend from school, and you were studying together, or something."

"Uh, school's out right now, holidays and all that."

"Well, you must have projects to work on over the break, right? I don't know much about human schools, but they do that sort of thing, right?"

Jilly sighed again. "Yeah, fine, I'll make up something." She looked at Lluck. "My mum's cooking is rubbish, but if you can stand that, you'll at least get something to eat."

"It's fine, whatever," he said. "Beats living on bacon sandwiches and flapjacks."

"I wouldn't be so sure," Jilly replied. She looked at Qwyrk again and pointed a defiant finger at her. "One night, one dinner, and you're going to owe me for this."

"Oh, I'm so bloody sorry! It's not like I expected to find him. But I did, and here he is, and we have to do something for now. I thought we were a pretty good team, or has that whole 'helping people' thing gone out the window in the months that I've been away?"

Jilly felt a little ashamed. "No it hasn't." She smiled weakly at both of them. "I'm sorry. Come on, I'll take you downstairs and introduce you to my mum; I don't think my dad's home yet. I must warn you though, they're, well, strange."

"Couldn't be any stranger than my foster families so far," Lluck said.

"We'll see. Just let me do the talking and everything will be fine."

＊　＊　＊

"Well, that was a complete, utter disaster!" Jilly fumed.

"Come now, my dear. It can't have been that bad!" Blip tried to reassure her as they sat in her bedroom after dinner. "Where is the lad now?"

"He pretended to leave, and Qwyrk is going to collect him in a few minutes and blink him back up here."

"Blink?"

"You know, teleport, whatever that thing is she does."

As if on cue, the two of them materialized in a flash of violet next to Jilly's bed.

"Sweet sacrosanct stones of Sisyphus, girl! I do wish you'd give us a bit more warning before doing that!" Blip clutched at his chest, obviously feigning some sort of jirry-jirry version of a near stroke. He wasn't very convincing.

"Are you kidding?" Qwyrk beamed. "Seeing the look on your face is what makes it worth doing!"

Jilly stood by the window scowling, refusing to acknowledge them.

"What?" Lluck whispered, looking at her. "I said I was sorry!"

"Yeah, well, that doesn't cut it, does it?" she snapped. "I told them you were a friend from school, and then you had to go and say you live in York, and then they were all mystified about how we could go to the same school, and then you had to cock it up even more by saying you were visiting up from Leeds, and then they wanted to know why you were living in two places, so you told them your parents were divorced but they send you to school up here, and then they looked at me like I was lying and they hardly ever notice me and when they actually do, I would appreciate if they didn't think I was some lying, potential criminal, thank you very much!"

That Jilly got all of that out in one breath was rather astonishing to her and probably to everyone else in the room.

"If they find out you're back up here," she lowered her voice to a whisper, "I'm in deep shite. I nearly blew it last summer with these two mucking about like idiots in the living room one morning—um, no offense—and I'd rather not repeat that."

"Nor I," said Blip. "Qwyrk broke my prized opera-singing walking stick on that little adventure, and I'd rather never relive that."

"Does he have to stay here?" Jilly turned to Qwyrk.

"Jilly, I have no other choice right now. You know why I can't take him to my world…"

"Because I'll go crazy?" Lluck sneered. "Because I'm a freak? I'm either not human enough for my foster family and everyone else, or too human for whatever all of you are, and I don't fit in anywhere. You're just like everyone else, so sod the lot of you! I'm leaving." He stomped over to his rucksack.

"I can't let you do that, Lluck," Qwyrk said in a commanding voice. "Don't make me stop you against your will; you wouldn't like it, trust me."

"Go on then, give it a try," he countered. "You know what I can do. I can take you. Try using your magic on me, and see how far it gets you."

Qwyrk hesitated for just a moment, her face bristling with anger.

"Look, nobody's going anywhere," Jilly said with a sigh. "Can we all just calm down a bit?"

"Quite right," Blip interjected. "You're making fools of yourselves. It will do no one any good at all if we quarrel amongst ourselves. We face a new mystery, one that should be uniting us, not tearing us apart. I, for one, want to know more about this lad; who he is, where he really comes from, who his true parents are. Young man," he said, addressing Lluck, "despite what you have seen so far, these folk, though a bit rough around the edges, are of a good sort, an excellent sort, even. I believe that with our help, you can reclaim your proper heritage and learn who you are. You stand a far better chance of it with us on your side than on your own, where there are many dangers awaiting you. So then, what do you say?"

Lluck seemed hesitant and looked back and forth between them before dropping his bag on the floor with a resigned sigh.

"Good lad."

Qwyrk flashed a relieved smile to Blip. "That was quite a speech."

"Well, someone had to be the adult, after all."

Jilly rolled her eyes and looked at Lluck. "Fine, stay the night, but we're fixing this tomorrow, so that you can get to wherever you're supposed to be. And like I said, you're sleeping in the corner."

"Whatever. I wouldn't want a girl's bed, anyway."

"And what's wrong with it?"

"Kids," Qwyrk interrupted with a strained smile, "let's try to be civil, all right? Lluck, have a seat. I want you to tell us everything you know about yourself and about the goblins that were chasing you. I know you've already told me, but Blip and Jilly need to get up to speed."

With another (and quite possibly overdramatic) sigh, Lluck recounted the same story he had told Qwyrk.

"So basically," he concluded after retelling it all, "I don't know who I am, I don't know who my parents are, I don't know who's been watching me, and I don't know why those things were chasing me. Any ideas?"

The room was unusually silent, given this trio's proclivity toward verbosity, strong opinion, and argument.

"Yeah, didn't think so! Well, good luck figuring it out then. I haven't been able to in thirteen years; let me know what you come up with."

"Look," Qwyrk said, "this may take a while. I suspect it's more complicated than it seems, and..."

"What was that?" Jilly whispered in a harsh voice.

Everyone stopped bickering for the moment and listened.

"Something's outside, in the backyard," Qwyrk said. "Stay here, all of you; I'll check it out."

* * *

Dill sniffed the chilly night air, inhaling deep, closing his eyes and thinking. He turned his head, trying to ascertain any clues from the area. He had no doubt that something significant happened recently.

"There is magic here, Mr. Chives," he said to his companion who surveyed a close with shuttered office buildings, "and it is not only the young fellow who we are pursuing. I catch a faint whiff of lavender, which tells me that something more is participating in this chase."

"Fae, Mr. Dill?"

"Possibly, Mr. Chives, but I am not completely convinced. I would hazard a guess that it may even be a Shadow, and given the unpleasantness that this world recently endured with one of those folk, this is potentially a cause for some concern."

"Should we tell our client about this unfortunate development, Mr. Dill?"

"I do not believe that will be necessary... yet. However, should things become more complicated, it would be incumbent upon us to inform her of this new situation. It is possible that a Shadow has crossed paths with the lad whom we are seeking. It is also possible that said Shadow is merely on the trail of the boy, as are we."

"And what would a Shadow want with him?"

"That, Mr. Dill, is a mystery that we cannot yet unravel. I suggest that we find ourselves a good local public house, sample a pint of something regional, and discuss our options further. The chill in the winter air is getting a bit much, don't you think?"

"I do indeed, Mr. Chives, and an excellent suggestion you have, might I add."

"I do try, Mr. Dill. All work and no play makes one a bit of a dullard, after all."

"Too much of the local libation, and we might become dullards, anyway."

"That is a risk I am willing to take, Mr. Dill."

"I share your sense of adventure, Mr. Chives."

CHAPTER FOUR

Qwyrk melded into the shadows along the back wall of the Pleeths' home. Sure enough, she saw two bloated figures, one large and one small, on the other side of the yard, crouched down by a tree and partially hidden behind the random shrubbery.

"They couldn't look more conspicuous if they tried." Rolling her eyes, she readied herself to give them a good pounding, when the smaller of the two spoke.

"Do you reckon he's up there, then? In the room with the light on?" It was a rough voice that wasn't really a whisper.

"It's likely; I can smell him." The taller one with the deeper voice motioned to his oversized nose.

"Get out! You can't, you're just sayin' that to sound all fancy like."

"Shut your mouth, numbskull. I can, too. I have a highly-developed olé factory sense."

"You what?"

"Olé factory. I think it's some place in Spain where they make fancy perfumes, or extra noses, or somethin'. Anyway, I got it, and I'm tellin' you, he's up there."

"I don't care about your big schnozzle, you git! But if he's there, let's just get 'im and get out of here. The boss don't want no more screw-ups."

"Yeah, well he's a bit of a tosser, ain't he?"

"Watch yer damned mouth, you mongrel!" the smaller one hissed, looking around. "If anybody hears you talkin' like that, we're pooka kibble."

"Relax... there ain't no one out here. And if there is, they'll just be tasty little human morsels and we'll eat 'em right up; a perk of the job."

"Actually, lads," Qwyrk said, emerging from hiding and ambling across the snow-covered yard in their direction. "I'm here, too. I'd just like you to know who's going to be handing your arses to you before I actually get on with it. You're welcome."

"Hey, get stuffed, Shadow bint! We ain't got time for the likes of you," the taller one said. "This ain't no business of yours, so be off with you before it gets ugly."

"Oh, it's going to get ugly, all right," Qwyrk said with a wicked smile, rubbing her fist into her palm. "I haven't kicked enough of you lot in the nadgers recently; that needs to change!"

Sneezewort and Silktassel lumbered out from under the old oak tree and plodded through the snow, pounding their chests and growling.

"Wait, no seriously: am I supposed to be intimidated by that? A couple of bloody baboons thumping themselves and thinking they look fierce? Fine, but just don't start wanking in front of me, or something, all right? Because that's where I draw the line."

"You talk tough, little girl," the larger one grumbled. "But let's see what you're really made of."

"Yes, let's."

The bigger goblin lunged at her, but she easily ducked out of his way and delivered a solid punch to his belly, knocking the wind out of him and sending him sprawling on his back into the snow in a grand thud. She skipped to one side and smirked.

"Oh, come on, if you're not even going to try, why are we doing this? I could have stayed home and had a nice bath, you know, with candles and one of those fancy scented bombs that dissolves in water: 'Voluptuous Violet' or 'Sensual Strawberry'... you know, that sort of thing? I could be halfway to being blissed out right now, but instead, I'm stuck out here with you twats."

Sneezewort dragged himself to his feet and growled at her, thumping his chest again.

"Then again," she went on, "I tried one once called 'Dark Chocolate Orgasm.' It was right disappointing, really. I mean, if you're going to sell it like that, it'd better deliver, right? Turns out, I just ended up smelling like malted milk powder for days, and I didn't even have one good org..."

Silktassel jumped at her and, though he evaded her next punch, he failed to score his own hit as she ducked out of his way. She slid to her left and stood up again.

"Honestly, really? We could have a good scrap here in a nice backyard with lots of plushy, comfy snow on the ground. It'll make even your most embarrassing falls not look so brainless. See how nice I am? The least you could do is make this a bit more challenging. Or amusing. Or less smelly, or something, whatever. Seriously, what's up with the cheap cologne?"

"Keep talking, you cow!" Sneezewort grumped as he got up. "That's gonna make it even nicer when I... oof!"

Qwyrk delivered a kick to his belly and danced out of the way as the smaller of the two took another swipe at her, but again failed to connect. Sneezewort doubled over and fell to his knees, gasping.

"See? This is what I'm talking about. If you're going to go down that quickly, why am I even bothering? I'd have more fun getting a slingshot and going somewhere to pick off Nighttime Nasties. At least it's funny when they get knocked over. They make this hilarious little squeak when you ping them on the arse with a stone. Seriously, you've got to hear it to believe it! It's like 'eek!' It's a right laugh."

She crouched down as the bigger goblin stood up again and swung his arms at her head. She also landed a punch on Silktassel's nose as he approached, and he stumbled backward, his clawed hands clutching his lumpy face while he swore profusely.

"Look, I think I'm just gonna go back inside. You two can finish up without me. Run into each other or something and just get it over with. Honestly, this is most boring fight I've had in... ugh!"

A harsh, burning blow struck the top of her head and she tumbled forward, seeing stars and tasting copper in her mouth. Pain surged around her head, and she felt dizzy. Something pulsed through her like an electric shock, something magical. She caught herself and turned around to see Sneezewort sporting a yellow toothy smile, his right hand lit up with some sort of magical energy. Silktassel joined him, and his claws were also glowing.

"Not so talky now, are we," the little one boasted. "See, the boss figured we might run into your kind, so he gave us a little somethin' extra to take care of you. The only question is, are we going to rip your pretty head off, or just beat you to a pulp?"

"Maybe we should rip her head off first, and then beat *it* to a bloody pulp?" Sneezewort said.

"A fine suggestion, Mister Sneezewort. Carry on, then!"

Qwyrk stumbled away from them, clutching the top of her head, which she could feel was bleeding; the pain was terrible. She swore, struggling to shake it off. She pushed through it and turned around, standing up to face them again. "It figures you'd need some help; a little magical ED medication, eh? What's the matter lads; can't perform on your own? Had to make sure you'd be ready when that 'special moment' arrives?"

"What's she talkin' about?" Sneezewort paused and asked. "I ain't takin' no stupid medicines, even if they are easy!"

"Good Goddess, you're so dumb, I can't even insult you. Right, let's try that again, without the sucker punch this time. Let's see how far you get when you have to... oof!"

A wave of enchanted light shot from the smaller goblin's palm, throwing her back to crash into the wall of the house. Crumpling to the ground, she breathed with difficulty as pain surged through her chest and shoulders. Gasping, she tried to pull herself to her feet, but couldn't get off her knees.

"Bloody hell, it really does work!" Silktassel squealed with an amazed smile, looking at his hands. "I've got powers. I'm a soddin' superhero!"

"Can I go bite her head off now?" Sneezewort asked.

"You know, I was hopin' she'd give us a bit more of a fight, but what the hell, we need to wrap this up; go on, then!"

Sneezewort grinned his toothy grin and stomped toward Qwyrk. His sharp teeth were starting to look rather terrifying.

"Think, damn it, think! What do I do?" But she was having a

hard time focusing, and light-headedness threatened to overwhelm her. The bigger goblin closed in on her, all teeth and terror.

"No!" Qwyrk heard a voice behind her cry out. Looking up, she saw Lluck, Jilly, and Blip standing outside the open back door.

"Get out of here," she hissed. "All of you, run!"

"Yeah, no chance!" Jilly answered as Lluck spread his arms out, waving them at the goblins. Nothing happened at first, so Qwyrk forced herself up, shaking off her injuries.

"Hey!" Sneezewort stopped in his tracks. "What's goin' on?"

Before Silktassel could do anything (or Qwyrk could, for that matter), the bigger goblin slipped and fell flat on his behind. No matter how hard he tied, he kept falling over again. It would have been funny, Qwyrk thought, if she weren't in such pain. As he flailed around trying to get up, she landed a fierce kick to his side, sending him rolling over and over, and sprawling several feet backwards.

"Thanks for the assist!" she nodded back to Lluck, descending on Sneezewort and unleashing a torrent of fierce kicks and punches on his still-prone body.

He yelped and began unleashing erratic bolts of magical energy from his right claw, taking off some small tree limbs and snapping the clothes line. Qwyrk barely dodged them as one shot just missed her.

She saw him try to aim for her again, but instead, he shot another blast backward, hitting Silktassel square in the face... and burning his head completely off. The rest of his body stood there for a moment, wavering back and forth, while the empty space where his head was until just a moment ago smoked and steamed. Then the little body fell forward with a sickening thud into the snow.

Qwyrk stared in disbelief.

"Oh, bollocks!" Sneezewort growled. He was at last able to

scramble to his feet and hobbled over to his diminutive companion. Looking back to them with fear on his face, first at Lluck and then at Qwyrk, he growled, scooped up Silktassel's headless body, and in a surprisingly dexterous move, jumped over the back fence in one bound, disappearing into the freezing night.

Qwyrk sank down into the snow, her head throbbing. She looked back at Lluck who still stood in the doorway, clearly just as astonished about what had happened as she was.

"Um, thanks again," she whispered.

Lluck looked confused, shook his head, and just shrugged.

* * *

"Ow!" Qwyrk swore, as Jilly dabbed her head with a wet cloth. She sat on the edge of Jilly's bed as her young friend examined the wound.

"Well, it doesn't seem too bad," Jilly said. "Not that I know that much about these things, though, especially not with you magical folk."

"I'll be fine," Qwyrk said. "It's more wounded pride than anything else, and I heal quickly. But I'm really worried about how and why those two tossers got that kind of power."

"Agreed," Blip said. "Such miscreants could not possibly have access to those abilities under normal circumstances. It seems they barely knew how to use them as it was."

"Someone gave them that energy," Qwyrk said. "Someone with significant power, and there aren't too many Darkfae who could do that."

"So what does it mean?" Jilly asked, making sure that Qwyrk's blue-green blood wasn't getting on her duvet.

"It means that someone very powerful and very not-of-this-world, not to mention very evil, is looking for you," Qwyrk glanced at Lluck, "and this situation is now a whole lot more complicated. Bollocks! Why is it that every time I come to this flipping town for a holiday, I get caught up in some bad bastard's plot? Can't I just have a few days off?"

"It's very troubling, I agree," Blip pondered. "The idea of sorcerously-enhanced goblins does not bear thinking about, to say nothing of what may be empowering them."

"Look, I swear I don't know anything about it," Lluck burst in. "Like I said, I've always felt like something was watching me, and sometimes it seemed nice and sometimes it was creepy, but in the last few days those—whatever those things are—showed up and tried to kidnap me."

"When exactly did you first see them?" Qwyrk asked, wincing again as Jilly dabbed her wound.

"A few days ago, just before I got to Leeds, I guess. I thought I was being followed and I noticed them out of the corner of my eye, but they were never there when I looked for them. I stayed in a hostel one night and the next day, they found me again and came after me. Don't know why they would try going after me during the day, though. Wouldn't everybody see them?"

"No," Blip said. "Even with their enhanced powers, they're invisible to mortal eyes, thus making it easier for them to pursue you."

"Great," Jilly said. "So they can just run around town eating whoever they want in broad daylight, and there's nothing we can do about it?"

"Well, one of them is missing his head now," Lluck said with a confident smile. "He won't be doing anything else again."

"Oh, that's not true," Qwyrk said.

"What?" Jilly and Lluck both looked at her, confused.

"He's a goblin. He just lost his head, it's no big deal. It'll grow back."

"Oh, come on!" Jilly said. "Are you kidding me?"

"No really, it's not like it's a vital organ or anything. A new one will grow back in a day or two, probably just as ugly. He'll be back, right cheesed off, and nastier than ever."

"Crap!" Jilly swore. "You know, the more I learn about your world, the less I like it."

"I never promised it was all tea cakes and roses, dear. Last summer's little adventure should have taught you that."

"Fair enough. So what do we do?"

"Well, they know Lluck's here, and that's not good. They'll be back. Not tonight, but probably soon. And whoever sent them apparently also knows he's here, which is even worse."

"I concur," Blip added. "It won't be wise for the lad to stay here after tonight."

"Right, so much for being safe then," Lluck said. "Thanks for nothing! I knew I should've just gotten on that train!"

"And they would have found you and taken you, if not tonight, then soon enough," Qwyrk said flatly. "Coming here was our best move, because now we know we're up against something big. And bad. And not fun at all. And good Goddess, why does this keep happening to me?"

"So, what are you going to do then?" Lluck asked, still eyeing his rucksack like he'd be happy to snatch it up and dash out of the room with no warning.

Qwyrk sighed. "I'm going to have to take you home. I don't like it, but I really don't have any other choice."

"Home?" Jilly looked at her, shocked. "You mean like, your

dimension? The world you come from? The one I never got to see? Oh that's great, thanks a lot! I help save the world and I never get to visit, but this twat causes a big mess for everybody and you whisk him right off. That's just great!"

Lluck sneered at her.

"It's not a vacation, Jilly," Qwyrk said. "I just don't have any other options. I don't like bringing your kind over to Symphinity, either, but it's all I can think of until we can stop this."

"My 'kind'? Oh, that's real nice, Qwyrk. Do you lot just spend your days looking down on us?"

"I didn't mean it that way." Qwyrk scrunched up her face. "It's just that you know I've told you how dangerous it is for mortals to spend too much time there."

"Wait," Lluck interrupted. "So you're going to take me some place dangerous? Isn't that the problem already? Why I'm sitting in this room? Why should I go to this 'symphony' place if it's no better than here?"

"Not dangerous from getting chased by big, stupid goblins," Qwyrk answered, increasingly exasperated. "It's dangerous for mortals because of the enchanted nature of our realm. If humans stay there for too long, they become charmed to the point that they never want to leave."

"Well, what's wrong with that, if it's such a nice place?"

"Because if that happens, you'll wander around in a stupor, grinning like an idiot for the rest of your life, completely unreachable, and we won't be able to undo it. Worse, you may not even want to eat or drink anything, so you'll be dead in a week or two, anyway." She looked again at Jilly. "And that's why we don't like taking mortals over there, got it?"

"All right, but what about Thomas?" Jilly asked.

"The Rhymer? Yeah, he was an exception from hundreds of years ago, but he doesn't come back here very often, does he? And it took everything Star Tao had and more just to get him to inhabit his body for a little while so that he could show up. I'm not happy about it, but I'm not sure there's another choice right now. At least Lluck will be hidden from whoever's looking for him, even if just for a bit. That may throw them off the trail until we can figure out what to do."

"Jilly? What's all that noise?" The voice of Jilly's mum sounded from the hall, startling them.

"Crap!" Jilly whispered. "Um, nothing, Mum! I was just... watching a video on my laptop and then chatting with a friend using a new voice program. I'm almost done."

"All right, then," her mum answered. After her footsteps faded away down the stairs, the four of them gave a collective sigh of relief.

"Right," Jilly said in a hushed and harsh tone. "Can everyone just shut up now? The last thing I need after that shipwreck of a dinner is mum coming in here and seeing you," she pointed at Lluck, "in my room after we pretended to sneak you out. I can't believe you ran back downstairs; what were you thinking? In fact, you know what? I'd like you all just to piss off for a while, all right?"

She grabbed her laptop and stood up. "I'm going downstairs for a bit, so work out whatever it is you're going to do, and be quiet about it. I don't care. Just leave me alone!"

"Jilly..." Qwyrk started, but Jilly left the room without saying another word.

"What's her problem?" Lluck asked, plopping himself back down on the floor and looking quite done with all of this.

"I don't know," Qwyrk said, "but I don't like it. She's a bit stroppy sometimes, but there was something meaner in her voice just now, almost hostile." She shook her head. "I'll deal with it later."

"Should I go and talk to her?" Blip suggested.

Qwyrk shook her head. "No, this is something that even Hegel can't fix."

"Hmph, well that would be a first."

"Blip, remember when I said 'never change'?"

"Yes?"

"I take it back."

*　*　*

She moved silently through the frozen city streets, her long purple cloak flowing about her with mystic elegance as she fairly glided over the snowy pavement. It was late, and if anyone out at such an unpleasant hour saw her, they paid little attention, or maybe they deliberately averted their eyes, which suited her just fine. The fewer distractions, the better; she was in no mood for a fight. As she explored the streets in dim light, she kept a constant eye out for trouble. She was cold, uncomfortable, and wanted to retreat to her own safe and warm haven to forget about her concerns, but she couldn't. The investigators were doing their work, to be sure, but not quickly enough for her.

She paused near the town hall. "He's here, or he was," she said to herself. She followed the trail through an alley and out the other side as it meandered through a twist of new-old streets.

At some point, she found herself in a close, a group of buildings long since shuttered. She sensed him; she smelled the traces of his magic still wafting about, but there was something else here, too.

Closing her eyes, she took a deep breath of the freezing night air and exhaled a long puff of steam. Her face registered a surprise.

"A Shadow? Why would one of them be here?"

And there was something else in the air, too, something nearby. It was threatening, monstrous, and almost... familiar? She calmed herself and tried to get a fix on its location, but couldn't. It seemed to be in all places and none at the same time. She gripped the small stick on her belt with her right hand, prepared to use it if necessary. She'd heard the stories about what had happened last summer, about the murderous Shadow that had nearly succeeded in unleashing something horrible in this world, and she shuddered. The chill running down her back had nothing to do with the cold. Taking another deep breath, she turned in a swift movement to look behind her, but there was nothing.

"Gone now," she voiced to herself in relief. "But it must know he was here. And so do the Shadows, apparently. By Kubera, if any of them touch him, they will regret it!"

She left the area as silently as she had entered it, determined to find what was hers.

* * *

From somewhere, something watched her and smiled, because it knew that the time was almost at hand.

* * *

Jilly rolled over and opened her eyes; her clock said that it was nearly half past seven in the morning. She looked around her bedroom and saw Blip sitting cross-legged in a corner, his eyes closed and looking like he was meditating, or something. No one else was there.

"Um, sir?" she whispered. Blip opened one eye.

"Yes, my dear?"

"Where are Qwyrk and Lluck?"

"Oh, well, she decided to leave early, you see, and take the lad with her back to Symphinity. She, well, she didn't want to make a fuss about leaving with him, given the unfortunate tension that was intruding into our conversations last night."

Jilly scrunched her face. "You mean she didn't want to have to look at me before taking him away, so she snuck out while I was asleep."

"My dear, there are very good reasons for limiting mortal contact with our worlds, and though she and I have our disagreements—many of them; all the time, in fact—I support her decision in this instance. Our dimension is the one place the boy will be safe, at least for a short time. His magical nature may afford him some additional protection from the effects of our enchantments, but he cannot stay there long, just as you could not. I know that it is tempting to want to explore our realm and learn of its marvelous mysteries, but the mortal mind..."

"Cannot comprehend it and I'll go insane and turn into a drooling, gibbering blob, yeah, yeah, blah, blah, you've told me that a dozen times. I get it! But I haven't even had a look. Not even a peep! That couldn't hurt, could it?"

"Probably not, but..."

"But what? Am I really going to go mad by spending a few minutes there? Haven't I earned at least that much for what I did?"

"Perhaps, but she did give you that amulet, which allows you to see her in her natural form."

Jilly clutched the small trinket, which still hung around her neck, while a mixture of annoyance and guilt vied for top rotten feeling.

"I just don't like that all of a sudden, Lluck's the golden boy who gets all the attention because he can do whatever it is he does. He doesn't even know what he's doing, and he just wants to run away, and yet everyone's making this big fuss over him."

"In other words, you are experiencing pangs of jealousy because of his magical talents, and because Qwyrk's attention is suddenly diverted to him rather than to you."

"Oh that's nonsense!" Jilly said, rolling her eyes and offering up a heavy sigh. "I just, I don't know, it's like everybody's making too much out of something before we even know what it is."

Blip looked at her with a doubting face, one eye slightly squinted. It was so annoying.

"Fine, all right, yes, I'm jealous, all right? I just got her back into my life, and she's already jumping off somewhere again, this time with some boy she just met who doesn't even like any of us. I want to go with her! I want to help her!"

"You want to know that you're as important to her as she is to you..."

Jilly sighed. "All right, that's it. She was gone for months and I didn't hear anything from her, and I know it was because she was busy looking for whoever was helping de Soulis, but I felt left out, I don't know, abandoned. I finally had someone who mattered to me, who I... love, and she just disappeared. I know it's stupid, but it hurt, at least a little. And then she came back yesterday, and I was so happy, and now she's gone off again, helping a complete stranger."

Blip jumped up on the bed and sat beside her.

"My dear, there are only a few things in this existence of which

I am certain. One is that Aristotle's *Eudaimonia* provides among the finest of insights into how one should live an excellent and fulfilling life…"

Jilly shuddered.

"And another is that Shadows, for all of their impetuousness and let-loose-arrows-from-the-hip approach to things, are in fact, quite loyal and, I daresay, decent beings—Qwota and Qwarrel notwithstanding—who are very much concerned for others. Qwyrk cares deeply for you, and has told me so on several occasions. Her sense of duty is causing her to take these actions now, and you can be assured that when the immediate crisis has passed, she will return and renew your friendship most enthusiastically."

"I guess, but it just seems like it's all happening again, doesn't it? I mean, she's not even back one day, and now some evil something-or-other is out there again, sending monsters around and trying to cause more trouble."

"Alas, we don't yet know what is happening, so it would be prudent to be cautious at this point, but not overly anxiety-stricken."

"Well, it would have been nice just to have a few days to hang out with her and catch up, especially now that I can see her." She reached for her laptop. "Let's see if anything interesting is happening in the news."

"Barbaric way to find out the happenings of one's locality, if you ask me," Blip said. "Give me a good town crier any day!"

"Oh look, it's that Mr. Greylocke we saw in Leeds the other day. Apparently, he's donating a lot of money to some charity. Says here he's in the import business, or some such, and is opening a new shipping center on the outskirts of the city."

"Ah, a captain of industry and a philanthropist, as well! Good to know there are still some such gentlemen left in a world so absorbed in the shallowness and selfishness of virus videos and telegramming."

"Viral videos and texting," Jilly corrected, not looking up from the laptop screen.

"Eh? Hm, whatever, it's all rubbish and has turned the minds of today's youth into boiled turnip pottage, and a particularly dull and flavorless variety at that. What the young people of the world need is a good…"

"This is interesting," Jilly interrupted, as she so often did to save her own sanity.

"What?"

"It says here that he's also investing in protecting some sensitive habitats in the York Moors for restoration and scientific study and stuff. That's nice of him; seems like a decent bloke!"

"Indeed, someone who cares for the natural world as well as his own pockets is a well-rounded man. From where does he hail?"

"It doesn't say, but he seems like he might be local; he's obviously interested in the north."

"Well, he's a fine gentleman indeed, one with whom I would like to share a good brandy and discuss elevated topics."

"Except, he wouldn't be able to see you."

"A small trifle. When I am seated in the Lords…"

Jilly sighed. It was going to be a long day.

CHAPTER FIVE

After a flash of light, they stood in a forest clearing. Qwyrk glanced around, relieved that all was quiet and peaceful. Lluck didn't move, looking astounded.

"So, this is..." he started to say.

"My world? Yeah, nice, eh?"

"Yeah, it's all right!"

"Come on," she said, pointing to a path leading into the trees. "I'm going to take you some place really interesting to meet someone rather, um, odd. But he's a good man, one of the best I know."

"Who is he?"

"He's an old mentor of mine. I've learned a lot from him over the centuries."

"So, you lot live for a really long time, then?"

"Forever, actually. We don't even know how long, but that seems to be the case. I mean, we can be killed, but otherwise, we don't really age, don't get sick, that sort of thing."

"That's brilliant!"

"Well, it's not always amazing and fun. It can get lonely sometimes." Qwyrk looked off into the forest for a moment. She brought her attention back to him. "Let's go meet Qwyzz. He's a strange one, but I think you'll like him! Oh, and this is very important: if you start feeling odd in any way, let me know, all right? I think you'll be fine here for a bit, but if I see that you're starting to get affected, I'm popping you right out of here and back to Earth."

Lluck nodded. "Fair enough. If I get a sudden urge to wear my underpants on my head, or something, I'll let you know."

"Good, but just don't actually do that, all right?"

"Wasn't planning on it."

After an uneventful stroll through some impossibly beautiful woods for the next quarter-hour, they arrived at quite the sight: a two-story mansion that was a curious mix of medieval castle, Tudor manor house, Roman villa, and the fevered imagination of every role-playing game enthusiast who ever lived.

"Um, what's that?" Lluck asked.

"Yeah, I know, it's all rather bizarre, but that's part of the fun, I suppose. And it changes every time I visit. Come on."

They sauntered up to the wooden front door, which was currently painted a dark red color and set in a medieval Gothic stone archway. A large bronze bell hung in front of it.

"So, do we ring it?" Lluck asked.

Qwyrk smiled. "Just wait; it gets even more... interesting." She reached out, dinged the bell three times, and then stood back, looking up at the roof.

"Allooooooo!" A scratchy, stony voice sounded from somewhere beyond their field of sight.

"Gargula, it's me, it's Qwyrk!"

"Qwyrk? I do not know zat name! Who are you really, and why have you come here?"

"Well, why don't you come down and see for yourself, and I'll tell you. Maybe that will jog your memory, you annoying gargoyle. And what's with the extra phony French accent today?"

"Gargoyle?" Lluck shot her a look of incomprehension.

She held up one finger. "Wait for it..."

A moment later a small figure peered down from the overhang and looked at them. It was made of stone, a little crumbly around the edges, with a dog-like face, tiny horns, and wings that it occasionally flapped, sending a scatter of small pebbles raining downward. A few of them hit Qwyrk on the face, but she just blinked and gave him an impassive expression.

"So, how long are we going to do this, then?" she said in a calm voice. Well, the kind of calm that says, "I'm going to break you into little pieces with a hammer if you don't let us in," that is.

"I do not know who you are," her little stone adversary countered. "You could be Napoleon Bonaparte or Suleiman the Magnificent, come to conquer. I must stand as zee last line of defense. I will be rock solid. Ha ha ha! Oh, zat is a good one!"

Qwyrk sighed and closed her eyes.

"And as for how long you must wait, I can do zis all day! It is my task, my duty, my sworn oath, my, owww!"

Another gargoyle appeared next to him, giving him a good swat with one of its wings, sending another flurry of pebbles earthward.

"That's Babewin," Qwyrk explained to Lluck. "She's like his wife, or something; whatever it is gargoyles do."

"This is right strange," Lluck said, looking at them.

"Isn't it just?"

"Gargula! Stop it now!" Babewin said. "You know very well

who this is, and she has brought a guest. Be nice to them, or I will smack you again!" She called down to them: "I am very sorry, dear Qwyrk; you and your young friend are most welcome. I will alert the master." She turned back to Gargula and raised another wing. "And not another smart-ass comment from you... Trop me fistes longement, a moi proiier ent!"

"Oh, oh... is zat so?" Gargula said in defiance. "Well then... Si ne m'en caut comment, on m'aparaut laidement!"

"Um, what are they saying?" Lluck asked in a hushed voice.

"They're arguing in medieval French, I think. I don't actually want to know. But don't worry, it shouldn't be long now."

"Are you sure this is the best place to be?"

"I know, I know, but it'll all work out, trust me."

"Maybe I should have just taken my chances with the goblins."

More pebbles scattered from their scuffle, fell from the roof, and hit her on the face. "I'm not entirely sure you're wrong about that."

Fortunately, all such doubts were banished a moment later (well, maybe not), when the door opened, and an older-looking man emerged. He had long white hair and a neatly-trimmed beard, thin golden, wire-framed spectacles, and he wore a wine-colored velvet robe. Various medieval illuminated animals were embroidered on it in various places, but they seemed completely free to move about all over the fabric randomly: a horse trotting, a falcon soaring, an ape jumping, a snail... snailing, and rather quickly.

He smiled a warm smile. "My goodness, Qwyrk, it is you!" He held open his arms and she rushed to his embrace, laughing.

"It's so good to see you, my dear friend," she said. "As usual, it's been too long!"

"Since the end of human summer season, I believe," he confirmed.

"I've had a lot to do since, you... know. Oh, Qwyzz, I'm sorry, I didn't mean to bring it up."

"No, no it's fine, my dear. My wife's role in that perfidious treachery is well known now, and I have completely denounced her. I'm still melancholic, of course, but I'm learning to make peace with it, day by day."

"Um, this is my friend, Lluck." She was eager to change the subject and not forget her main task. "He's rather special."

Qwyzz squinted through his glasses and then his eyes widened. "He is, indeed! Come here, young man, and let me greet you properly."

Lluck set down his rucksack and approached the older-looking Shadow. "Hello, sir." He extended his hand, which Qwyzz took.

"Oh, no need for formalities, my young friend. If you are with Qwyrk, that is good enough for me. Call me Qwyzz, and come inside, both of you."

Moments later, they were in his splendid sitting room, a mixture of Tudor dining area and Viking mead hall, embroidered together in improbable ways. They sat on his comfortable velvet sofa and beheld the swirling scene. The room was a menagerie of the magnificent, with everything from a suit of armor in one corner that compulsively polished itself, to a chess game where the Viking pieces played by themselves and got into heated arguments—in Old Norse—which was just as well, given the amount of apparent cursing going on. Oh, and occasionally, what looked like a tiny dragon flew through the room leaving a trail of smoke behind it as it flitted about before exiting.

"Oh, don't mind the miniature wyvern," Qwyzz said with a wave of his hand. "He's just patrolling. He'll settle down when he gets a bit older... in a few decades."

Qwyrk was amused to see Lluck's reaction to all of it.

"So," she said, "we find ourselves in yet another messed-up situation back on Earth, and as usual, I could really use your advice. And he needs a safe place to stay for a bit." She and Lluck relayed what had happened in the last day, while Qwyzz took it all in. He looked at the boy.

"You're a special young man, indeed. Half-human and half-Fae."

"So he *is* half faerie?" Qwyrk interjected.

"Oh yes, very clearly. The facial features are the giveaway, and also this remarkable talent you mention, of course. Tell me, lad, do you know which parent was which?"

Lluck shook his head. "No clue. Sorry."

"Well, that is a pity. I could narrow it down a bit if I knew, but we'll just have to make do with what little we know."

"How safe is he here, from, you know, spellshock?"

"Oh, I should think that, given his unusual parentage, he could manage here for a good few days, perhaps four or five. He is welcome to stay, of course, and I'll see to it that he doesn't eat the wrong kinds of food."

"That's a relief. I'd really rather have him here while we're trying to figure out what the hell sent those goblins after him."

"Yes, that's a concern. If a Darkfae is enabling others of its kin with enhanced magical powers, we could be looking at something very worrying. Whoever it is might be building an army or planning some kind of larger attack."

"Lovely. Any idea which one of those bastards it could be? Think it might be a stray de Soulis supporter?"

"The latter is a very good question and it's possible. While as to the former query, I simply don't know. There are a number of possibilities. Tell me, lad: you said that you've sometimes felt like you're being watched, and not always in a good way. What were the less pleasant incidents like?"

"Don't know, they just seemed like there was someone, something nearby. I might be walking to school or going to the shops or something. I never got a look at anyone; it was more like a feeling, you know. Chill down your back, that sort of thing."

Qwyzz nodded. "And when did your powers first manifest?"

"Well, I've always been able to do it a little, but yeah, it's gotten stronger in the last year or so."

"With the onset of adolescence," Qwyzz said. "Yes, this makes sense. Something has been watching you, has been aware of your gifts, perhaps for your whole life. But it's taken a greater interest in you now that your powers are beginning to blossom."

"But who would know about them? About me?"

"That's where knowing who your parents are would be of great help. Whoever is spying on you may have some connection to your Fae parent. But, we cannot be certain until we learn more."

"So," Lluck said. "You don't know who my parents are, you don't know who I am, you don't know who's after me, and you have no idea how to fix any of this. Great, I feel so safe. I should've just gone to London."

"Could you excuse us for a minute?" Qwyrk said to Qwyzz, before yanking Lluck to his feet and marching him back outside. She was holding back her anger, barely.

"I didn't say we were going to have all the answers right away," she started in on him when they had stepped outside.

"Doesn't sound like you have any of them."

"It's a start, and believe me, Qwyzz is one of the wisest of all of us. If he's committed to helping you, he will. He has access to all sorts of things: books, scrolls, important Shadows who know things. You just need to lie low here, and we'll get it sorted out."

"So you say, but how long am I supposed to stay in this magic museum of his? A few days? A week? Until I start going mental? Because that's a real risk, isn't it?"

"Lluck..."

"No, I'm serious. All I hear is talk about how 'special' I am and how valuable I might be. But nobody's actually listening to me! You're not being chased by those things. You're not the lad without an identity. You're not the one who's had to live without your parents and grow up feeling like an outsider."

Qwyrk looked away in a flush of anger, but held her tongue.

"You're not leaving here. Not until we figure out what's happening," she said, still not looking at him.

"Fine, whatever, I'll stay," Lluck said after a pause. "Beats going back to England, anyway. And if I do end up one brick short, then at least I won't have to worry about all this crap anymore."

He turned away from her and stormed back into Qwyzz's home.

* * *

A freezing dawn broke over a bleak and barren vale in the Yorkshire Moors, lonely and hopeless in the early morning mist. Two figures made their way to the appointed meeting place, the larger one carrying the smaller, his rough feet crunching through the ice that clung to the ground. He stumbled a few times, but pushed up the final hill, where his master stood.

An enormous figure, clad in a tattered dark robe, awaited them.

FIVE

A hood shrouded his face, but his exposed hands were grey, with black fingernails like talons. He said nothing as the two approached him.

The larger goblin dumped the headless body of the smaller one on the ground, where its impact crunched the ice with a loud thump. He kneeled before his master.

"You were generously given great power," the master said in a deep, commanding voice with a faint Germanic accent, "a task to complete. Yet I see that the youth is not with you, and your smaller companion is missing something, though nothing important."

"I'm sorry my lord. We ran into some trouble we weren't expectin'. A Shadow girl got in our way, and we had her, with the power you gave us. We was all prepared to tear her apart, but the lad got to us again, usin' his tricks."

"He's thwarted you twice, even when you possess the gift of my sorcery. This is most... unfortunate."

"Yes, my lord. But we was... we was not expectin' him to have help. Down in the city, we were thrown off by a jirry-jirry and a child, who were far braver than they should've been."

"They must have been formidable opponents."

"It was more than we thought, my lord."

"Clearly."

"So, so, we um, we'd like another shot at gettin' him, if you'll permit us. We can do it, I'm sure of it. We can show you we're worthy. Me mate here just has to regrow his head, that's all. Won't take long. Should be back in a day or so."

"I should strike you both dead now. But I'll be merciful and permit you to have one final chance. Retrieve the boy, and soon, or do not bother returning to me, for you shall have nothing to live for."

"We'll do it, my lord. I've a finely developed nose, and I can sniff him out."

"Fail me again and I will boil that nose and feed it to you before turning you inside out. Then I shall kill you. Perhaps."

Sneezewort gulped.

"The Shadow woman's presence is an interesting development," their master continued. "If her kind are involved, they must know how important the boy is. It is imperative that they do not discover his true value, at least not until I have him. Then it will no longer matter. The time is near, and I will not have their interference, not after all of this preparation."

"Understood, my lord. We'll kill her if we see her again. As I said, we nearly did it last night, with your help, of course. She didn't know what hit her." He grinned, but it quickly faded.

"Where is the boy now?"

"Um, well that's the thing, my lord. I don't know, exactly. But he's gotta be close. He was staying with that girl and the jirry-jirry in a town called Knettles, which is a little place north of..."

"I am aware of it. Go back and bring him to me. Fail me again, and die."

"Um, right, sir. Very good. I'll um, carry off me friend here and let him get better, and we'll head back there tonight."

The master said nothing.

"So, um, good talkin' with you, as always. Lovely day, eh?"

The master said nothing.

"We'll uh, we'll chat again soon, eh?"

The master said nothing.

"Right then, off we go!"

✳   ✳   ✳

After they were out of view, the master motioned with a tal-oned finger, and a young man with long black hair wearing a long black leather coat joined him.

"They will fail, and I will kill them. But they are useful for the moment, especially if they can eliminate any of those around the boy. The Shadow is an annoyance that I would rather not have to contend with."

The young man nodded.

"Forget those two fools. I want you to oversee the boy's capture. Find him and bring him to me. But beware; *she* is looking for him, as well. Her interest in him is intense, and she will have resources at her disposal, but she must not find him first. Do not underestimate her or how dangerous she can be."

"Understood. If the boy is on this Earth, I'll find him and bring him back, and if she crosses me, she will regret it."

Beneath his hood, the master smiled.

* * *

Qwyrk took a deep breath. Facing two angry goblins with enhanced magical powers was one thing. Facing the wrath of one angry twelve-year-old girl with strong opinions was another entirely.

"Right, let's get this over with. I've already stalled long enough."

She walked up to Jilly's front door and knocked. It took a moment for a response. Jilly opened the door a crack and peered out.

"Qwyrk?" she said, looking confused. "Why are you knocking? Why didn't you just appear up in my room?"

"Well, I thought it might be a bit rude, just showing up again, seeing as how I ran off this morning and all."

"Yeah, that was a bit shite of you. Come on in before some

neighbor sees you and panics and calls the police or something. Last thing I need is them coming round."

Qwyrk stepped in and Jilly closed the door behind her. A cacophony of plaintive words sounded as each tried to apologize at the same time.

"Um, you first?" Qwyrk offered.

"Yeah, fine. Um, I was stupid last night. I don't know what got into me. I think it was just having my space invaded and having you back, only to see you dive off on another adventure, I couldn't go on. And I didn't like all the attention you were giving Lluck; I was jealous, I admit it. It was childish. I'm sorry."

"I'm sorry, too. When I found out there were super-powered goblins in your backyard, I panicked a little. I guess after all that business with de Soulis, I didn't want you in harm's way again, so I used Lluck's problem as an excuse to whisk him away so you wouldn't be hurt. I mean, I know what you're capable of, but I still get overprotective. And yeah, I snuck out while you were asleep, and that was a cowardly thing to do, but it really was for the best. He'll be safe with my old mentor, at least for a few days. Whoever's after him can't touch him there."

"Yeah, that's something. Any idea who's after him?"

Qwyrk shook her head. "Not yet. I'm probably going to have to go shake down some Nighttime Nasties to get answers. I'm kind of looking forward to that, actually."

"Excuse me ladies," Blip stood at the entryway to the living room. "Far be it from me to disrupt ongoing negotiations of peace treaties or détente or what have you, but Qwyrk, there is a message that I think you must hear."

Qwyrk was hit with a sudden wash of worry, and she headed into the living room in haste, followed by Jilly. In the middle of the room, floating in mid-air, was a ghostly image of Qwyzz's face. He seemed distressed.

"Qwyrk," Jilly said with hesitation. "There's an old man's face in my living room..."

"Qwyzz? What's wrong?" Qwyrk asked, ignoring her. "What's happened?"

"We've had an unfortunate development, I'm afraid," he said. "I was showing young Lluck around my home and explaining various magical devices to him. He seemed particularly interested in the Peregrination Orb."

"The what?" Jilly asked.

Qwyrk sighed. "It's a device for teleporting. It lets those who can't, do what we can do naturally. What happened?"

"Well, I thought his interest was purely academic. He seemed quite keen to examine all of my devices, so I was happy to explain how each worked. It's rare that I have a student these days."

"Yeah, and then?"

"And then, I went to make some tea from the starberry fruit, a lovely and fragrant blend that has a scent almost like..."

"Qwyzz?"

"Oh, terribly sorry! I came back some time later to ask him how his studies were going and he was..."

"Gone." Qwyrk filled in the sentence. "And I imagine he took his things, too. Where's he gone off to?"

"Well, the orb only takes one to a place they've already been. So I would have to assume that it's somewhere near you."

"Bollocks! I'll bet he's gone back to Leeds. He wanted to get a train to London, and it'd be quicker from there. Damn it, if he gets on one, we may lose him!"

"Why wouldn't he just teleport to London, then?" Jilly asked.

"He wouldn't be able to if he hasn't been there before."

"So what are you going to do?" Jilly asked.

"It's getting dark already, so I'll have to go back to Leeds now and find him, won't I? Bloody nuisance!"

"What if the lad won't return with you?" Blip asked. "He seems adept enough at using those powers of his, and that might well make things very difficult for you if he has no desire to come back here."

"I'll just have to cross that chasm when I come to it. Qwyzz, did he give you any indication of what his plans are? What he might do?"

"None at all, I'm afraid. I would agree that your suspicions about the lad wanting to flee to London are sound, foolish as that course of action might be."

"Right, thanks for letting me know. I'll be in touch if we learn anything."

Qwyzz nodded and his ghostly face faded.

"Well that was odd," Jilly commented.

Qwyrk sighed. "Things can never be simple, can they? No, there always has to be some spanner in the works, cocking up everything. He was just fine there, everything was set, and now we're right back to square one. And those stupid pillocks are probably already back on his trail, assuming the short one's head has grown back."

"All right, that's still really weird," Jilly said.

"Yeah, isn't our world just full of fun, peachy surprises?"

"So, you're off to Leeds, then?"

"I don't really have a choice. I'll be back later, with or without him, but I have a really bad feeling about everything. If I don't find him soon, we might be absolutely screwed."

"I concur," Blip said, after a surprising length of silence. "This all sits wrongly with me. I'm going to make a few enquiries of my own. I still have a few contacts you know, from my robust days in espionage."

"Oh, is this another part of your mysterious past that I've managed to know nothing about until just this moment?" Qwyrk asked with a sarcastic grin.

"I'm not an open codex, girl! There are whole sides of me that you've not seen."

"Well, mainly the side I see is the pot belly and the knobbly knees, but all right, if you say so."

Blip let out a decisive "Hmph!" He folded his arms and turned away.

"See?" Jilly smiled. "As soon as you two start fighting again, I know things are going to be all right!"

"I wish I had your confidence." Qwyrk managed a weak smile in response. "Right then, I'm off. I'll be back later. Cross your fingers and toes and everything else you've got that I find him, or at least something useful. Bye for now."

And with that, she disappeared in a flash of violet light, just hearing Blip say, "Knobbly knees, indeed!" as she whisked herself away.

CHAPTER SIX

Lluck wandered through mostly empty streets in a Leeds suburb, rucksack on his back. He hadn't quite ended up where he planned, but at least it was in the city, sort of. The sky was already getting dark, and he was keenly aware of the cold, but he hadn't yet made his way toward the city center and the train station. Something was holding him back. Guilt? Qwyrk and the others were trying to help him, he knew.

"I'm putting them in danger," he kept telling himself. It was justification enough for betraying her. He meandered up a cobbled lane between two rows of brick houses, still trying to decide what to do.

"Hm?" Out of the corner of his eye, he noticed a slim figure in a long, black leather coat, with long, equally black hair and dark sunglasses, hovering across the street. "All right, this is the third time I've spotted you in the last quarter-hour. What's your game?" he said. He clenched his fists but kept on walking. The figure had already disappeared again.

Lluck stopped at a newsagent's kiosk and flipped through a magazine, hoping to draw out his stalker. He didn't have to wait long. He felt an icy cold hand touch the back of his neck.

"I could snap it if I wanted to," a voice said behind him, barely above a whisper. "Walk with me."

Lluck put down the magazine and backed up. They ducked into another of Leeds' endless alleyways and connecting streets, away from prying eyes.

"So," Lluck said. "You in town for a vampire convention or something? Or is it retro wannabe goth night at some club down in the city center?"

"You're funny, mate. Move."

"Who are you? What do you want?"

"We're going to see my... employer. He has a keen interest in you and your talents. And he'll no doubt be grateful you made such a magic splash, coming back to this world like you did. You may as well have had a bull horn. It was easy for me to find you."

"Was he the one that sent those two idiots after me? You must've heard what I did to them. What makes you think you'll have any more... luck than they did?"

His captor chuckled. "Well, I'm not stupid, for one thing. I keep this grip on your neck, and the instant you try something, I turn your head around to face mine. Got it?"

"Except your boss obviously wants me alive, so you kill me, I reckon he's going to be right pissed off, yeah? Try again."

"I can also crack just enough of your neck to paralyze you. You only need your arms to do what you do, not your legs. Move."

Lluck scowled; he had no choice but to keep going as his captor pushed him forward.

SIX

* * *

The air was icy under the dark sky. Qwyrk stood again in the close where she'd met Lluck the day before and shut her eyes, trying to get a sense of him again: if he'd returned, or where he might be. She paced around trying to find something, anything. But his trail was as cold as the wintery air.

"Damn it! Nothing left. At least I know he didn't come back here."

As she scanned the area, she sensed someone behind her; her peripheral vision suggested a cloak of purple.

All right, who are you? Someone magical, obviously.

"I'm so not in the mood for this!" Qwyrk said, as she turned to see a figure standing behind her, about fifteen feet away. It was a woman, dressed all in black: leather jacket, form-fitting jeans, short boots, all that is, except for her long purple cloak. The hood was drawn back from her head, revealing that she looked young, except by her faerie visage, Qwyrk knew that she was no mortal. She had long, raven-black hair, with one slim purple streak trailing down her front left side; her mane flowed about her with an almost eerie perfection. Her skin was brown, a pointed ear just showed under her tresses, and she had dark eyes that seemed to sparkle even in the dim light. Qwyrk decided that she was one of the most gorgeous women she'd ever seen; she could hardly move. But that fascination was quickly shattered.

"Back off, Shadow!" the woman said in a rather posh accent, raising her hand in a threatening manner, snapping Qwyrk back into the moment. This newcomer held a short stick that expanded in an instant into a long staff. She gripped it with both hands and swung it all about herself in masterful ways, leaving trails of light and sparks in its wake. She ceased her display and held it in front of her, pointed at Qwyrk as if in warning.

"I'm impressed!" Qwyrk said. "Look, I'm honestly not here to fight. I've a feeling we're both looking for the boy for the same reasons."

"I highly doubt that. He's no concern of yours, and you're getting in the way of my search. It's my duty to protect him, so stand aside and leave this place."

"Excuse me, but he *is* a concern of mine, considering that I took him to Symphinity this morning to keep him safe from those damned goblins that were chasing him."

"Wait, you took him? Goblins?"

"Yeah, to get him away from those things, the same ones who nearly took my head off last night with some crazy enhanced powers they shouldn't even have, thank you very much. So ease up on the attitude, all right? I want to keep them from getting to him, and I'm guessing we're on the same side here."

The stranger gazed at Qwyrk, and a look of hurt and regret flashed across her face. She lowered her arms, and her weapon reverted to a small wand, which she tucked away in her belt.

"I'm sorry," she said. "I'm just so on edge at the moment. I don't know what's happening or who I should trust. It's like I've been stabbed with a dagger and it's just getting worse every day."

"Who are you?" Qwyrk asked.

She sighed. "That's a rather long story. You can call me Holly."

"I'm Qwyrk," she said, taking a few tentative steps toward this newcomer.

"Qwyrk? *The* Qwyrk? The one who defeated William de Soulis last summer?"

"Uh, yeah, well, about that: I had help, from quite a few others, actually. I wasn't nearly as brilliant as some people have been saying. I wish I were. Honestly, it was quite the mess and we almost failed. In fact, it's a bit of a miracle that we aren't all dead right now."

But Holly strode up to her and took her hands in hers. "This is brilliant. This is amazing. This is more than I could have hoped for! I feel like I should be asking for your autograph, or a selfie, or something!"

"Well," Qwyrk answered with an embarrassed guffaw, "that's not necessary, really. I mean, unless, do you, do you *want* my autograph?"

"Some other time, perhaps? But you saw him? I mean, you talked to him? Helped him? You took him to Symphinity? Is he still there? Oh, please tell me he is! That would be ever so wonderful; I must put my mind at ease!"

"Um, well, that's the problem. He was there, all settled in at my old mentor's home, and then, well, he ran off, and I thought maybe he came back here, where I first met him. He said he wanted to go off to London by train."

"London? Whatever for?"

"He thinks he'll find what he's looking for there; his real family, he said."

Holly gave her a pained look. "No, no he won't. Qwyrk, we have to stop him. He can't leave. Is he at the station now?"

Qwyrk shook her head. "I was just there. There's no sign of him. No trace of that magic he leaves behind. It's extra strong when he does his 'lucky' thing. He leaves a ripple that's as obvious as street lights, at least to me. It's how I found him to begin with. Trust me, he hasn't been anywhere near there today; I'd know. If he's still in the area, he's definitely not in the city center, so he hasn't gotten on a train or a coach, at least not from there."

Holly let out a sad sigh and looked down, dejected; she still held Qwyrk's hands. "Can we go somewhere and talk?" she said, looking back up at Qwyrk. "There are things you should know about him, about me."

Qwyrk looked at her with concern and sympathy, and somehow she knew. "You're his mother, aren't you?"

* * *

"Right, youngling," the man in black whispered into Lluck's ear. "We're heading toward that park over there."

"Then what? You gonna sacrifice me, or something? Ritual knives and stone altars and all that crap?"

"Not even close. Like I said, my employer has plans for you."

"Yeah, I'll be he does. Some sort of dark lord keen on taking over the world or something?"

"Something like that. Keep moving."

They crossed the street and made their way into the park. It was two blocks long with snow-covered grass, surrounded by a veritable forest of winter-barren oaks, birch, and maples. Lluck glanced about the grounds, barely lit under a pale moon, long shadows dancing over the snowy earth, cast by the wraith-like limbs of sleeping trees.

"So, is your employer a gardener, or something? Because frankly, he's doing a bit of a rubbish job."

"Quiet!"

"Sorry! It's just that being kidnapped makes me want to yell for help, or something. Not like you can blame me."

"Cry out and you'll never walk again."

"Yeah, about that. I don't think you quite get what I can do," Lluck bragged.

SIX

"I've heard stories."

"Well, the thing about stories like that is, they're usually pretty much crap."

Lluck jerked both elbows into his captor, whose grip was broken at once as he was sent flying backward a good ten feet, crashing into the snowy ground. Lluck was already bolting for the other side of the park. "Told you!" he yelled back.

He was pleased with himself as he reached the first tree cover, only to hear commotion above him, a swooping noise, like a hawk circling for its prey. Looking up, he saw the young man, arms outstretched and his coat spread out like wings, soaring above him in menacing circles. It almost would have been funny if he didn't look so furious.

"Shite!" Lluck cursed. He took off running again in the opposite direction, heading for a larger clump of trees.

"Bad idea, youngling!" his kidnapper called down to him as he turned and pointed his flight path toward the fleeing youth. "As long as I don't kill you, I can do whatever I like to you now, and you're going to be sorry for it!"

"Yeah, we'll see," Lluck yelled back. He headed toward one especially large oak, glad that the snow wasn't deep enough to slow him down. He didn't look back, but he knew his would-be captor was closing in. Good. "A few more steps," he panted. As he reached the tree, he pushed himself to one side and swept his hand back toward his pursuer. At once, the flying man crashed into the same tree and fell to the ground in a crumpled heap.

Lluck let out a laugh. "Not so tough now, are you, goth boy?"

Taking a deep breath, he ran back in his original intended direction. He could see an open field in the distance and more trees beyond. He picked up his rucksack. "Get out there and get lost in nature. Gonna be right cold tonight, though."

He left the park and crept along a dry stone wall edging a road alongside it.

"No traffic right now, no lights, all good. Time to disappear."

"Don't think that's going to happen."

Lluck saw his enemy standing farther up the road, his long black coat flowing about him like a bird's wings folding in after landing. He held stiletto daggers in each hand.

"Now, it's possible that you can use your luck powers on me again, knock me over, make me look foolish, but these," he flashed both weapons, "I'm really good with these. I can't kill you, but I can hurt you, and I'm sure I can get both blades into you before you can magick me again. Want to see who's faster? You win, I fall on my arse and look stupid; I win, you fall to your knees and bleed. A lot."

Lluck weighed his options, swearing to himself. He was about to put his hands up in surrender, when lights appeared behind his opponent, from an approaching car. The vehicle screeched to a halt behind his would-be captor, who glanced back, while keeping one hand aimed at Lluck.

Its lights still on, the right door opened and out stepped, well, someone odd.

Lluck and his nemesis both looked in astonishment at the figure striding toward them. He was wearing a pale lavender-colored unitard, a green cape and boots, and a purple mask. He was slightly balding and not in the best shape.

"Stand down, villain!" he ordered in a surprisingly commanding tone, given the ridiculousness of his outfit.

"Who the bloody hell are you?" the young man in black demanded.

"I am the Phantom Phennel: righter of wrongs, protector of the innocent, and dispatcher of evil-doers. As the defender of this city, I order you to surrender and take yourself at once to the local police station for incarceration and eventual punishment as rendered by judicial process!"

"Um, yeah mate, not going to happen."

"You don't want to cross me."

"Not exactly quaking in my boots, which admittedly aren't as fancy as yours," he taunted with a laugh.

"Whom am I addressing?"

"My name's Longwing, and just because you're kind of mental, I'll let you get back in that car and speed on out of here. This is no concern of yours, and you don't want to get involved. Trust me."

Longwing looked back at Lluck, who was ready to knock him on his arse again if he could just get a bit closer. "Don't move, boy!" He pointed one dagger to back up his threat.

"Where there is injustice, I must fight," the Phennel said in a commanding tone.

"Mate, this is your last chance. Leave while I still think you're a bit of a laugh."

The Phennel gripped his green utility belt and stood defiant.

Longwing shrugged and lifted the other dagger to throw it. "Right then, it's your funeral. I didn't want to do this, but now you're bothering me."

In a move that surprised Lluck, the Phennel drew what looked like some sort of bad science fiction ray gun and pulled the trigger. It shot a stream of gas straight into Longwing's face. Even from where he was, Lluck could tell that it smelled of rotting vegetables. Longwing collapsed to the ground and doubled over, violently gagging and retching, struggling to breathe.

The Phennel looked at his gun in shock. "It's never done that before." He looked over to Lluck. "Quick, lad! Get in the car, while he's down." He motioned to his vehicle.

"Um, I'm not sure that's a good idea..."

"You want him to recover? Come on, I'm rescuing you!"

"Yeah, all right." Lluck sighed and ran to the car, sidestepping Longwing, who was still heaving. He couldn't resist and gave his would-be abductor a good kick in the side, which only made his coughing worse.

"Sorry, 'mate.' I had to do it."

The Phennel motioned to him again. "Come on, come on!"

Lluck stepped over his fallen foe and got into the stranger's car. "This is probably a bad idea, but it beats staying out here with this creep."

The Phennel hopped in and started the car. He backed up and turned around.

"Come on, lad. I'll take you home. Where do you live?"

"Well, that's a bit of a problem..."

* * *

Qwyrk and Holly stepped through a light snow on the pavement to a festively-decorated pub near the main Leeds train station. Qwyrk was amazed at how graceful Holly was, even in slippery conditions, and it made her feel clumsy in comparison, even though she didn't stumble on the icy ground, silly things like gravity having little effect on Shadows. But she still hoped Holly didn't notice.

"Why are we going in here?" Qwyrk asked, as she pulled open the pub's door and held it for Holly. "This isn't exactly the kind of place for folks like us to be chatting about supernatural dangers."

Holly smiled. "Not a problem. I find that these places always seem to have a spare room where I shan't be disturbed."

Sure enough, they entered the pub and no one even looked at them, which amazed Qwyrk. "All right, we're a Fae woman in a purple cloak and a Shadow with glowing eyes, and everyone's ignoring us, and this is just a bit odd," she said.

"Over there." Holly pointed to a doorway. She took Qwyrk's hand and gently escorted her into what proved to be an empty room with a large window with multi-colored lights draped all around it. It looked out at the train station. "Perfect!" she added.

"How did you do that? Walk in as if you owned the place, be completely unnoticed, and find this spot that we can have all to ourselves, where we can also see the station perfectly?"

"Just lucky, I suppose. I've always been able to do things like that."

"So, that's why he can do what he does?"

"Well, it's much stronger in him. It's his mixed heritage."

"So, he does have a mortal father!"

Holly nodded and looked down, as if embarrassed.

"I'm sorry," Qwyrk added. "I didn't mean to pry. If you'd rather not talk about it..."

"No, it's fine," she smiled. "Come on, let's sit and chat."

They settled in across from each other at a tiny table, well-worn by years of pint glasses and elbows, though from a decidedly more mundane clientele. Qwyrk situated herself so that she could keep an eye on the station's entrance.

"I'm guessing you're not from around here. Northern England, I mean?" she said.

Holly chuckled; Qwyrk thought it was adorable.

"Right. I'm a Yakshi, one of the forest Fae of... well, what everyone now calls India."

"You're a long way from home!"

"Well, it's not my home any more, not for a long time. We left when I was very young, centuries ago. We were in danger from an especially vicious Darkfae attack; they were very brazen. It was a chaotic time. My mother believed that we should retreat back to Faerie for safety and then bond with a new realm on Earth. She chose England because it was so far away."

"And your father?"

"He... didn't make it. She said he died in the attack."

Qwyrk was touched by sympathy. "I'm so sorry."

"It's all right; it was a very long time ago. I was only about forty Earth years old, not even an adolescent."

Qwyrk gave her a weak smile. "There's a mortal joke about how the first fifty years of childhood are the most difficult. If only they knew..."

Holly smiled in response and Qwyrk got rather lost in it. She made herself come back to the moment. "So... um, you ended up here, in the north?"

Holly nodded. "It was the sixth century, according to European reckoning, and the thick, primal forests seemed a perfect place for us to bond with."

"Who attacked you? Back in your home..."

Holly shook her head. "I don't know, I don't think mother knows, either; if she does, she's never told me. But once we escaped, she saw to it that I was kept safe. She wanted me to be able to defend myself, so she trained me in silambam."

"Silambam?"

"An Indian martial art; that's the fancy stick work I was doing before, when I was trying to scare you off."

"Oh, that was brilliant! Yeah, I'd think twice about taking you on."

They both laughed. Qwyrk reached out to touch Holly's hand but withdrew it just as quickly, embarrassed.

"Sorry!" she said.

"Not at all," Holly said with a welcoming smile. "My real name is Vishala. I was named after my mother. But after we fled, my mum wanted me to adopt something more like the local names of the Fae folk who welcomed us here. So she made up a ridiculous, Celtic-sounding name: 'Haelleidhfoelleidh.' I thought it was gibberish."

"Wow, yeah, that's a mouthful!"

Holly nodded. "She wanted it to be difficult to pronounce to prevent mortals from summoning me. Not an easy thing for them to do, mind you, but a few wizards and druids had the power, old Merlin and his lot. She wanted us to stay hidden and be safe.

"Still, I never could say it right, so I just said 'Holly Folly.' It kind of stuck and became my nickname. Now, I just go by Holly, and if I have to be in this world and pretend to be human, I call myself 'Holly Vishala.' No one ever questions it... as long as they don't see my ears!"

Qwyrk grinned. "Who knew naming could be such a complicated process?"

"You should hear my mother expound on the proper titles of deities and devas some time; that will make your head spin!"

Qwyrk laughed. "It's a date! I mean, so, what about Lluck, then? What's his story, if I may ask?"

Holly frowned. "It's not a very happy one, I'm afraid, and it's my fault, all of it."

"Tell me. I mean, only if you want to."

"No, it's fine. About fourteen years ago, I was in a very bad way. It doesn't really matter why, but I was despondent. I needed to escape from something and I just... ran. I didn't know where I was going, only that I had to get away. I mean, I can't stay away from trees for long without getting tired and drained, but I wanted to lose myself for a bit in a sea of mortal life, the chaos of the modern human world, just forget things for a while."

Holly looked out the window towards the station.

"I ended up in Manchester, at a science fiction and fantasy convention, of all things. It was actually perfect. I could walk about with no disguise, and if anyone saw my ears, they'd just assume it was part of some elaborate costume."

Qwyrk chuckled.

"It was a wonderful gathering of the fantastic: celebrities, people in fancy dress, whole rooms of books and films dedicated to the human imagination. I love seeing how mortals imagine us to be; sometimes it's spot on, sometimes it's splendidly bad."

"I swear," Qwyrk said, "the next person who calls me an elf is so getting slapped!"

"Oh, you get that too? Yeah, that one's a real treasure, isn't it? I mean, come on, elves are just a bit, well..."

"Silly?"

"Yes!"

"That's what I always say! Drives me crazy! Anyway, we're digressing."

"Right. Being there lifted my spirits for a bit, but I was still distraught. I ended up in the hotel bar that night. I actually ordered an entire bottle of single malt scotch—the good stuff, believe me—and just sat there, drinking it by myself, glass after glass. Not that it had any effect on me, of course. I may as well have been drinking orange juice, but I liked the taste."

Her expression turned more serious.

"And then, he walked in. He seemed shy and awkward, but that made him rather adorable. I asked him if he wanted to join me, and he did. We sat chatting about all sorts for ages, I don't even remember what. It was just nice to talk to someone who had no idea who I was. He probably thought I was just some fangirl with really good prosthetic ears and a high tolerance for alcohol. Of course, I never told him the truth, not that he would have believed me, anyway."

She sighed, looked away, and ran her fingers through long black hair.

"At some point I suggested we go back to his hotel room, and the next thing I know, there we were, and one thing led to another. I just wanted to be connected to someone, you know? I wanted to feel something. It surprised him as much as me, but he was very sweet. I um, I didn't want any complications, so I left very early the next morning, while he was still asleep. I never saw him again."

"What was his name?"

"That's the thing, I have no idea. I didn't think to ask, and I didn't want to linger to find out later. I just felt like I needed to leave in a rush. That should have been the end of it, except it wasn't. You probably know, it's rare for a Fae and human coupling to produce offspring, but I found out soon enough that I was with child. My mother was quite sympathetic, and she helped me make arrangements for the boy. He couldn't stay with us, of course. Even though he's only half human, he probably would have gone mad and died, even as an infant. We wouldn't take the risk. And I had no way of contacting the bloke, so he couldn't go and live with him, either."

"That's heartbreaking."

Holly nodded. "So we decided to place him at a good foster home agency in York. I named him Lluck, with two 'L's, kind of as a little joke for how my mum had renamed me; I think I also hoped that he'd be lucky. It broke my heart to leave him, but I had no other choice. I checked in on him when I could, just to see how he was changing. Mortals grow up so quickly—seriously, puberty as a teenager? What's that all about?

"Right?"

"Anyway, he was taken in by a human family, and I was relieved. Sad, but happy. I figured that it was time to let him go, to let him be in a real human home, but he ended up getting shuttled from one place to another. It upset me, but there was little I could do. I guess I just wanted him to be mortal and have a good life. I thought my being around would only bring him pain. But then recently, things changed. I knew something was wrong; that mother's bond never really goes away. Sure enough, I found out that he'd fled from his current family, so I hired some fellows to look for him."

"Not those two goblins!"

"Goddess, no! They're private detectives of the paranormal. They specialize in, shall we say, unusual cases. Troll protection rackets, gnome-nappings, mermaid ransoms, that sort of thing. Pay them well and they ask no questions. They've kept me updated, but I was impatient, so I came here tonight to look for myself, and then I met you. But please tell me, how did you find out about him?"

"Oh, well, those goblins that were chasing him happened to run into a couple of friends of mine while they were down here the other day. They saw your son too, and talked with him, so I decided to come and look for him. And I found him."

"And he was well? He was all right?" Her face was pained and she looked as if she might cry. Qwyrk almost melted inside.

"He seems healthy enough, but he's got quite the attitude, let me tell you!"

Holly rolled her eyes and smirked. "Takes after his grandmother."

"I took him back to my friends in Knettles, and then we decided I should whisk him off to Symphinity for a few days, but not long enough for spellshock to set in. I just wanted to get him out of immediate danger while we figured out what was going on. It was a perfect plan, but then he ran off this morning. So here I am, looking for him again."

"Oh Qwyrk, what if he's really in trouble? Why are these creatures chasing him?"

"We think it's because some Darkfae wants him, probably to try to force him to use his luck powers. He's hitting his teenage years, and that means his ability will be blossoming in full. He said it's gotten much stronger in the past year."

Holly nodded. "Yes, I thought that might happen. I mean, the odds against him existing at all are high, and it's even stranger that he seems to have such good luck and that he can control it."

"That's quite a power. In the wrong hands, it could be really bad."

"So what do we do?" Holly looked distressed. Qwyrk reached to take her hand again, but held back.

"I'm going to do everything I can to find him, and honestly, I could use your help."

Holly nodded. "Of course."

"Where can I find you?"

"I'm staying at a little inn just outside the north part of the city, so I can be connected with the natural world. I shan't go home again until I've fixed this. But I don't have your natural ability to teleport, sad to say."

"Wait, you're staying at a B&B? Seriously?"

"Of course, why not? It's easy enough to exchange faerie gold for human money, so I might as well be comfortable while I'm looking for him! It's also how I'm paying Dill and Chives."

"Dill and Chives?"

"The investigators."

"Oh, right. Where are they now?"

"I've no idea. They come and go as they please and contact me when they have new information."

"Are they any good?"

"Quite. Though, they are a bit odd."

"Well, all right then, we'll let them do what they do, and we'll work on our own."

Holly shivered, and drew her cloak about her.

"Darling, you're freezing!" Qwyrk said. *Darling?*

"I'll be all right. I'm just drained from being away from the forest all day."

"Let me take you back to that B&B."

"You needn't if you don't like. I can call a taxi..."

"Oh please, don't be daft! I can have you there in a few shakes if you focus on where it is and give me a description. You need to take care of yourself."

Holly smiled. "Well, I can't refuse an offer like that! Thank you."

Qwyrk took her hands again. "Come on, let's get you nice and warmed up."

CHAPTER SEVEN

"So, you're not from around here, then?" the Phantom Phennel asked as they sped down the icy road. He'd doubled back and headed into the city again, to a different suburb than where they'd been.

"Well, kind of, outside of York, 1 mean. But it's a bit of a mess." Lluck shifted around in his seat, not really wanting to have this conversation.

"Look, if you've run away, 1 understand. It's nothing to be embarrassed about. Sometimes things just get to be too much. If you've done something, or you're in trouble with the law, you don't have to worry; 1 won't say anything."

"Yeah, it's a bit more complicated than that."

"So, who was that bloke? He seemed dangerous, with those knives. Why was he after you?"

"Don't really know. He said his boss wanted me for something; didn't say what."

"Is it some sort of kidnapping or slavery ring thing? You should go to the police!"

"No, I don't think it's that, it's just, never mind." He looked out the window and back, eager to change the subject. "Hey, why are you running around in that get-up? Are you some kind of superhero or something?"

"Well, I try. I've got to do something, but I'm not quite there yet. I go out for a bit of practice; it's training. By the way, do you play a musical instrument?"

"Hm? No, sorry. Why?"

"Oh. Too bad. I need a theme song."

"Uh, okay. So, you don't have like a superhero car or plane, or something?" *Is this conversation really happening?*

"I'm more incognito in my old Vauxhall, and to be honest, those would be pretty expensive."

"Yeah, I suppose. You do this a lot?"

"Some nights. This was the first time I've seen anything really bad. Finding you was just luck, I guess."

"Hm. Just luck." That word again. "The trick with the gun was brilliant, though."

"That's the funny thing; it's not supposed to do that, at least not like that. It's just supposed to squirt bad-smelling vegetable juice, enough to distract someone, so the victim can get away."

"Seriously? Bad-smelling vegetable juice?" Lluck struggled not to laugh.

"Well, it's also got a bit of pepper spray, but not much. But that was amazing! It left him completely incapacitated."

"Yeah, that might have been me." Lluck immediately regretted saying anything.

"What do you mean?"

"Long story. Look, can you take me to the train station in the city center?"

"I suppose. What's there?"

"I need to get a train."

"Where to?"

"Don't know, London, maybe."

"What's in London?"

He looked out the window again, thoughts of his foster care life swirling around in his head. "It's just away from here."

"That doesn't sound very promising."

"It'll do."

"Look, it's dark and cold. Why don't you stay at my house for the night? Sleep on it. If you still want to get a train in the morning, I can take you then."

Lluck shook his head. "I don't know. I mean, come on, you have to admit it seems a bit sketchy, a bloke in a weird get-up and mask asking me to go back to his house. That basically screams axe-murdering perv who's going to put bits of me in his freezer."

The Phennel chuckled. "Yeah, it does, doesn't it? Look, I promise I'm harmless. You can even take my vegetable gun and keep it pointed at me if you don't believe me. Apparently, it works a lot better than I planned. Here, go on, take it."

Lluck sighed. "No, it's all right. Fine, I'll sleep on your sofa, or something. I'm kind of knackered, anyway. So, who are you, really?"

"Well, I can't tell you, secret identity and all that. But I'm one of the good guys, honest. I'm just tired of seeing so many petty crimes go unanswered. I want to make sure that people get out of bad situations. I mean, I'm not much of a fighter, so it's not like I'm going about pounding criminals into the pavement or anything."

"It sounds kind of dangerous."

"Well, we all have to step up and do our part."

Lluck rolled his eyes. "I guess."

"I'll need you to do something before we get to my house, though."

"What?"

"Reach into the glove box and get the blindfold."

"Blindfold?"

"For my secret identity, I can't have you seeing where I really live."

"Look mate." Lluck felt more than a twinge of annoyance. "I'm not going to tell anyone. I don't even know this part of the city."

"Just a precaution."

"So, it's like your own personal bat cave, then?"

"Yeah, something like that. Once we're inside, you can take it off."

They drove on in silence for a bit. Lluck had no clue where they were going, and started second-guessing his decision. Eventually, he felt the car come to a stop.

"Right, we're here," the Phennel said.

"You do realize that if anyone sees you, it's going to look like you're kidnapping me and taking me to your house to do weird and probably illegal things."

"Yeah, well no one's out right now. I checked as we drove up. It'll be fine. Besides, I have a raincoat I slip on to hide the costume."

"Yeah, 'cause a bloke in a raincoat taking a blindfolded minor into a house is not at all suspicious." Now he was third and fourth-guessing his decision.

"It's a quiet neighborhood most of the time."

"Fair enough, but if we end up at a police station and I have to tell them what happened, I'm not gonna lie and say we're old mates. I'll probably just tell them you're a perv with a vegetable fetish."

They made it inside without any such awkward incidents, and once the door was shut, the Phennel sighed in relief. Lluck slipped off the blindfold and found himself in an ordinary, semi-detached house. No superhero headquarters, no fancy computer terminals, nothing special about it at all, other than inordinately large amounts of science fiction, fantasy, and comic book memorabilia, books, DVDs, and the like.

"Right, I see why you want to be a superhero."

The Phennel smiled. "Make yourself at home. I'm going to run upstairs and change."

Lluck flopped down on the sofa and thumbed through a movie magazine. In a bit, he heard steps on the stairs, and his host appeared in civilian clothing, which was fine, except for the black ski mask on his head.

Lluck almost dropped the magazine. "Mate, you *do* realize that you've just gone from potential perv to full-on serial killer, right?"

"Yeah, sorry about this, it's the only thing I could find to hide my identity."

"But, I don't know who you are, and even if I did, I wouldn't tell anyone."

"Just to be safe, can't let word get round, you know?"

Lluck shrugged. "Suit yourself."

"You want a cup of tea or something?"

"No, I'm all right, thanks."

The Phennel sat down in a chair.

"Well, help yourself to any food you like."

"Cheers."

Lluck wandered into the kitchen and was delighted to be confronted by an enormous bag of...

"Jalapeño crisps? Mate, these are my favorite!" He reached for them.

"Really?" His host wandered in behind him. "Huh. I don't normally eat them, but something made me want to pick up the biggest bag I could find today. Have at them. They're all yours. What luck, eh?"

He chuckled as he tore open the bag and almost inhaled the spicy, potato goodness waiting within. What luck, indeed!

"Look, I'm not sure what happened tonight," the Phennel said, "but you had something to do with it. I mean, you said so, right? You can do things, right? You affected my gun, made it better. We took that creep down, left him flat-out on the pavement, we saved the day! You could help me, be my assistant, my sidekick."

"Yeah, I don't know, sounds a bit dodgy," he said between crunches.

"No, no! It would be brilliant! We could get things done! Stop petty crimes, make the streets safer! I mean, it's not like you'd need to live here or anything. Go back home, or wherever; I can be in touch when I need you."

"Um, not really my thing, sorry." He barely got the words out through his crisp-filled mouth.

"There was something about that bloke who was after you, wasn't there? He wasn't normal. I saw him swoop down out of the sky, like a hawk. It was terrifying, but amazing. He has abilities, doesn't he? So do you. People with powers exist, don't they? I'm not imagining it."

"Yeah, I guess there's some of us around." He set the bag down. For the moment.

"Oh, this is brilliant, I knew it! So, are there hidden leagues of superheroes? Avenging justice legions? Are there aliens and para-humans?" He clenched his fists and pumped them in the air.

"I think it's more like faeries, and elves, and goblins, and shite, really." He picked up the bag again.

"Oh, that's brilliant, too! Tell me about them, please? What are they like? Do you know them? Are they all around us?"

"Don't really know. I've seen a few strange things, but she knows more about them than I do." He gave into temptation and scooped up more crisps.

"Who?"

"Oh, just this lady I met," he said through his crunching. "She's some kind of shadow being, like, you can't see her unless you have the Sight, then she looks pretty much human, except for the pointy ears. She's kind of fit, though."

"Is she a friend of yours?"

"No, not really. I bailed on her while she was trying to help me out, and now I feel a bit bad about it."

"Is that why you're running now?"

"Sort of. I really want to try to find my mum, my real one." He stopped eating for a moment, mindful of how impossible his story sounded.

"And you think she's in London?"

"Don't know, maybe? She's not human, so I figure that's the best place to start looking."

"So she's..."

"A faerie or something, yeah, and that's probably why your gun went all extra disgusting on that bloke. I can change things, make them luckier for myself and other people."

Carl gasped. "That's incredible!"

"Yeah, it's all right, but everyone else that knows about it wants it, too, you know?"

"And that's why you're being chased."

"Yeah, I reckon. I just want to get away from it all." He set the bag down, no longer hungry.

"I'm not surprised. Look, why don't you stay here for a few days, help me out on my patrols, see how it goes. You'd be safe here; no one knows where you are. We might make a good team. I mean, if you don't know who your parents are, it's not like you're running away from them."

"I don't know, mate. I mean, your heart's in the right place and all, but..."

"Maybe sleep on it, see how you feel tomorrow?"

"Yeah, all right, then." He looked at his greasy hands. "Um, can I have bath? I mean, as long as you're not going to sneak in all Psycho-like and stab me."

"I promise that won't happen."

He pointed at his host. "I'm gonna hold you to that mate, or else you're getting a face full of vegetable gas!"

*   *   *

Jilly was up early the next morning, pacing about. Not only had Qwyrk not returned, Blip was also nowhere to be found. She was anxious; even spending time on her laptop wasn't helping. She wandered back and forth in the living room after her parents had left for the day. She wasn't in the mood to draw, and checking her Twitface account was equally unsatisfying. Odin was blissfully asleep in his new heated dog bed in the corner of the room. She looked over at him with envy.

"Show off. Damn it all, where are they?"

As if on cue, Qwyrk appeared in flash of purple light. "Hi love, sorry, to be away. Things last night took an, um, unexpected turn."

"Qwyrk! Did you find him? Is he with you?"

She sighed, frustrated. "No, I'm afraid not. There was no sign of him in the city, at least nowhere near the train station. Qwyzz gave me a magical alarm to set up around it; if Lluck had entered, I'd have known. But something else interesting happened."

"Oh?"

"I ran into his mum, almost literally."

"His mum? Who is she?"

"Well, it's like we thought. She's Fae, from India, funnily enough; it's a long story. He doesn't even know her, but she's worried sick about him and looking for him, too. Seems like several folks are trying to find him, and not all of them have good intentions. She and I chatted for a bit in a pub and then I took her back to her B&B outside Leeds."

"She's staying at a B&B?"

"Like I said, long story. I dropped her off, then went back to my home in Symphinity."

"You have a home?"

"Yes, I have a home. I don't live in a magical mulberry bush or in a hole in the ground, thank you very much."

"No, it's just that you've never mentioned it before."

"Oh, well, I don't stay there as often as I'd like, so it's not as 'homey' as it should be. But I needed to enter Reverie."

"What's that?"

"It's like a deep meditation; it's what we do instead of sleep. It revives us, and I've been really bad about not doing it enough in recent months. I was exhausted, which is why I've been crankier than usual."

Jilly grinned. "Hadn't noticed."

Qwyrk shot her an annoyed look. "Anyway, I came straight back here as soon as I was rested; feeling so much better now. Sorry for not checking in sooner."

"No, it's fine. So, she's a real faerie. What does she look like?"

"Who?" Qwyrk fidgeted, looking at the floor.

"His mum, silly!"

"Oh, you mean other than being gorgeous with luscious, long black hair, flawless skin, amazing dark and sparkling eyes, and absolutely charming in every way?" Qwyrk blurted out all at once. "Yeah, didn't really notice all that much."

"Wait a minute," Jilly said with a cheeky grin. "You *fancy* her, don't you?"

Qwyrk flashed a sheepish grimace. "No! I mean, well, maybe a little? Hang on... how do you know I like girls?"

"You told me you like boys *and* girls, ages ago."

"I did?"

"Yep, last summer, when you were fawning over that Templar bloke at Jimmy's."

"Excuse me, I was not 'fawning'! I was admiring a work of art, that's all."

"If you say so."

"So," Qwyrk said with hesitation, "you know all about, um, reproduction, and all that?"

"Yes, Qwyrk. I'm twelve, not five."

"Oh Goddess, you didn't learn about it from Blip, did you?"

Jilly burst out laughing. "Thank goodness, no. Can you imagine how that would have gone?" She put on a scowl and lowered her voice: "My dear, there comes a time when two beings who are, how shall one say, orbiting in each other's paths, not unlike a planet and one of its satellites, may find that they are drawn to one another for reasons other than mere intellectual discourse and stimulation, for whom Hobbes and Kant no longer suffice."

"All right, stop, you're scaring me."

Jilly giggled. "What's her name?"

"Holly."

"And she's nice, then?"

"More than nice. She's smart, sophisticated, seems like one hell of a fighter, and charming and sweet on top of all that. Pretty much amazing."

"Qwyrk, this is wonderful! You're both magical, right? You both come from Faerie, or whatever. I mean, I suppose you're different... species or something, but that doesn't matter, does it?"

"We're all part of the same magical tapestry, I suppose."

"Well, there you are! Like you said, perfect!"

Qwyrk flopped down on the couch next to her. "Jilly, first of all, she's a distraught mum looking for her lost child. That's the most important thing to her right now, not looking for someone to date. And I'm totally on board with that; the poor thing is worried sick, and we have to help her. And second of all, I don't even know if she likes women!"

"Come on, what's not to like? I mean, you're funny, intelligent, strong, gorgeous. I mean, I'm saying that as someone who loves you like a sister, so I'm biased, but still."

"You're sweet, but now isn't the time. We have a job to do, and I don't need distractions."

"I think this is exactly the kind of distraction you *do* need!"

"Wait, weren't you just annoyed that my attention was directed at Lluck and not you?"

"Yeah, but that's different. You've already got a side-kick, namely me, thank you very much. But this is about you being happy, which I totally want for you. Promise me that when all this is sorted, you'll talk to her? At least see if she might be keen on you?"

Qwyrk sighed and rolled her eyes.

Jilly folded her arms and titled her head.

Qwyrk glared at her.

Jilly, unperturbed, glared right back. "I will scrunch up my face and pout if you don't say yes! Don't make me scrunch up my face and pout!"

"Fine, okay, all right, fine! I'll see if she wants to go get a coffee or something."

"Oh come on, that's pathetic! Do something daring, something romantic. Coffee's boring. And you don't even drink coffee, or anything else from our world."

"Yeah, all right, but I can if I want to. I just don't *need* to, that's all; you know that. And besides, it's symbolic; asking someone out for 'coffee' just means going somewhere and sitting and chatting. You can have tea, or fizzy water, or a fermented yak butter smoothie; the drink's not the point."

"Is that even a thing?"

"What?"

"A fermented yak butter smoothie? It sounds dreadful!"

"Oh, I'm sure some hipster juice bar in London has one at an exorbitant price, along with kale and beetroot chai; and yes, I actually *have* seen that on a menu." She shook her head. "Look, we're getting way off track here. If we get this whole mess sorted, and the world doesn't end—again—I'll chat her up a bit, all right?"

"You promise?"

"Yes, I do."

"I'm going to hold you to it."

"I have no doubt."

"Fine then."

"Fine."

"Ahem," Blip interrupted, having just appeared from a corner of the living room, walking right out of the wall. "If you two are done arguing about frivolities, I should like to report that I've found something."

"Blip! Don't *do* that!" Qwyrk snapped, clearly startled at his sudden intrusion.

"Oh, you mean like when just your head suddenly appears in a wash of light, floating in mid-air? I jolly well near had a conniption when you did that, I'll have you know."

"Yeah, all right, fair enough; payback and all that. We're even. So, what is it?"

"I was off doing some martial arts training, to keep myself toned and ready, delving into the ancient mysteries, becoming as one with the..."

Qwyrk glared and even Jilly sighed.

"...and I overheard some of my colleagues in the dojo talking of something happening."

"The dojo..." Qwyrk said.

"A training facility for the martial arts."

"I know what a bloody dojo is, Blip. I'm just trying to get my head around what you were doing in one."

"It is an interdimensional school for all seekers of ancient wisdom, open only to the chosen."

"You said something's happening," Qwyrk interrupted. "'Something' is not helpful. What is it?"

"There's rumor of a powerful Darkfae emerging from hiding and gathering forces. Nothing firm yet, but his presence is said to be causing some terrible unease among the Nasties and even others of his kind. He may be making a play for a higher position of power. It occurred to me that a certain young man with the ability to bend providence in his favor might be just the means of doing that."

"That's exactly what it sounds like," Qwyrk agreed. "Did you hear anything else, like who it might be?"

Blip shook his head. "I didn't wish to pry. It seemed wise not to tip my hand that I know anything at all at the moment."

"You know how much I hate agreeing with you, but good call. It's a start, anyway. We have to find Lluck, and soon. I mean, even with his powers, he's not safe! Just in the area around the Leeds station alone, someone gets mugged several times a week!"

"How dreadful," Blip offered. "Has this individual filed a report with the local constabulary?"

Qwyrk gave him a blank stare.

"So, what should we do?" Jilly asked.

"Well, I could go back and chat with Qwyzz, but right now, maybe some of that new-fangled tech of yours can help us out," Qwyrk said. "Can you search for websites that might talk about evil faeries? I mean, we found stuff on de Soulis that way."

"No problem," Jilly smiled. "Let me just check my toplap."

"You're quite unfunny, I hope you realize," Blip retorted.

They sat down on the sofa, Qwyrk and Blip huddled on either side of Jilly. "So, what should we search for?" she asked.

"Good question," Qwyrk said. "Anything too esoteric might not give us any answers."

"And anything too obvious, too many," Blip added.

Jilly saw Qwyrk grimace, but remain silent. "How about: 'evil Fey?'" she suggested.

"Worth a try."

She typed the words into Goggle and looked at the top results:

Evil fedoras, just what you need to make a splash at your next fancy dress event or 1940s gangster theme party.

Come to the Medi**eval Fey**re in Little Retching, Nottinghamshire, during the first two weekends of June. Jousting! Food! Music! Fake stick-on plague sores! Simulated heretic burnings! Mock beheadings! A fun family day out!

De**vil faji**tas, the authentic Mexican food in Sheffield with a diabolical bite; one taste and you'll be possessed.

Evil Fay's Dungeon of Pleasure. Accepting new slaves now for training...

"Bloody hell, it never changes, does it?" Qwyrk swore.

"Why would being in a dungeon be pleasurable for slaves?" Jilly asked.

"Never mind," Qwyrk answered. "Let's try something else."

"Wretched contraption," Blip said. "I have no desire to indulge in puerile *schmutzwortsurche*, thank you very much. How about 'depraved faeries'?"

"Right, I'm going to stop you right there and suggest 'goblins in history' instead," Qwyrk blurted out.

Jilly looked back and forth at each of them as they exchanged nervous looks, then shook her head and typed in Qwyrk's suggestion. "Right," she said, "here we are: this site has a list of some of the most famous and notorious goblins and creatures of the night! Hey look: it's our old friend Redcap, except he wasn't a goblin."

"Yeah, well, better off if they don't know that." Qwyrk said. "Who else is there?"

"The usual things. You've got your imps, your kobolds, your hobgoblins, nothing out of the ordinary. Wait a minute, what about this one: the Erlking?"

"Oh yeah, I've heard of him," Qwyrk said. "He's not been around for a long while has he?"

"He created quite the ruckus across England and the continent at various points many centuries ago, if I recall," Blip offered. "A nasty figure, fancies himself a king; some call him the 'king of the elves.'"

"Are you flat-out kidding me?" Qwyrk said. "So we can presume that he's quite silly then, and just move on?"

"Well, he hasn't been heard from in some time, I grant you, but no one knows what became of him or what he may be up to."

"Well, I'm not going to suffer from any disrupted Reveries over the monarch of the flipping elves, thank you very much."

Rather than watch the two of them go back and forth like a surreal ping pong match, Jilly wisely tuned them out and read on. "It says here some believed that at certain times of the year he led a great hunt that went after not only animals, but humans as well, and that he was jealous, ambitious, and eager for revenge on anyone he thought had wronged him. Apparently, some version of him was even the model for Harlequin, you know, the Italian comedy bloke with the patchwork shirt."

"Well, comedy and tragedy do sit side-by-side," Blip said. "Arlecchino is at times quite the sinister figure in the Commedia dell'arte, humorous though he may be."

"I admit, it's a bit interesting," Qwyrk said, "but seriously, if he's really just the king of the bloody elves, then we've got nothing to worry about, honestly."

"All right, what is it with you and elves, anyway?' Jilly asked.

"I don't know, they're just... *silly*, that's all."

Jilly ignored her and finished reading. "Well, it's not much, but maybe there's something to it. We could take another trip to the *Swapping Shop* and look around."

"I shall remain here, thank you very much," Blip said. "Given the failure of the last reconnaissance mission, my time is better suited to other matters than traipsing through inclement weather on wild goose chases to an establishment that apparently can't be bothered to stock even the most basic tomes."

"What are going to do instead, then?" Qwyrk asked. "Hone those martial arts skills back at the interdimensional dojo? Judo-throw a bunch of brownies? Karate-kick some kobolds?"

"Hmph! You may jest as you like, girl, but one day soon you will be astonished at my abilities."

"Believe me, I eagerly await that astonishment." Jilly saw that Qwyrk was struggling to suppress a smile.

"I wish Granny were home," Jilly said, hoping to ward off another argument. "She might be able to help us out."

"Yeah, that would be nice," Qwyrk agreed. "You haven't seen her at all?"

"No, she's been in and out of her house for months. The place has been dark at night, so I'm guessing she's gone off somewhere. It would be good to have her back."

"I'm still baffled as to why she's here at all," Blip interjected. "Living directly across the street, I mean. It seems far too coincidental to me. Not that I'm complaining about her help, of course, but some random occurrences seem not so random, if you get my meaning."

"Well, I've learned not to look a gift horse in the mouth," Qwyrk said, "even when it's an unlikely and unimaginative plot twist. If she comes back, it'd be well worth picking her brain a bit to get any more info we can."

There was a knock at the door. Jilly furrowed her brow. "Who'd be coming around here at this hour?"

"Be careful child! We don't know who it may be. Fiends and foes may be arrayed against us!" Blip jumped down from the sofa and assumed a pose involving making fists, crossing his arms in front of himself, and bracing both feet firmly on the floor. Jilly and Qwyrk looked blankly at him. Then at each other. Then back at him.

"Um," Qwyrk said, "You look, uh, wonderful—like an Amazon warrior, really—but I'm going to go out on a limb and say it's probably not those two goblins coming back for more in broad daylight. Just a hunch, especially since one of them is still waiting for his head to grow back. Also, pretty sure the Erlking and his bad-arse elves aren't spoiling for a fight in a residential neighborhood of an English market town, but by all means, carry on doing... whatever that is."

Blip dropped his position and turned up his nose at them, pouting.

"Um, I'm going to answer the door, if that's all right," Jilly offered to ease the tension.

"Sounds like a good idea to me," Qwyrk said.

Jilly went over to the door. "Who is it?"

"It's a surprise, except not really, 'cause I just gave it away!"

Jilly's eyes widened with excitement. "No! It can't be!"

She flung open the door, and was delighted to see a young man with long brown platted hair (tied back), a scraggly beard, and an eyebrow and nose piercing. He wore a tie-dyed shirt, olive green baggy pants, purple Doc Marten boots, and a long grey wool coat over all of it. He threw open his arms and smiled.

"Hello Jilly, all right?"

She laughed and reached out to hug him. "Star Tao, it's you!"

From the living room, she heard Blip say, "What? Splendid! A fine young man, indeed," while Qwyrk just blurted out a "bloody hell."

No matter, Jilly thought. The gang was back together at last, and all was right again!

CHAPTER EIGHT

Jilly laughed as Star Tao, her quite strange but delightful New-Agey friend from last summer's adventure, strode through the door and into her living room. Upon seeing Blip, he immediately fell to his knees and stretched out his arms, bowing in prayer.

"Hail, oh lord, and thank you for deigning to bless me with your presence once again! I remain your humble servant. May Jim Morrison in his celestial form serenade your wondrousness to your eternal bliss."

"Yes, well, good to see you again, lad," Blip beamed. "Fine young man, the very finest!"

Qwyrk smiled through a pained expression. "All right, mate? How goes it?"

"Not bad at all, thanks," he gave Qwyrk a hug that she slithered out of with all haste. "In fact, I have some brilliant news!"

"And that would be?" Qwyrk raised one eyebrow.

Star Tao pointed at her. "I can see you now, as you really are! And my lord there, too!"

"Wait, what?"

"Yeah, it's brilliant!" He reached into a pocket and pulled out a little crystal. "Qwypp asked a mate of hers over in your neck of the woods if he could help us out, so I could see her as more than just a spooky shadow with red eyes. I mean, no offense, there's nothing wrong with that, but I figure since we're together and all..."

Qwyrk cringed.

"...I should be able to see her so I can enjoy and fully appreciate all there is to see, if you get my meaning." He nudged Qwyrk with his elbow.

Qwyrk felt ill. "What is it?" she managed to blurt out, eager to change the subject. And not feel sick.

"Right, it's a crystal."

"I can see that. What does it do, and who gave it to you?"

"Well, it's enchanted with some kind of elf magic or something."

Qwyrk clenched her jaw.

"But it came from a friend of hers, Qwartz?"

"Oh yeah, I know him, makes jewelry and such, right?"

"That's him. He came up with a way to use crystal magic to let mortals see shadows, but it only works for a while. It has to be recharged every few weeks by putting it under moonlight."

"I have something, too," Jilly smiled proudly and held up the pendant around her neck. "Qwyrk gave it to me as a birthday present, and it means I can see her!"

"Aw, that's brilliant, Jilly," Star Tao said. "Now we're all on the same level. Oh, and happy birthday!"

"Thanks!"

"Right, lovely, anyway how's she doing?" Qwyrk interjected, "Qwypp, I mean. I haven't heard from her in ages."

"Oh, she's all right, yeah! Her mate Qwykk's fine, too; I think she's off in Majorca or some island like that, enjoying the warmer weather."

"Yeah, that's one of her favorite haunts. She always comes back with some new crazy story, usually one I'd rather not hear."

"Oh, and Qywpp's got a new name," Star Tao announced with pride.

"A new name?" Qwyrk really didn't want to know.

"Well, not like a permanent change, or something legal or anything, just a workshop name, really, to facilitate guiding seekers more properly."

"And this new name is..."

"Freedom Rainbow Love Bongos."

"Freedom... Rainbow..."

"Yeah, groovy, eh?"

"That's one way of putting it."

"I helped her pick it out."

"Why am I not surprised?"

"Anyway, she might be able to come round soon, and then you two can catch up."

"Yeah, that'd be lovely; and maybe I can slap her silly."

"What?"

"What?"

"Anyway," Star Tao bobbed back and forth between each foot. "We're up north for a few days promoting a new workshop over in Manchester next month, and I figured it was well worth a drive over to Knettles to put some flyers up in the shop, and call round and say hello to Jilly. I didn't expect you all to be here, so that's a nice surprise, too. It's a reunion!"

"It's lovely!" Jilly said, but Qwyrk was not so thrilled.

"Ahem," Blip said. "Now about that obeisance, young fellow. It has been some time since you directed any prayers to me, you know, and don't think it has escaped my attention." He held up one froggy finger in admonishment.

"I do apologize, my lord, things have been very busy lately."

"Understood, but do remember that devotion is the cornerstone of a proper god-supplicant relationship."

"Oh, for feck's sake," Qwyrk grumbled. "Look, it's lovely of you to drop by—completely unexpectedly and all—but we're in the middle of another mess and we need to get back to it so that things don't go balls-up again."

"Oh yeah? What's going on? Maybe I can help."

"I highly doubt that."

"Qwyrk," Jilly squinted and said in an annoyed voice. "Are you forgetting he channeled Thomas the actual Rhymer?" She smiled at him.

"No, I haven't, but I don't see how channeling anyone is going to help us find Lluck."

"Why do you need luck?" he asked.

Qwyrk sighed and relayed the events of the last few days, while Star Tao took it all in.

"Crap," he said after she'd finished.

"Yeah, exactly, and I suspect there's a lot more going on that we don't know about yet. So unless one of your channeling buddies has built-in satellite navigation and can locate runaway teenagers, I don't know how much use you'll be."

"Well, you never know. I could plug into the cosmic multi-web and try to find out something."

"The what?" Qwyrk winced.

"The cosmic multi-web. Well, that's just what I like to call it. The real term isn't really pronounceable by the human mouth, so I had to come up with something that would work."

"Wait," Jilly said. "We can't even pronounce it?"

"Yeah, the real name was coined by an ancient interstellar race that now lives in the seventh dimension. They don't even have tongues, actually, just long snouts shaped a bit like saxophones."

"Shaped like... saxophones?" Qwyrk had already had enough.

"Well, approximately; maybe more like a cross between a saxophone and a crumhorn. Their voices are a bit buzzy. Anyway, I could do a bit of plugging in and see what I can come up with, but I really just wanted check in here for a bit before I dash up to the store and leave some adverts for the workshop."

"Is this class a sequel to your highly successful Atlantis-Dolphin-Pyramid-Reiki-Wakey thing from last June?" Qwyrk, of course, didn't actually want an answer.

"Oh no, this one's entirely different. I'm not teaching at all; I will be but a willing student. No, this one's put on by a mate of Qwypp's actually, a witch. It's a whole two-day workshop in witchcraft witchery called 'Which Witch is Which?' I actually liked 'Which Witch is Witch?' better, but I was outvoted. Her name's Morgana; good lass, really. Here, have a look."

He held out the ad for all three of them to see:

Join the thousands of people who've already made a dynamic change in their lives, and attend our **Insta-Witch** weekend seminar, coming to your area soon.

World-renowned witch and motivational speaker **Morgana Starlight Glittery Golden One,** High Priestess of the Temple of Nu-Avalon (based in Greater Farting, Wiltshire) will guide you through an intensive two-day training session that will give you all you need to become the certified witch of your dreams!

For only £799 (plus half VAT), you'll receive all these materials: a robe in one of four eye-catching colours (black, dark grey, gun metal, or charcoal; your choice while supplies last), our luxury mini aluminium cauldron (not meant for making tea), twelve scented power candles (fragrances come and go), a cosmic crystal (actually, it's from Dorset), a ceremonial knife (dulled for safety—do not use for slicing cheese), the Glittery Golden Book of Sparkly Shadows on a digi-witch memory stick (save paper, save the trees, save the world), and a straw flower-adorned pointed hat (one size fits all, most of the time—don't wear in the rain), as well as our bonus anointed broom (not meant for actual flying) at no extra charge!

Classes include:

- **Which witch is which?** – An introduction for those who don't know their Wiccans from their Warlocks.

- **Horned god or horny god?** – Why not both?

- **Aphrodites and tighty-whities** – Goddesses and Gods in many beliefs.

- **The call of the cauldron** – Let the cauldron's call call to you like a caller calling on you. Call now!

- **Let's sit down for a spell** – During this lunch break, we'll learn about tyromancy (divination by cheese), with some proper Stiltons, Cheddars, and Wensleydales. You can have your cake (cheese, actually) and eat it, too! After divining, you can use your cheeses to make a "sandwitch" for a proper lunch.

- In the afternoon, we will experience a talk by our very special guest, **Lady Quintessa Apple Fairybottom**, Esteemed High Priestess of the Great Rosedongle Coven, Fifth Holder of the Silver Garter, and Friend to all Fey. The topic of discussion is hidden behind the veil for now.

Why wait? Summon your mobile, or invoke your WiFi, and phone the number below. Conjure up your reservation, and see what a difference our seminar can make in your life right now! Which witch will you be? Come to the coven and find out!

1 12 35 81 38 53 211

Insta-Witch is a registered trademark of **Fluffy Bunny Productions, Inc.**

Note: all payments are final, no refunds. There are no guarantees in life.

"Right cool, eh?" Star Tao said with an ear-to-ear grin.

"Let me guess, you actually have people signed up for this?" Qwyrk said.

"Oh yeah! A dozen or so already. I want to see if we can get a few more seekers from over on this side of the Pennines. Every little bit helps, you know? Witches do not live by spells alone."

"So, these... new witches," Qwyrk went on. "What will they do once they're, um, certified? So to speak."

"Oh I don't know, good things, I suppose. Help the Earth, do what you will but harm none, that sort of thing."

"Lovely. Now, if you don't mind, we have to get back to what we're doing. Feel free to contact your saxophone-nosed friends a few dimensions over and see what they have to say. I'll await their wisdom with bated breath, really."

"Well, it'll take a bit of preparation, but I can do it after I drop these off."

"I'll look forward to it," Qwyrk fake-smiled, lying through her teeth and ever-so-slightly shaking her head at Jilly.

*　*　*

Lluck yawned and turned over. It was already morning.

"Well, I'm still alive, that's a good sign."

"Of course you are; I told you I'm a man of honor."

Lluck, still half-asleep, turned to see his host, once again sporting that vile black ski mask. It was enough to jolt him the rest of the way up and make him almost fall off the sofa.

"Bloody hell, mate! That is *not* what I want to see first thing in the morning! You almost scared the crap out of me!"

"Sorry, I'm just protecting my identity."

"Look, I don't give a toss who you are, but if you want me to stay here any longer, that thing has to go. For real, it's creeping me out."

"But..."

"No buts, mate. The scary-arse mask goes, or I do." He stood up.

The Phennel sighed. "Fine, all right, but understand this is a big step for me."

He pulled the mask off his head, revealing an ordinary-looking man of about forty, with a sparse mustache and a thinning head of brown hair, now sculpted by the mask removal to look a bit like the Matterhorn.

"My name's Carl. Carl Woldham. I'm not special, really, just trying to do my bit for the community. During the day, I own a fandom shop: sci-fi, fantasy, comics, that sort of thing."

"I never would have guessed," Lluck smirked, sitting back down again.

"Yeah, well, it does all right, I suppose, but I just need to contribute more, you know? Give something back; and that's where you could come in."

"Mate, I still don't know about this. It sounds dodgy, and if you get caught by the police, we'd both be in deep shite."

"Yeah, but with you around, that won't happen, will it? I mean, that's what you do, right? Change people's luck for the better?"

"I guess, but I don't really even know how it works. I can't promise it would keep you—keep us—out of trouble." Carl's insistence on this crazy idea was testing his patience.

"Fair enough, but it's worth a try, isn't it? Tell you what? Why not give it a couple of days, just a few, and if it's still not your thing, I'll take you to the train station, or back home, or wherever you want to go. Sound good?"

Lluck thought about it for a moment and then sighed. "Fine, but right now, I'm really hungry, and I'm happy to announce that breakfast is on you."

Carl smiled. "Sounds good to me! Let's stuff ourselves!"

* * *

"What are you doing?" Qwyrk asked.

"Preparing." Star Tao's eyes were closed.

"For what?"

"To make the inter-dimensional bond. It's kind of like one of those old internet connections, you know, where you heard the static and then the funny beeping and then you got plugged in."

"Actually, no I don't know." Qwyrk stared at Star Tao as he sat cross-legged on Jilly's living room floor, having dropped off a stack of ads at the *Swapping Shop*, inviting one and all to the grand witchery shindig, and trudging back through the snow in all haste. He started flapping his arms like a bird.

"Ssssssssssssssssssssssssssssshhhhhhhhhh! Ooooooooooooooooomamamamama... eeeeeekaykaykaykaykay! Gwok! Gwok! Gweebokkk!"

Qwyrk didn't say another word, but got up and walked over to the cabinet where the Pleeths kept their bottles of hard liquor.

"What are you doing?" Jilly asked.

"I want to see if something in here will actually have an effect on me. Maybe if I downed a whole bottle..."

Star Tao's pseudo-bird-flapping ceased, and he began to sway back and forth, his eyes rolling back.

"Well, this is not at all disturbing," Qwyrk snarked. "I'm not sure I want to know who's in there."

"Be quiet, and let the boy do his work." Blip advised.

"Oh, and since when did you get on board with all this?"

"Since the lad successfully channeled Thomas the Rhymer, or have you forgotten that?"

"That's what I said!" Jilly interjected.

Qwyrk looked at them both and shook her head. "Maybe if I mix brandy, gin, *and* scotch together I'll start to feel something."

"Greets!" Star Tao announced in an odd, high-pitched voice.

"We've met you before, haven't we?" Qwyrk asked. "You're the New Age song lyric bloke, right?"

"Songs are songy! Ages are ever anew, new-new! We bring love-life from the deepest cosmos to embrace you with all-knowing heart wisdom."

"Yeah, that would be the same one." Qwyrk cringed. "So, what can you tell us about this mysterious Darkfae and his plans?"

"Dark is dark, but fades in the light. Plans may be planned, but not all planning pans out."

"That's so helpful! Thank you!" Qwyrk fake-smiled. "We'll be in touch if we need any more information. Bye then! Byeeee!"

"Touch, touch, touch, touuuuuurrrrrrrghghgh..." His voice lowered to a growl and took on something like a Germanic accent as he continued:

"Waul, Waur, Wode, and Wotk,

Frie and Fuik and Fu.

Hellequin and Herla named,

To search by night for you!

Death it rides in Wild Hunt

Across the Moorland bare,

It seeks the one who brings all luck

To take back to its lair.

Bound and bled, torn and rent

His vitalness consume,

And then Erlkönig will arise,

And bring this Earth to doom..."

The three of them stared at him in shock as he swayed about in a violent trance, arms thrashing about in random directions, but saying no more. He expelled an occasional growl in a voice not quite his own, one that sounded horrific.

"Qwyrk?" Jilly said with a trembling voice.

"Crap," Qwyrk whispered.

"For once, my dear, your vulgarity is utterly called for," Blip said.

Star Tao calmed down and rocked back and forth, taking a few deep breaths. In a moment, he opened his eyes, and looked about. Their wide-eyed gazes were still fixed on him.

"What?" he asked. "Did you learn anything?"

"Oh yeah," Qwyrk answered. "I don't know what you did, mate, or who was babbling through you—actually, I don't want to know—but it worked, and basically, we're in deep shite."

She told him what he'd orated in the trance, and he stared at her for a moment, confounded, before gasping, "Bloody hell!"

Jilly picked up her laptop again, saying, "Um, right. I'm going to search for some more information. That was so creepy! Please don't do that again!"

"I can't help it, Jilly, I'm sorry. I'm only a conduit for what comes through." He resumed his arm flapping and bird noises.

"What are you doing now?" Qwyrk asked, wondering if this situation could get any worse.

"Oh, I have to complete the ritual to make a fully safe return to our plane. Otherwise, I could end up trapped between dimensions, with my body here and my mind over there."

"Probably over there most of the time, anyway..."

"What?"

"Nothing. Carry on with... whatever it is you have to do."

"Oh, this is horrible!" Jilly made a face.

"What is?" Qwyrk asked, tearing away her gaze of morbid fascination from Star Tao's avian display as he started to bring himself fully out of his trance and back to the mortal dimension, arms fluttering about.

"I clicked on the local news. There are police at a place in the York Moors."

"The Moors? Are you kidding me? As in, what he just mentioned in that torture-flick poem?" Qwyrk pointed at the still-flapping Star Tao, and stressed-sighed.

"Yeah. It says they've uncovered a whole bunch of animal bones and mutilated carcasses; rabbits and sheep, and such. There are markings and symbols burned into the ground and signs of other activity, like discarded beer bottles and chocolate wrappers. They think it's some kind of ritual-cult thing. Beer and chocolate?"

"Well, that is very distressing news," Blip said. "About the ritual, I mean, not the libations and confectionary, unless they are of inferior quality, of course."

"Let me see," Qwyrk sat down next to Jilly, ignoring Blip, and perusing the story. "Crap, that's definitely Darkfae business, well, probably; the beer makes it more likely. That's exactly the sort of thing they do when they're trying to achieve something by magic, but it's usually on a much smaller scale than this. A ritual this size means they're after something big. Like helping the Erlking increase his power."

"What do you think they're doing?" Jilly asked in a timid voice.

"Pretty sure it has to do with our boy Lluck; nothing whatsoever to do with learning faerie scouting skills or having beer-drinking competitions. Our mate over there said as much in his nightmare sonnet. Right, I need to go check this out, now. You three stay here."

Qwyrk was met by incredulous stares from all three of them.

"What? This is dangerous! You heard what Star Tao said, er, growled. I need to go and have a look out there and see what's going on."

"Yeah," Jilly said, "and we're going with you."

"Absolutely not!"

"Ahem." Blip spoke up. "I must agree with..."

Qwyrk started to smile in triumph.

"...Jilly on this occasion."

"Blip, are you out of your mind? I mean, more than usual?"

"Oh, very droll. Listen: Jilly and the lad have more than earned their places as paranormal warriors by our sides. Without the boy's connection to the ether, we wouldn't even know what we now do. You cannot keep coddling them."

"*Coddling* them? Are you freaking kidding me? Look what happened the last time they snuck into the middle of a battle with us!"

"Um, we *are* sitting right here you know," Jilly snarked.

"I know full well what happened," Blip snapped. "They saved the lives of three mortals by keeping them out of harm's way, while we failed at our task and had, to put it crassly, our arses handed to us."

"That's not the point..."

"Then what, pray tell, is?"

"It's the site of a ritual sacrifice? Get it? The Erlking seems to want to eat people, get it?"

"And these two have skills that helped us defeat an ancient sorcerer, *get it?*"

Jilly and Star Tao looked at each other and then to the floor, over and over, with increasing frequency.

"Um," Star Tao started, "right before I disconnected, my spirit guide *did* tell me that I might be of use in all this. Just sayin'."

"And I've been studying this sort of thing since last summer," Jilly added. "Maybe I can identify some magical symbols or something? Figure out how to disrupt whatever they're planning? I don't know, but I've kind of done that before."

Qwyrk threw up her hands. "All right, fine, you win. We'll all go together and it'll be a morbid picnic, a gruesome day out on the Moors. Crushed beer cans, spent chockie wrappers, burnt markings in the earth, dead sheep, and gnawed organs; fun for the whole damned family!"

"Sounds brilliant!" Star Tao smiled. Qwyrk glared at him, and his smile disappeared faster than a politician's campaign promise.

"But we're not using your freaky rainbow hippie van to get there," Qwyrk said to him as a follow-up.

"What do you suggest, then?" Blip asked.

"We don't really have a choice, do we? I'll have to teleport everyone home and then on to the Moors. I can move about by myself just fine now, but with the extra people, I'll need to get a boost."

"Really?" Jilly squealed. "Oh, this is fantastic!"

"Don't get too excited," Qwyrk said in a blunt tone to quell her young friend's enthusiasm. "We'll only be there for a minute, so get a good look, and then we're out of there and on out to where the gruesome fun apparently never stops."

* * *

"Best of winter days to you, ma'am," Dill took a seat at a table in the same room where they had met their client a few nights before. Chives joined him a moment later and both looked at her, dressed as always in black, bedecked in her purple cloak, the hood drawn over her face once again to conceal her identity.

"Good afternoon, gentlemen. I trust you are well?"

"Pleasantly adequate, all things considered," Dill replied, "though I would be happier if we had more information to give you. What we do have is troubling, if I may say so."

"Why? What have you learned?"

"The boy seems to have left this world for the other at some point, but then returned."

She remained impassive.

"Upon returning, which we believe was somewhere in the north side of Leeds, he seems to have been beset by an adversary of a magical nature, different from those bumbling goblins who were previously in pursuit of him. Whoever is behind this game of cat-and-mouse may be upping the game, so to speak."

"What happened?"

"Unknown, ma'am. We have not heard anything regarding his being abducted, so we must presume that for the moment, his luck holds again, so to speak. But whoever seeks him may be becoming more determined."

"I see. Do you have any idea of where he may be now?"

"We are pursuing a lead, ma'am, and we hypothesize that he is still somewhere in the north of the city, hiding out with a mortal man in a nondescript house. That is our next objective, to seek out a probable location."

"That's all you know?"

Dill nodded. "For the moment, ma'am."

"Thank you, gentlemen. Contact me again when you learn more." She rose up and left the room with grace.

"Do you think she knows more than she is leading us to believe, Mr. Dill?" Chives asked, after she was well departed.

"Undoubtedly, Mr. Chives, undoubtedly. The question is: will we need to do something about it?"

* * *

A flash of light brought the four companions into a lovely wood. Holding hands, they emerged from the swirl of magic and set foot on enchanted ground.

"Is this...?" Jilly asked.

"Home," Qwyrk said.

"Oh, Qwyrk, it's gorgeous, it's magnificent!" Jilly turned in every direction, looking about, her eyes wide with delight. Star Tao stood gazing into the distance, mouth open.

"Yeah, all right, but don't get comfy, either of you," Qwyrk warned. "Get your good look in, and then we're on our way to somewhere far less pleasant."

Jilly, seemingly oblivious to Qwyrk's warning, took a few steps forward, still turning about. "It's, it's..."

"Nice, yeah, I know. Take it all in, quick!"

Jilly laughed. "I've never seen anything like this! It's like even the air is full of magic. I can see it. I can smell it. I can almost taste it!"

"A common reaction," Blip said. "Over time, as one becomes more accustomed to the surroundings, that sensation fades, in fact..."

"Blip," Qwyrk interrupted, "we're not staying long enough for that sensation to fade, remember?"

"Quite. Yes, she's right. Jilly, we must prepare to leave now."

"Just another minute, please?" Jilly said.

Star Tao spoke up. "What harm is a little longer gonna do, eh?"

"Yeah, 1 think that's about enough," Qwyrk said, starting to worry. "Come on then, both of you, let's go."

"No…" Jilly said wandering a little farther away.

"Jilly," Blip cautioned. "Qwyrk is quite right; it's time to go."

"1 don't want to yet…"

"Jilly," Qwyrk ordered. "Now." She walked up behind Jilly and took her arm to pull her back.

Jilly resisted a little but looked at Qwyrk, rolled her eyes in annoyance and said, "Fine, all right let's go."

"Blip, grab our air-headed friend there, and let's be on our way."

Blip easily guided a near tranced-out Star Tao over to her and took Qwyrk's hand. "A very good idea, I should think."

With Jilly still reluctant, Qwyrk concentrated on their next location and in a flash, they were gone as quickly as they had arrived.

CHAPTER NINE

"So," Lluck asked, standing opposite Carl, "what exactly do you want me to do?" He'd moved the furniture in the sitting room back against the walls and out of the way.

"Whatever it is you do," Carl answered. "You know, wave your arms, summon your good luck, that sort of thing. I mean, if you can make bad things happen, you can make good things happen, too, right? Like when you changed the contents of my veggie juice gun."

"Mate we *have* to get a better name for that."

"Yeah, you're right, maybe something like the 'Bean Blaster.'"

"That's even worse."

"The 'Parsnip Pistol'?"

"Um..."

"The 'Mustard Musket'?"

"The thing is..."

"I've got it! The 'Fennel Flintlock'! Perfect!"

Lluck considered reviewing his recent life choices. "Uh, yeah, fine. That'll do, I guess."

"And you, you need a name, too. We could call you the 'Avenging Aubergine' or the 'Caped Courgette.' You know, something like that."

"Yeah, probably not." Really reviewing his recent life choices!

"Well, there's plenty of time to come up with a good one."

"What's with all the vegetables?"

"What?"

"Why are you using those as your theme?"

"I don't know. I guess no one's used them before, so I wasn't at risk of copying anyone else. Calling myself 'Power Pasty' seemed odd; I mean, I'm not even from Cornwall."

"Fair enough."

"So, go on then."

"What?"

"Do it. 'Luck' me."

"I don't know..." He winced, sure he was going to fail before even starting.

"Come on, just give it a try, and see what happens. Here, I'll jump up and you wave your arms at me, or whatever."

"I don't think that's going to do anything."

"Humor me."

"Fine." Lluck was already imagining what he'd have for lunch.

Carl jumped up but landed before Lluck could wave his hands.

"Right," Carl said, "let's try that again. I'll let you know when I'm jumping. 1... 2... 3... jump!"

Lluck flicked his hands. Carl did a mid-air somersault and landed on his back with a thud.

"Damn. Sorry, mate!" Lluck said, genuinely regretful.

"No worries," Carl grunted. "I think this is going to take a while to perfect."

* * *

In a flash, Qwyrk, Jilly, Blip, and Star Tao were in the Moors, standing on a low hill. They were quite exposed and all but Qwyrk felt the biting chill of the air around them. She immediately motioned for Jilly and Star Tao to crouch down.

"Over there," she pointed to a low-lying area marked off by yellow police tape. A car was parked on the nearest road, much farther away.

"I do not like this, not at all," Blip remarked.

As they'd seen on television, it was an area of ritual sacrifice: bones, burnt offerings, animal carcasses, patterns, and archaic alphabets etched into the frozen ground. An officer was going about and trying not to disturb things. He seemed to be the only one there.

"No sign of anyone else, at least," Qwyrk said.

"It looks like the reporters and cameras have gone away," Jilly whispered.

"Thank Goddess for small favors," Qwyrk answered. "Look, Blip and I are going to check this out, you two stay here."

"But Qwyrk..."

"Because he's invisible to them, and I can hide myself well enough. Unless you've discovered a way to make yourself disappear, too? In which case, please tell me, because I'd love to know how and when you concocted that one!"

Jilly shook her head and folded her arms in a huff. "You don't have to be such a smart arse about it, you know."

"Of course I do, darling!" Qwyrk winked at her.

"Come on, Jilly," Star Tao said. "Why don't we check out what's over there?" He pointed to the hilly area behind them. "There might be some clues the cops ain't found yet a little farther out."

"A splendid idea, young man," Blip beamed. "I knew we could count on you."

Qwyrk hesitated, but conceded. "Yeah, he's got a point. Why don't you go and see what's out there, but stay hidden! If you're found out, we're really screwed."

"Don't worry, we'll be fine," Jilly said as they left.

Qwyrk watched as Jilly and Star Tao made their way over to another knoll, climbing to the top and descending out of her sight. She turned her attention back to the crime scene and spotted the police officer in the distance, wandering about, taking photos, and writing things in a small notepad every now and then. She got the impression he was being too thorough and trying to act more important than he actually was. She watched him for a few minutes, making sure there were no other officers and that no other police cars pulled up.

"This should be easy enough," she said to Blip. "Hop on down there and wander about. Have a look around and see if there's anything interesting that he might not notice."

Blip clasped his hands together. "I do rather like this! A bit of sleuthing, teasing out the undercurrents of the attendant skullduggery, assisting in the uncovering of evidence for a heinous crime, bringing the guilty to justice! Perhaps I missed my calling. Inspector Blippingstone... has a rather nice ring to it, don't you think?"

"Yeah, I'm sure the Yorkshire police would love to have an invisible magical being on the force. It would really help with all those investigations into the nefarious activities of evil sorcerers under the age of thirteen."

"Scoff all you like, but if not for said magical technicality—my being invisible to human adults, that is—it would take us much longer to figure out what may be happening here."

"Just get on down there, and tell me what you see."

"Right then, off we go a-sleuthing! It shall be elementary, I daresay!"

A horrible cry from some distance away stopped Qwyrk from retorting with a witty comeback.

"Damn it!" she hissed, turning in the direction of the voice, and then looking back at her froggy companion. "Blip, get down there and distract that police officer! Now!"

"Oh? And just how am I supposed to do that?"

"I don't know, make something up! Kick him in the shins, throw rocks at him. I don't care!"

"That's impolite and puerile, to say nothing of being disrespectful to an officer of the law, and I would rather not take part in such a childish exercise."

"Blip, if he heard that yelp and heads on over and finds Jilly and Star Tao out here, we're in big trouble! Not to mention that wasn't even close to a human sound."

"Fine, very well! I shall be a precocious brat, but I do so under protest. Go and see to Jilly and the young man!"

Qwyrk bounded up from her hill to land on the side of the one nearby. She searched the area but didn't see her friends. She heard a second howl, echoing from beyond the next hill over.

"Crap! Something magical's out here. Bollocks, bollocks, bollocks. Hang on Jilly, I'll find you!"

*   *   *

"Well, well, look who we meet out here, all by her little lonesome?"

Jilly turned around and saw those two damned goblins, yet again. Except the short one had a tiny head resting atop its shoulders. Very tiny. Like, about the size of a kumquat, but fully-formed, and trying to look angry and scary. As angry and scary as a goblin with a kumquat-sized head could look, which to be honest, wasn't very frightening at all.

Instead of crying out in fear (or even surprise), she actually suppressed a guffaw.

"Oh, yeah, you think this is a right laugh, eh?" the big one said, pointing to his smaller friend. "Gets his soddin' head torn off by accident, and we all have a good chuckle."

"Um, excuse me, *you* were trying to kill my friend and kidnap someone, so he got what he deserved," Jilly said. "I mean, logic's obviously not a strong point with you lot, but do try to keep up at least a bit, all right?"

"Bite your tongue, little girl," the big goblin growled. "The magic that beat the crap out of your Shadow mate?" He raised his clawed hand. "I still got it, right here, and I wouldn't be averse to using it and having a tasty little snack, if you don't stop with the sassy lip."

The smaller goblin opened his mouth and tried to say something, but it just came out as, "Meep."

Jilly put a hand over her mouth and choked back a laugh. She tried to force it down, to glare at them and be defiant, but it was no use; the urge the giggle was just too strong. She let it out, bursting like a dam, half doubling over.

"Oh dear, I'm sorry," she said through mirthful tears. "I know I'm supposed to be scared and all, but this..."

She dissolved into fits of giggling again as she gestured toward the mini goblin head that responded with, "Meeeeep!"

Sneezewort, for his part, put his fists on his hips and scowled. "Young folks! Back in the day, we used to strike terror into their tasty little hearts, but now they just mock us. It ain't right. It ain't proper. Mortal children should know their place."

"Oh come on," Jilly said, gasping for air. "You've got to admit, he looks pretty funny!"

"Jilly, I think I might have found—bloody hell!" Star Tao stumbled up to her, wide eyed and too surprised to say anything else after beholding the bizarre sight of 1.8 goblins looming over her.

"Oh right," Jilly said, "you haven't met these lovely gentlem... goblins... things, yet. Boys? This is my mate, Star Tao. He's an ace channeler. He can contact spirits, aliens, even Thomas the Rhymer; you name it!" She motioned towards the goblins. Star Tao, this is... sorry, I've forgotten your names. Weren't they something like 'Snotnose' and 'Stupid'? Something like that? Oh no," she pointed at Silktassel, grinning. "'Stumpy,' that was it!"

"Right!" Sneezewort bellowed, stomping toward her. Silktassel made some punching motions in the air, but stayed where he was, though he managed an indignant, "Meep!"

"I've had enough of you, little girl!" Sneezewort continued. "I'm gonna put you in my belly, and it's gonna be a lovely and tasty thing!"

He reached out to grab at her, but she ducked under his grasp and dove to one side. She hit the hard, frozen ground and gasped; it hurt more than she thought it would. So much for those action heroics on television and in films. Star Tao swore and took a few steps back.

"Go get Qwyrk!" she ordered, scrambling to her feet.

"But I can't leave you here alone with those things."

"Just do it, I'll be fine!"

"Nah, you'll be digestin' in my belly," Sneezewort taunted, making for her again.

"Go!" Jilly commanded. Star Tao nodded and made his way up the hill, glancing back a couple of times as he fought to get up the icy slope.

"Right then, lovely," Sneezewort said. "Ready to be an appetizer?"

"No," she said, refusing to show any fear. She reached into her coat pocket and pulled out a small knife. "I think I'll do this instead!"

She dropped down into a crouch and lunged at the goblin, landing at his feet on her stomach. "Ouch! Seriously, why is this so much harder in real life?"

Before he could react, she plunged the knife down into his foot. It sank deep and black blood spurted out, coating her hand and spraying on her face.

"Gah! Oh, that's disgusting!"

Sneezewort howled in pain, flailing his arms around. His yell echoed about, and Jilly knew it would attract Qwyrk's and Blip's attention, and probably the police officer's as well. He lifted his foot up and incidentally managed to kick her, sending her into a roll a few feet away. At least she managed to keep hold of the knife. Sneezewort hopped about on his uninjured foot and yelped again. Nearby, she saw Silktassel looking on with his very tiny, pinpoint, yet wide yellow eyes as he gasped something. Or rather, "meeped" it.

But Jilly was too busy wiping goblin blood off her face and swearing and feeling sick to even notice that his kick had actually hurt. She stood up, disgusted and pained and furious and started slashing the knife madly in the air in front of her. "You want more of this? You want more, eh? Come and get it! I'm not afraid of you, you bastard, I'm not..."

"Jilly!"

She looked up to see Qwyrk at the top of the hill, who in one bound, leaped down and landed right in front of her in a crouch with one fist planted on the ground. Star Tao hadn't even made it to the top of the hill yet, but Jilly heard him say "bollocks" as he turned around and started working his way back down, slipping and sliding all the way.

"Right," Qwyrk said, clenching her fists and bringing them up in front of her. "I have had more than enough of you two. Magical enhancements or not, I'm going to kick your bloated arses to Durham and back! Twice! And I'm going to enjoy every minute of it!"

With a swiftness that astonished Jilly, Qwyrk landed a vicious punch on Sneezewort's nose, knocking him on his flabby bum. She stormed over to Silktassel, who was waving his hands in front of him for mercy, chirping like a mad little bird. She yanked him by one arm, threw him over her shoulder, and sent him crashing into the icy ground next to his fallen companion. Qwyrk grabbed Sneezewort's throat and pinched Silktassel's tiny head between her fingers.

"Now then," Qwyrk said in a calm but threatening voice. "You're going to tell me absolutely everything you know, and maybe, just maybe, I won't tear your heads off and stuff them up your arses, which in your case," she said, looking at Silktassel, "won't be much of a challenge."

Jilly choked back another laugh, momentarily forgetting the grossness of being smeared in goblin blood. To her surprise, Sneezewort started to bellow, as if he was crying. She approached them with caution, trying to be quiet so that Qwyrk wouldn't order her away.

"We didn't have no choice!" the bigger goblin sobbed. "We heard there was this new player in the game, right? So we figured, why not? Look into it, see if he's worth our time. But, but, we kinda got wrapped up in it, and then he gave us these super powers, which was brilliant at first, but he said he'd torture and kill us if we didn't deliver the boy, so we went after him. We was in over our heads!"

"Why does he want the boy?" Qwyrk asked.

"No idea, I swear! We just did wot we was told. He made it more than clear that too many questions meant death. We don't even know who he is. I'm tellin' you the truth, honest!"

"Oh, I have a fairly good idea of who he is," Qwyrk said.

"Please don't send us back to him," Sneezewort begged, sobbing again. "He said if we didn't bring the lad back this time, he'd do all sorts of horrible things to us, make it real painful before he kills us; turns us inside out and that sort of thing. I mean, you wouldn't want that on your conscience, would ya?"

"Honestly? I'd be happy to let him do whatever the hell he wants to do with you."

"Qwyrk..." Jilly walked up behind her. "We can't do that. I mean, they're horrid and all, but, but that's not us, is it?"

Qwyrk turned to look at her, not releasing her grotesque captives from her grip. Her gaze softened. She sighed. "No. No it isn't." She smiled a little. "So what should we do, oh wise one?"

Jilly looked down at the goblins. "Right then, we're not sending you back to your master, and we're not going to kill you, so you'd better run and hide somewhere until this is all over. I don't care where, just leave us and the boy Lluck alone."

She wisely didn't mention that Lluck was missing once again.

"Qwyrk here will deal with your master, and then you won't

have to worry about him anymore, all right? You'll be safe, but if you get in our way again, we'll take care of you," she raised her knife, "permanently."

Qwyrk grinned and stood up, releasing them. They followed suit, scrambling to their feet.

"Thank you! Good on ya!" Sneezewort gasped, rubbing his throat. Silktassel twittered and chittered and gave something like a tiny nod and another "meep."

"You won't be hearin' from us again, I promise! We're layin' low until all this crap is over. I'm done with the lot of it!"

"See to it," Qwyrk said. She stomped the ground at them and they yelped and ran off, Sneezewort limping on his one good foot. Their lumbering forms crunched the ice as they hopped up an adjacent hill and disappeared.

"Qwyrk, I'm sorry if I got in above my head. I'm sorry if I..."

"Actually, that was very impressive, Ms. Pleeth," Qwyrk smiled.

"Yeah?"

"Yeah! Nice little knife you've got there, by the way. Where did you get it?"

"Oh, it's only a little ritual blade I bought at the *Swapping Shop* a few months ago; I just liked the look of it. Figured it might come in handy someday. Guess I was right."

"Can I see it?" Qwyrk reached out, and Jilly offered it to her. "It's odd. I wouldn't have thought a simple human knife would be able to pierce goblin skin, especially since they're dripping with their master's magic. But it seems to have done the job just fine. Normally someone has to have magic in them to hurt one of those creatures."

"Never really thought about it," Jilly answered with a shrug. "Just lucky, I guess."

"Hm," Qwyrk said as she handed it back.

"What the bloody hell were those things?" Star Tao came jogging up to them, panting in the icy air.

"Remember the goblins we told you about?" Jilly said. "Yeah, that was them."

"Gruesome looking buggers, ain't they?" he said.

"You have no idea," Qwyrk said. "Come on, let's get out of here. I left Blip to handle that police officer, and I don't think that was a very wise choice."

"Handle?" Jilly asked.

"Distract him, so he wouldn't head on over here and see you, and who knows? Maybe even the goblins."

"Oh dear," Jilly said.

"Yeah," Qwyrk agreed. "Probably not my best idea."

* * *

"So, we're really not getting anywhere, are we?" Carl said as he flopped on the living room floor.

"Maybe we just need a couple more tries," Lluck suggested, trying to sound hopeful, but secretly agreeing with his odd host.

Carl shook his head. "No, we've been at this all morning; it's hopeless. I'm useless. Honestly, I should have gotten the crap beaten out of me, or maybe even been killed by now. I suppose that's the only luck I actually have. I just wanted to do something, you know, Make a bit of a difference. But I'm just a failure at it."

Lluck felt sorry for him. "Look," he offered, "maybe I just need to change my focus a bit. I mean, I don't really know how to control this lucky stuff I do, right? I just throw out my hands and things happen. But what if I actually focus on something, like try to concentrate my thoughts on a result? Maybe if we start small, that'll make a difference?"

"Have you done that before?"

"Never tried. Didn't really think about it. Fact is, it's gotten stronger in the last few months, so who knows?"

"All right, then, what do you suggest?" Carl asked as he stood up.

"Well, try a simple move, like a jump into a somersault, or something, and let me just see what I can do." Lluck found himself surprisingly eager to continue.

"You realize if it fails, I'm going to look right stupid. And probably hurt myself."

"Yeah, but at least I'll have a laugh," Lluck smiled. He was starting to like Carl, in spite of his misgivings.

Carl sneered. "Fine, but my reputation, to say nothing of my neck vertebrae, is in your hands. Literally, I'd imagine." He backed up a bit to give himself a few more feet.

"Just give it a try," Lluck said. "But let me get settled first."

He sat down on the couch and rubbed his hands together, breathed deeply a few times and shook his hands out. "Right, I'm going to think only about making this work..."

"Brilliant, off I go!" Carl said and lunged forward.

"Wait! I wasn't..."

Carl faceplanted with a thud on the floor, letting out a painful "Oof!"

"...ready. Mate, seriously, you've got to stop being so impulsive."

Carl roused himself. "Well at least my neck is still in one piece."

"Yeah, but it won't be if you keep on like that. I'll tell you when to lunge."

"But in the heat of battle, I can't wait for your signal."

"Um," he looked around, "we're not in the heat of battle, as far as I can see. And can we just try starting small and see where it goes from there?"

In answer, Carl got up and reset himself for another try.

"Great! Now just wait for a minute." Lluck went through the same ritual as before, telling himself that it might mean something. He closed his eyes and breathed in, opened them and exhaled. He brought his attention to Carl's feet and how he would move, and tried to block out everything else.

"Right, okay, I think I have it," he said.

"You think? These falls are getting painful."

"No, I'm sure; give it a shot. Go on, then."

Carl looked at him with distrust and hesitated. But he clapped his hands together and said, "Right, let's do it!"

He ran three steps and lunged for the floor. Lluck kept his attention on that one small space and tried to follow his movement. He called on his inner intention, tried to direct it to that one point, unsure if it would work, or was just a load of bollocks. To the surprise of both of them, Carl landed into a perfect somersault and sprung to his feet on the end of it, jumping up far higher than he could possibly have done normally, landing in one smooth motion, like a master gymnast.

He turned around, looking at Lluck in shock.

"How? What? I don't believe it! That was totally brilliant! I've never done anything like that. That was full-on superheroics! Did you really do that?"

"Well, *you* did it. I just helped, I guess."

"This is amazing, spot on!" He was shaking with excitement. "Can we try it again?"

"Sure, why not?"

A second attempt yielded a bigger flip and a higher jump. Carl pumped his fist in the air and yelled in triumph, and Lluck was rather proud of himself.

"This is it, we're on our way!" Carl announced.

"It's a start, anyway." Lluck was thrilled to exercise more control over his power. Maybe this wouldn't be such a bad place to work on that, after all.

CHAPTER TEN

"Now then," Blip mused as he hopped down the hill to the unwitting police officer. "How shall I go about this unpleasant little display? Let me see. I suppose I could attack him with a modal argument against the very concept of singular propositions. No, no, not unless he's well-versed enough for proper counter-argumentation, which, looking at the poor chap, I presume is not the case. Perhaps I could simply stall for time with a discussion of haecceity and quiddity in the sense of their ontological meanings. This fellow looks as if he could use a good dose of whatness."

A terrible screech startled him out of his pontification, followed by... was that a faint little "Meep"?

The officer jumped at the sound and reached for his radio, radioing someone about something radio-related. Blip, confirmed luddite though he was, realized that if the dimwit were calling for back-up...

"Damn it all! No time for pleasantries. Goddess, this is

distasteful!" Blip picked up a small rock and threw it at the officer, striking him on the leg. He yelled out, turning in every direction, looking rather peeved.

"All right, whoever you are," the policeman called out. "Get your arse on out here now. I'm in no mood for your games."

"I, too, am in no mood for recreation," Blip muttered, ambling on up to the officer and kicking him in the shin.

"Ow!" the officer yelled, gripping his leg and trying to find the perpetrator of this affront against the law.

"Arrghghgh!" Blip yelled at the same time, hopping away and clutching his foot. "Why am I always injuring my damned feet on these wretched adventures?" He hopped into a rather large rock, crashing unceremoniously, and falling flat on his face on the cold, hard ground. Pain shot through him. Rolling over and sitting up, he glimpsed the policeman rubbing his leg, but he was already back on his damned radio, doing more of those damned radio things that radios do, apparently.

"Right, no time to think it through." He stood up and hobbled back over to the officer, lunging for his midsection. The two connected, and the man went over on his back, Blip landing on top of him. Both let out "Oofs!" at some considerable volume. Blip had the sense to roll off and scamper away, his toes still throbbing.

"What the bloody hell is happening?" the man yelled, rousing himself into a sitting position and darting his stare in every direction. "I'm warning you! You've assaulted an officer of the law; this has crossed the line and..."

An anguished yelp echoed from somewhere over the hills.

"What the hell is going on?" the hapless policemen shouted. "This isn't funny anymore!"

"You're damned right, it isn't," Blip muttered. "And since brute force isn't doing the trick, I'll resort to something a bit more subtle, if garish."

He grabbed a stick and, marching up to the policeman (who was still sitting on the icy ground, looking ever more confused), began to scrawl something in the dirt. The man's eyes widened as words appeared on the ground out of nowhere:

Leave us now, mortal. The dead do not countenance your trespass. Perhorresce at our power, and be gone from our sacred domain or suffer the eternal, damnable, and utterly non-supernal consequences!!

"Two exclamation marks should make the point well enough," Blip announced, quite satisfied as he held his crude writing implement in triumph.

Indeed, the officer's mouth dropped open and his eyes widened in horror, just as Blip had hoped. He scrambled to his feet, whimpering and shaking his head, and he ran all the way back to his patrol car. He jumped in and sped off at a good pace.

Blip watched with a satisfied grin. "The pen—or rather, the stick—most truly is mightier than the sword."

* * *

Holly breathed in the fresh, cold air of the woods behind the B&B as she finished meditating in front of a rather large old oak, now bereft of leaves for the duration of the wintry season. Despite trying to calm herself, she was restless and agitated. This wasn't going well, not the way it was supposed to at all.

She sighed in frustration and began to wander back to the welcome warmth of her chosen temporary abode, when she was stopped short by one of the stranger sights she had seen in a while—and she'd seen some strange sights recently.

Standing in front of her, apparently having materialized out of nowhere, was a mottled green creature, roughly one foot tall, looking something like a tiny version of a mortal's idea of a devil. He had stubby horns protruding from his bald head, an oversized and bulbous nose, and wore a burlap sack that was a bit too large for him. His yellow eyes were rather unsettling, and he sported a toothy grin that was both comical and creepy.

"Top of the day to ya, lovely lady," he said in a voice much deeper than it should have been, given his tiny stature.

Holly glared at him. "And you are?"

"My name is Horatio, representing the local Union of Nighttime Nasties, Yorkshire Chapter." He made a slight bow.

"And I care because?"

"Because, I have some information wot might be useful to you, regardin' your son."

Holly reached down in an instant and jerked him up into the air, her hands under his arms, as if he were a puppy or baby; a very un-cute puppy or baby. One that she had no qualms at all about shaking with some vigor.

"Tell me what you know, and perhaps I shan't throw you into that tree behind you."

"Whoa, whoa, whoa!" Horatio flailed his arms about, his eyes wide in genuine fear. "A bit more decorum, please. I would hope that one with your elegant and graceful nature would comport herself with a fair bit more good manners to a bearer of tidings. Don't shoot the messenger, and all that."

"I'm in no mood to comport myself in any way to your liking," she said, her anger growing. She set him down again, but not too gently. "All right, you said you have 'tidings', so tell me what you know."

"I keep me ear to the ground, right? I make it me business to know wot's goin' on when the big stuff starts shakin' out. And believe you me, miss, this business with your boy is big. That thing after him? It's bad, real bad. Real scary. Now we Nasties, we like to have our odd bit of fun, right? Scare the kids, cause some chaos, that sort of thing. But this ain't that. This is hell on earth, death and destruction, and all the rest. If the thing chasin' him gets ahold of your boy, things are gonna go to shite, and pretty damned quick. I can promise you we Nasties don't want that any more than you do. In fact, this is the second time the world has been in danger of ending this year, and I for one, am bloody sick of it. Your girl, Qwyrk, she can confirm I'm on the level."

"What do you know about Qwyrk? And how do you know she and I have spoken?"

"Like I said, I make it me business to know when powerful beings such as yourselves have a bit of social intercourse. And she and I go back a long way. I helped her out last summer with the de Soulis affair."

Holly gave him an "I don't believe you, you twat" glare.

"All right, not directly helped, but I gave her mates info and off they went and helped her and next thing ya know, old Willie was dead, and the world was back to normal again. I'd very much like for that to be the case this time around, too."

"Fine. So what do you know?"

"Word has it that your lad is currently staying at some bloke's house in the north of Leeds. Been hold up there for a day or two."

"I already know that. I have my own resources."

"Yeah, but do you know who the mortal is?"

"What difference does that make?"

"Maybe none. Maybe a lot."

Holly drew out her stick, which transformed at her touch into the staff she wielded with such precision. She pointed it at Horatio in a threatening manner.

"Who is he?"

Horatio gulped. "Don't know for sure, ma'am, but he seems like he might be connected to your boy somehow."

"Connected? Connected how?" It hit her as she said the words. "No. No, it can't be."

"Can't be what?"

She looked away and let her arm fall to the side of her, retracting the staff. She glanced back down at him.

"Nothing. Never mind. Um, thank you. That's actually far more helpful than I expected."

Horatio bowed again. "Always happy to do me part to help prevent the end of all things. If I should hear anything else, I'll happily pass it on to you."

"Uh, fine. Good. Thank you again." She turned toward her B&B, more troubled than ever.

Horatio grinned. "I'll give your regards to Qwyrk, should I see her. She's quite somethin', ain't she?"

"Meaning?" She looked back at him with impatience.

"Meaning that she's quite somethin', and one could do a fair bit worse. Just sayin'. Cheers!"

And with that, he hopped away into the woods, leaving her to stare after him in irritation and a bit of confusion.

* * *

"Oh, this is brilliant! Brilliant!" Carl's face was alight with glee as he accomplished more and more complex maneuvers in his backyard: jumps, rolls, kicks, fancy superhero landings, all with Lluck's concentration and help, of course. Lluck was worn out, but didn't want to interrupt the older man's fun.

As if sensing the boy's fatigue, Carl said, "I mean, we've been at it for a while now. We can take a break if you'd like."

"Yeah, I wouldn't mind, actually," Lluck said. "It seems easy enough, but it takes lots of concentration. I've never actually done anything like this, not for like a full hour, anyway. It's exhausting."

"No worries," Carl said, standing up from a particularly impressive backflip. "I could do this all day, but I understand. Let's take a break, have some lunch. We could pop down the pub at the end of the street."

"Sounds good. I could murder a pie of some kind."

"They've got lots of those down there. Come on; it's on me."

Lluck breathed a sigh of relief and followed Carl back into the house.

"I'm just going upstairs to change. Got a bit hot doing all those acrobatics. Back in a few ticks."

"Sure, fine, I'll wait here." Lluck plopped himself down on the sofa and picked up another selection from the endless magazines, comics, and fan material strewn all about the living room. Well, not strewn, exactly. They were in semi-neat piles and seemed to be sorted by category.

As he flipped through a sci-fi magazine, doubts crept into him again. What about school and legal stuff, and all that? His foster family would only ignore him for so long. Even they would start looking for him in another couple of days. He couldn't just disappear. Carl acted like this could all be taken care of, but Lluck doubted he had any plan at all.

"Oh well, at least I'll a get a good free lunch."

A few moments later, Carl came bounding down the stairs, looking light and airy and full of happiness. Lluck was oddly sympathetic; he liked this odd fellow in spite of himself. There was something about him that appealed, which was the only reason he hadn't bailed already.

"Right! Shall we go gorge ourselves on pies and chips?"

"I'm ready, mate!"

There was a knock at the door.

"That's odd," Carl said, scrunching up his face in confusion. "Who'd be here at this time of day?"

A bit of worry hit Lluck in his hungry stomach, and he readied himself.

Carl walked over to the door and opened it. Lluck couldn't see who the visitor was.

"Yes?"

There was no answer, but Carl flew backward, crashing into the foot of the stairs and slumping over, knocked out. Lluck was on his feet as Longwing stepped into the living room, slamming the door behind him. He looked the same as the previous night, only far more pissed off.

"Hello, youngling. You gave me quite a chase there for a bit, so I give you full credit for that. But you didn't think you were going to get away, did you? Your superhero there was less than useless, just as I'd figured he'd be without his stupid gun."

Lluck flung his hands outward at the intruder with all the force he could muster, channeling everything he had into the most explosive burst of his power that he'd ever tried to conjure.

And nothing happened.

Longwing smiled. "Spent all morning draining yourself, didn't you? You obviously don't know, but magic is a bit like a well. Use too much at once and it depletes until it can be replenished."

"Magic?" Lluck stammered.

"Of course! What did you think it was, idiot? You're half-Fae. The stuff is practically dripping off you, which is how I found you, by the way. But given that whole part-human business, you'll never be as strong as a pure-blood, so all I had to do was wait while you used up your power making that fool jump about, and then it was time to pounce. This is the part where I abduct you and you try to flee, but fail miserably, by the way."

Lluck sneered. "Yeah, right, mate. I got away before, and I can do it again!"

He dashed toward the kitchen and the back door, but Longwing was too fast. The hunter-in-black tackled him and sent him crashing into the floor. He hit it with a thud and a loss of breath, as pain surged through him. Longwing grabbed him by the hair.

"See, if you'd come quietly last night, I'd be nicer about this. But since you delayed me, which makes me look bad—and I really don't like looking bad—I'm in no mood to be pleasant. So, this is going to hurt, and if I'm being honest, I'm going to rather enjoy it."

He slammed Lluck's forehead into the floor.

A momentary sharp burst of agony shot through Lluck, and then blackness took him.

* * *

"Bloody hell, Blip! What did you do?" Qwyrk surveyed the crime scene as she and the others made their way down the hill, having left the fleeing goblins long behind and best forgotten. She saw no policeman or car anywhere.

"I sent the fellow packing. Did a rather damned good job of it if I do say so myself!"

"What? How?"

"I made him think that some malevolent but unseen ghoul was possessing the place and wanted him gone. And believe you me, he left in a great hurry." Blip showed her his handiwork scrawled in the dirt, a smug smile on his froggy face.

She read it and exhaled a sharp puff of air. "You *do* realize that nobody is going to believe him, and they're likely to order him back to the scene along with backup. Probably soon."

"Yes, yes, but we'll be long gone by then," he replied.

"But we need time to look about and see if there are any other clues! What if he comes back with a whole damned squad?"

"Well, what do you suggest? We had to get rid of him somehow. I was improvising in the moment!"

"Yeah, all right, fine. We'll do a quick search and get the hell out of here. I don't think there's that much to see, anyway. Scratch out that writing so when his mates come back, he'll look right foolish, and there won't be any evidence we were ever here."

"Fine." Blip scowled, but set about rubbing out his warning.

Star Tao wandered over to him. "If you don't mind me saying so, my lord, I think that was a very clever plan. Did the trick and made the officer all terrified. That's two wins, in my book! I'd have loved to see his face!"

"I do not engage in petty hooliganism, young man, just remember that! The law is the law and deserves proper respect. I only did what needed to be done to further the accomplishment of our task. As my acolyte, I expect better from you."

Star Tao bowed. "Forgive me, my lord. I spoke rashly."

"Yes, well it is the way of mortal kind. You are forgiven."

TEN

Qwyrk watched this absurd dialogue, half relieved that things were at least somewhat normal (for this group, anyway), and half ready to throw in the towel and relocate to Aruba. But she motioned to Jilly to join her, and they scouted up and down the ritual site in some haste.

"You don't think any people were sacrificed here, do you?" Jilly asked, more than a little fear in her voice.

"No, not yet, anyway. But you can be sure that's on the program."

"So, Qwyrk and friends have to save the world. Must be Tuesday." Jilly smiled.

"Wait, it's not Tuesday, is it?"

"No. It's just an expression."

Qwyrk looked at her, confused.

"Like, it happens so often, it could actually be once a week," Jilly scoffed.

"Right! Of course, sorry. I know that. I'm just a bit distracted right now."

Jilly raised an eyebrow. "Got a pretty faerie on your mind, maybe?"

Qwyrk glared at her. "No, I do not! Not really. All right, fine, but I can't worry about it right now. I may not even really like her, that much, sort of, I don't think."

"Whatever you say," Jilly said with a smug smirk.

"Look, we should get out of here," Qwyrk said, trying to change the subject. "I don't think we're going to find anything else, and I don't want to have to deal with a whole posse of Yorkshire's not-so-finest rolling up and seeing you two. You getting arrested is the last thing I need right now. Let's gather up the other two members of the 'Farce Force' and get out of here."

"Are we passing through your home again?" Jilly's face brightened.

"Yes, and we're *not* staying, so don't get your hopes up."

Jilly's face fell as quickly as it had lit up.

"Blip! Star Tao!" Qwyrk motioned to them with a wave of her hand. "Come on, there's nothing else to see here. Let's go."

They ambled back over.

"Right," Qwyrk said. "Everyone join hands again."

They did as she asked and she closed her eyes to concentrate; it always took a bit more effort when transporting so many people. It was like she was providing some sort of inter-dimensional replacement bus service. Still, after a moment of directing her intent, a flash surrounded them and they were once more in the magical, golden, glowing forest of Symphinity, where the air just seemed to ooze magic, but not in a gross way.

Jilly flashed a wide smile, and her eyes seemed to glaze over as she let go of Qwyrk's hand and started to wander off into the forest.

"Jilly, no! Come back!" Qwyrk reached for her, but Jilly shrugged her off and picked up her pace.

"Bollocks," Qwyrk swore, coming up behind her and grabbing her hard on the shoulder.

"Hey, let go of me! Bugger off!" Jilly shook her arm free.

"Jilly!" Qwyrk snapped.

"Ms. Pleeth, cease this nonsense now!" Blip commanded from behind them.

"I will force you if I have to," Qwyrk said.

Jilly turned around and with a look of spite, punched out at Qwyrk, missing but shocking her. "I'm not leaving!"

"Right, I knew this would happen. That's it, we're done." She grabbed Jilly, threw her over her shoulder, and dragged her back to the others. Jilly started kicking and yelling, struggling in Qwyrk's grip.

"Let go of me, damn you!" She pounded on Qwyrk's back.

"We're getting out of here, right now! Blip, grab that moron and take my hand."

"Hey!" Star Tao protested. "I didn't do anything."

But Blip did as she asked, and in a flash they were gone almost as soon as they'd arrived, leaving all temptation behind.

※　※　※

The door was ever so slightly ajar when they arrived, as if it had been opened and shut with some force. Two figures in long, black trench coats, their faces obscured by sunglasses, quietly surveyed the scene.

"I would say that this looks suspicious, Mr. Dill."

"I quite agree, Mr. Chives. Shall we enter and remove ourselves from prying eyes?"

"I think that is an excellent course of action."

Dill and Chives slipped into the house and shut the door properly behind them. In front of them, lying prone at the foot of the stairs was a man, breathing but not stirring.

Dill sniffed the air. "Magic is most definitely here, or rather it was," he observed.

"I concur," Chives said. "And I do believe it bears the essence and hallmarks of our lucky young target."

"Indeed it does, Mr. Chives, but there's something else, as well. Can you detect it?"

Chives sniffed. "I can. I would hazard a guess that it is not Fae, not exactly, perhaps an amalgamation of said magic and some other ingredient, something very old?"

"Were I to hazard a similar guess," Dill said, "and I will, if that is acceptable to you..."

"It is."

"...I would hypothesize that it is Darkfae, but mingled with human."

"Are you suggesting that said individual is supernatural, rather like our quarry?"

"That would be my immediate suspicion, my esteemed colleague."

"A most unusual blend."

"Indeed, but then, so is our young man."

"Clearly, neither is here now. Based on the unconscious fellow lying behind us, may we assume that there was some altercation resulting in the boy being taken against his will by this curious new player in the game?"

"We may well assume such. Look," Dill pointed to a spot on the floor where there was a small splotch of blood. "I would hypothesize that the aggressor overpowered the boy and, rendering him as unconscious as this human, abducted him, most likely at the behest of the real culprit."

"I would agree. Should we tell our client?"

"Which one?"

"The *actual* one, of course."

"Let us hold off, just for the moment. I want to speak to the mortal. Help me rouse him."

They kneeled down and picked up the poor victim, carrying him to the sofa where they laid him down gently. He stirred a little, and Dill tapped the side of his face. His eyes opened. He blinked and squinted and blinked again. He was clearly not prepared for the presence of two strangers in dark sunglasses standing over him, so, naturally, he panicked. He shouted, flailed his arms, and tried to get up, but Dill placed a finger over his mouth and shushed him, easily holding him down with the other hand.

"There is no need for alarm, I promise you, sir," he said. "At first, that may seem unlikely, given that we have entered your domicile without your express permission and moved you from the stairs to your place of lounging without your consent, but I can assure you that we mean you no harm, that whoever did this to you is long gone, and that we are here to try to assist, in whatever way we can."

"Who are you? What are you doing here?" He looked around. "Where's... where's Lluck?"

"All very good questions, sir, and we shall endeavor to answer them as best as we can. However, it is apparent that there is more occurring here than you are probably aware of, and therefore we believe that we need to have a little chat first."

"About what?"

"About the end of the world as we know it, among other things, sir."

CHAPTER ELEVEN

In a violet flash of light, the Farce Force was once again standing in Jilly's living room. Odin looked up from his comfy bed, momentarily curious, and then settled and went back to sleep. Qwyrk set Jilly down and backed away. Jilly took a few deep breaths and looked up at her; she was on the verge of tears. She put a hand over her mouth and ran up the stairs and into her bedroom, slamming the door shut.

"What happened?" Star Tao asked, after an uncomfortable silence.

"Something's wrong. Very wrong," Qwyrk answered, the gravity in her voice betraying her own fears.

"With Jilly?"

"I don't know," Qwyrk said, looking up after her.

"Do you want me to go up?" Blip offered, for once not sounding at all sure that he could remedy the situation.

"Not yet. Leave her be for a bit," Qwyrk said, looking away from both of them. "I'll come back later, after I've thought about it some more. I'm going to set up a meeting."

"A meeting? With whom?" Blip asked.

"Bogtrotter."

"Who?" Star Tao asked.

"Bah! That scoundrel?" Blip spat. "What on Earth do you hope to learn from him?"

"The Nasties make it their business to know the latest magical gossip," Qwyrk answered, "and even though they're a pain in the arse, they might just know a bit more about what the hell is going on. At this point, I'll take help from anywhere I can get it."

"Well, be careful. I don't trust them," Blip warned.

"Oh, I don't either," she answered, looking down at him. "But I have to try something."

"Who's Bogtrotter?" Star Tao asked again.

"Long story," Qwyrk answered. "Basically he's the head of a group of magical creatures who aren't as evil as the Darkfae; they're more just annoying. Still, they're really good at finding out bits of information that no one else seems able to dig up, so I go to them for tips and such every now and then."

"Do you need us to come along?" Blip asked.

"No, I've got it. Just stay here with Jilly. Keep an eye on her, but don't disturb her for a while. I also need to go talk with, um, someone else first, and then I'll meet with the Nasties. I'll be back later."

* * *

Jilly sat on the edge of her bed, fidgeting. She'd washed the goblin blood off her face, but that didn't wash away her guilt. She looked over at the door, expecting Qwyrk to come storming through it at any moment to tell her off and announce that she was leaving and would never come back. It was like waiting for an execution. When a knock finally came, she almost fell on the floor.

"Come in," she managed to say. She was relieved when Blip poked his head around the corner. But maybe that just meant that Qwyrk had already left without saying good-bye and would never come back.

Blip entered and closed the door behind him. He said nothing as he strode across the room and hopped up on the bed to sit beside her. She couldn't bear to look at him, but he didn't speak, which just made her more nervous.

"I'm... I'm sorry," she said, looking down at the floor. "I don't know what happened back there, but I turned into a right pain, didn't I?"

"I'm afraid your behavior was rather pugilistic."

"Is Qwyrk...?"

"She's gone off on some errands, but she'll be back later."

Jilly sighed in relief. "So, she's not going away then, like never coming back?"

"Good gracious, child, why would you think that?"

Tears came to her, and she looked up at Blip. "Because I was horrible! I was awful! I've been nothing but terrible to her since she came back, and then I snapped at her, and now I'm worried I've ruined everything and she hates me and..."

She broke down and sobbed, not caring what Blip thought of such a blatant display of emotion.

"There, there, child." She felt his hand on her back, and his touch was surprisingly light, given her previous encounters with his attempts to be comforting. "It's not nearly as bad as you think it is."

She looked up again. "But what happened back there? I mean, I know I wanted to see your home, but that was crazy! Once I was there, I couldn't take my eyes off it. It was like I was trapped and was just fine with being trapped, you know?"

"It's not unusual for mortals to become entranced with our world. I've seen it happen many times over the centuries."

"But this was mental, like extreme, like I was a drug addict, or something. I mean, Star Tao's been there a few times now and hasn't reacted that way at all, has he? This doesn't seem right."

"No it doesn't. I believe there may be other forces at play here."

"Where is he, by the way?"

"The lad? Oh, I think he had some more errands to do for that ridiculous workshop of his, or some such. He said he'd call around tomorrow."

"Ah, all right. I don't know, I've just felt off for the past few days. Like really aggressive and angry. I mean, I'm always kind of annoyed by everything, but this is more, way more than it should be. It scares me."

"When did you first notice it manifesting?"

"Maybe after we met Lluck in that alley in Leeds? I don't know. It might have been after Qwyrk came back. Do you think one of them brought something bad with them? Like a magical disease or something, and I caught it?"

Blip looked away for a moment as if thinking hard, but shook his head. "I'm not aware of any such infection, but that's not to say that there couldn't be one. All sorts of unfortunate impediments have been cropping up lately, it seems."

"So, what do we do? I don't want it to happen again, and I'm really afraid if it does, Qwyrk is going to hate me and never want to speak to me again." She started to cry again.

"My dear," Blip said in a surprisingly comforting tone. "Ms. Qwyrk is never going to hate you. You have shown remarkable courage and heroism in the face of great evil, and that is not something lightly forgotten. I assure you, if there's a problem, she will want to get to the bottom of it as much as you do, and I've no doubt that you will work together to enact a solution that will be highly satisfactory to all parties. I can confirm that she is presently quite concerned for you and will check in on you again once her other duties are complete."

"What's she doing?"

"She is arranging a meeting with a certain Nighttime Nasty, or rather, the leader of the Yorkshire faction, to try to obtain more information about the Erlking and his agenda."

"Is that safe?"

"Oh, I wouldn't worry overly. You see, Bogtrotter..."

"Bogtrotter?" Jilly let a smile peek through her tears.

"His name, yes."

"That's funny!" she giggled.

"How so?"

"You know!"

"I'm afraid I do not."

"*Bog*trotter..." Jilly made a funny face, raised her eyebrows, and waved her hands around.

"One who walks over the marshes and fens, yes. It probably has Anglo-Saxon origins. Possibly something to do with Grendel, an apt comparison."

"You don't, you don't get the joke?"

"Is there one?"

"Yes!" Jilly couldn't believe it wasn't clear, but Blip just stared at her, uncomprehending. She sighed.

"A bog... it's slang for a loo."

"Is it?"

"Yes! Also, 'trotter.'"

"I'm failing to see the humor."

"When someone has 'the trots,'" she said as she tried making some sort of hand movements that might convey the expression's meaning, without being too obvious.

"What? They have a compulsion to skip about?"

"Well, they might, but no. It's when someone really has to..."

"Yes?"

"You know, when they need to..."

"What? Jump? Caper? Dance a galliard around a toilet?"

"When they really need to use the loo, like after a bad curry or something. So bog, trotter: having the trots on the bog!"

"I see. How vulgar."

"I've just wasted the last minute explaining this to you, haven't I?"

"I'm afraid so."

* * *

Qwyrk materialized in a shower of violet sparkles near Holly's B&B, into a decent smattering of barren trees that concealed her magical light show well enough. A thin layer of icy snow blanketed the forest floor. Though she wasn't cold, she could see her breath, an odd effect she always enjoyed.

"Just hope she's here," Qwyrk said, as she wandered toward the charming old stone building in the distance.

"Out for a bit of a winter stroll, or is there some breaking news?" Qwyrk almost jumped and turned to see Holly wandering toward her, a smile on her face. She wore a long purple overcoat, a voluminous grey scarf wrapped around her neck, while her silky black hair flowed all about her with the ever-present slow-motion perfection of a shampoo commercial.

"How did I not hear you?" Qwyrk asked, trying not to look ridiculous.

"I'm 'one with the trees,' remember? I'd have been surprised if you had. I was just out for a wander myself; clearing my head. Hello, by the way."

"Right, sorry! Hi, how are you?"

"Better for seeing you."

Qwyrk swallowed and smiled. A stupid smile that she was quite sure was the stupidest smile she possibly could have stupided.

"It *is* rather cold out, and the sun's setting." Holly continued, graciously ignoring Qwyrk's awkward reaction. "Shall we retire to the inn? My room has its own fireplace, which I lit before stepping out. It should be lovely and toasty now. Oh, but you don't get cold, do you?"

"No, but I wouldn't say no to a nice fire and some charming company." *Oh shut it, you prat!*

Holly smiled. "Come on, then!"

As they wandered back, they made small talk, Qwyrk trying not to stare at Holly like a creepy stalker, and they soon found themselves at the old building. Holly put her index finger over her lips.

"Best not talk until we get upstairs," she whispered. "I mean, we wouldn't want to attract attention and scare anyone. I assume anyone else can't see you as you really are?"

"No," Qwyrk confirmed in a low voice. "Only you can."

Holly smiled. "Lucky me."

Qwyrk bit her lip and followed her new friend upstairs and down the creaky hallway to a room with an old green door. They entered and, as Holly predicted, the room was warm and cozy, though the flames in the small stone fireplace had burned down to embers.

"Please, have a seat," Holly said, taking off her coat and hanging it on the old-fashioned hanger in the corner, motioning to an equally old-fashioned, four-poster bed. She wore a woolly, grey jumper over her black trousers. She left her scarf on for the moment, which made her look adorable.

"On the bed?" Qwyrk fidgeted and fretted.

"Of course, why not? It's large enough for two."

Qwyrk hesitated, but sat down on her hands in one awkward motion.

"So, how are you holding up?" she said, realizing that sitting on said hands probably made her seem odd, or at least odder than usual, which was already odd. She removed them from under her bum and placed them in her lap, trying not to look conspicuous. Or odd.

Holly sat down near her. Not that Qwyrk was complaining, she mused. *Mused?*

Holly sighed. "Not well. I mean, I've worried about him every day since he was born. Always afraid that someone would find out who he really is, *what* he really is, and then he'd be in danger for the rest of his life."

"You can't blame yourself for that."

"I can and do. It's not his fault that he's who he is. But it's all because I had to run off and have a fling with some mortal I never saw again."

"Don't beat yourself up about it. You said you were in a bad way. Anyone might have done the same thing. In fact, I have a couple of mates who absolutely would've done the same without the excuse of being distraught!"

Holly laughed. "Honestly, it was silly and impulsive; it's not like I go around doing that sort of thing often, or even rarely, for that matter."

"What, hooking up with random blokes in hotel bars?"

"Well, yes, *that*, but I meant with men in general. Don't misunderstand me, they're lovely—mostly—but not really to my taste."

"Oh? Oh! So you prefer..." *Oh crap. Hang on. Is this? Is she? Could we?*

"The feminine? Quite."

"Brilliant! Um, I'm quite all right with that, just so you know. I'm right there with you, actually!"

"Really?" Holly raised an eyebrow.

"Well, yeah, you know, 'the feminine' is my sort of thing, too. Blokes are fine, dandy in fact, lovely, for the most part. Can't deny I've fallen for a few great ones over the centuries. But ladies are just as nice, even nicer, if I'm being perfectly honest, which I honestly am, honestly. Um, power to the girls!" *Could we? Is she? Is this? Hang on. Oh crap.*

"How lovely, I didn't know."

"Well, I like to be full of surprises."

"I think you do."

"Yeah, it's all good, but, um, we should, we should chat about your boy before we digress too far, you know?" She hoped Holly didn't notice her hasty attempt to change the subject.

"Do you have any idea what might be happening now?"

"I'm looking at a few possibilities, based on what we know."

"Have you found anything at all?" Holly seemed sad and worried again.

"Not as much as I'd like, but it's early yet, and I'm sure more info will turn up as we go along. And you've got your own detectives working on the case, too, right? Between all of us, we're bound to figure it out."

"They said they're quite sure he's in north Leeds right now, but that could be anywhere. Oh Qwyrk, what if we can't find him? What if, what if he's already..." She started to cry.

"Hey, it's all right. We're going to do everything we can," Qwyrk answered in a gentle voice, trying to be as reassuring as she could, if not all that convincing. Almost on instinct, she held open her arms. "Do you need a hug?"

She was surprised (shocked, really) when Holly leaned in to embrace her. Holly rested her head on Qwyrk's shoulder. She held Qwyrk tightly and cried. Qwyrk caught the scent of her hair, a mixture of rose and amber, with a hint of cinnamon. It was almost intoxicating and most definitely magical.

Qwyrk held Holly for a time, quite content to stay there. For her part, Holly nuzzled her cheek against Qwyrk's left ear.

"Um, I don't have any tissues, I'm afraid," Qwyrk blurted out in panic, ruining the moment.

Holly smiled through her tears and separated herself from their embrace. Qwyrk hoped Holly hadn't felt her heart racing.

"I've made a bit of a mess, haven't I?" Holly said with a sniff. "Sorry about that."

"There's nothing to be sorry for. Honestly."

Holly stood up. "I'll just go clean myself up and be back in a moment." With that, she went to the washroom.

"Bloody hell," Qwyrk said to herself and shook her head, crossing her legs and then uncrossing them, fidgeting and un-fidgeting.

She closed her eyes and sighed in exasperation. "I don't want this right now. But I do, and it's distracting me from everything, and I can't have that. Her boy's in danger; she needs help."

Holly emerged a minute later from her ablutions, tears dried and looking as good as new, even better, really. Qwyrk marveled at how she could do that.

"Uh, right, so I have a plan," Qwyrk said, eager to bring the conversation back to their immediate concern.

"Good, a plan is good," said Holly, breaking eye contact and sitting herself back down on the bed. "So what is it?" she asked.

"Hmm?"

"The plan, your plan. What should we do?"

"Right! The plan! Plans are good!"

"They are."

"So, I'm setting up a meeting with Bogtrotter."

"Bogtrotter?"

"One of the leaders of the Nighttime Nasties. Head of the Yorkshire chapter of the Union."

"How strange! I just had an encounter with one of those Nasties earlier today."

"Really? Where? Who?"

"In the forest behind the inn. He said his name was Horatio?"

"Oh, Goddess," Qwyrk brought her hand up to her face.

"Is that not good? He said you'd vouch for him."

"No, he's all right, I suppose, as Nasties go. Good for the odd bit of information. What did he tell you?"

"That Lluck seems to be hiding out with some mortal in north Leeds. But he implied there might be a connection between them."

"Connection?"

"I know it's ridiculous, but what if, what if through his luck powers, he somehow found his father?"

"What? That's quite a long shot!"

"It is, but stranger things have happened. You're the last one I need to remind of that."

"Fair enough. Did he have any idea where Lluck is, exactly?"

"He didn't say."

"Of course he didn't." Qwyrk sighed in frustration.

"But, it's a start, at least. Maybe this Bogtrotter will know something more?"

"Possibly. They do seem to have their nasty noses into all sorts of things they shouldn't. When I talk to him, I'll mention it."

"When *we* talk to him."

"Oh, I can't let you come with me. It's too dangerous."

"Qwyrk, this is my son's life we're talking about. I'm not going to sit on the sidelines like some helpless damsel and let you rescue me. I can more than take care of myself."

"Believe me, I have no doubt of that. But are you sure you're up to it? If he knows anything bad, it may be hard to hear."

"I'm going to find out eventually, anyway, so I'd rather it be sooner than later."

"All right then, we'll do it. We'll go up to the Moors together. I just have to sort out a few things, and set up a meeting."

"Thank you, ever so much. I know it may not seem like a lot, but everything you're doing means the world to me." She took Qwyrk's hand. They gazed at each other for a moment.

"Um, right!" Qwyrk said. "I should probably get on with arranging that meeting and let you know when it's on for. And honestly, it's nothing, really. I just want to help. I don't like seeing you like this. You shouldn't be sad and worried. You should be happy and relaxed and not sad and not worried and, you know!"

She stood up, breathed out sharply and got ready to go. Holly followed her to her feet, planted a quick kiss on her cheek, and threw her arms around her.

"Thank you again," she said through the hug.

Qwyrk held onto her—quite sure she was about to faint, or something equally awful—but she keep her composure. After too short a time, they parted, and she smiled at Holly. "I'll see you very soon."

Holly smiled back. "Horatio said you're quite something. I think he's right."

Qwyrk's face flushed in embarrassment, but she managed a nervous grin that she was sure looked just as awkward as everything else she'd said and done so far. She stepped back and waved, before vanishing in a dazzling display of purple lights. She might have made her exit a little more impressive than it needed to be. In an instant, she was back in the woods near her home.

"Crap," she swore as she paced back and forth, a bundle of nerves and anxiety. "Just, bloody hell!"

* * *

"What do you mean 'the end of the world'?" Carl rubbed his head and sat up a bit.

"Do be careful sir," one of his visitors said. "You've taken a rather nasty hit to the head, and you might be a bit concussed."

"No, I'm all right," he looked around. "Lluck, where's Lluck?"

"Try to remain calm, sir, and we will try to explain. The boy in question is more than he seems."

"Yeah, I know that already."

"He is more than human, but less than a creature of pure magic.

He is highly unusual and as such he is, shall we say, in demand with various factions."

"Factions? You mean like the Soldiers of Superdom versus the Horrific Horde?"

"That may be something of an oversimplification, sir, but yes, essentially. Teams of quite powerful and very malevolent folk are trying to gain the upper hand in this world and other teams of heroic folk are trying to stop them. It's been an ongoing struggle for millennia, though most humans remain blissfully unaware of it, and that is by design."

"I knew it!" Carl said in triumph. "But what does that have to do with Lluck? I mean, he was being chased by that vampire-looking bloke when I rescued him, so I figured there was a lot more to him and his lucky powers than he was letting on."

"You saw his pursuer, then?"

"Oh yeah, I got a good look at him."

"Can you describe him, sir?"

"Sure. He was pale, dressed all in black, long coat, long straight hair, also black. It was odd; under his arms, it looked almost like wings were folded up, but it must have been a part of the coat, I suppose. Does that ring any bells?"

"A veritable carillon, sir. Suffice to say that all is not well, and you are fortunate to have emerged from this encounter with only a bump on your head."

"So, is this bloke bad, then?"

"It's more that he's not especially good, sir."

"So, what are you going to do? I mean, did he kidnap Lluck? If so, I want to help!"

"I would advise that you rest and take the proverbial back seat, sir. We shall take care of this. It is beyond mortal assistance, even one with the apparent vigilante skills that you possess."

"So, you know about my secret identity, then?"

"We are investigators, sir."

"Right, um, don't tell anyone, please?"

"We are known for our discretion, sir."

"Right, good, thanks. Can you at least tell me if you find him? I'd like to see him again; he's a good lad."

"I have no doubt that you would, sir. In fact, it all makes sense, now. We will contact you again in due course. Good day, sir, and perhaps put something cold on your head for a while, just in case."

With that, they nodded and let themselves out, leaving Carl with a sore head and feeling very confused.

*　*　*

"Sorry, I didn't get your name," Qwyrk said to the little fellow sitting on the dry stone wall in front of her.

"Scribblemutt, madam," he said, still focused on his miniature book. He was about a foot tall, covered in green fur, with two black horns on his head and a face like a corgi. He had a small ledger and was writing something in it with a tiny quill pen. The snow-covered landscape of the Dales behind him only made the scene that much more surreal.

"Fine, so it's set then?"

"Yup," he answered, looking up. "The boss'll see you at four o'clock sharp this afternoon, near the sight of the recent sacrifice on the Moors."

"Do we really have to do it there? I mean I was just out there and there's not a whole lot to find."

"Well, we want to have a look-see ourselves, don't we? Get the lay of the land, obtain a sense of what's happening, so's we can react accordingly when the time is right."

"You mean find out what's going on and who did it, so you can all run and hide until it's over and then try to cut a deal with the perpetrators later if they happen to win."

"I'm wounded, madam. You make it sound so craven and cowardly."

"Hey, if the shoe fits."

"I don't wear shoes, thank you very much. Odd little things, really. Besides, they pinch my toes."

"Um, fine, suit yourself. So, do I need to do anything? Prepare anything before meeting with his most royal pompousness?"

"Nothing of note, though—and this is strictly off the record, you understand—he is most partial to sticky toffee pudding."

"Sticky toffee pudding?"

"Yeah, especially if it's got a nice chocolate glaze drizzled over it, and is sprinkled with fried and sugared crickets."

"Fried..."

"I mean, it's short notice, so if that's not possible, I hear he also has a fondness for raw iguana tongues in aspic. Though, that may be even more difficult to procure at the last minute."

"Yeah, just a bit. Look, mate. I'm not meeting him for some great big British bake-off thing, all right? I just want some answers to some serious questions, and then he can bugger back off to his cricket puddings and aspic tongues with spider juice or whatever."

"Oh, you don't want to do that."

"What?"

"Spider juice. It's quite bitter; ruins the taste of everything. Except for maybe a drop or two in some spider fritters. Now *those* can be lovely, but they do take a certain touch. I find black widows a bit more appetizing than funnel webs, but tarantulas are just far too heavy..."

Qwyrk grimaced, grossed-out. "Right. I'm going to give you until the count of five, because I'm feeling generous, and if you're not gone by then, I'm going to pick you up and throw you over that little hillock behind you, got it? Tell your boss I'll meet him at the appointed time and place, and I'm bringing someone else along, just in case he's got any stupid ideas about double-crossing me. Ready? One... two..."

The little creature had already hopped off the wall and scampered away through the snow as she was finishing counting.

She grinned. "Threatening to kick their tiny little arses never gets old. I should have brought my slingshot!"

CHAPTER TWELVE

In a familiar flash of the now-usual violet lights and sparkles (honestly, it's always lights and sparkles with these inter-dimensional pop-ups, isn't it?), Qwyrk and Holly materialized out on the icy Moors, near where Qwyrk had her earlier unpleasant encounter with Silktassel and Sneezewort. The shadows were growing long, with a looming sense of forbidding.

"No wonder the Darkfae make their sacrifices out here; it's positively ghastly," Holly said, looking around with revulsion. "Mortals are right to be terrified of it. I am!"

Qwyrk nodded. "It's a bit of a ghoulish and creep-inducing old place, that's for sure."

As usual, she felt nothing of meteorological discomfort, but Holly was well bundled up in her coat and scarf, and Qwyrk was glad for it. The coat's purple color, while quite fetching, wasn't the most intimidating of choices, perhaps, but her martial arts skills were formidable, and that was enough should they have the need.

Still, she hoped it wouldn't come to that, fun though it was to pound Nasties into the ground. She started to fantasize about herself and Holly fighting side-by-side, back-to-back, and front-to-front. She had to bring her thoughts back to the situation at hand.

"So, that thing you do," Qwyrk said, looking around, scouting for any runners or heralds or kazoo players for the big boss they were about to meet. "Silly Balm, was it?"

Holly smirked. "Not quite."

"Simple Barn?"

"No."

"Sick Lamb Bomb?"

"You're getting worse, but please continue. It's ever so amusing."

"Sorry, I've had a lot on my mind lately, as I'm sure you can appreciate. I can't remember it properly. What's it called?"

"I won't tell you, just to see what else you can come up with."

"That's very kind of you."

"Not really, but it is rather funny."

"Just watch yourself."

"What if I'd rather you watched me, instead?"

Qwyrk chuckled. Or upchucked. Or something equally undignified, but before she could answer, she was semi-relieved to see a passel of odd figures appear on the horizon.

"Well, there's as rotten a pack of unloveliness as you're likely to see. At least they're on time," she noted, again happy to change the subject. "Nasties are strangely punctual, if mostly repulsive."

"I'm glad the company here makes up for it," Holly said with a smile.

Qwyrk was almost starting to get annoyed at how charming her companion was, but she managed to say "likewise" without sounding like a complete fool. Maybe.

"Stand your ground, and don't let them intimidate you. They look like right mean bastards, but they're honestly not very impressive. Bogtrotter's only the boss because he's the biggest and the scariest looking. But honestly, if you kicked him in his tiny shins, he'd probably fall to the ground and cry. Just don't tell him I said that."

"I wouldn't dream of it, though I'm tempted to try it, if they aren't helpful."

"Just whip out your... Sill and Ball stick?"

"No."

"Slick Land Bog?"

"I think you're just trying to wind me up at this point."

The Nasty entourage approached. Bogtrotter was just as she remembered him, for better or worse: a good seven feet tall, about five feet wide, with muscled arms, but tiny little legs no more than a foot long each, ending in cow's hooves. He sported horns like a Highland cow (with a mane to match), set atop a wide face with a cow's nose (complete with a bull's ring) and beady yellow eyes. In fact, he was essentially a bipedal Highland cow. His fur was a mottled red-brown color and he was dressed in a dark blue doublet, with a matching kilt and a large silk sash worn over his left shoulder.

He strutted toward them with an entourage of mini-Nasties, including one that marched in front, his herald. He looked a bit like Horatio, except that he was sickly yellow color, and playing his trumpet-shaped nose, which sounded rather like a kazoo. Oh, and a small cloth banner hung from it with a gothic letter "B" embroidered on it.

This ramshackle assortment stopped a good fifteen feet away from Qwyrk and Holly, while the herald wrapped up his tune, which went on. And on. And on.

"Look, sorry to be rude," Qwyrk said, shuffling her feet, "but can we get on with it?"

The herald concluded his fanfare and gave her a slight bow. "Greetings from Bogtrotter, President-for-Life of the Loyal Union of Nighttime Nasties, Yorkshire Chapter. Trotter of Bogs, Frightener of the Frightened, Daunter of the Daunted, and Scarer of the Scared Shiteless. Fifth of the Bogs, Sixth of the Trotters..."

Qwyrk rolled her eyes. *Bloody hell.*

Another minute went by as the titles continued to roll out in an endless blur: "Squonker of the Squozen, Frigger of the Fairies, Bonker of the Brownies..." Bogtrotter said nothing, but inclined his head forward just a bit, looking quite pleased with himself. Finally, the herald finished his enthusiastic encomium. Several moments of uncomfortable silence followed.

"Well?" Qwyrk asked with raised eyebrows.

"He wants ya to sing the song," the herald whispered.

"What? No, no! I'm not singing the song!"

"Come on, ya gotta sing the song."

"I'm not singing the damned song!"

"What song?" Holly asked.

"Oh, it's a stupid-arse 'anthem' of praise that he insists everyone sing, as a sign of respect, or some crap like that."

Bogtrotter motioned again, and his herald nodded and looked back to Qwyrk. "He says sing the song, or no audience."

"Bloody hell," Qwyrk cursed.

"How bad can it be?" Holly asked. "I mean, I assume you already know it?"

"Oh, I know it; I'm just in no mood to look ridiculous." *Especially not in front of you.*

"Go on, then," Holly urged with a smile. "I promise I won't laugh, too much."

"Oh, thank you for your support."

"Of course. Besides, I think it might be charming."

"That's because you haven't heard it yet." She sighed and turned to the herald. "Fine, all right, fine! I'll sing the flipping song."

Bogtrotter flashed a broad smile and nodded. Then he pointed to the ground.

"What?" Qwyrk asked. "What is it now?"

"He wants you to kneel before you sing it," the herald insisted.

"Not a chance!" Qwyrk fumed, ready to pick up the mini-Nasty and toss him as far as she could. It was the second time today she'd had that compulsion. "No, no flipping way! If he wants the damned song, I'm jolly well standing up to sing it!"

She glanced over at Holly, who tried to cover her smirk with her hand and failed rather badly. The herald looked back at his master in confusion. Bogtrotter frowned, but gave a grudging nod.

"The boss says you may stand, just this once," he announced.

"Oh, how gracious of him," Qwyrk made a mock bow in Bogtrotter's direction. "Fine, let's get this over with."

"I can't wait to hear it," Holly teased under her breath and folded her arms.

Qwyrk tried to ignore her. She couldn't. But she cleared her throat and started to sing in a very quiet voice: "Hail be to Bogtrotter…"

"Um, excuse me, excuse me!" the herald said. "We can't hear you at all over here, ya know. Gotta project a little bit better; protocol and all that."

Bogtrotter flashed a toothy, bovine grin.

Qwyrk grimaced and rolled her eyes again. She started over, determined to be loud, obnoxious, and out of tune:

"Hail be to Bogtrotter, Lord of the Backwater

He's a right stink-rotter, likes to maim, then to slaughter.

Boss of the nasties, fancies Cornish Pasties,

As long as the meat's raw, never cooked, but let it thaw

He's so scary, he's so evil, likes his tortures quite
medieval

Nothing like a good upheaval, and some chaos, most
primeval

Watch your back when he is hunting, you won't like
what you're confronting

If you let him win the chase, then he might bite
off your face

(Chorus): Munch, crunch, brunch, lunch

It's a gory bloody story

Brain sprain, veins drained

You'll never be the same again!

Flash flood, full of blood

Now your head's in the mud

Checkmate, decapitate

What a way to lose some weight!

Hail Boggie, cheers Boggie.

Go, mate, go! Arrrrrrrghghghghgh!"

Qwyrk flailed her hands around in the air at that last bit,

finished, and looked around. "That was the most mortifying thing I've done in a very long time," she whispered to Holly.

"It was quite appalling, it must be said," Holly answered, her smirk bubbling into full-out laughter.

The herald clapped his tiny hands. "Brava! Well done. Now, verse two."

"Verse two?" Qwyrk stammered.

"You *do* know all eighty-seven verses, I assume?"

"Eighty-seven?" Qwyrk clenched her fists and stepped forward. "You get that one, mate, and I'm just about done with your crap!"

The herald made a hasty retreat behind Bogtrotter, and the two seemed to confer for a moment. Finally, he stepped out again. "The boss says that under these strange and unusual conditions, one verse will suffice, this time."

Qwyrk made another mock bow. "Thank you so much for your generosity. Now, can we get on with the meeting, please?"

Bogtrotter trotted toward her, raising one hand in greeting and nearly stepping on his herald with a hoof, but the little fellow managed to duck out of the way just before being crushed.

"Right then, I've done your song and dance—" Qwyrk started.

"You didn't do the dance," Bogtrotter interrupted in a low, gravelly voice.

"What?"

"The dance, you didn't do it."

"There's a dance, as well?" Holly raised an intrigued eyebrow.

Qwyrk shook her head with vigor and cringed. "Trust me, you don't want to see it."

"I think I do."

"I should insist you do the dance," Bogtrotter mused, stroking his furry chin with a clawed hand, "but I am prepared to overlook that pleasantry just this once."

"How disappointing," Holly quipped. "Perhaps some other time?"

"Don't hold your breath," Qwyrk said.

"A girl can wish, can't she?"

"Shhh!" Qwyrk shushed. "Right," she said, addressing Bogtrotter, "so, help us out here. What's going on with the Erlking? You lot always have your ears, noses, various other appendages to the ground, on the ground, in the ground, whatever. What the hell is happening and how do we deal with it?"

Bogtrotter rubbed his ringed nose, stared off into space for a moment, squinted, rubbed his chin some more, snorted, and looked down at her.

"Haven't a clue, sorry. Lovely to chat. Ta, then." He turned around to leave.

"Wait just a damned minute! If a twat as unimportant as Horatio has an idea about what's happening, then you definitely know a hell of a lot more. I'm not leaving here until you spill it." She lowered her voice. "Don't make me kick your arse in front of your herald and your stupid little underlings!"

Bogtrotter stopped in his tracks, considering her words, rubbing his chin yet again. He turned around to face her. "Fine. You and I can chat alone. Your girlfriend will have to wait here."

"Oh, she's not my, I mean, we're not, I mean..." Qwyrk felt her cheeks get hot and couldn't look Holly in the eye. So she skulked off behind Bogtrotter as they wandered away from prying ears, certain that Holly was watching her intently, and probably grinning that sarcastic grin that she seemed to love to grin so grinningly.

"Right, I'm only saying this once," Bogtrotter half-whispered as they walked out of ear-shot and came to a stop. "This is bad stuff, as bad as de Soulis, if not worse. De Soulis was an arrogant pillock, but the Erlking's way more clever. He's mustering an army of Darkfae and seeking out some kind of magic weapon—a boy with powers—and word on the dirt road is that he's got the tacit and very off-the-record support of a few of the good Fae, elder Shadows, and such. And that makes him even more dangerous."

"What? Who? Why?"

Bogtrotter shrugged. "Honestly, I don't know and I don't want to know. Apparently, it's all happening tomorrow night, the winter solstice, in case you forgot. I'd suggest keeping yer head down for a bit."

"Yeah, not really an option, mate."

He shrugged again. "Suit yerself, but me and me folk are sittin' this one out. I've ordered the whole union to stand down, to not even scare any little children until further notice, which gutted quite a few of the Nasties, believe you me; they had some lovely night terrors all dreamed up for the little darlings in Leeds and York this week. But alas, that will have to wait. We officially don't exist as long as that freak is out and about."

"How brave of you."

"Keeps us alive, love. Despite me fierce-sounding anthem, I'm no killer. Ain't even much of a fighter. That's all just for show and keeps the rest of the Nasties in line. I'd suggest you and your girl-friend stay out of sight, too, if you want to keep your necks."

"She's not my, I mean, we're not, we're just..."

"Sure love, whatever you say. Just remember: we Nasties? We know stuff. We see it. Now, if you'll excuse me, we're gonna have a look at where that gruesome little soirée took place; call it a threat assessment." He trotted on his tiny legs past her and went back to his sycophants, who cheered and burst into applause at his arrival, as if he'd been gone for days. They started off toward the site of the sacrifice, and as he left, he waved his hand behind him. Dozens of sparks, flames, fireworks, rockets, thunder-booms, bolts of mini-lightning, and various other pyrotechnic tricks filled the air, all of them barreling right toward Qwyrk and Holly in claps and snaps of sound and fury.

"That's for not doing the dance," he called out. "Next time, do the dance. And bring a sticky toffee pudding."

Qwyrk swore and made a dash for Holly as the missiles exploded all around them.

"What on Earth is happening?" Holly shouted above the explosions, holding her hands over her ears and trying to avoid falling showers of sparks and random blasty detonations.

"Boggie's a gobshite!" Qwyrk yelled back. "Come on!"

She grabbed Holly around the waist and waved her free hand in the air, throwing them both into a funnel of purple light. A moment later, they appeared just outside Holly's B&B, and promptly slammed right into it.

"Oof!" Qwyrk gasped as her back hit the stone wall hard. Holly smacked into her, and they found themselves standing face to face, Qwyrk's arms around Holly's waist, Holly's palms resting on Qwyrk's shoulders.

"Are you all right?" she said to Holly as they panted and caught their breath.

"Yes, I think so. You broke my fall, thank you." Holly blew a strand of hair out of her face. "So, that was, um, different."

"Yeah, the Nasties are a right pain in the arse, aren't they? They've always got some wanky trick to play, like those damned faerie bombs going off everywhere for the hell of it. Luckily, I got us out of there. I imagine that little fireworks show will be going on for some time, just to make a point."

"It was quite the rescue, in any case."

"Well, I don't know if I'd call it a *rescue*. Do you... want to call it rescue?"

"That suits me."

"Right then, good, a rescue it is!"

"So..."

"So."

"Here we are."

"We are here." Qwyrk swallowed. "Here is where we are, indeed. Right here. In this spot. At this moment. Here. Nowhere is more here than here, as they say, or maybe they don't, because that's a bit of a naff expression, if it even *is* one, which I don't think it is, to be honest."

"I'm sure I don't know." Holly hadn't yet moved her hands and seemed to show no interest in extricating herself from Qwyrk's embrace. "So, what did he say?"

"Hm? Who?"

"Bogtrotter? It must have been very important if he didn't want your 'girlfriend' to hear it."

"Oh, right, that!" Qwyrk felt her cheeks turn hot again. "That was, well, you know. He was just being facetious, fatuous, flatulent, something. Just a nasty little joke, heh, a little Nasty joke. You know."

Holly raised one eyebrow but didn't say anything.

"He, um, he just said what we already know: that the Erlking is serious business, and we should stay out of his way because he's up to something tomorrow on solstice night, and he's trying to find a boy with powers, to which I said we couldn't walk away because we're heroes or some such like that, and he was like 'well suit yourself, I'm off,' or something."

"That was a dreadful impression of him."

"It was a bit shite, wasn't it?"

"You should probably stick to saving the world. So, are you sure you're all right?" She rubbed Qwyrk's shoulders.

Qwyrk's eyes widened and she nodded. "I'm fine." Now she was sure she sounded like a chinchilla who'd been sucking helium.

"I'm glad. I should..." Did she inch in just a bit closer? Qwyrk felt immobile, and mildly terrified.

"I should probably get inside, if that's all right? I know you've a dozen other things to do, and wasting time with me can't be a priority."

"Oh, it's, it's not a waste, I promise." Qwyrk found her voice. "I mean, *this* is a waist, ha ha!" She patted Holly's lower back with her hands. "But you, you're not a waste of time, not at all."

"How lovely. I'm glad."

"Me too."

A moment or two (or three) of lingering glances ensued. Qwyrk leaned in closer. Holly answered by doing the same and moved ever so slightly forward.

"Um..."

"Um..."

Qwyrk's heart began to race as they edged closer still...

The sound of a gate slamming around the corner drew their attention and ruined the moment.

"So, I really should go in, then," Holly said. "We shouldn't be seen by mortal eyes out here."

"Right, yeah, that works. In to the inn, as it were. Heh. Off you go, then; in and all that. Lovely afternoon out with you. Sort of."

"I've had worse."

"Yeah, well, comes with the territory, investigating paranormal crimes and such. Right, then, bye for now."

"There's just one thing," Holly added.

"Yes?"

"Your arms are still around me, and you're very strong. I'm quite trapped."

"Oh, right, of course. Sorry! Yeah, I forget that sometimes."

"I mean, you *were* rescuing us and all, and I'm ever so grateful. I can think of far worse ways to wrap up that odd little encounter."

"Me too! I mean, there could have been all sorts out there. He could've conjured up exploding bags of rubbish, or flying purple piranhas, or..."

"Qwyrk..."

"Yes?"

"I still can't move."

"Right, sorry! Gosh, I'm foolish!" She let go of Holly, who took one slow step back.

"You're not foolish at all. As far from it as I can imagine. Anyway, I really am going to go; ta for now, darling!" She leaned in and kissed Qwyrk on the cheek. That was the second cheek kiss today. It was Holly: two, Qwyrk: nil.

"We'll talk soon?" Holly suggested.

"Yes, yes of course, absolutely! I'll do what I need to and get back on you... *to* you, as soon as possible."

"Lovely," Holly said as she went to the back door and took the handle. "By the way," she looked back at Qwyrk. "I still want to see that dance."

"Heh, in your dreams."

"See you there tonight, then. Good night." She smiled again as she opened the door and went inside.

Qwyrk slumped to the cold, hard ground and stared off into the trees, shaking her head. She was frustrated, flustered, and wanted to be done with the day. "Bloody hell. Just... bloody hell!"

* * *

"So, what should we do?" Jilly asked. Her attempts at toilet humor were completely lost on Blip, so she decided to return to the problem at hand. He was nothing if not predictable.

"I'm not yet sure. It seems that each day brings us new situations for which we are not fully prepared. There is something nefarious at work here, but I cannot yet suss out what it may be."

"Wait, what did you say?"

"What?"

"You just said 'suss out.'"

"And if I did?"

"But that's not proper English. It's slang."

"Nonsense! It's a perfectly acceptable term to describe when one is trying to determine the answer to something. I think it dates back to the seventeenth century, or some such."

"No, it's not! It's 'improper' English, and you just used it!" Jilly grinned wide.

"I take umbrage at the suggestion, Miss Pleeth, that I would stoop to indulge in vernacular vulgarities, even in times of great duress, but that is hardly the point. I fear we are straying far off-topic, and we could better use our time trying to solve the mysteries at hand. It's extremely unpleasant to be constantly confronted with new peculiarities. This whole situation is really getting on my wick!"

"You, you just did it again!"

"What? Did what, damn it?"

"You said 'getting on my wick.' That's pure slang!"

"Good heavens, did I?"

"Oh, you did!"

"Oh dear. This may be more serious than I had first surmised. If some pernicious spell-work is at hand, it may be altering our personalities in ways that we are not made up about. Good Goddess, I did it yet again!"

Jilly suppressed an urge to laugh, but she knew Blip was right. "We're both starting to act strangely, like out of character, and that can't be good."

"No, it most certainly cannot! It's becoming a ginormous problem! Oh, bollocks! Gaaaah! Bollocks, I'm starting to sound like Qwyrk! Before long, I'll be speaking like that miscreant disciple of mine. I may even begin to skive off my duties. Skadi's skis, I can't stop myself! It's a right nightmare, gaaaah!"

"We have to do something," she said, not even trying to hide her amusement. "It might be for the best if you didn't talk for a bit? It seems to be making things worse." Jilly couldn't believe she got to say that. It pleased her very much.

Blip nodded, the look of mortification on his froggy face growing with each passing moment. Jilly was shocked that he actually agreed with her idea. It pleased her very much.

"I don't know why this is happening... hang on a minute!" A memory dawned on her. "I think I recall seeing something when we got back here. Let me just go check."

She hopped off her bed, opened the door, bounded downstairs, and went to look out the living room window. Sure enough, there was a light on in the house directly across the street. And that could only mean one thing.

"Mr. Blip!" she called out to him in excitement. "Come down and see this! I think she's back. Granny's home! Let's go talk to her; maybe she can help!"

* * *

Lluck groaned and opened his eyes, but didn't see much except gloom in his still-hazy vision. The front of his head hurt, and he was on his side on a cold, concrete floor. His hands were bound behind his back with thick plastic ties. His legs were tied up, too. The air was chilly and smelled damp.

He squinted and shook his head to try to clear it and get his bearings. He twisted himself around to get a better look. A flickering lightbulb hung from the ceiling.

A tall figure sat on a large chair nearby, wearing a long, dark grey robe with a hood obscuring its face. The sleeves fell past the hands, concealing them, too.

"Ah, you're awake at last," a deep voice addressed him with an accent that sounded vaguely Germanic.

"Nice robe, mate."

"Thank you. It was rather expensive, but I did purchase it at a discount."

"I was being sarcastic."

"Ah, well, never mind. I am sorry that Longwing was a bit harsh with you, but you really gave him no choice. If you'd just come along with him willingly the other night, you wouldn't have that nasty bump on your head. It was not my wish to inflict harm, not to one as special as you. Do not worry, though; you will heal up in enough time."

"In enough time for what? Who the hell are you? Where am I?" He struggled with his ties, but realized with a sinking feeling that he couldn't undo them. The more he fought against them, the tighter they seemed to become. He tried to focus on manifesting his luck to break the bonds, but nothing came of that either.

Damn it!

"In time for the solstice event, of course. Oh, and you will not be able to use your powers to free yourself. I've dampened them, using an arcane spell that I am pleased to see has worked perfectly. The spell is like a baking recipe, only with less sugar and flour and more cobra venom and crushed werewolf skull. Though a sprinkling of nutmeg on top complements the mixture perfectly, especially when... um, never mind, we are getting off-topic."

The figure stood.

"This binding will not last forever, but it will hold you for long enough. As for who I am? That's not your concern at the moment, though I suppose I can reveal that to you when the time is right. You do have a right to know, I suppose. As for where you are? Simply some place where those annoying friends you've made cannot find you. I will not have them interfering after all my hard work—werewolf skull is hard to come by, you know. Besides, they have just enough ability and smarts to cause me no end of problems."

"Hard work for what? What do you want? Look, if you think I'm going to help you, you're mental, mate! I'm not going to be like your little flying goth errand boy, or help you rob banks, or cheat at the dog races, or any shite like that. I'll figure out a way to get free, yeah? And then you're gonna be dead sorry you brought me down here!"

"Oh, you needn't worry that I want you to help me to commit petty crimes, young man. Human money is the least of my concerns. And I had no doubt that you would not be willing, even if that were all I required. No, my good young sir. I do not want your assistance, or even your servitude. You see, I am going to rip your powers out of you and take them for myself."

CHAPTER THIRTEEN

Qwyrk wandered in the woods behind Holly's B&B, alternating between blissful infatuation and egregious anxiety.

"Bollocks, crap, shite, crap, bollocks, crap. Does she fancy me? I'm pretty sure she does. She *did* say she wants to see me dance and she was going to dream about it and what if I actually do the dance but it's not as good as she dreamed it would be and I'm a complete tosser and screw it up and what am I thinking it's a Nighttime Nasty dance for bloody Bogtrotter and of course it's going to look like complete utter rubbish no matter how much I practice it and do I even want to practice it? No, no I don't, because that would be daft but if I don't practice it then I'll look completely stupid as I try to work my way through it without knowing it properly but how will she know because she's never even seen it before and bollocks, crap, shite, crap, bollocks, crap!"

Such was the shambolic state of her thoughts when she came

to the realization that she'd been meandering for some time and it was already dark.

"I should go and check in on Jilly," she said, guilty at being preoccupied with her own mini melodramatic catastrophes and all but forgetting about her young friend. "The poor thing's probably worried and scared with no one but Blip to comfort her—there's a thought!—and here I am obsessing over something I don't have time to even think about until this is all sorted, if it ever gets sorted."

She waved her hands in a circle to make a light portal to step back to Knettles.

Only instead, she stepped into a dimly-lit room that looked like an office. She found herself near a desk, in front of which was standing a man, a mortal by the looks of him. He wore a long, grey coat, accented with a charcoal scarf, and his short silver hair was neatly groomed.

"I don't mean you any harm," he said, approaching her slowly, his hands held up to show that he was unarmed.

"Where the hell am I? How did I get here?"

"You're in my office, in Leeds. Don't worry, you're quite safe. I've been tracking you. Or rather, one of my incanters has. Your teleportation leaves a trail, rather like that of a jet, only made of magic, of course. So, it was a simple matter of studying that pattern and seeing where it would show up next, and then interrupting your path and redirecting it. Not easily done, I might add. But I do apologize. It's rude of us to interfere with your affairs, and I assure you that we're not trying to kidnap you or hold you against your will. You're free to go, but I would like to talk with you first, if I may."

"Who are you?" Qwyrk looked around for anyone else who might be hiding in the shadows, but saw nothing out of order. Still, she kept her fists clenched and raised to show this prat that she meant business. "How do you know who I am?"

"Well, that's just it," he said. "I don't know who you are. But your form shows me that you're magical, and I've heard from reliable sources that you know about the boy."

"What boy? I don't know what you're talking about."

He gave her a look of disbelief. "The boy who has been causing no end of trouble, apparently; the one they call Lluck."

Qwyrk hesitated and frowned, fists still clenched. "What business is it of yours?"

"Well, in fact, I do have a vested interest in him."

"And that would be?"

He paused for a moment and sighed. "I'm his father."

*　*　*

Jilly put on her coat and motioned to Blip, who was waiting at the top of the stairs.

"What if your parents come back?" he asked.

"Oh, they're off again at some boring meeting-dinner-function thing. They left me a note on the kitchen table, saying they won't be back until after eleven at the earliest. As usual, there's something horrid in the fridge for me to warm up and eat."

"Have you seen it?" he asked, making his way down.

"I had a quick look; it doesn't bear talking about."

"How do you survive, child? It's all very not on."

Jilly smirked. "It's only when they're out late. Most nights, the food's not that bad around here. I mean, it's not great, but..."

"Good enough, I suppose. Has your hound been fed?"

"Odin? Yeah, he's had his dinner, and he's sleeping quite nicely," she said as she pointed at the dog.

Blip moved with caution, keeping his eye on the animal as they made for the front door.

"He won't hurt you, you know," Jilly said, letting them both out into the chilly night.

"I prefer not to take my chances. It's good to see that he's right knackered. Gah!"

"Remember what I said," Jilly said as she suppressed a laugh. "You might want to keep quiet for a bit."

He nodded and off they tromped across the street to Granny's front door.

Jilly rang the bell, which set off a medley of chimes inside. "Well, that's different," she said, looking down at Blip, who opened his mouth to say something, but obviously thought the better of it and let it remain forever unspoken. She was almost sorry he did.

They waited for an answer, which seemed to take longer than one would reasonably assume that answering the door of a rather small home would take. The wait was made worse by the wintry air around them growing chillier by the moment. At last, the door opened a crack, and a pleasant-looking older woman dressed in a cashmere jumper and long skirt looked out at them and smiled.

"Well, I was wondering if you might stop by. Do come in!" She opened the door and they happily stepped inside. "Please, go into the sitting room, and I'll put on the kettle."

"That's very nice of you ma'am," Jilly said. She looked at Blip, who merely nodded and smiled. Jilly decided to enjoy his embarrassment for as long as she could.

Soon, they were all sitting in a nice, warm room, sipping hot tea and munching on digestive biscuits, which made Jilly realize that she was rather hungry, after all.

"So," Granny said.

"So," Jilly answered.

Granny looked at her with a raised eyebrow, but said nothing. Jilly looked over at the normally-vociferous Blip, but he just stared at the floor and twiddled his outsized thumbs.

"Bit chilly tonight, isn't it?" Jilly said.

"That's rather normal for this time of year, I should think."

"It is, isn't it? Funny that!"

"Amusing."

"Jilly," Blip said as he looked up and seemed to implore her with his eyes.

"Oh bollocks. I'm very sorry ma'am, but things are in a really bad way right now, and I was hoping that maybe you could shed some light on them?"

"Well, it all depends on what 'things' you're referring to. I mean, I'm very old and somewhat wise and all that, but I don't know everything."

"But you must know about what's happening?"

"I've heard whispers, though I must admit, I've been away a lot lately, so I may not have a very clear picture."

"It's the Erlking, ma'am. We think he's back and wants to do something quite terrible."

She nodded. "So it seems. And you're right to be concerned; he is not someone to trifle with if one is unprepared."

"Qwyrk is out trying to find answers about what he's planning, where he is, who he's working with. He's got a keen interest in a boy we've run into, named Lluck. Lluck's, well, lucky, you see, and this

Erlking wants him for something. We're afraid he's going to kidnap him, and then who knows what will happen?"

"Who indeed? Yes, I'd wager that the Erlking is making his move now, especially since de Soulis failed to return to power last summer, thanks to you all. That it's happening right before the winter solstice suggests that he's got some kind of ritual in mind, and if he's seeking out this boy, that can't be good."

"You think he might try to sacrifice him, or something?"

"I'd say there's a very good chance of something bad happening."

Jilly shuddered. "So, what do we do?"

"You stop him, of course."

Jilly shook her head in frustration. "How?"

Granny smiled. "My dear child, you really don't know who you are, do you? Why I'm here, living right across the street from you?"

Jilly shook her head, looked to Blip, who seemed likewise uncomprehending, and then back at her.

She sighed. "I was hoping you'd figure it out on your own; it's always more satisfying that way. But you haven't stopped by once since last summer. It's terribly frustrating."

"Figure out what?" Jilly was growing anxious and impatient.

"My dear, you're a descendent of mine, and from what I suspect, a very powerful young witch in the making."

*　*　*

"Wait," Qwyrk said. "His father? Are you kidding me?"

"Quite the opposite, I promise you. My name is Simeon Greylocke, and after years of searching and studying, I'm now convinced that the lad is mine."

"But that doesn't fit at all with what I know. Why should I believe you?"

"Because I can prove it, all of it. Years of research, having the best students of the occult at my disposal, all of whom can testify to the work we've done trying to determine the identity of the boy."

"How do I know you're not some spy or a Darkfae posing as a human?"

"A what?"

"Never mind. Hold out your hand."

He looked at her with suspicion.

"Now. Do it! I don't have time to waste if you're having me on, and if you are, I'm going to beat you senseless."

"Fine," he said, rolling his eyes and thrusting his right palm at her, face up. He raised his eyebrows as if to say, *can we get whatever it is over with?*

She held her own hand above his, and a white light appeared between them, and began to grow hot. She grimaced and grunted as its intensity increased, and her palm trembled. She held on, fighting the pain, forcing it out of her mind. But her effort was no good; in a moment, she jerked her own hand away, swearing and shaking out the burning sensation.

"What was that?" he asked.

"Just a test. It's a heat that only magical creatures can feel, not mortals. The fact that you didn't even flinch tells me you're not one of us. Damn!" She shook her hand again and blew on it.

"Sorry, I felt nothing."

"Fair enough. So, what do I look like?"

"You're a shadow with a pair of glowing red eyes. It's rather unnerving, if I may say. I assume that's not your real form?"

"No, no it's not. All right, fine, you're human. So how did you find out about me? Us?"

"As I said, I've employed some of the best occult researchers and practitioners in the country. Even so, it was very difficult for them to find any sort of information about you folk."

"Yeah, that's kind of the point, really. We don't like being spied on."

"But the more intrepid members of my team have succeeded in teasing out some pertinent facts."

"There're always a few wankers out there who are too smart for their own good."

"Well, their private activities aside, they were most helpful in finding what I was looking for. I knew he was out there somewhere, but his mother has kept him effectively hidden from me with her magic."

"Who, Holly?"

"Is that what she's calling herself now? I knew her as Vishala, but it makes sense that she would want to change her name."

Qwyrk grimaced. "What are you talking about? She told me that she met a young man at a science fiction convention at a hotel in Manchester, that they had a night together, and then accidentally out popped Lluck at the appropriate time."

"Well, it *was* a hotel in Manchester. Perhaps there was some sort of convention going on; I don't recall. I was traveling on business; I'm an importer. I was relaxing in the bar when she came in. Beautiful young woman, South Asian-looking, but different somehow; unlike anyone I'd ever seen. She walked right up to me, sat down, and began chatting, as if we were old friends. I think I only realized later that there was something off about her. Underneath her friendliness, she was very upset about something. But I allowed myself to be won over by her charms, and the next thing I knew, we were back in my hotel room, where one thing led to another. At the time, I couldn't believe my good fortune, but afterward, it became evident that she was unstable."

Qwyrk shook her head in disbelief. "What?"

"The next morning, she accused me of deceiving her," Greylocke continued. "I wanted to calm her, but she started yelling at me, becoming ever more angry. Honestly, I thought someone from a neighboring room might call security. I tried to do something, but she eventually broke down in tears and admitted that she had murdered her own father. I was shocked."

Qwyrk stared at him in horror. "What?" This couldn't be true. And yet...

"It was dreadful. Of course, my first thought was to call the police, but she drew a knife and threatened me, and then ran off. I tried to find her, but it was hopeless; she was gone. In any case, I phoned the police and gave them a statement, but nothing further came of it. It was as if she had vanished without a trace, which I later found out was essentially the truth; she's not from this world."

Qwyrk felt light headed. She saw darkness creeping in to the edges of her vision.

"I was concerned for myself, so I naturally underwent a battery of tests for various transmitted infections, but fortunately, I was fine; I'll never be that foolish again! In any case, much about her bothered me, so I began trying to find out more. I'd noticed at some point that her ears were pointed, but I assumed that was the effect of the alcohol altering my perceptions. Nevertheless, I investigated, and I eventually found evidence of a world beyond our own. Your world, I presume."

Qwyrk wobbled, reeling at his words.

"Also, just before she ran away, she insisted that we had 'created life.' I began to fear that this little tryst was a plan for her to conceive a child for reasons unknown to me. More recently, the two private investigators that I have on retainer have informed me that a boy with unusual abilities was seen in Leeds. When they described him, I was fairly certain who it was."

"Two private investigators..."

"Yes, an odd pair, to be sure. Dill and Chives, they call themselves. They actually found her, much to my astonishment, but of course, I wanted to keep my distance. So now, they work for me and pretend to work for her. That way, they can tell me what she's planning and doing."

It was all too much. "Wait, they *pretend* to work for her?"

"A clever ploy we concocted. She has no idea, you see, but with their help—giving her small amounts of information along with some misinformation—I may be able to keep my son away from her, keep him safe, until we can find a way to neutralize her and bring him back to me."

Qwyrk could hardly think straight. "What do you know about the Erlking?"

"The what?"

"Just... something we're following up on; it's a magical being that's chasing Lluck."

Greylocke shrugged. "I've never heard of him. But it wouldn't surprise me if she has allied herself with someone evil from your realm to further her goals. Oh, I just remembered: Dill and Chives did say something about her planning to kidnap him and offer him up to someone, maybe this Erlking of yours? I do believe he's in danger if she gets a hold of him."

"This can't be true. It just can't," she protested. Her head seemed filled with cobwebs, and she had a hard time focusing. His words wove their way into her mind, and she believed him, even though she desperately didn't want to.

"Look, I can prove everything I've said. Find him, bring him back to me, and I can show you all of my research, everything I've discovered over the past decade. There may even be something in there that can help you defeat this 'Erlking.'"

He took a step toward her.

"I must warn you, though: be very careful with her. She's not what she seems, and from what I've learned, she's quite dangerous; I was lucky to escape our encounter with my life. She may appear sweet and kind, but underneath that lovely exterior is someone very cold and scheming. If she murdered her own father, there's no telling what she would do to get her son back. And if she's allied herself with this enemy of yours, maybe she's planning to do something terrible to the boy, as well."

He looked at his watch. "My apologies, I must go." He handed her a business card. "Ring me at this number if you find out anything else, or if you discover where he is. I assume you have access to phones or some such? We may yet be able to save him. Goodbye for now." He turned and left through the office's only door.

Qwyrk fell into a chair by the desk and just sat, alone and dejected, her stomach in knots and her mind whirling with thoughts, all of them bad. Her mind was cloudy, but the truth of his words seemed beyond doubt. Tears stung her eyes, and everything good started to fall away from her.

"How? How could she do this? How could I have been so utterly stupid?" Those tears rolled down her cheeks, and she buried her face in her hands and sobbed.

* * *

Jilly's mouth hung open, and she stared at Granny in shock. "I'm a witch?"

"Well, you've the potential to be one, of course. Now, don't go getting ideas about boarding a train and going off to some secret school somewhere; it doesn't work that way. This form of magic is specific to chosen humans and is passed down through families."

"But, my mum's not. I mean I don't think so."

"No, she's not. These gifts can skip generations, just like someone might have the same eyes as their grandmother, rather than their mother or father. But you have the talent, dear, and with you about to become a young woman, you'll be noticing more changes in yourself than just those you're expecting, I can assure you. I want to be here, to help you, to train you, if I may."

"I just, I don't, I mean, I've always been kind of sensitive, I suppose, but this is, I don't know. I'm kind of gobsmacked right now. So you're my..."

"Great-grandmother many times over, yes." She smiled and took a sip of her tea, as if there was nothing mind-bending about this little tidbit of information at all.

"But this is bonkers. It makes no sense!"

Granny turned to Blip. "You're uncharacteristically quiet tonight."

"Oh, that," Jilly said. "Yeah, um, in addition to everything else, we have another problem, which is why we came over, actually. Over the last few days, we've both been, I don't know, acting strangely? Like, out of character. I'm getting really angry, and when we were in Symphinity for like less than a minute earlier today, I just couldn't tear myself away from it. It was like it was a drug, and I couldn't give it up. Qwyrk literally had to drag me back here and I was screaming at her, hitting her. That's so not like me, not at all."

"I see," she said, looking concerned. "And him?" She motioned to Blip.

"Oh, he's started using slang words, not speaking proper English."

"Oh dear," she said. "This is worse than I thought. What's changed in the past few days?"

"Well, Qwyrk came back after being gone for six months, but she's the same as always. Um, our mate Star Tao popped by, but he's as lovably odd as ever."

"Any magical happenings? Did you try to work any spells?"

"No, nothing. Honest."

"Have you acquired any items that are magical in nature?"

Jilly's eyes widened. "My amulet!" She pulled it out from under her shirt and held it by the end of its cord. "Qwyrk gave this to me as a birthday present. It lets me see her as she really is. Not, you know, just as a shadow with glowing eyes."

"Well, that's your problem, right there, my dear. You're a witch, and you're wearing something meant for non-enchanted mortals. It's causing a disruption to the enchanted power around you and affecting those in your vicinity. Since Mr. Blip..."

"Mr. Blippingstone."

"...is with you regularly, it's rubbing off on him, as well. I would suggest removing it immediately and only using it when absolutely necessary."

Jilly lifted it over her head. "Wow. I feel, I don't know, lighter, somehow?"

Granny nodded. "Save it for when Qwyrk is around and wear it at no other time, or your moods will start getting much worse. And don't let a magical creature wear it."

"Why not?"

"Well, it would enhance their powers greatly, probably heal them if they're injured, but it would have the same effect as on you, only much more quickly. Best put it away for now, and perhaps give it back to Qwyrk when you can."

Jilly slipped the item into her jean pocket.

"Excellent!" Blip clapped his hands together. "Good to get to the bottom of this mystery, I'm well made up! Gaaah!"

Granny chuckled. "Its effects will take some time to wear off, Mr. Blippingstone. Speak as freely as you wish, but just understand that you may yet utter a few more colorful vernacular phrases before the balance is restored."

"Then I shall remain silent." He folded his arms and sulked. "Sorted."

"So, this whole witch thing," Jilly said. "What do I have to do? I mean, do I have classes? Books to read? Exams?"

"We'll talk about it in due course," Granny answered with a reassuring smile. "But in the meantime, you're going to need to stop whatever the Erlking has planned."

"How?" Jilly asked, frustrated.

"I'm going to have you do something. Consider it your first assignment. Down at my old cave, there are some symbols and sigils carved on the side of a wall. Those with the gift can activate them, and transfer those images to paper, parchment, whatever, simply by touch. They will then be something you can carry away with you and use."

"What do they do?"

"Different things. Sometimes different for each user or each circumstance. You should be able to intuit what they're for when the time is right."

"How will I know when the time is right?"

"I would assume when you and your friends are battling the Erlking to stop whatever he has planned."

"Lovely."

"Your world is about to get a whole lot bigger, my dear."

"It's already gotten quite big enough, thank you."

"If I may," Blip interjected. "Madame, thank you. And I remain in awe of your skills, heritage, and abilities. But even if Ms. Pleeth is one of your good folk, do we really need to traipse all the way down to your former domicile at this moment, just to retrieve some sigils? It's approaching freezing outside, and I would prefer to return to the comfort of the young lady's home and wait until sunrise, late though it is at this time of year. I really can't be arsed about this. Argh! Slanged again!"

"She can't work her magic in the daytime when there are curious onlookers," Granny replied. "Now is the only time you have. And the sooner she retrieves the sigils, the better."

"She has a point," Jilly said, shrugging.

Blip sighed. "Fine. We'll go, but I do so under protest. It's definitely dodgy." He clenched his mouth shut.

Granny smiled at Jilly. "Off with you then and have at it, my dear. Let's see if you can work your first real magic!"

* * *

Qwyrk was back in the woods outside Holly's inn, lingering, stalling, trying to do anything except go in there and say what she needed to say. Her eyes were swollen from crying, and she was so angry she almost punched a nearby tree, but thought better of knocking down the innocent sylvan bystander.

She took a deep breath and strode to the back door, which was locked. She pulled it open anyway. *I'll leave them some cash for a new lock later.*

She climbed the stairs, taking care that her fury and heartbreak didn't make her too stompy. She swallowed hard as she reached the top and started down the hall to the green door on the right at the end. She took another deep breath, went up to it, and knocked.

"Who's there?"

"It's me," Qwyrk said, but she wanted to run away.

The door opened.

"Qwyrk!" she smiled. "This is an unexpected pleasure. Please, do come in."

Qwyrk stepped inside and shut the door behind her, resisting the temptation to slam it, but only just. She was edgy and ready for a full-on fight, if need be.

"I hope you're well," Holly said. "Is there news? I hope nothing's wrong. Also, I seemed to have misplaced a ring, probably lost out on the Moors during that ruckus, but I thought I'd check. It's how I communicate with…"

"Right, I'm only going to say this once, so listen up," Qwyrk interrupted. "I know what you are and what you've done. I also have a good idea of what you're trying to do, and there's no way I'm going to let it happen, understand?"

"Qwyrk, what are you talking about?"

"Really? You're going to act all innocent and make me go over everything? Sorry, I'm not going to give you the pleasure, because you're probably getting off on seeing me so angry and upset as it is."

She regretted her words, but the black cloud passed through her mind again, urging her to walk away from Holly and never speak to her again.

Holly shook her head. "Why would I take pleasure in hurting you? What are you saying? I don't know what you're talking about, but I swear to you, I haven't done anything since I saw you, certainly nothing to hinder you."

"I can actually believe that. It's everything else you've done that's been messing us about. Lying, deceiving, pretending to care, all the while working against us and hiding your past."

"Qwyrk, what..." Tears formed in Holly's eyes.

"No! Enough! I'm done with you, at least for now. I don't have the energy to kick your arse at the moment, or believe me, I would. Just stay away from us and everything we're doing. But when this is over, we're going to have it out, and you're going to be very sorry you lied to me."

"I don't understand what you're talking about. Please, tell me what's happened. What's going on?"

"Spare me the crocodile tears, missy; I am in no mood for your crap. Goddess, I don't even want to look at you, right now! Go back to your Erlking mate and tell him he's failed. You both have!" *This can't be true!* Her mind still rejected what she was saying, and yet...

Holly tried to reach out to her, but Qwyrk held up one hand in warning. "Stay back, I mean it! I don't want to fight you here, but I will if I have to, and it will hurt like nothing you've ever felt before."

"Qwyrk..." Holly said through a sob.

Qwyrk just backed away, shook her head, and in a flash, she disappeared, willing herself to return to her own home, only moments before she broke down and cried again.

CHAPTER FOURTEEN

Dampness seeped into his clothing. After the creepy robed figure had left, Lluck had the chance to inch himself around and get a good look at his surroundings. He now spied one window, and reasoned that he was in a basement by the looks of the limited light coming from it; he also realized that it was after dark. The window was barred and looked well sealed.

"No chance of getting out that way," he sighed. He also noticed some kind of pattern on the floor, which he guessed might be a magical symbol.

"Probably what's keeping me from using my powers."

He managed to roll over and sit up, but he felt both his hands and feet going numb. Every time he tugged at his bonds, they seemed to get a little tighter.

"Deliberate. More damned magic something or other. I wish it would all just go away!"

He sat in frustration for a while longer, when he heard footsteps outside. He tensed, but realized that they sounded different from those of his captor. The handle turned, and the door creaked open.

Longwing peered through the opening. He crept inside and closed the door behind him. As he walked up to Lluck, he held up one finger over his mouth and sat down beside him.

"All right?" he said in a half whisper.

"Yeah, no, not really!" Lluck answered. "I mean, I would be fine, except for that bloody pounding you gave me on my head, you tosser!"

Longwing held up his hands. "Look mate, I'm sorry. I didn't want to do that, but he kind of made me."

"Who?"

"The boss, the one in charge."

"Who is he?"

"He's not a good bloke, that's for sure. He's got an agenda, right? And he's determined to see it through. I was down with that because he seemed to be on the winning side, and I wanted to join that team, but that was before..."

"Yeah? Before what?"

"Before I found out what he's planning. What he wants to do to you. It's all bad, really bad."

"Oh yeah, he mentioned it. He's gonna separate my power from me somehow with more of that stupid magic of his."

Longwing shook his head. "No, mate. That's not what he's going to do."

"Yeah? So what is it, then?"

"He's going to rip your beating heart out of your chest and eat it tomorrow night in his bloody ritual for the solstice."

Lluck stared in disbelief. "Oh. Oh, shite."

"Yeah, not great. And I'm not all right with that. I mean, I've got a past, yeah? Done some bad things, petty crime and such. But murder? That's a whole other level; not on. I had no idea what he was planning."

"Maybe next time, check out the full job description first?"

"You're a laugh, mate. Now, keep your voice down, and I'll help you escape."

"How? These damned ties are so tight. I can't even move. They won't budge."

"Yeah, here, let me have a go."

Longwing reached down to his feet and fiddled with the ties for a moment. Lluck was amazed when they slid off like nothing.

"How?"

"All in the wrist, youngling," he said with confidence. "Here, let me get the others on your hands."

A moment later, Lluck stood up and grimaced as he shook off the pins and needles in his extremities. "So, now what?"

"Not a big deal, really. You're being held in a basement in Leeds, so it'll be easy enough to get lost in the big city again once you're out of here."

"What about you?"

"Eh, I'll be all right. I can probably make up some whinge about how you overpowered me, or something."

Lluck was skeptical. "You're not telling me something."

Longwing shrugged. "I've told you everything I know."

"No, I can see it. What is it?"

"Fine. I can't run off with you, because he's threatened to kill my sister, all right? It's how he makes sure I stay in his 'employ,' as he likes to call it."

"Who are you? What are you?"

"It's a long story."

"Well, you can fill me in as we're getting out of here. Also, I know people. Powerful people who can help. You should see what they can do." *If they even want to speak to me again.*

"We'll talk about it later. For now, let's just get you out of here quietly, all right?" He opened the door again and they stepped into the hallway.

"Crap," Longwing said, looking around.

"What?"

"This isn't the same hallway I used to enter the room."

"Wait, what? But there's only one door!" Lluck had had just about enough of today.

"I know."

Lluck threw his arms up. "What the hell does this even mean?"

"It means that there are magical traps set to prevent you from getting out, and we're likely to be somewhere else in the building now. And I have absolutely no idea where."

* * *

"It's damned well freezing out here, I hope you realize!" Blip shivered even though he was bundled up in his large scarf and tall Regency boots. He hopped up and down as he walked, hugging himself and rubbing his arms.

"I'm sorry, sir," Jilly said, "but Granny really wanted us to come down here and copy the symbols tonight. I mean, I understand why, but if it's any consolation, I'm pretty cold, too."

"No, it is not. The only consolation I am taking at the moment is that I seem to have full control of my verbal capacities again, thank Goddess. No more low-brow crudeness from me, I daresay. Gracious, what an ordeal that was!"

FOURTEEN

"Yeah, it was terrible." Jilly teased as they made their way along the dark, deserted river bank to Granny's old cave. "I could tell you were right cheesed off."

"Stop it."

"I mean, you were sounding positively narky at times."

"You're not funny."

"Any more of it I'd have gone right off you and buggered off somewhere else."

"I'm not listening."

Jilly giggled. "Come on, it's just up here. I know you're going to be right chuffed when we get there."

"Blah, blah, blah, la, la la." Blip covered his amphibian ear holes.

They trudged through a fresh dusting of snow as the path veered off to the right, away from the river, and soon found themselves at the entrance to the old cave. Tiny icicles hung from the roof of the mouth, giving it a magical, if rather creepy appearance.

"Is going in here really a good idea?" Blip asked. "I mean, we could be back at your home right now, nice and warm, you doing your media socializing and what-not, while I sip a fine glass of brandy to the accompaniment of Bach's *Art of Fugue*, as we contemplate our next move in this vexing game of chess. But no, instead we are out here in this positively inclement weather looking for enchanted symbols in a cave or some such, which apparently you will just know by the sight of them, because—oh yes!—you just happen to be an alleged descendant of the greatest witch and mystic the north of England has ever seen. How do we know that? Because she told you so herself! Just now, this very evening. She decided to spring it upon us in all of its unexpected glory. 'Oh, hello Mr. Blippingstone. Hello Ms. Pleeth. Good to see you. By the way, Jilly, you're my great-great-great-great-however-many-times removed granddaughter, huzzah!

Well, off into the bitter cold you go to prove yourself with your first assignment on the path to witchdom. Go on, then.'"

Jilly rolled her eyes. "Come on, you do have to admit, it's all rather exciting!"

"For you perhaps, and yes, I suppose congratulations of a sort are in order. Welcome to the magical side of reality. Properly, I mean."

"Thank you. I mean, it would explain why all this weirdness keeps happening to me, why I even met Qwyrk, and you, for that matter."

"It's possible, I grant you."

"So let's have a look inside, find those symbols or whatever they are, and see what happens. The sooner we get it done, the sooner we can go home. I'll even see if I can scrounge up some brandy for you."

Blip sighed. "Very well, but do try to make some haste, will you? I'm already rather frost-bitten."

"I think you're exaggerating."

"I am merely offering a reasonable enhancement to garner sympathy for my dire predicament."

"I figured. It didn't work."

"Hmph."

"Come on, let's go in."

"Do you have a source of illumination?"

"No, I thought we'd just feel along the walls. Of course, I do, silly. I brought a torch." She clicked on her flashlight. "We won't be stumbling around in the dark."

"There's some small comfort, then."

"In we go!"

"Charming."

FOURTEEN

* * *

As they entered Granny's former abode, they didn't notice a tall, dark, robed shape watching them from the top of the castle hill in the distance.

* * *

Carl fretted. He stood up. He sat down. He paced (but only while standing up, of course; pacing while sitting down would have been silly). He looked outside; the sun had set in the wintry sky, the day before the longest night of the year. The situation gnawed at him: the lucky boy, his apparent kidnapping, and especially those two oddball investigators who never removed their sunglasses. They said they'd contact him, so why hadn't they? He had their card. He picked it up, looked at it, set it back down, paced again, looked out the window, sat back down, looked at the card.

"Right, enough of this." He pulled out his mobile and dialed the number. Instead of a standard ringtone, a series of chimes rang in a melodic pattern. "Well, that's rather nice."

"Greetings, valued potential customer." A woman's voice answered the phone.

"Hello?" Carl said. "I'd like to speak to one of your two investigators; they visited me earlier and..."

"Welcome to Dill & Chives Investigations, the finest in other-worldly detective work. If you know the extension of the party you are trying to reach, please enter it now."

"Damn it!" He almost hung up, but decided to sit it out. This was his first mistake.

"Otherwise, please listen to the menu for your options. Instructions will now continue in Elder Fae."

"Wait, what?"

A voice said something in a language he'd never heard before.

"I don't... I don't understand."

The voice spoke again.

"Um..."

A different voice seemed to ask a question.

"Wait..."

A third voice seemed rather put out.

"Oh, this is pointless..."

"To hear this menu again, press fffththtp." The line went fuzzy.

"No, damn it!" He started pushing random numbers with the faint hope that something might get him through; he nearly dropped the phone in the process.

"Welcome to the menu in English."

"Oh, thank heavens."

"For help with ghosts, press or say '1.' For poltergeists, press or say '2.' For goblins and other assorted household pests, press or say '3.' For trolls, ogres, and Fomorians, press or say '4.' For warlocks and necromancers, press or say '5.' For banshees, press or say '6.' For elves (though they are a bit silly), press or say '7.' For all other paranormal disturbances, such as cursed tomes, possessions, missing time, evidence of changelings, etc., press or say '8.' To speak with a representative, press or say '9.'"

"Nine, nine, damn it!"

"Please hold while we connect you."

More chimes. Several minutes of more chimes. Twelve minutes, to be exact. Twelve minutes of incessant chimes, playing the same six notes over and over and over.

"Dill & Chives Investigations, how may I direct your call?" A friendly-sounding woman with an Irish accent answered at last.

"Yes, hello! I need to speak with Mr. Dill or Mr. Chives. Either one is fine. I'm not even sure which one is which, to be honest."

"I see. And what is this in regards to?"

"They were at my house earlier today. See, I was attacked by a young man who can fly. He kidnapped someone who's really lucky, and I should've seen it coming, because I'm a superhero. All right, that all sounded ridiculous."

"Not at all sir. You should hear some of the complaints we get around here. Just this week, we had a potential client complaining about two goblins fighting with a shadow in their neighbor's back yard. One lost its head, apparently."

"Fine, well, can I just talk with one of them?"

"I'll see if either is available for you."

"Thank you."

"Please hold."

More chimes. This time only five notes, over and over. After four more minutes, Carl was ready to throw the phone across the room. But just before he did...

"This is Mr. Chives, so good to hear from you, sir. Again, terribly sorry about the knock to your head earlier today from the perpetrator. I hope you have not found yourself to be overly-concussed or otherwise inconvenienced because of it."

"Oh, that? No, no, I'm fine, really."

"I am overjoyed to hear it, sir."

"Uh, yeah. Look, I want to meet up again. I can't just sit idly by. I have to do something about Lluck."

"Sir, I do assure you that we are working on the case and will contact you when and if..."

"Listen up, damn it!" Carl interrupted. "I'm not waiting this one out. I'm a superhero, yeah? I want to meet as soon as possible."

"I'm afraid it will not be possible until tomorrow morning, sir."

"Fine, tomorrow it is. Wherever you like. I have a car; I can get there."

"And what is this in regards to, if I may ask, sir?"

"I've thought about it all afternoon, and I'm pretty sure that Lluck is my son."

* * *

In a flash, Qwyrk was back in Knettles—more precisely, back in Jilly's home, in her bedroom. Though the light was on, Jilly wasn't there. Qwyrk felt a little relieved; her eyes were still swollen from crying and she didn't want to have to face Jilly and offer a lengthy explanation of why and tell her all about the appalling whirlwind of a day she'd had. She took a deep breath, composed herself for a few minutes, dried her eyes, and stepped out into the hallway to go downstairs to where Jilly was likely watching telly or putting up with one of Blip's philosophical lectures, or some such. Except, she wasn't down there, either.

"Jilly? Blip?" She wandered into the dimly-lit living room. Nothing. No one. She was about to go check in the kitchen, when a force slammed into her left leg and nearly knocked her over.

"What now?" She whipped around with her fists clenched.

She looked down, and Odin was at her feet panting and wagging his tail.

"Oh, bloody hell, mate, you scared the crap out of me!"

Odin brushed against her and started rubbing.

"Oh no... no, no. None of that!" She stepped away and pointed down at him. "Sorry, you'll have to find another leg to get off with. This one's spoken for. Except, it really isn't, is it? Oh crap."

A new wave of sadness crushed her, and she was about to cry again, but forced herself to stop thinking about Holly. For the moment.

"Focus! Now's not the time for crying over schoolgirl crushes. Where would Jilly go? Think, damn it!"

She went into the kitchen and saw the note that Jilly's mum had left for her on the table, telling her that, yet again, they were going to be out for much of the evening. She sighed. "That poor girl. I swear I want to smack her parents silly sometimes."

She wandered back into the living room and happened to gaze out the main window, where she saw a light on in the house across the street.

"Wait, does that mean Granny's about?" She looked back down at Odin who was surreptitiously maneuvering himself into position for a second humping.

"Look, I'm warning you mate! I don't care if you're Jilly's dog. Try again and you'll be sorry!"

Odin seemed to get the message. He squinted at her with one eye, turned around, and retreated to his heated bed.

"Good lad. Well then, I guess I'm paying Granny a visit."

She closed her eyes and made a circle with one hand, emerging outside in an instant, noting the cold night air that surrounded her. She strode across the street, bounded up to the door, and rang the bell, which produced a pleasant sound, rather like singing bowls, which complemented the wintriness of the weather.

A moment later, Granny answered the door.

"Hi, you're Granny Boatford, right? I'm Qwyrk, not sure if we've ever properly met before, but I helped save the world last summer from William de Soulis. You may have heard of him. Anyway, we have a new big pain in the arse—calls himself the Erlking—and apparently he's about to do something really bad, destroy everything and all that, and I'd like to stop him, if possible, and you haven't seen a girl named Jilly, have you? About this high," she held up her hand to her shoulder, "blonde hair, quite the attitude? She's probably accompanied by a jirry-jirry named Blip. Looks a like a bullfrog? About this high," she said, holding up her hand to her waist. "Victorian facial hair, quite the attitude? Yeah, I know it sounds mad, but I suppose you've seen some right strange things in your time, right?"

Granny just smiled. "Come in, dear."

* * *

"How long is this going to take?" Blip whined. "I fear that if my extremities are exposed to too much more of this gelid malaise, you might be carrying me back to your home after your scribal activities are completed, as I shall be unable to move a muscle."

"I'm sure it's not as horrid as you're making it out to be," Jilly said, scanning the wall with her flashlight. She grinned and looked at him. "But look on the bright side."

"Which is?"

"At least you didn't say you were freezing your nadgers off."

"Oh, ha ha, and hardy har, and slap my knees. Don't think I haven't noticed your petulance and growing insubordination, young lady! I've a strong suspicion that your wretched amulet is still exerting an undue and entirely vexatious influence over your young mind. Are you sure you have not hung it around your neck again?"

She rolled her eyes. "It's still right here in my pocket." She patted her jeans, as much as anything to be sure that it was indeed still there.

"Good, good. Well, then, carry on and find these confounded sigils, if you'd be so good as to do so."

"They have to be around here somewhere, maybe... here!"

She pointed to a section of the wall a bit father down and shone her light on it. Blip stepped forward to look, and they both examined the strange glyphs carved into the wall. There were ten of them in two vertical rows of five each.

"I've not seen their like before, I must say," Blip commented, his potential hypothermia and other irritations apparently forgotten for the moment. "So, what are you supposed to do?"

Jilly shrugged. "Granny said I'd know when I saw them, remember? But honestly, I haven't a clue."

"Hm. Perhaps you're supposed to trace them onto paper or some such?"

"Well, she gave me this journal." She pulled a small cloth-bound book out of her coat pocket. "But it's just blank pages."

"Maybe you're supposed to copy the signs into the book?"

"That's what I was thinking, but that hardly seems like the kind of thing we'd need to come down here at night for. I mean, I could've done that during the day, when it's a lot easier to see."

"Exactly my point! So perhaps we should return in the morning when this will be far less tedious and uncomfortable."

"No, there has to be something more to it." She opened the book to the first page. "Here, hold the torch and shine it on the wall."

Blip took the flashlight and held it up.

"I wonder..." She put her hand on the first carved sigil. At once, it lit up, and she gasped, pulling her hand back. The light went out as quickly as it had appeared.

Blip nearly dropped the flashlight. "Merciful mimosas of Mercury, girl! What in perdition did you just do?"

Jilly looked at him in shock. "I... I have no idea."

"Well, try touching it again, but be careful."

"How can I be careful touching a wall?"

"I don't know, but just, well, don't bring the whole structure crashing down on us, please!"

"I wasn't planning on it." Jilly reached out and touched the symbol again; sure enough, it started glowing, a golden light that illuminated the darkness all around her. A surprisingly comforting warmth emanated from it, enveloping her hand.

"Ms. Pleeth, I did warn you to be careful!"

"No, no, it's all right. I think it's supposed to happen." She looked down at the book still open in her other hand. "What?"

"What, what? What are you 'what-ing' for?"

"Look!"

Blip strode up to her and peered at the open book. The first symbol was inscribing itself on the page, as if burning the image into the paper.

"Extraordinary!" Blip said.

Jilly watched, wide-eyed in wonder and disbelief as whole sentences began writing themselves underneath the first symbol. The page turned as new paragraphs appeared, all in some arcane language.

"What does it say?" she asked.

"I don't know. I don't recognize the words, I'm afraid. At least it's in the Latin alphabet, so that's something, I suppose."

After two more pages of auto-written sentences, the writing stopped.

"Now what?" she asked.

"Try turning to a blank page and then putting your hand on the next symbol."

"Good idea. The one next to it, or beneath it?"

"Try the one beneath it. Just a hypothesis."

She did so, and sure enough, the astonishing spectacle repeated itself. Jilly found it no less wondrous the second time. Or the third. Or the fourth. In fact, each transfer of a sigil into her book seemed like a new experience, one that became more fascinating and just plain fun with each manifestation.

"Well, I guess we figured out what to do."

"And not a moment too soon," Blip said, once more hopping in place. "Now, when you've finished, I would dearly like to retreat to some place warm, i.e., your home, post-haste."

"I think I would rather you stay here for the moment," a deep voice with a Germanic accent echoed from behind them.

Blip turned around and shone the torch out at the mouth of the cave, but there was enough of an ambient glow from outside that they didn't need it. In that half-light, Jilly saw a tall, hooded figure in a dark robe, floating a few feet above the ground. He flexed his long fingers, revealing nails splaying out like talons.

"How fortuitous that I find you here, child," he said. "I was hoping that an artificer of the arcane arts might make themselves known to me, and it's truly fitting that you are here now, just before the solstice rite."

"Who are you?" Jilly demanded. "We're not afraid of you!"

"Oh, I do not want you to be afraid of me. Well, that's not true. I always enjoy when mortals are afraid and run for their puny lives; it amuses me, rather like listening to a cheerful Top 40 pop tune. But in this case, it is not strictly necessary. As you are a descendant of that ancient hag, I simply need to subdue you and bring you under my control. Or, if that's not possible, I will kill you. I would say the choice is yours, but it is really not."

"I knew we should have waited to come here until tomorrow," Blip groused.

*   *   *

"Wait, what?" Qwyrk exclaimed, standing up from the sofa and looking at Granny in shock.

"It's true. I've suspected it for some time, and it's why I arranged to move into this house across from her a few years ago. Jilly is my descendant, and she's potentially a powerful witch. I'm not yet sure of the precise nature of her gift, but it's probably what's drawn all of you to her."

"I... I don't even know what to say," Qwyrk stammered, sitting back down. "I mean, I know she helped dupe de Soulis, but I just assumed that was because she's a good artist."

"That was probably true. I think her powers are only starting to manifest now, even if the forces around her were always aware of who she really is."

"Of course, puberty and all that, as if she doesn't have enough to deal with as far as all that goes. Goddess, how do humans cope with the change at such a young age? I couldn't imagine not staying a child until at least fifty!"

"Well," Granny said with a knowing grin, "a lot of humans seem to still be children well after fifty and beyond!"

"True enough. So, what's she off doing?"

"I sent her and Blip down to my old cave. She needs to undergo a simple initiation, which she needs to figure out on her own. Magical glyphs on the cave wall will recognize her and write themselves into the blank book I gave her. She'll be able to meditate on them and eventually use them to work magic of various sorts. There are instructions, but they're written in a very old language that she'll have to learn and decipher over time."

This news was a lot to take in, Qwyrk decided. Too much, given everything else that had slammed her today. "I feel bad about yelling at her earlier. If she's undergoing physical *and* magical changes, she's probably having a rough time of it. That explains why she was such a cow earlier."

"Oh no, her belligerence came from the amulet you gave her."

"Wait, what?"

"Yes, sorry to say. Because she's already enspelled, she doesn't need it. As she grows into her abilities, she'll be able to see you without additional magical help."

"Of course! It's like getting a double dose of some nasty medicine."

"That's a good enough analogy, I suppose."

"So, they're down there now, then?"

"I would imagine so. I haven't seen them return yet, though it has been a while."

"Hm, maybe I should check in on them."

"If you like, though I'm sure they're fine."

"Yeah, well, I'm not quite sure of anything right now." Despair tugged at her heart, but she resisted the urge to tear up, but only just. "I think I'll go have a look, just to be sure."

"If it will make you feel better, then by all means, do so."

Qwyrk nodded. "It will. Look, thank you so much. I've had a lot of really upsetting rubbish to deal with today, but this is a small bit of good news, at least."

"Not a problem at all, dear. And if you'd like to chat about any of that rubbish, I'm always here."

"Thanks, maybe I'll take you up on that. Eh, probably not. Bye, then."

She left Granny's and bounded over several rooftops, heading down toward the river and then on to the old cave. She breathed a sigh of relief to be out in the night, for the air to be rushing against her face. She felt a touch more relaxed, like her old self.

"Maybe it's all for the best, anyway. I mean, this is what I do, and it's better when I'm on my own. And it's not like I don't have enough on my..."

She landed some distance away from the cave, but could see the entrance was blocked by a tall figure in a long, grey, and hooded robe, floating above the ground and flexing taloned fingers that protruded from voluminous sleeves.

"Oh, crap!"

CHAPTER FIFTEEN

"So... where are we, then?" Lluck asked. This was worse than running away and living on the streets. If anything, he felt more trapped now than before. The cold, musty air stung his nose, and he'd had just about enough of everything and everyone.

"Like I said, I have no idea," Longwing answered, looking around.

"Are we even in the same place?"

"Um, what part of 'I have no idea' didn't you pick up on? I can explain it better if you want."

"Yeah, all right, I'm just thinking out loud!" he snapped, mindful that other people never failed to spectacularly disappoint him.

"Wherever it is, we have to get out of here as fast as we can. Then we can figure out how to get to the center of Leeds again, safety in the crowds and all that."

"Wow, you're like a genius, or something, mate! Brilliant! Why didn't I think of that?"

"You know, I could just leave you here, if you're keen on getting your internal organs eaten."

"Fine, sorry, but I'm only here to begin with because of you. Do you have any sort of plan?"

"Keep moving and stay hidden until we find a way out of here."

"Seriously, I'm blown away." This failure seemed even more spectacular.

Longwing shot him a dark look and motioned for him to follow down the hall.

"Why this way?" Lluck asked.

"Shhhhh!"

"Why this way?" Lluck repeated in a whisper.

"Why not?" he whispered back.

"Fair enough."

They crept along, but the sound of rough and rumbly voices in conversation stopped them in their tracks. Longwing gestured to Lluck to pull back into a nearby dark alcove.

"Quick!" he whispered. "Hide here."

As they crouched and waited, the voices came closer.

"Why'd we get stuck doin' this, then?" one said, growling and grumpy.

"Don't know, I think we were volunteered," the other answered.

"That ain't how it works."

"What d'ya mean?"

"You can't be volunteered for something. You gotta volunteer for it yerself, willingly and all that."

"You what?"

"You have ta want to do it, or it ain't volunteerin', you're just ordered around by someone who's got more authority than you. Yer bein' 'voluntold', or somethin' like that!"

FIFTEEN

"Well, that don't seem fair!"

"Of course it ain't fair, you muck-wit! That's why we're here!"

"Oh. So we coulda said no, then?"

"For cripe's sake, shut yer trap!"

Lluck and Longwing watched as two squat hobgoblins with spears trundled on by, hobbling and gobbling along and complaining about their sorry lot in life.

"My feet are sore. I want a break."

"Awwww, your little footsies gettin' tender? I can hack 'em off for ya!"

"Eh, shut yer drink-hole!"

After they'd wandered far enough out of earshot, Lluck whispered, "Should we take them out?"

"No, probably best not to. We don't want to attract any more attention, and there's bound to be more of them around. Come on!"

They slipped out of the alcove and headed down the hallway in the opposite direction of the grumping guards. After a minute, said hallway took a ninety-degree turn to the right. Following it around, they saw three more halls branching off in different directions.

"Crap," Lluck swore. "Any ideas, genius? Or do we just pick one at random?"

Longwing didn't answer, but he seemed to be weighing their options.

"The one on the left," he said after a moment of concentration.

"You sure about that, or are you just trying to look impressive?"

"I'm using logic, mate. The farther away we get from your cell and any sign of trouble, the better."

"Maybe you've forgotten, but we're apparently not in the same set of halls you were in before. You said so yourself." *I should've just gone to London.*

"No, but they'll still have to follow some kind of pattern. Magic's not so random that it just makes shite up as it goes along."

"You could've fooled me."

"That's just because you don't know enough about it yet, or about your own power."

"So how do you know, then? Who are you? What are you?"

"Like I said, it's a bit of a long story."

"Well?"

He sighed. "My sister and I, we're special. We were ordinary people once, but things changed."

Lluck let out an irritated sigh. "That makes literally no sense at all."

"I know it sounds crazy, but we were taken by some less than reputable Fae, who replaced us with changelings. We were both babies at the time, twins, so we were raised in a different world by a couple of cranky old creatures, who were more like fairy tale villains than real parents. It wasn't pleasant."

"Hold on," Lluck stopped and stared at him in disbelief, "if you're human, then how did you manage not to die or go crazy? I thought that was a problem with humans spending too much time in their world?"

"Yeah, it's a bit complicated."

Lluck held out his hands, palms up. "Yeah, and?"

"There are certain old spells, old magics that can be cast on humans when they're babies, right? They're not approved of, apparently, and in some places they're flat-out forbidden, but they exist. Once used, those infants become more like Fae and can never go back to being fully human again. It's why I can fly and have extra strength; apparently you never quite know what powers you'll get. The problem is, we're enchanted, but we're sort of between worlds, not really human or otherwise. Plus, my sister and I, we had enchanted blood already, so we relied on each other when we were young. Until we ran away."

"Ran away?"

"Well, our abductors were bastards, and by the time we were older, we'd had enough, so we snuck out one night and never went back."

They started walking again.

"How did you manage not to get captured?" Lluck found himself wanting to know more now.

Longwing smiled. "We're good at not being seen when we don't want to be."

"So your sister; where is she now?"

Longwing shrugged. "Haven't seen her for two years."

"And that doesn't bother you?"

"Of course it bothers me, you wanker! But we decided it'd be safer to keep apart for a while and not to stay in touch unless we absolutely had to. When I met the Erlking, he seemed like a right powerful bloke—and he is—someone who could shake things up, maybe help me get more power so I could find her and fix things for us. But after a bit, he started asking me to do stuff I wasn't happy with, like kidnapping; remember that? He told me he knew where my sister was, and that he'd torture her or even kill her if I didn't go along with whatever he wanted. So I did."

Longwing sighed and shook his head, as if angry with himself.

"But now, I'm realizing that she's way more clever than that, and he probably has no idea where she is, or maybe he *has* tried to hurt her and she kicked his arse. The few times I pushed back against his commands or outright refused, he'd rough me up, but he never came back and said he'd done something to her. So, I'm guessing he's been bluffing the whole time. Also why I decided to help you out, by the way."

"It's appreciated, mate."

"No worries, but the sooner we find an exit, the better. Like I said, those hobgoblins won't be the only ones down here."

As if in answer, they rounded a corner and a short flight of steps led up to a door. A chilly draft passed by them. Longwing smiled. "See? My intuition was on point. Come on, use your fancy gifts and unlock it. They should work now; we're far enough away from that floor sigil, and you've had enough time to recharge."

Lluck stepped up and concentrated for a few moments before flicking his hands. Sure enough, when he tried the door handle, it opened with ease.

"Brilliant, mate!" Longwing said. "I told you it wouldn't be that hard to get out of here!"

They exited and bounded up the staircase in front of them.

"Seems awful quiet for Leeds," Lluck said, apprehension tugging at him. "This, this isn't right, is it?"

"Are you fecking kidding me?" Longwing grumbled.

The cold night air surrounded them, under a dark sky. They saw stone buildings, a church in the distance, a standard street, a few street lamps lighting up the dark. The only problem was that the buildings were old, short, and squat, and in the distance they could see hills and countryside. And the quiet of the place suggested that the whole town had gone to sleep for the night.

Longwing shook his head. "When I went into the building, it was part of an office complex just off Leeds city center. But this...

this looks like some town out in the Dales or Moors. Mate, we must be at least twenty or thirty miles from where we were when I found you!"

* * *

"Now you listen to me, you rebarbative ruffian!" Blip bellowed, shining the torch at the robed figure's hood, though unable to illuminate the darkness obscuring his face. "I don't know who you are, and I don't particularly care; you lot are all alike, anyway. But if you are going to come in here and insult and threaten this fine young lady in my presence and in the house of her esteemed ancestor, no less, you are sadly mistaken if you think you won't receive a resounding rebuke! What have you to say to that, sir?"

"I say, little pompous one, that I admire your spirit, truly, and your willingness to defy me even in the face of your own demise. In fact, I could use one such as you, should you be tempted."

"Use me? Whatever for, you nefarious levitating freak?"

"Why, to join my hunt, of course; to scour this world and cleanse it of the unworthy."

"Your hunt? Why on earth would you be hunting to... oh! You mean the great hunt of the lost souls? The Wild Hunt?"

"None other."

"Then, that would make you..."

"At your service." The figure bowed slightly. "Except not at all. Rather, you are at *my* service, should I so permit it. Now, stand aside, and let me see the youngling, so newly imbued with her great-mother's enchantments."

He floated toward them.

Blip stepped back and stood in front of Jilly.

"Is that who I think is?" she asked, panicking.

"I fear it may well be," Blip whispered back. "If there is anything in that new magical grimoire of yours, now might be a very good time to use it, my dear."

"But I have no idea how! I was just supposed to come here and collect the symbols and take them back to Granny. Then she was going to train me, or something. I'm ages away from being able to do anything, maybe years!"

The figure drifted closer.

"We don't have years, Miss Pleeth! I doubt we even have minutes!"

"You know," a familiar and welcome voice sounded from the entrance. "I've had a really crap day, like one of the worst in decades, and it's mostly due to you, you hovering pillock. So, I'm thinking that an arse-kicking is in store, and I'm going to make it extra painful and drawn-out, because right now, I can't think of anyone who deserves it more than you do."

Jilly almost laughed out loud as she heard Qwyrk's voice and a Shadow with glowing red eyes stepped into view. She grabbed ahold of Blip and edged backward, dragging him with her. "See, Mr. Blip? Everything's going to be fine!"

* * *

"Well, this is a bit of a pain in the arse, isn't it?" Lluck looked around at their new surroundings: a small town in the snowy countryside in the dark. Everything had gone wrong again; what a surprise. "I mean, it's not like we're going to get a taxi back to Leeds at this time of night. So, what the hell happened?"

"He's probably set some magic on the building that lets it serve as a teleportation mechanism, bending space-time and such so that one spot can open up onto several others, some of them really far away. Good for getting around fast."

"Of course he has. I mean, that's exactly what I figured." Lluck rolled his eyes and looked around again.

"You're funny, youngling. Just be glad we're not that far away from where we started. We could've ended up in London, or maybe even back in the faerie realm. My guess is that this village is close to his sacrifice site."

"And you would be correct in that assessment." They turned to see the two hobgoblins standing at the bottom of the stairs, smiling at them with jagged yellow-toothed grins.

"Bollocks," Lluck said as he flicked his hands forward. The would-be captors yelled out in surprise as they slipped and fell on their bloated bums and slammed into each other, spears clattering to the stone steps.

"Come on!" Lluck yelled, as he dashed away. Longwing followed right behind him, and they ran down the main street for a block before dipping into a side lane.

"We're not gonna stay hidden for long in a small place like this," Lluck wheezed, as they stopped for a moment, once they were sure they hadn't been followed.

Longwing nodded. "And if two of them are already here, I can guarantee there will be more."

"So, what do we do?"

"No idea."

Lluck let out an exasperated puff of vapory air. "That's real helpful."

"Well, I didn't think we were going to get whisked off for a sight-seeing side-trip to wherever the hell we are, did I? Remind me not to rescue you next time."

"Remind yourself not to kidnap me, first."

"Yeah, fair enough."

"You can still fly, right? Can't we just soar on out of here?"

"Yeah, but I don't think I can carry the extra weight."

"I don't weigh *that* much!"

"It's a question of weight distribution and lift and all that, you know, like with airplanes. Just because it's magic doesn't mean that the laws of physics don't apply."

Lluck put a hand over his mouth as if talking on an intercom. "Longwing International Airlines. Welcome aboard, just don't bring anything with you, including yourself."

"You're a right laugh, mate."

"It's one of my gifts."

"No, it really isn't."

"Well, we could at least try, right? I mean, if you get a running start or something, maybe we can sail far enough that they can't run after us." It seemed like a sound enough plan, even if he secretly doubted it would work. .

"Maybe, but we'll just end up in the middle of the countryside, not exactly ideal on a freezing December night."

"Better than getting caught and dragged back down into that cell."

"Fair point. We'll head back to the main street and give it a go."

"And if they see us?"

"We'll just have to outrun them."

"And what if they have spears and arrows and all that?"

"Don't get hit?"

Lluck shook his head. "You're like a genius at tactics, mate."

Longwing shot him another annoyed look, and they headed back to the main street.

"The snow-covering will make it harder to get a good run going," Longwing said.

"So, what's the plan?"

"We take off, run as fast as we can. I'll grab you and lift off, and with luck—pun a little bit intended—we might make it a half-mile or so before I give out. But it should give us enough of a head-start. I don't think I'll be able to get much altitude, though."

Lluck was surprised that this crazy plan was maybe not so crazy. "Hey, as long as it works, I'm good."

They heard a chorus of angry, growly voices in the distance and turned to see a mob of hobgoblins and an assorted array of unsavory atrocities barreling down the street toward them, swords, axes, and spears waving about.

"Right, if we're going to go, now's the time," Lluck said.

Off they dashed, struggling not to trip and fall on the snowy, icy street. Lluck chanced a glance behind him; somehow, not only were the bloated beasties keeping pace, they were gaining on them.

"Um," he huffed and puffed, "any time!"

Longwing grabbed him by his coat and pulled him in. He jumped up, and they were airborne. They rose to five feet, then ten, maybe fifteen, and sailed ahead faster than they had been running. They were flying! Lluck's stomach felt like it remained on the ground, but the whole thing was a visceral thrill unlike any he'd ever experienced. Soaring through the air! He delighted in the cold wind rushing toward his face and the ground speeding by below them.

"Hah! This is brilliant, mate! You did it, you did..."

An explosion of pain knocked him across the head, and then he was falling. He had the sense somehow to flick his hands out, slowing their descent and landing them gently on the snowy pavement. He groaned and looked over to see Longwing lying face down, out cold. He heard footsteps approaching and a monstrous hobgoblin came into view, who reached down and picked up the giant wooden club he'd just belted them with.

"That was highly satisfying," the creature said with a smug look on his face. "I know I can't kill ya, but makin' ya hurt is the next best thing. Thanks, by the way, for doin' that lucky thing of yers and landin' like you was on a nice comfy pillow. Now you ain't roughed up so bad that we can't rough you up a little bit more."

Several goblins arrived, cackling and muttering.

"Take 'em back below, boys and be quick! Don't want no stupid mortals catchin' sight of any of us accidentally, 'cause then we'd have to kill 'em and the master wouldn't be pleased with us ruinin' the secret of his little country hideaway."

Lluck felt light-headed and delirious as grabby hands wrapped themselves around his arms and legs and lifted him up. He caught sight of more of them doing the same to Longwing and felt himself being carried along roughly just before he blacked out.

❄ ❄ ❄

"So you're the big, bad Erlking, master of the Wild Hunt, lord of the ghosties and ghoulies that endlessly wander the night skies, looking for those unfortunate souls to join in the eternal pursuit, blah, blah, blah. No wait, aren't you that numpty in those Italian comedies, always falling on your arse and getting the crap beaten out of you for being so stupid? I can get on board with that. When I'm done with you, you'll wish that's all you were."

The Erlking turned to Qwyrk, and though she couldn't see his face, she thought she caught a glimpse of a mocking and unsettling smile.

"Recently," he said, "two of my minions clashed with you. If they are to be believed, they nearly killed you with their enhanced powers. Now, who do you think gave them those powers, and if they had them, don't you think it likely that I have them, as well?"

"All right." She put her hands on her hips. "First of all, those stupid prats sucker-punched me, and I'm way more ready and pissed off now than I was then. And second, 'minions'? Really? Couldn't you come up with something better? Flunkeys? Henchmen, hench... goblins, whatever? Factoti? Sycophantic toadies? I don't know, just something a little less naff and boring?"

She clenched her fists until they practically shook.

"Oh, and by the way, that girl in there and I thoroughly thumped the two of them until they ran off to hide, in case you're wondering where they are now. And no, I have no idea where they went, but as far away from you as possible, I would imagine. So, Mr. Grand-and-Scary Cull-Meister, maybe you might want to tone down the arrogance a bit, all right? We're the same little band that took down William de Soulis last summer, and I see nothing in your flying circus trick there that tells me you're in any way more impressive than him. So why don't you give it your best shot, because I have a whole lot of anger and frustration to work out, and your ugly mug would be a lovely place to start!"

The Erlking laughed and drifted back toward her.

Good! Qwyrk thought. *Get him away from Jilly and Blip. Keep him distracted.*

"I think you will find," he said, "that my power far exceeds those of two imbecilic... factoti, did you say? Yes, I like that word; it should be worth extra Scrabble points."

Qwyrk gritted her teeth, his voice already sounding like his long claws on a chalkboard. She glared, so ready to commence the pummeling. "Give it your best shot, ugly. Well, I don't know for *sure* that you're ugly; you might be really fit under that hood, but looking at those nails, I'd reckon probably not. Seriously, what's up with those? You need a manicure, like, last week! I'm guessing your toenails are pretty disgusting, too. I don't even want to think about it, to be honest, so please don't show them to me!"

She held up her hands as if pushing him (and his awful toenails) away.

"Also," she went on, "what's with the cheesy old German accent? I mean, I know you're like some ancient Frisian spirit-thing, but honestly, it's the twenty-first century; we've all moved on. I mean, these days, I sure as hell don't talk like I did 1,500 years ago. That'd just be crazy! Have a go with a new accent, maybe Scouse or Geordie, or something? Why not give it a try? It might not work, but it could be a right laugh for a bit."

"You talk quite a lot."

"Yeah, I do that when I'm nervous. Or excited about kicking some pillock's arse. It's the latter of the two, in this case, just so you know."

"I welcome your attempt to defeat me."

"Aw, I'm touched. If you didn't want me to do it, I've no idea what I'd do."

The Erlking flung a bolt of pale blue lightning from his hand, but she ducked and jumped to one side.

"Yeah, I'm not getting caught out with that crap this time, Creepy Claws."

He launched another at her. She jumped up in mid-air to avoid it, but she knew the shot was a little too close for comfort. She landed near enough to him to get off two punches to his gut, making him gasp and shoving him back several feet. She pressed the attack and lunged at him, delivering several more hits to his mid-section that knocked him clean out of the air and onto his back. Not waiting, she jumped on his stomach, trying to land as hard as she could. He gasped again, and she was thrilled to have winded him, if such a thing were possible with an ancient spirit. Though his face was still covered by his hood (somehow), she punched what little she could see of his jaw, left, right, and left again.

"Get... off... me, you little rat!"

He flung his arms forward, and a force knocked her several feet into the air, landing her on her behind. She exhaled as pain surged through her backside but jumped to her feet at once, alert and very angry.

"Not this time, you twat!"

But the Erlking was already up. He brought his hands together, and a sickly purple light began to swirl between them. He uttered some words Qwyrk didn't understand and shot a beam at her with a violent jerking of his claws. She ducked, and it passed over her head. *That was far too close.*

"So" she said, standing back up, "you're not actually Odin, are you? I mean I've heard some rumors to that effect. I think they're silly, of course, but I just wanted to check. You know, it's funny; the girl in there you're so keen on? She has a bulldog named 'Odin,' because he squints. I'm thinking it would be a right laugh if you pulled back that hood and your face was a big squinty dog."

"Ha! I have nothing to do with that old Northern wizard. And when I have claimed my power, even those gods will fear me as much as you are about to."

"Yeah? 'Cause I have to be honest, mate: not really feeling the fear. Now, you know what *would* scare me? If you told me that fifteenth-century men's bowl haircuts were making a comeback. Those things always freaked me the hell out; that's one fashion trend we do *not* need to revisit, thank you very much!"

The Erlking growled and brought his hands together again, palms facing each other. He bowed his head, face still hidden under his cowl's darkness, and uttered more words in the mysterious and ancient tongue, a language that didn't sound like it would be on offer in any university course anytime soon.

"Wait, so you're praying, now?" she taunted. "I thought *you* were the god, the dog, whatever."

She lunged at him, fists poised to deliver more hammering blows.

But that was a big mistake.

He flung his arms out wide, and a shadowy mist erupted from the void of space left by his hands. It caught Qwyrk full-on in the face, and before she knew what had happened, it sent her flying backward through the air, across the river and crashing down on the far side.

She hit the pavement hard and rolled several more feet. Her vision exploded in stars as pain slammed through her. But the mist wasn't finished. It surrounded her face, obscuring her sight and choking her. She coughed and gagged, but couldn't dislodge it from her throat. Not able to see, she dragged herself to her feet and jumped straight up as far as she could, trying to shake it off. It followed her for a moment but melted away the higher she rose. She paused about thirty feet up, smiled at her plan, and started to fall. Which, of course, was not supposed to happen.

"Bollocks! Must be whatever the hell that was."

She traced her hands in a circle and passed into a glowing violet vortex, emerging inside the cave and stepping out only a few feet above the ground. But her momentum hadn't completely slowed and she hit the rocky floor harder than she intended, stumbling forward and coming to a stop right in front of Jilly and Blip. Somehow, she didn't fall flat on her face.

"A very elegant entrance," Blip remarked.

"Oh, shut it!" she answered.

"Hi Qwyrk. Um, everything all right out there?"

"Could be better, could be worse. But I think I've got it under control. Listen, don't do anything stupid, all right? Honestly, I've got this."

"But I can help…"

"No! I mean, it's *him*, Jilly, and he's bad news. I'm going to try to stop him, but you've got to run. Get yourselves on out of here, now."

"But I'm still trying to figure out these symbols in my book. Granny sent me here to…"

"I know, I know. But you can deal with that later. Seriously, just go!"

She turned around and started for the entrance to the cave, before she could hear Jilly protest any more.

The Erlking was already waiting near the cave's mouth.

"I trust you found that at least somewhat frightening?" he mocked.

Qwyrk just shook her head and offered a grim smile. "Not even a little."

"That's a shame. It's so much more entertaining when my victims beg before I take them."

"Take me? Take me where? Out for a drink after a good scrap? You know, I'd almost be tempted to take you up on that, but you probably drink blood, or fermented yak butter tea, or something."

The Erlking chuckled. "You have quite the wit, Shadow. I do

appreciate your bravado. It's a shame we are not on the same side. A warrior such as you would be most welcome in my legions."

"Legions? Are you a flipping Roman general now? Is that why you wear the hood? To hide some funny helmet with plumage? You know, I think it's all starting to make sense now."

"No. I mean, these legions."

"What are you... oh crap!"

All around him, beings began to materialize. Dark and twisted forms: goblins, trolls, snake-men, skeletal birds of prey, zombies, armored honey badgers, horned satyrs, minotaurs, giant floating eyeballs with fangs (wait, what?), and much worse. Well, there's not much worse than a giant floating eyeball with fangs.

"Now," the Erlking said, "I would have offered you a chance to surrender, but I think I will just let them rip you to shreds, and then I will take the little girl with me."

"Joke's on you, feck-face! I already told her to get the hell out of here."

"That is a shame. I suppose I will just have to do with watching my army tear you apart. And then I will find her, anyway."

The creatures moved on her as a mass, hissing, growling, scratching, shrieking, giggling. Qwyrk waved her hands in front of her to blink away... and nothing happened.

"Oh, did I not mention?" the Erlking taunted. "The mist you inhaled should be taking full effect about now. It inhibits your powers, only for a short time, but more than long enough for them to kill you. You see, I have no interest in fighting fairly."

"Shite!" Qwyrk cursed, backing up, only to see more enemies materializing right behind her. She looked around in every direction, trying to find an escape route.

"You are starting to feel... afraid? Let the desperation overtake you. Fall to your knees. Beg. Cry. Maybe I'll command them to kill you quickly."

"Look, you bullying prick! I've just gone through one of the worst days I've had in a *very* long time, and if you think I'm going out on my knees, you are sadly mistaken. I may not make it out of here, but I'll damn well take a pile of these bastards with me."

"A warrior to the end," the Erlking bowed his concealed head; there was something oddly sincere about it. "I respect that, truly. Farewell, Ms. Qwyrk. You were a worthy adversary, though, perhaps too trusting."

"What? What are you talking about?"

The creatures converged on her. It was over.

Except that it wasn't. A blinding light shot out of the cave, and the beasties all around her cried out and fell to their knees (or equivalent limbs), cowering and covering their faces. Qwyrk herself had to shield her gaze, but she could see the shape of someone emerging from the mouth of the cave. Two someones, actually.

"Bloody hell! Jilly, Blip! What did I tell you?"

But Jilly stepped out, one hand clutching her book, the other held in front of her, the source of the magic light. She winced, and Qwyrk could tell she wasn't going to be able to keep up the effort for much longer. But that girl, that amazing young person, with Blip at her side, she walked confidently right into the middle of a gaggle of gargoyles, a murder of monsters, and a flock of fiends, all of whom recoiled as she passed by them.

The Erlking growled and launched bolts of magical energy toward them, but these bounced away as soon as they hit the light. Jilly reached Qwyrk, and still their enemies held back.

"Jilly, we have to get out of here! Blip, I can't teleport right now. Can you manage all three of us?"

"It will be an effort, but I think so."

"That's not filling me with a lot of confidence."

"Well, what do you want me to say? Shall I instill false hope, only to have it dashed at the last possible moment, when..."

"Just do it. Take us away, now!"

"But what about the town?" Blip said. "Do we leave it at the mercy of these hellions?"

"He needs Jilly, for some reason. There's nothing else here he wants, or he would have come here a long time ago. Now please, hurry up!"

"Fine, fine. Everyone hold on." Blip placed one hand on Jilly's back and gripped Qwyrk's hand with his other. He closed his eyes, his face stern with concentration.

"Any time would be good."

"Don't rush me, damn it!"

Qwyrk looked back at Jilly. She was straining and Qwyrk knew she wouldn't last for more than a moment or two.

"Blip! Now!"

Blip yelled out something approaching profanity, and in a flash, they were gone.

CHAPTER SIXTEEN

Qwyrk opened her eyes. It was still nighttime. She was in a tree, hanging over a branch, to be precise. About thirty feet up from the ground. But the lack of wintry weather, the smell of the air, and the vibrational pattern of the place told her she was home.

"Jilly? Blip?"

"Um, over here," she heard Jilly say. Turning to look in the direction of her voice, she saw Jilly in a similar situation one tree over.

"I'm just fine, thank you for asking," Blip said, his voice revealing him to be two trees down in the opposite direction.

"Nice job there, Mr. Ninja House-of-Lords-Candidate," Qwyrk said.

"Oh, I am so terribly sorry!" Blip fired off. "Next time I'll be sure to put everyone down in front of a roaring hearth fire on a comfy sofa with a plate of hobnobs and a mug of hot cocoa in their hands."

"That does sound rather lovely, right about now," Jilly said.

"I was being facetious for ironic and comic effect, Ms. Pleeth."

"I never would have known," Jilly said, rolling her eyes.

"Look, let's just get down and figure out exactly where we are," Qwyrk said.

"How do you know if your powers have returned?" Jilly asked. "I heard him talking about it from inside the cave."

"Well, I'm home, so I'll have to assume everything is fine here."

"And if it isn't?" Blip asked.

"Then it's going to be a right painful landing when I drop out of this tree, isn't it?"

She swung herself over and dangled off the branch by both hands.

"Right, here goes nothing. Or maybe everything."

She let go.

She fell.

But slowly, in a gentle descent that allowed her to land on both feet with only a slight knee-bend.

"Yes!" She clapped her hands. "All right, Jilly, I'm coming up for you." She walked over to Jilly's tree, and jumped into the air, where she hovered by her friend and reached out to her.

"Take my hands." Jilly did so, and in a moment, they had descended to the ground in the same graceful manner.

"Ahem. Now me," Blip announced.

"Of course!" Qwyrk grinned. She jumped up to him, took his hand, and started to descend. But she pretended that her hand slipped, catching him again, holding him upside down by one leg.

"Gaaaaah! What in Nergal's nefarious name are you doing, you mad woman! Put me down safely at once!"

She landed and set him down with all care on the ground. Well, she did "slip" again and drop him a foot or so onto the earth.

"That was decidedly not funny! Is that the thanks I get for saving our hides?"

Qwyrk felt a twinge of guilt. "All right, I'm sorry. I just needed a bit of a laugh after the crap day I've had."

"What is it, Qwyrk?" Jilly asked, her smile at Blip's misfortunes fading. "What's wrong?"

"Well, first there was the fight you and I had..."

"Yeah, that was caused by the amulet you gave me; Granny said so. I guess since I'm some sort of witch or something, it was too much power all at once and was making me bonkers."

Qwyrk nodded. "Yeah, she explained that when I stopped by, after you'd already left. I'm so sorry, by the way. I had no idea."

"It's not your fault; you couldn't have known. I mean, I had no idea until tonight. You just wanted for me to see you, and, and I love you for it." She hugged Qwyrk, who relaxed as relief washed over her.

"And now, the Erlking is after you," she said as she held Jilly. "But I promise you, he's not going to get you!"

"It's all right," Jilly said, looking up at her. "It's not like it's the first time some evil tosser has wanted my help for his big plan."

"Yeah, you do have a fair bit of talent for attracting these twats," Qwyrk said with a smile. "Watch out when you start dating." Her smile fell to a concerned frown. "There's more, though. It's Holly. She's betrayed us; she's been playing me the whole time." She blinked back the tears forming in her eyes.

"Wait, what?" Jilly said in shock. "No! How?"

"The boy's mother?" Blip said. "That's very distressing news, if true. She's a Yakshi, correct? Allying herself with the Erlking sounds very out of character."

"How did you find out?" Jilly demanded.

"It's a long story. Look, let's get out of here, go to Qwyzz's home, and I can tell you about it there, all right? Blip, where are we?"

"I'm not entirely sure." Blip said.

"You don't know?" Qwyrk asked.

"Well, we were in a bit of a hurry, if I recall? At least I've transported us somewhere safe."

"I know. I'm sorry. Thank you. You saved our lives."

Blip nodded. "Happy to do so, of course."

"Come here," she motioned to both of them. "I'll take us to Qwyzz's home."

"I can see you, by the way," Jilly said as she wrapped her arms around Qwyrk's waist.

"Well, you are *here*, after all," Qwyrk said. "How do you feel?"

"Fine. Completely different from earlier."

"Good. We'll need to keep an eye on you, but your new-found powers probably mean you won't have too many future problems."

"Does that mean I could come here whenever I want?" Jilly bounced up and down with an eager smile.

"Maybe. But we'll talk about it later, all right? Let's just get somewhere safe for now."

"You don't think the Erlking and his minions could follow us here, do you?" Blip asked.

"I doubt it, but let's be safe, just in case. Qwyzz will have all sorts of protections around his home. No one gets in there without his allowing it, believe me!"

She waved her hands in the air as Jilly and Blip held on to her, and in a moment, purple lights flashed around them. Shortly after, they found themselves standing in front of a peculiar mansion-sized home that was a hodge-podge of architectural styles, currently mostly medieval and Tudor.

"What an amazing place!" Jilly said, looking up in wonder.

Qwyrk sighed. "Hang on, there's just one thing before we can go in."

"Alloooooo!" a voice rang out from the roof top. Qwyrk closed her eyes and shook her head. A little stony being with a dog's face and short horns popped its head over the ledge.

"Right, Gargula, we have absolutely zero time for your nonsense right now and..."

"Do you know ze password? None shall speak to my master without ze... ack!"

Qwyrk levitated into the air, grabbed him by the neck and descended back to the ground in front of a wide-eyed Jilly and an equally bemused Blip.

"Everyone, this is Gargula, the gargoyle. He's the so-called guardian of Qwyzz's home and he's a right pain in the arse! So listen up, mason-mouth: you're going to tell your master I'm here and that it's urgent, as in, life-or-death, and then we're going in, got it?"

The little creature grunted and nodded.

"Good," Qwyrk said with a smile. "Off you go, then."

Grumbling, the diminutive stone monster flapped his wings, sending a spray of pebbles to the ground and flew back up to the roof, where he disappeared.

Qwyrk stood in front of the entrance, literally twiddling her thumbs, not bothering to explain anything else to Jilly or Blip. A moment later the door opened, and Qwyzz poked his head out.

"Qwyrk? My goodness, my dear, why are you here so late? My gargoyle said it was urgent."

"I'm afraid it is, old friend. Can we come in?"

"Yes, yes! By all means, please. Join me in my sitting room, and tell me all about it."

A quarter of an hour later, Qwyrk had given him a suitable summary of the day, while Blip sipped a small glass of port. Jilly looked around in amazement at the suit of armor polishing itself, the self-playing chess game, the diminutive wyvern, and a dozen other quaint and fantastical curiosities.

"Oh dear, it's worse than we feared," Qwyzz said after a moment of silent contemplation.

"Yes, the Erlking may already have Lluck," Qwyrk said, "and he's going to do something at the solstice, probably at the sacrificial site we visited earlier. It's likely going to end up in a lot of death and him gaining even more power than he has, which was already considerable, I have to say. That whole draining me of my magic thing? That was scary as hell, and I don't want to repeat that ever again, thank you very much. Is there anything you can do to counter that?"

"I don't know," Qwyzz answered. "Perhaps. I'll consult a few tomes and see if I can find a precedent for it."

"Oh, by the way, Jilly here? She's a witch and a descendent of Granny Boatford. And that amulet you made for me to give to her? Turns out it was driving her crazy, because she's already got magic inside of her to begin with."

"Ah, yes, yes," Qwyzz answered with a knowing nod. "That will happen when one is already enchanted. It can enhance the energy of a magical being considerably, and not in good ways. I'm terribly sorry, child. I hope it didn't cause you too much distress?"

"No, not really," Jilly replied, "but it is quite nice to be able to see Qwyrk as she is, thank you."

"Well, it seems that you won't need such a trinket for much longer," he said with a smile.

"What do you mean?" Jilly asked.

"You soon should be able to see her just fine on your own all the time, I should think, given your magical lineage."

Jilly's eyes widened, and she looked as if she might explode in excitement. "Are you serious?"

"Yes, quite. It's always been the way of those with the elder gifts and the Sight to be able to see our world and those in it."

"Oh, this is brilliant! Qwyrk, this is incredible!"

"Yeah, it's really good news," Qwyrk said in a decidedly not excited tone. "Sorry, but we've got to focus on what to do now, all right?"

Jilly nodded, understanding.

"You're staying here for the time being," Qwyrk said. "He wants you and this is the one place he can't get you."

"Qwyrk, we've been over this how many times? I've already helped out loads before, and now that I've found out that I can do magic..."

"Which is exactly why you need to stay out of the way. If he gets a hold of you..."

"He won't!"

"You don't know that! Qwyzz, please tell her how dangerous this all is."

"She's right," Qwyzz said. "It's a dreadfully dangerous situation."

Qwyrk smirked, expecting him to take her side.

"One that calls for young Jilly to be involved, I'm afraid." Jilly pumped her fist and smirked back at Qwyrk.

"Bloody hell!" Qwyrk swore. "Is everyone just going to override me on this?"

"Qwyrk," Jilly pleaded. "I need to help. Granny said I'd have to go and prove myself."

"Yes, but not by going up against a malevolent forest spirit that can wipe out my magic! And probably yours, incidentally."

"We saw what Ms. Pleeth did before, at the cave," Blip offered, sniffing his port. "She made them all cower and gave us cover to escape. That's not to be dismissed lightly."

"Thank you, sir!" Jilly said with a smug smile.

"Yes, but that might not work again, not if he can rob her of that power, like he did me," Qwyrk objected.

"You're going to need all the help you can get," Jilly said. "It's a risk we have to take."

"The Erlking is a sly one, to be sure," Qwyzz said. "He's a formidable enemy. He thrives on trickery, on working in the dark, on deceiving. In fact, I believe he's been in England for ages, now, biding his time. Excuse me."

Qwyzz left the room for a moment and came back with a book. Blowing dust off of it, he opened it up and scanned a few pages.

"He's been masquerading almost in plain sight, as far as I can tell, probably waiting for this chance to put his terrible plans in motion."

"What do mean, 'plain sight'?"

"Oh, he's been posing as a human, apparently for years. Imagine that! A man of business, or some such, probably amassing enough human wealth to buy influence and servants without being detected. It says here that he calls himself 'Simeon Greylocke.' Now there's a rather sinister sounding name, eh?"

"What?" Qwyrk's jaw dropped and a sick feeling pummeled her stomach.

"Yes, I know. You'd have thought he would have chosen something more meek sounding, like 'Phineas Pigglesworth' or something."

"No, no. That can't be right. It just can't." She started to shake.

"Wait," Jilly said. "You mean the bloke that Mr. Blip and I saw in Leeds lighting up the big tree a few days ago was really the Erlking?"

"That is quite the shock," Blip said. "He seemed a decent fellow. He must be damned good at playing the role."

Qwyrk sat down in a nearby plushy chair. She was sick, dizzy, and she knew she might pass out, something that Shadows didn't normally do. The black cloud that she'd felt with his words appeared again in her mind, but now seemed to dissipate, as the truth came to her.

"Qwyrk, what is it?" Jilly asked, coming over and putting a hand on her shoulder.

"I, I talked to him, for a bit, actually, earlier. He's the one who told me that Holly was working against us. I was teleporting back to Knettles and somehow, he summoned me to his office in Leeds instead, right in the middle of my transference. He told me he'd had sorcerers tracking my magical trail because he needed to talk to me. He said he was Lluck's father, he told me that Holly tricked him into spending a night with her all those years ago, that she murdered her own father, and now was trying to hurt Lluck, maybe even deliver him to the Erlking."

"Oh, Qwyrk! Oh, no! What did you do?"

Qwyrk shook her head and almost laughed. "I believed him. For some stupid reason, I didn't doubt him, because I thought he was human. He even passed the test."

"The faerie fire?" Qwyzz said.

Qwyrk nodded.

"Hmm. It is possible to cheat it, though it takes considerable power to do so. But the Erlking probably could, I'm afraid."

"What's faerie fire?" Jilly asked.

"A way of determining if someone is magical or human," Qwyrk explained.

"And you thought he was human?" Jilly asked.

Qwyrk nodded, tears flooding her eyes again. Her face grew hot as the awful realization set in. "Oh crap. Oh Goddess, no!"

"Qwyrk, what happened? What did you do?"

She looked up at Jilly. "I went to her, to Holly. I confronted her. Accused her. Didn't even give her a chance to defend herself or explain anything before I just went off on her, threatened her, and stormed out. I thought she was a traitor, that she'd been deceiving me. But she hadn't, it was his magic. She really does want to find her son and help him. And she, she probably does fancy... oh Goddess, I'm such an impulsive idiot. What have I done?"

Despair overcame her, and she buried her hands in her face as her tears erupted. She sensed all hope draining away. Jilly put her arms around her, but it didn't help. Nothing would. She cried for a few minutes and looked up, only then noticing that Jilly was still there.

"I'm sorry. I'm such a fool," Qwyrk said.

"Don't you even apologize," Jilly said, leaning her head against Qwyrk's.

"Honestly, what the hell have I done?" Qwyrk sniffed. "I can't believe I was that stupid."

"The Erlking revels in deception," Blip offered. "The lies are enhanced by his magic, I would assume. There's no shame in being caught out by it. In this time of heightened emotion, anyone might have been ensnared by his trickery, myself included. Don't despise yourself over it."

Qwyrk was grateful that he was trying to be kind and understanding, his formal approach notwithstanding.

"What am I going to do?" she asked to no one in particular.

"Well, you might try going and talking to her," Jilly said, still nuzzling Qwyrk's head with her own.

"She's never going to want to see me again, much less talk to me," Qwyrk protested, more tears coming.

"You don't know that," Jilly replied as she hugged her friend tighter. "You've got to try. At the very least, it sounds like she's amazing with that martial arts thing, and we need all the help we can get right now. Plus, she wants to save her son as much as we do."

"I'm too scared. I don't know if I can even look her in the eyes. Those gorgeous eyes."

"Just go and apologize," Jilly said. "Tell her what happened, that it was magic. Tell her you're sorry. I think she'll understand."

"And if she doesn't?"

"Well, then at least you'll know, but it would be a lot worse never finding out, wouldn't it? And if we're going to stop whatever the Erlking has planned, she has just as much right to be there. More than any of us, really."

Qwyrk hung her head, certain that nothing she could say would make up for her awful behavior. But she agreed with Jilly. "You're right. I'll go see her in the morning. Maybe by then, both of our heads will have cleared a little."

"You won't regret it," Jilly encouraged, hugging her again. "I have a good feeling about it."

Qwyrk returned Jilly's embrace. "I hope you're right, because right now, everything sucks worse than I could've possibly imagined, and that's saying something."

"Right then," Blip said, setting down his empty port glass and hopping off his chair. "I'm going to attend to a few things."

"What things? What are you on about?" Qwyrk wiped her eyes and furrowed her brow.

"If we are to go into battle on solstice eve, I need to be better prepared than last time."

"Better prepared how?"

"No need to worry," he held out one hand and waved it as if dismissing her concerns. "But I assure you, that when the time again comes to march toward our destinies, I shall be fully ready to do my duty! Master Qwyzz," he turned to his host, "you make a truly excellent port sir, one of the finest I've had in a very long time. If we survive this debacle, I should very much like a tour of your cellar."

"I'd be happy to oblige you, Mr. Blip… pingstone."

Blip nodded. "Excellent. Now then." He turned back to Jilly and Qwyrk, "I shall see you later, when I am properly kitted out, er, attired for war. Cheerio!"

And with that he strolled into the wall and vanished.

"Properly attired? What did he mean?" Jilly asked.

"I don't even want to know," Qwyrk sighed, shaking her head.

❉ ❉ ❉

Dawn broke over Nicewood Park in West Leeds. Carl stepped out of his car. The sky was clear, but it was freezing cold and there was a new dusting of snow on the ground. He shook off a shiver and wrapped his coat around himself tighter as he strode toward two figures standing by their black sedan in the distance. No doubt about it, these were the same two he'd spoken to the day before, dressed in their black trench coats, bowler hats, and wearing sunglasses, even though the sun wasn't all the way up yet.

What an odd pair, he thought. "Good morning, gentlemen,"

he said, not offering his hand in greeting. *They might be aliens, or something.*

"And top of the morning to you, sir," the one he thought was Dill, said.

"He has my face," Carl said, not interested in small talk. "I mean, better looking, but yeah, I could see it. He's got her eyes, her complexion. It took me a while, but I figured it out. He's my son, and you know, too, don't you? You already knew?"

"We had a suspicion, sir, that your relationship to the boy was paternal in nature. It seems that his luck guided him right to you."

"So, he's special, then? Magical and whatnot?"

"Of course sir, those talents were inherited from his mother, our client."

"Wait, what? Your client?"

"She's been trying to find him since he ran off from his foster family in York. The boy is now, we fear, in grave danger. It is imperative that we locate him and rescue him today, what with the solstice coming."

"What's that got to do with anything? What are you on about?"

"We believe that his kidnapper, whom we pretend to represent, intends to do him harm, probably during some sort of ritual, set to take place after sunset tonight. We also believe that we know where, but we are not completely certain of the details."

"Well then, we're going and we're rescuing him."

"Out of the question sir, this is far too dangerous an affair for mortals to be entwined in."

"Now you just hold on," Carl snapped, pointing an angry finger at both of them. "This is my son, who I didn't even know I had, and I'll be damned if I'm gonna sit on the sidelines while you lot talk about maybe, possibly rescuing him if you can find him. Wherever you're going, I'm coming with you, and that's final! I may not be the superhero I want to be, but at least I can do something right for once!"

"As you wish, sir, but we cannot be responsible for whatever may happen to you."

"I don't care about you being responsible. I care about finding him and saving him! And if he's so special, there must be other folks like you looking for him, right? Where's his mum now? Who's his mum? *What* is his mum?"

"In answer to your first question sir, she is at the moment residing at an inn outside of Leeds, where we meet with her to give her periodic updates on our findings. We weren't quite sure who she was at first, but our sleuthing eventually revealed her identity. In answer to your second question, she frequently goes by the name of Holly Vishala when in this world. And in answer to your final question, she is a Yakshi."

"A what?"

"A tree spirit of the lands of India, rather like the Fae of these northern nations."

"So, those pointed ears are real?"

"Quite so, sir."

"So, I spent the night with a faerie?"

"I am not privy to those specific details, sir, but assuming that the two of you successfully consummated your evening, then yes, Lluck was the unintended consequence of such a union, delivered at the appropriate time."

"Why didn't she try to find me?"

"It's very complex, sir, and you'll have to ask her about all of her reasons, but humans and Fae cannot dwell in each other's worlds for long, and she probably felt it was best to hide the boy away, for his own safety, and for yours. In all likelihood, she didn't even know how to find you."

"Well, we never exchanged information, that's true. I was pretty drunk at the time. To be honest, I don't remember much of it. I thought for a while I just dreamed it, since she was gone when I woke up. I mean, an average bloke like me, an incredible lady like her; what are the odds, eh?"

"I am unable to calculate them at this precise moment, sir."

"Where is she now?"

"We are uncertain, sir. Our usual method of contacting her seems to be malfunctioning, and she was not at her usual domicile last night when we checked in to inform her of this distressing news."

"Hm. So it was all true. I have a son. And all this time, I never even knew it."

"It would seem so, sir. But at the risk of sounding insensitive, and I assure you it is not my intention, your son is at great risk, so if you wish to accompany us to the probable location of tonight's ritual, you will need to be ready by midday. Shall we meet back here again at precisely noon?"

"Yeah, yeah, that's fine. I'll see you then." He turned to walk back to his car, but looked back for a moment. "Thank you, really."

Dill nodded, and then Carl watched as both entered their own vehicle.

"This is it, mate," he said to himself as he trudged back to his own car. "This is your moment. You wanted to be a hero, now you're going to get to be a hero. Tonight, the Phantom Phennel rises for real!"

He paused.

"Damn it, I need a theme song!"

* * *

Qwyrk appeared back on Earth, outside the now-familiar sight of Holly's B&B, and realized her stomach was already in knots. It was almost mid-day and sunny, but the chill inside her rivaled that from the elements. That morning, she'd sent word to Holly via a Fae-gram, asking if they could meet. She'd explained all about Greylocke and what he'd told her, and assured Holly that she now knew the truth. The reply she'd gotten back was just one word: "Noon," which didn't seem very promising.

She exhaled and let herself in through the now-broken back door, and then ascended the stairs, heading up to the first floor. It was like she was wearing lead boots that got heavier with every step she took.

About three months later (well, maybe a half-minute or so), she reached the top and stared down the hall to that familiar green door; it was slightly ajar. Assuming she was expected, Qwyrk went to it, knocked, and pushed it open. Holly was pacing in the middle of the room, arms folded around herself in a self-hug. She wore her familiar black outfit, and the sight of her would have made Qwyrk's heart race a little, if she didn't feel so awful. She could see that Holly was just as nervous and uncomfortable. They gazed at each other for a long, quite nerve-wracking moment.

"Um, hi," Qwyrk said at last, almost inaudible.

Holly let out a little sigh and looked away, pained. Qwyrk's heart sank.

"I, um, I did something really stupid, really crap," Qwyrk continued, her voice shaking. "I fell for a ridiculous lie, and then I said things to you that were horribly hurtful and very wrong. I'm sure now I didn't mean them, really, and even then it felt bad saying what I did, deep down, I mean."

Holly stared back at her, but Qwyrk couldn't tell how she felt.

"You, um, you don't even have to even look at me if you don't want to; I'll completely understand. I just, I just want you to know that I was wrong about everything. I've never been so wrong in my life, in fact, and you didn't deserve the terrible things I said, not one bit of them, at all."

Holly's gaze softened, just a little. She looked like she might be ready to say something, but Qwyrk couldn't hold back any more and took a step toward her.

"Oh, Holly, I'm so, so sorry!" The too-familiar sting of tears was in Qwyrk's eyes again; now she could barely bring herself to look at Holly. "If you never want to speak to me again, I get it. Hell, I don't want to speak to myself right now, if you know what I mean. And if you want to beat me up, I'd totally get that, too. In fact, I'll help. Just tell me what part to punch first. Get out that stick of yours and smack me, if you want to, as many times as you'd like. I completely deserve it."

She risked a couple of steps forward.

"But please understand that I just didn't know, didn't know what to believe, and his magic, his lies, he was *so* convincing. He managed to make himself appear totally human; it completely threw me. I even tested him with faerie fire and he passed; I've no idea how he did it. His magic really had me thinking that he was the real deal, that you were evil, crazy, something, I don't know. I can't say enough how sorry I am; I don't think I'll ever be able to. Please, please forgive me if you can, and if you can't, please at least don't hate me. I couldn't bear that!"

"Why didn't you just talk to me?" Holly said in a broken voice, tears forming in her eyes. "I didn't sleep last night. I was so upset. I ended up going out and wandering around in the forest until dawn. I half-froze."

The thought of how much she'd hurt Holly stabbed at Qwyrk like a knife.

"I wanted to talk to you," she answered. "I meant to, I *did* come see you. But then, I was so angry and frustrated and confused, and it felt like we were running out of time, and I just snapped and said all those awful things, and I couldn't even believe they were coming out of my mouth when I said them. The more I yelled, the angrier I got. I just lost it. But I never wanted to believe anything bad about you. I don't think I ever really believed any of it, but it seemed so logical in a weird sort of way, you know? I just didn't know what to do, so I lashed out like a, a horrible lashing-out person. But I'm so, so, sorry. I'm so..." She thought she might break down entirely.

To her surprise and immense relief, Holly gave her a gentle smile, even as her own eyes were rimmed with tears. "It's all right, you don't have to apologize. Well, yes, you *do*; but you just did, and it's brave of you to do it. Thank you. I knew when you went off on me that something was wrong. I think the Erlking clouds everyone's minds; his words are like poisoned sugar. He'll say and do anything, no matter who gets hurt. He obviously tried to drive a wedge between us, and he almost succeeded. That tells me he's scared of us, of what we might do together. I'm just glad you learned the truth, before it was too late."

Qwyrk managed a weak smile.

"Though you should have just talked to me," Holly said, grimacing. "I'm actually quite easy to chat with, you know!"

Qwyrk nodded. "I know. Goddess, I'm such a gormless idiot!"

"No, you're not. Impulsive? Yes. Headstrong? Absolutely! A bit of pain in the arse? Probably. But we can't worry about all that now. He probably has Lluck by now, and we have to save him. I don't know exactly what he has planned for tonight, but it's not good and I know that I need your help, Qwyrk, I need *you*. If there's anyone at all that I'd want by my side to stop this, it's you!" She laid a gentle palm on Qwyrk's cheek.

Qwyrk sniffed and placed her hand over Holly's, which rested with such ease on her face. Holly's touch was like a soothing balm. "Thank you," Qwyrk said. "Really, thank you so much. I was afraid I'd messed everything up. I may as well have delivered your son right to him, but I will fix this, I promise!"

"*We'll* fix this." Holly said.

Qwyrk nodded. "I was so stupid to let myself be fooled into thinking you'd betrayed us; I mean, how ridiculous is that? I'm so bloody gullible. And then after I talked with him, I was just angry and hurt and let down because I fancy you like crazy and... bollocks! I need to shut up now, don't I?"

Holly let out a nervous laugh and looked away. "Well, the feeling might just be mutual, even if you did act like an arse!"

Qwyrk's heart skipped a beat, and she let out a teary chuckle.

"How about this?" Holly said, looking back to her. "We save my son, stop the Erlking from doing whatever he has planned, save the world from ending and so on, and maybe we can have a chat about all that. Deal?" Her hand fell from Qwyrk's face, taking Qwyrk's hand with it.

Qwyrk gave her an embarrassed look and wiped her tears with her free hand. "Right, fine, good plan, that! I guess I've got an incentive to help save the world again, don't I?"

Holly just stepped up on her tip toes, leaned in, and kissed

Qwyrk on the forehead; Qwyrk nearly swooned. Holly: three, Qwyrk: nil.

Holly smiled, taking Qwyrk's other hand. "I think a certain 'Master of the Wild Hunt' is due for an arse-whipping, wouldn't you say?"

"Oh, you have no idea how ready I am to deal out some poundings!"

"Actually, I think I do. And I'd very much like to help with that."

Qwyrk laughed. And cried. And laughed a bit more. "Right then, let's go save everything and everyone together, shall we?"

CHAPTER SEVENTEEN

"Good midday to you, sir, I trust you are ready?"

"As ready as I'm going to be." Carl walked with purpose toward Dill and Chives, who waited in exactly the same place they'd been at dawn. In fact, he wasn't sure if they'd moved at all since then.

"I am glad to hear it, sir. May I enquire as to the contents of your briefcase? Purely for safety's sake of course, if we are going to be transporting you in our vehicle. Unknown items are an unacceptable risk in our line of work, as you can probably imagine."

Carl looked down at the case he was carrying and then back at Dill. "It's just my gear and my costume, for tonight," he announced with confidence. "It isn't much, but it's what I've got, and maybe it'll help me save my son. You can have a look if you like."

"I do hope you realize, sir, that the most likely outcome of tonight's endeavor will result in you dying a horrid and grisly death, possibly impaled on some sharp instrument, or perhaps torn in half by a hoard of nefarious creatures, or maybe even sacrificed and eaten alive by the perpetrator of these events himself?"

Carl winced; a momentary inclination to chicken out seeming like a fine idea. "Uh, yeah, all right, but it's a risk I'm willing to take. I have to."

"I am both glad and sad to hear it, sir, but I felt it prudent to warn you of your probable fate, given that you have no special powers to speak of."

"But that's just it. When I was near him, my son, he enhanced the effects of my Produce Pistol, and allowed me to completely subdue his would-be kidnapper!"

"Produce Pistol, sir?"

"Yeah, it's a weapon of my own making. I finally decided on the name, just last night. If I can just get close enough to Lluck, he can probably do it again, and we might have a chance."

"And what exactly did said Produce Pistol do, if I may ask, sir?"

"It produced a noxious gas of rotting vegetable fumes that completely overwhelmed the assailant, allowing us to make a getaway. I mean, normally, it's just a squirt of old juice with some pepper spray, right? But Lluck, he made it into something special, a weapon of real force."

"I see, sir. That would be an interesting and potentially helpful piece of firepower. I wish you good fortune in your quest, regardless. Shall we be off?"

Carl got into the back seat and strapped himself in. "So, where are we going, then?"

"Out to the Moors, sir, and to the site of a recent sacrifice, which we believe was something of a trial run for tonight."

"Sacrifice?" Carl swallowed hard.

"Indeed, sir. If you would rather remain behind, this is your last chance to do so."

"No, no, I have to see this through, no matter what happens. I couldn't live with myself if I didn't at least try."

"As you wish sir, though I do hope you have set your affairs in order. Just in case."

* * *

Qwyrk flashed back to Jilly's bedroom, but Jilly wasn't there. She opened the door and stepped into the hallway. The whole house seemed oddly quiet, which worried her a bit. No sign of the parents, not that they were ever home to begin with.

"AAAIIIEEEEE!!!!"

Jilly! Qwyrk dashed downstairs to the living room, only to see her young friend holding her mouth in terror, while Blip postured proudly beside a large lizard, some six feet long, lounging and seemingly minding its own business. It was wearing a saddle and some kind of reptile armor. For his part, Blip was sporting a Roman centurion's helmet, a shiny breastplate, his Regency boots, and he was holding his sword cane proudly. He tried twirling it, but gave up after dropping it one time too many.

"Blip, what the bloody hell is *that*?" Qwyrk blurted out. She rushed to Jilly's side and put her arms around her young friend in as close to a comforting hug as she could muster in the moment.

"You brought a dinosaur into my house!" Jilly said after another moment of whimpering.

"Pssh! Hardly a 'dinosaur,' my dear child, though yes, I do suppose there may be some phylogenetic connection through untold millions of years of evolutionary descent."

"Blip, what is a giant iguana, or whatever the hell that is, doing here?" Qwyrk demanded.

"She's my mount!" he announced with satisfaction and a broad smile, pointing to the creature's saddle.

"Your... mount." Qwyrk shook her head, not understanding; not wanting to understand, actually.

"The previous times that we went into battle, things went rather poorly for me, if you recall. Therefore, I was determined that, before we plunge headlong into this campaign, I should equip myself better and be thoroughly prepared for any and all dangers that may arise. Having a war beast beneath me seemed the best means of ensuring my success, which will be our success, as well. There is no 'I' in 'team,' after all."

"A war beast." Qwyrk raised one very skeptical eyebrow.

"She's a very well-trained Komodo dragon who is utterly ruthless in combat. And the best part is: she's not even fully grown! Hurrah!"

"Not even fully grown," Jilly stammered.

"Blip, you brought a flipping Komodo dragon into Jilly's home? You *do* know that their spit is diseased, right?" Qwyrk asked.

"Wait, what?" Jilly gasped. "What the actual..."

Blip held up his hands and shook his head. "No need to worry, my young friend, none at all. While yes, plague-laden spittle is an effective weapon in the creature's natural state, it is rather uncouth, it must be said. So I've had her modified."

"Modified?" Qwyrk asked.

"Quite."

Qwyrk gave him a questioning glare.

"With magic, you silly Shadow! My associates at the dojo took away that particular aspect of her natural physiology and gave her something in exchange, something far better."

"So," Qwyrk mused, "you're going to be riding a GMO lizard into combat."

"I prefer the term PEM."

"PEM?" Jilly asked.

"**P**rovidentially **E**nhanced with **M**agic."

"So, it was changed?" Jilly asked.

"Yes," he said with pride, patting the lizard on the back. "She now breathes fire through her mouth instead of spitting bacteria. A jolly good substitution, don't you think?"

"Wait," Jilly said. "You brought a fire-breathing dragon into my parents' living room? Yeah, that's not a good idea. It's not even a *bad* idea! It's a totally crap idea!"

"There is no need for worry, my dear," Blip waved away her concern. "The beast will not unleash its flames unless I command it, or unless she is really startled."

"Define 'really startled,' and please tell me that's a very rare thing," Qwyrk demanded.

"Very rare, indeed," Blip assured her.

Qwyrk scowled at him, but he seemed unmoved.

"Um, does it, does she have a name?" Jilly asked.

"Of course, behold: Snickerwocky."

"S-Snicker..." Jilly looked hopelessly confused.

"An amalgam of two words from the work of Lewis Carroll: the Jabberwock and the vorpal blade that went snicker-snack. It seems to fit her, don't you think?" He smiled with pride. "I cannot wait to ride into battle, blade drawn and held high, ready to charge into the fray, to right wrongs and to save this land once again!"

Qwyrk looked at Jilly, who looked at her, and then they both looked back at Blip, who was now in his own world, gesticulating in the air with his sword in hand. He leaped into the lizard's saddle. "Onward, Snickerwocky! To victory and glory!"

"We're so screwed," Qwyrk said.

*   *   *

Lluck groaned and opened his eyes, to find that his hands and feet were bound again. Cursing, he realized that his whole body ached. He rolled over to find himself back in the same room, back in the middle of the sigil painted in the floor. Longwing was lying nearby, also bound.

"Psssst! Mate! You all right?" he whispered. Longwing groaned but said nothing else. "Bollocks!" He couldn't tell what time it was, but the light shining in through the window made it seem like sometime in the afternoon. "Have we really been lying here all night?" he said. His aching body told him so.

He heard the handle of the door turn and the door open. Twisting himself around, he struggled to see his visitor. It was one of those bloated hobgoblins from last night.

"Oh, yer up," the hobgoblin growled. "Pity. I was hopin' we'd just be able to carry you out when the time is right." He thrust a spear point perilously close to Lluck's face. "Don't make no sounds, and don't try to escape."

"You're not gonna kill me, you bastard," Lluck said with defiance. "You can't, so don't try to scare me!"

"No, I can't kill ya, but I could still hack yer nose off, so shut your cottage pie hole, brat!"

"Fine, so what's happening now? What's the next item on the menu of this stupid horror show?" Lluck asked, rolling his eyes.

"Oh, you and yer mate there are gonna be moved out soon enough. It's gettin' late in the day, and the master wants you primed and ready for tonight."

"So, you're gonna do what? Baste us in herbs and cooking oil, or something?"

"Oh, I like that idea, actually!" The hobgoblin tapped his chin and pondered the possibilities. "Maybe he'll let us have the leftovers when he's done with you; I reckon you'd be quite tasty with some garlic and radishes! Maybe with a nice side of baked maggots and cheese? Cheers for the suggestion!"

"Happy to help," Lluck sighed with sarcasm.

The sound of more flappy feet and convoluted conversations at the door told him that the rest of the grisly goon squad had arrived to take them wherever they were going. And wherever that was, it wasn't good.

* * *

Blip was apparently so delighted with his martial display that he failed to notice that the lizard soon started rocking back and forth in an even rhythmic pattern. Jilly's eyes widened as she saw the source: her dog was having a go, humping the creature's hind quarters. She and Qwyrk grinned at each other and tried not to laugh. It didn't work.

"What? What's so damned funny?" Blip demanded. "And what is that unnatural motion?"

"I think," Qwyrk managed to get out through her giggle, "Odin's trying to have a romantic interlude with your beast. Personally, I think they make a cute couple, don't you? Mmmpphphphhahahahahahaha!" She nearly doubled over and Jilly joined right in with her. Guffaws and tears abounded.

Blip looked behind himself and was plainly horrified to see the family canine doing the deed on his prized war dragon.

"Away from her, you perverse canine!" Blip swore. "Step away from my steed and take your morbid and libidinous desires elsewhere!" He shook his fists, but Odin just happily rubbed away. Snickerwocky, for her part, seemed not bothered one way or the other.

Qwyrk and Jilly attempted to stifle further laughter, but failed rather miserably, opting to hold each other for support.

"This is not funny!" Blip protested. "This is an assault on my very dignity. A man's beast is his pride and joy!"

"Well, your 'pride and joy' is getting a bit of a workout at the moment," Qwyrk guffawed. "I think it's true love! He has been fixed, right?" She looked over to Jilly.

Jilly nodded and covered her mouth, but couldn't contain her giggles. In a moment, she had doubled over, too.

"Depraved mongrel!" Blip shouted, hopping down. "Gah! Confounded croissants of Charon!" He shook with rage and stomped about.

"Careful now, Blip," Qwyrk said, trying to catch her breath, "wouldn't want to spoil the moment." Another round of tear-filled hysterics ensued.

"I think she's rather taken a shine to him, to be honest," Qwyrk sputtered.

"Yes, well, while you're off wooing the lad's mother, some of us are taking battle preparations seriously!" Blip bellowed.

"Speaking of which," Jilly finally seemed to gain some control back, and turned her attention to Qwyrk, "how did things go, with Holly and all that?"

"Fine," Qwyrk smiled, relieved by it all. "Better than fine, actually. I threw myself at her mercy, figured I had nothing to lose. It was one of the hardest things I've ever done. But she forgave me, said she figured I was deceived or ensorcelled, or some such, called me an arse, and kissed me. On the forehead, I mean."

Jilly grinned and pumped her fist. "Yay! See? I told you! So, what's next?"

"Well, I'm going to go retrieve her in a bit and bring her back here, and then we'll all head off to the Moors after sunset and try to put a stop to this nonsense."

"Wait, you're bringing her *here*? As in, we'll get to meet her? Oh, this is brilliant, I can't wait!"

"Yeah, well, before you get too excited, let's save the world first, all right?"

"Fine," Jilly rolled her eyes. "Oh, Star Tao's coming over in a bit, so the whole gang will be here. I feel better knowing that we're all in this together."

Qwyrk smiled. "You know what? I do, too, despite... this."

She motioned and glanced back over at the zoological spectacle still ongoing in front of them; a nature documentary it was not.

"Your hound's got some stamina, I'll give him that," Qwyrk quipped, and Jilly descended into another fit of giggles, while Blip uttered a string of curse words that Qwyrk was quite sure she'd never heard him say before.

* * *

Dill stopped the car at a roadside pull-out. The sun was setting and the Moors seemed even more ominous in the fading light. An otherworldly chill descended over a frosty vale, and hills and peaks in the distance seemed to grow around it in the shadows.

"This is as far as we can go by vehicle, I'm afraid," he announced. "And it's a fair walk to the place of the sacrifice, where we will have to wait for cover of dark."

Carl stepped out and breathed in the air of his frigid surroundings. Retrieving his case, he shut the door and awaited further instructions.

"You can still wait here if you wish, sir. No one will hold you to blame, nor will you be seen as cowardly if you choose not to pursue this course of action."

"No, nice try, but I said I'd see this through and I mean to do it, no matter what. I owe him that."

"A noble sentiment, sir, and one to be commended. I just hope that it does not result in you being decapitated and your cranium being put on a spike and paraded around to the tune of 'Raindrops Keep Falling on My Head.'"

"Wait, that's a possibility?"

"It has happened in the past sir, at least twice that we know of."

Carl swallowed. "Well, it's just a risk I'm gonna have to take, and that's that!" He only wished he felt as overconfident as he sounded.

"It is your choice, sir. Please follow us this way, then."

They crossed the road and hiked into the low-growing shrubbery across the icy, crunchy ground. An awkward scramble up a small hill brought them to an unpleasant sight.

"We believe this is where the Erlking will attempt his rite." Dill said. "And it would behoove us all for him not to succeed."

"Fine. So what's the plan?"

"The plan, sir?"

"Well, you must have a plan, you know, for how to stop it, or some such."

"Since we are unfamiliar with the Erlking's particular set of combat skills, and since we are not yet sure of the exact nature of the rite and how many of his minions will be in attendance, it will take us some time to study the layout and the participants involved to formulate an appropriate response."

"Wait, you're saying that we can't do anything until we've actually watched it happen?"

"That is something of a simplification, sir, but essentially captures the problematic nature of the circumstances that we face."

Carl threw up his hands. "Oh, this is ridiculous! My boy is going to be murdered tonight in some black magic ritual, and we've got to sit around and watch?"

"Unless you have a better plan that you've not yet revealed to us, sir?"

"No, I bloody well don't. But you must have, like backup, or something, right?"

"As I said, we did try to alert the boy's mother, however, she seems to have disconnected the means by which we usually contact her, and our attempt to, how do they say, swing by her place and inform her of the dire situation yielded nothing. This of course, puts the remainder of our fee at risk, if she decides that we were negligent in our duty to inform her, but it could not be helped."

Carl seethed. "Puts your fee at risk? I don't ruddy believe what I'm hearing!"

"We are in a bit of a bind, it is true, sir."

"What about those others, the ones Lluck mentioned. He said they have abilities, kind of like him. Like they're some kind of supernatural Justice Brigade, or something. Can't you contact them?"

"Their specific identities are not known to us, sir, but if they are resourceful, they may yet find their own way here."

"So, we just have to hope that they show up?"

"In essence, yes, sir."

"Oh great, just brilliant!" He turned and stomped several steps away.

"You may still wait in the car, if you prefer, sir."

"Yeah, and if they massacre you lot, what's to stop them from coming for me, then?"

Dill offered Carl the car key. "Take the vehicle and leave now, if you wish, sir."

Carl shook his head. "I'd never be able to live with myself. I have to see it through, come what may."

Dill put the key back in his pocket and almost smiled. "I assumed you would see it that way, sir."

* * *

In a flash, Qwyrk and Holly stepped into Jilly's living room. They held each other close. Closer than was technically necessary to teleport, of course, but Qwyrk was happy not revealing that bit of information at this precise moment.

"I don't know if I'll ever get use to that," Holly said. "If I were human, I'd probably feel sick."

"It gets easier the more you do it," Qwyrk said. "You'll just have to bounce around with me more often."

"Sounds rather fun."

"Yeah, it'd be nice to jump you... jump *around* with you. Um..." Qwyrk's cheeks flushed hot again; that seemed to be happening a lot recently.

Holly looked at the floor as if embarrassed, but Qwyrk was sure she saw her trying not to smile.

"They're here!" Jilly said as she bounded into the room, followed close behind by Blip and Star Tao.

"Great," Qwyrk said with the slightest eye roll. "The Farce Force is all here. Um, everyone: this is Holly. She's Lluck's mum, and she's going to be helping us out tonight, for which I'm very grateful, because we need all the help we can get, and she's brilliant!"

Qwyrk motioned toward Jilly. "Holly, this is Jilly Pleeth, one of my best friends. She's amazing, and I don't know what I'd do without her."

"How do you do?" Jilly said, offering what almost looked like a curtsey.

"Lovely to meet you," Holly smiled.

Qwyrk grimaced just a little. "And this, um, is Star... Tao. He's actually a cracking channeler, helped us out in a big way when we took on de Soulis. Actually channeled Thomas the Rhymer, if you can believe that!"

"All right?" Star Tao grinned and waved.

Holly smiled again and gave a nod of her head.

"And this is..."

"Bernard Beresford Bartlesby Blippingstone III, my dear, at your service." Blip bowed and reached out to take one of her hands, kissing it lightly.

Holly glanced at Qwyrk in confusion, but was gracious. "Enchanted, I'm sure."

"So," Qwyrk realized that she and Holly were still arm-in-arm and gently let go of her companion, ignoring Jilly's big smile. "How's everything going?"

"Most excellent!" Blip asserted. "Young Jilly has been studying her new magical tome, the lad here has been meditating or some such to attract, er, whomever it is he attracts, and after some effort to dislodge the girl's canine, my war beast is now primed and ready!"

"War beast?" Holly asked.

"Long story," Qwyrk answered in haste. "Best not worry about it right now."

"Um, Qwyrk, can I chat with you upstairs for minute?" Jilly asked. "About that thing?"

"Thing?"

"Yeah, you know, the *thing*." She waved her hands around, as if it were so obvious. Qwyrk was lost.

"Just come upstairs with me for a few minutes, all right?" Jilly insisted.

"It's fine," Holly said with a smile. "I'm sure Mr. Blippingstone and I can chat in your absence. Perhaps Mr. Star Tao as well?"

"It would be my pleasure!" Blip announced, hopping up on the sofa, and clapping his froggy hands together. "My dear, do have a seat. Now tell me, what do you know about Hegel?"

Qwyrk rolled her eyes. "Fine, all right, let's go."

She followed Jilly up to her bedroom, where Jilly shut the door in haste and then almost jumped up.

"Oh. Em. Gee. Qwyrk!"

"What? What are you on about?"

"Are you mad? She's amazing! And she's nice, and smart, and kick-arse. And drop dead gorgeous. And she totally fancies you, too!"

"You don't know that. She might just be being friendly."

"She's *not* just being friendly. You two couldn't take your hands off each other!"

"I told her to sod off yesterday."

"And she forgave you when you told her you'd been tricked."

"Look, it's messy. She's worried about Lluck, we all are. It's not the right time for me to be getting distracted."

"Then make her your reason to win. I saw how sad you were before, when you thought she'd betrayed you. I've never seen you like that; it was awful. And look at you now. I mean, I've always thought you're gorgeous, but I don't think you've ever been lovelier than you are right now, even with all this crap going on. You're practically glowing, and not from magic. That tells me something, and it should tell you the same thing."

Qwyrk looked at her, this wonderful, wise young lady, who had such a talent for saying the right thing at the right time. She sighed and chuckled.

"You're right, as usual. This is all making me feel things I haven't felt in a long time. I did *not* expect to take a journey down that road any time soon, thank you very much. It's reminding me of all sorts from the past and how amazing and thrilling and horrid and completely stupid falling for someone can be, which is exactly what I don't want right now."

"No. Qwyrk, this is too important and you need to go for it."

"You've only just met her!"

"Doesn't matter, I have a good feeling about it. And I'm going to keep bugging you until you give in and ask her out."

"Jilly."

"Qwyrk! I'm a witch now, so I have to go with my intuition. You two are meant for each other." She folded her arms and grinned. "I have spoken."

Qwyrk sighed. "Fine, but can we at least save the world first?"

"Yeah, I guess that'd be all right."

They hugged.

"I got pretty lucky, what with you crashing into me last summer, didn't I?" Qwyrk said.

"Yeah you did," Jilly answered. "So don't cock it up, and you'll also be getting lucky with Holly soon enough!"

"You're not going to stop, are you?"

"Oh, not a chance!"

They headed back downstairs, where sure enough, Blip was in the midst of giving Holly and Star Tao an enraptured lecture.

"In the first mode of active reason, self-consciousness felt it was pure individuality; and over against this stood empty universality. In the second the two factors in the antithesis had each both the moments within them, both law and individuality; but the one factor, the 'heart,' was their immediate unity, the other their opposition."

"Woah," Star Tao sighed, his eyes wide and jaw hanging open.

"How utterly fascinating," Holly said, with less obvious enthusiasm, though she was polite enough.

Blip beamed.

"See?" Jilly whispered. "She even makes Blip smile. She's a keeper!"

Holly looked up and smiled. "So, is everything all right?"

"Hmm? Oh yeah, yeah, everything is great!" Qwyrk blurted out. "Grand! Brilliant! Just um, you know, a brief catch-up on things, and stuff and bits and bobs, you know."

"So, do we have a plan of attack?" Blip asked, apparently not too annoyed about having his Hegel lecture interrupted. Qwyrk was happy to avoid giving any more awkward answers to Holly.

"Well, I think we can all agree that whatever's going to happen will happen at the sacrifice site, you know, where we were before," she said. "So, that's where we should go."

"Sound reasoning," Blip agreed. "I daresay my war beast is ready to embark!"

"What kind of creature is it?" Holly asked.

"Um," Qwyrk interjected before Blip could launch into some Carrollesque panegyric about his new pet, "why don't we wait and you can see for yourself when the time is right? Uh, by the way, Blip, where is she?"

"Oh, well, yes, after a period of reflection, I agreed that it would be best for her to wait elsewhere, as in not on this Earth."

"Which means she's where, exactly?" Qwyrk glared.

"Well, um, I mean, that is to say..."

"Out with it."

"I tied her reins to a tree outside your home."

"You did *what*?" Qwyrk shouted. "Are you out of your bloody mind? What if her fire-breathing antics burn down my house?"

"Calm yourself," Blip said. "There's no reason whatsoever to infer that Snickerwocky will pose any sort of danger to your personal domicile. You are indulging in pure supposition exaggerated by your predisposition to dislike her!"

"Oh yeah, right. I'm so overreacting, because, in case we survive tonight, I don't want to return home to a pile of ash and cinders! How perfectly unreasonable of me!"

"Everything will be fine!" Blip insisted. "I muzzled her to ensure that she poses no danger except to the foes we will face. I will only unleash her true fury on the enemy at the appointed time."

Fine, but I'm warning you: if my home is damaged, we'll be having dragon burgers for the next few weeks."

"Hmph! You wouldn't dare, you insolent flibbertigibbet!"

"What did you call me, you gnomish pollywog?"

"How dare you, you... argh!" Blip hopped up and stomped

about. "Everyone has the right to be wrong sometimes, but you abuse the privilege!"

"Oh really? Well, no one is better than you at using more words to say less about nothing."

"About nothing? My mind is a library; it holds the complete works of some of the greatest thinkers who ever lived!"

"If you mean it's cavernous, wooden, and dusty, then yeah, you're absolutely right."

* * *

As their volley continued, Jilly sat down next to Holly. "See, when they do this? It means everything's going to be all right."

"Are you certain?" Holly glanced back and forth between them.

Jilly grinned. "Don't worry, it happens every time!"

CHAPTER EIGHTEEN

"Death it rides in Wild Hunt, across the Moorland bare, I seek the one who brings all luck, to take back to my lair. Bound and bled, torn and rent, his vital heart consume, and then Erlkönig will arise, and bring this earth to doom!"

The Erlking raised his clawed hands as he finished his chant. In flash after flash of magic and sorcery, they arrived: creatures summoned by his call, drawn to the lure of the master of the chase, the hunter of souls. Torches set about the place of sacrifice distorted their forms in the flickering light.

"Come to me, my beauties! My darklings and moon-beasts, my acheronian Unseelies. Come unto me, all cursed things of the blackest hours... except for orcs; I don't like them, they smell odd. But all others: come and join the eternal Wild Hunt! For tonight, luck is on our side, in a most literal way. Tonight, I become un-vanquishable and come tomorrow, we walk this world, free to work wickedness as we will!"

A roar of approval erupted from the malevolent mobs that gathered around the Erlking, with more and more creatures great and small phasing into this plane with each passing moment: horrific hobgoblins, nefarious nilbogs, perilous pookas, wirry-boggles and weary boggarts, gargles and gurgles, nixies and nacken, and every other kind of nefarious creature under the sun, er, the moon. And large, floating eyeballs with sharp teeth (seriously, how are these even a thing?) drifted about near the perimeter.

The Erlking bellowed a satisfied laugh as his monster-muster filled the sacrificial site to capacity. He held open an ancient tome in one hand while gesturing with the other, and began reciting words in some ancient and forgotten language. Lluck watched in frustration and fear—and a whole lot of annoyance—from the edge of the ceremonial site, bound hand and foot to a tall, wooden pole carved with arcane symbols. Longwing was tied to an identical pole next to him, though his head drooped forward and he was still unconscious. Lluck flicked his constricted hands, trying to cause the ropes to slip off, but to no avail.

"Keeping my powers dampened, eh, you bastard? Hey, Longwing! Mate, wake up... oof!"

"Shut yer trap, you little half-breed," a goblin guard said as he smacked him in the stomach with the handle of his axe. "Or next time, you might get the blade."

"Yeah right, you tosser," Lluck choked. "You kill me, your master over there isn't gonna be pleased. He'll probably roast you alive, or bite your head off and eat it, or something."

"Uh, well, just keep your mouth closed, then!" The goblin hobbled off to join others of his fell folk.

"Damn it," Lluck swore. "How are we gonna get out of here? Longwing, come on mate, wake up!"

EIGHTEEN

* * *

They emerged into the darkness of the Moors, the cold landscape made colder by a biting winter wind that blew with occasional fury and then died down before coming back again at unexpected moments, stinging their cheeks and chilling their exposed digits. Qwyrk held Jilly's hand; she also held Holly's, which was just lovely, thank you for asking. Jilly held Blip's, who in turn held Star Tao's (who was no doubt well made up about being touched by a god). As for Blip's mount...

"Good. I shall now go and retrieve my noble steed," he said.

"My home had better still be there," Qwyrk threatened.

Blip dismissed her with a wave of his hand, turned around and walked into thin air, disappearing.

"Bloody hell, that was brilliant!" Star Tao gasped, agape with wonder, falling to his knees in supplication. Qwyrk rolled her eyes for the umpteenth time.

"So what now?" Jilly asked, clutching her new magic book. Even though she was well bundled up, she jogged a bit in place to keep out the chill.

"Yes, I'm already cold," Holly said. "This is very unpleasant. I thought my longer coat would only get in the way. At least I have a scarf."

Qwyrk frowned in sympathy. "We need to get to the place of the sacrifice, over there," she said, pointing, "but we have to stay quiet."

"How are we going to get over there without any light?" Jilly asked. "We'll trip over everything in the dark and make tons of noise."

"Bollocks, you're right," Qwyrk swore.

"If only we could light a flame to a torch," Holly suggested. "It would also give us some heat.

"Well, when you unleash some of your Shrill Arm Bomb," Qwyrk said, "you'll probably warm up just fine."

"You're trying too hard, now."

"So, what *are* we going to do?" Jilly asked, looking over at the far hill and the faint glow emanating from beyond it.

"Well, I can get us a bit closer, but we'll risk being spotted," Qwyrk answered. "Teleporting leaves a trail and other magical creatures can sense it. Some of them can even smell it. Come on, then."

"What's it smell like?" Star Tao asked.

"What?"

"The trail, what's it smell like?"

"How should I know?"

"Well, you just said that magical creatures can smell it; you're like, magical, right? So can you smell it?"

"Not all of us can. Only some species, the more feral and earth-dwelling ones."

"All right, but if you could, what would it smell like?"

"I don't know, lavender, maybe?"

"Fair enough." Star Tao nodded, hopping up and down to keep warm.

"Fine, now look, I can get us closer, but..."

"Why lavender?"

"What?"

"Why lavender? Why not jasmine, or lime, or rhubarb pie?"

"Why would it smell like rhubarb pie?"

"Mmmm, some hot rhubarb pie would be lovely right now," Jilly said.

"Yeah, that'd be nice, wouldn't it?" Star Tao added, "Maybe with a couple of scoops of vegan vanilla ice cream?"

"Bit cold for ice cream, though," Jilly answered.

"Yeah, you're right," Star Tao said. "But some hot tea with a slice of pie right out of the oven, topped with custard would be spot on, I reckon."

Blip's face appeared out of nowhere, floating about two feet above the ground. "Earl Grey is the tea of choice in such a delectable dessert, of course," he said, before nodding and disappearing as quickly as he'd arrived.

"Oh, brilliant!" Star Tao fell to his knees again.

"For crap's sake, will you all just shut it!" Qwyrk snapped. "This is completely, totally, and *so* not the point at the moment! Let's just get over there; take my hands."

They did as she asked, and she glanced at Holly as if to say, "I'm so sorry." In another flash, they emerged most of the way up the hill in question. Behind them was a steep ravine that ended somewhere below in darkness. Strange chattering and ominous voices jabbered, and a dim glow lit the night sky.

"Right, everyone else stay here, I'm going to have a quick look."

Without another word, Qwyrk scrambled up the remainder of the hill and peered over the top. She could see a horde of creatures in all shapes and sizes milling about below: Darkfae, Korrigans, goblins, hobgoblins, pookas, and assorted other beasties and Unseelies, both familiar and strange, but none of them very inviting. Oh, and floating eyeballs with sharp teeth (are you bloody serious?). Torches on pikes dotted the terrain in a haphazard fashion, and their flames sputtered in a variety of colors, natural and otherwise. Two enormous wooden poles stood upright at the far edge of the site, each with someone bound to them. She recognized Lluck, but not the other one, who was all in black, his very long hair worn loose and obscuring his face. In the middle of it all was a figure in a voluminous grey robe, hood drawn over his head, and his exposed hands ending in sharp talons.

She scrambled back down to the others. "Yep, it's him all right, and a few hundred of his closest fiends."

"Don't you mean friends?" Jilly asked.

"Uh, yeah that, too."

"Qwyrk," Holly said as she put a hand on her arm. "Is Lluck there?"

She nodded in response and put her hand over Holly's. "He is, and he's alive, and he's going to stay that way, I promise you!"

"So, what now?" Jilly asked. "I mean, we're way outnumbered, right?"

"By quite a bit," Qwyrk said.

"Well, this might be a silly question," Jilly asked, "but why didn't anyone think to call the Templars? They were brilliant when they helped us out last summer."

"They were, indeed," Qwyrk said. "And the best answer to that is that I'm a right pillock and totally forgot to reach out to them, didn't I? You're welcome."

"But isn't Mr. Blippingstone going to fetch reinforcements?" Holly asked.

"Um, I wouldn't exactly call use the word 'reinforcements.'" Qwyrk grimaced.

* * *

He blipped back onto the Moors, sword cane in hand, helmet on head, astride his noble war beast.

"I have returned!" he announced with pride, eager to show off Snickerwocky in all her glory. "And I can confirm that your home is perfectly safe, Ms. Qwyrk, just as I said it would be, and..."

He looked around, but all was silence and darkness.

"Where are you? Where did you go? This is not amusing, if you think hiding from me is some sort of jest!"

There was no answer. He looked to the hill in the distance and the faint glow flickering from beyond. He sighed.

"Fine. Very well. I suppose it is to be just you and me, mighty mount. We shall make a showing that will be remembered in epics and songs until the end of time. Forward, then!"

Snickerwocky wouldn't move.

"Heh, any time now, dear steed. Glory awaits!"

She started chewing on one of the nearby clumps of frozen vegetation.

"Damn it and Gadsbudlikins! We'll not be late to the fray simply because you need to stop for supper. If you were hungry, you should have dined before!"

He leaped down and started tugging on her reins, but to no avail. "Onward, you otiose iguana! Bah! The Duke of Wellington never endured such indignities!"

* * *

"I want to see something," Jilly said as she climbed up the hill.

"Jilly!" Qwyrk hissed. "Get back here!"

But Jilly ignored her and in a moment, she reached the top. The scene was just as Qwyrk described it, otherworldly and surreal. She squinted and tried to make out some details about the two captives. She worked her way back down to the others.

"I thought so!" she said, lowering her voice. "The pillars holding

Lluck and that other bloke have writing all over them that looks a lot like what's in my book. They even have some of the same sigils."

"So what does that mean?" Qwyrk asked.

"I'm not sure, but I wonder if one of the reasons Granny sent me to her old cave to get these things is that she knew it might have something to do with this whole sacrifice thing. I'm guessing that those poles have signs and marks inscribed on them to stop Lluck from using his powers, and the other lad, too, if he's got magic. So, if I can get close enough, maybe I can undo whatever they're doing, and they can free themselves."

"No, absolutely not!" Qwyrk protested. "It's way too dangerous, and you have no idea if it will even work."

"I think you should let her try," Star Tao said.

"Well, I don't bloody care what you think!" Qwyrk shot back.

"Qwyrk," Jilly scolded in a whisper. "You don't have to be so mean to him. I know you're worried, but we've done his kind of stuff before. And what if this is a test Granny wants me to pass? If I can free up Lluck's power, he can save himself. I'll be careful, I promise!"

"It's not a question of being careful; if even one of these things hears you, you could be captured, or a lot worse. They may be patrolling all around here right now."

"Hey, we may be mere mortals, but we did all right for ourselves last summer," Star Tao protested. "I know Jilly's almost like your sister and all, but you gotta let go a bit. How about if I go with her? We'll just skirt the edges of the place and stay in the shadows."

"It might be good to let them try," Holly said. "We don't have too many other options, I'm afraid."

Qwyrk sighed. "Fine, but at the first sign of trouble, I want you to run like crazy and don't look back, all right? This is not a game, and these things *will* kill you."

"The things in Hermitage wanted to kill us too," Jilly said. She was glad for Holly's and Star Tao's support. "Besides," she said as she and Star Tao crept off, "you two probably want to be alone, anyway." Yes, it was a cheap shot, a childish taunt even, but she still enjoyed saying it.

* * *

"Right, so are we finally going to do something, or are we just going to sit here?" Carl was nearly done changing into his costume. He'd just attached his cape, and was fixing his mask in place.

"Are you sure that garb is quite appropriate for the potential proceedings of this encounter, sir?" Dill asked.

"Quite right! It's the only thing I'll wear to save my boy. I took an oath to defend the defenseless and arrest the... arrestless, and that's exactly what I'm going to do. Goblins and ghosties and whatnot make no difference. I have a duty!"

"To whom did you swear that oath, sir, if I may ask?"

"What do you mean?"

"You said you swore an oath, if I heard you correctly?"

"Well, yeah, sort of."

"Then it's more just curiosity on my part; to whom was it addressed?"

"Um, well no one. I sort of made it up in my secret headquarters."

"Secret headquarters, sir? Is this an abode of which we are not yet aware?"

"All right, no, it's my living room, but it's secret enough! It's not like anyone else ever goes there, except him." He pointed to Lluck.

"And there's no way I'm letting him languish down there. Looks like his kidnapper's being held captive, too, the one that knocked me for a loop. Shows you just how far he got, trying to be a henchman to a super villain! I've got to go down there and rescue my boy; rescue both of them, actually."

"I would not advise that course of action at this moment, sir."

"Well, I don't *care* what you would advise. I appreciate the lift out here and all, but this doesn't concern you, not the same way it does me."

"His mother is our client, sir, and we want to free him as much as you do."

"Yeah, so you can jolly well get paid! But he's blood! He's family. And I'll be damned if I'm gonna let something happen to him after all this time of not even knowing he existed!"

"Sir, if you will just follow our lead, we are seventy-nine percent of the way to formulating a suitable plan."

"Oh, that much, eh? Well that's impressive. Look, why don't I leave you two here to finish your formulating, while I pop down there and rescue them?"

"It would be an unwise course of action, sir."

"I concur." Chives nodded in agreement.

"I'll take my chances." Carl said as he brandished his weapon.

"Sir..."

He walked to the edge of the low rise and gave his cape a flip.

"We really must insist..."

He paused for a moment.

"That you remain..."

"Damn it! I need a theme song!"

"In the cover of darkness until..."

And then he ran into the fray and shouted, "There's no need to fear, the Phantom Phennel is here!" and started shooting the veggie gun randomly, squirting rotting juice in every direction at his astonished Unseelie foes.

* * *

"I believe that we have a bit of a predicament, Mr. Dill."
"That we do, Mr. Chives. That we do."

* * *

Jilly and Star Tao worked their way in darkness around to the poles, unseen by the rabble who were giving their full attention to their master, even the floating eyeballs with teeth (who came up with this ridiculous idea, anyway?). The two took care to stay in the shadows, just out of view of the flickering torchlight.

"Fortunately, they've got their backs turned," she whispered.

"Yeah, they're a nasty lot, ain't they?" he whispered back. "Those eyeballs are right creepy. Gotta stay out of their sight; I'll bet they can see a lot!"

She opened her book and thumbed through the pages, looking for symbols and signs that matched the ones carved into the wooden pillars.

"There!" She pointed at a sigil that matched one on Lluck's pole.

"Brilliant! So, what do you have to do?"

"I'm not really sure. I think Granny knew I was going to need these, but I still have to figure out what to do with them."

"Is it like what you said you did in the cave?"

"Yeah, I reckon it's something like that, but I don't want to get too close and get caught."

"I could try to channel someone to help us out…"

"All right, if you want, but I'll probably just have to work it out on my own."

Star Tao snuck farther back into the shadows. He sat cross-legged on the ground, resting his hands on his knees. Jilly glanced at him for a moment, shook her head at how endearingly strange he was, and then turned her attention back to the symbols at hand.

"Right, sod it!" She crept up to Lluck's pole, hiding in the shadow it created.

"Psssst!"

"Who's there?" Lluck asked, trying to turn his head.

"Quiet! It's me, Jilly."

"Jilly? What the hell are you doing here?"

"Trying to save your arse! Qwyrk's here too, oh, and your mum."

"What?" He was a little too loud, prompting Jilly to shush him again. "How?"

"It's a long story. Look, I think the symbols on these poles are cancelling out your lucky powers."

"You're right. Making me useless and my mate, Longwing, over there. Looks like he's out cold."

"Who?"

"Also a long story."

"Fair enough. Anyway, I'm going to try to undo the power in those things."

"How?"

"I've got a magic book that can help."

"Why does that not surprise me? Look, I'm glad you're here, but do what you have to do in a hurry, all right? He's gonna kill us!"

"I know, we're trying to stop the whole thing. Hang on!"

She opened her book again and matched the sigil nearest her

on the pole to one in her book. She held out her hand and tried to concentrate like she did in the cave.

"Maybe if I just..."

She trembled as a pulse of heat flowed into her outstretched fingers, passed through her, and exited through her other hand. As the magic entered the book, the sigil on the open page glowed for a moment and then faded back to black ink. She looked at the corresponding mark on the pole, and saw that it had gone out.

"That's it!" she whispered. "I can drain the power out of them, one by one, like turning off light switches."

"Brilliant, but you might need to get a move on; the ceremony's getting weirder and scarier by the minute."

"You're welcome," she said with a sneer.

She set about draining the next sigil, and sure enough, it worked again.

"If I can cancel enough of these, you'll probably be able to get your luck back."

"Sweet!"

She undid another.

He flexed his hands. Nothing. "Keep trying!"

She found a fourth symbol, straining not to stretch herself too far into the firelight. She focused on it and saw him move his hands again.

"I think it's working!" he whispered in excitement. "Keep going!"

She finished draining the symbol's power onto the page. "Try now."

He flipped his hands again, and just like that, the rope undid itself and fell to the ground.

"Yes!" she whispered.

"Brilliant!" he said. With his hands free, he flicked them at his feet. Sure enough, the ropes fell off, crumpling to the ground. He stepped out from the pile of discarded cord and dashed over to Longwing.

"Hurry!" Jilly whispered.

"Longwing," he said. "Come on, mate, wake up."

Longwing groaned a little and shook his head. Then Lluck flipped his fingers, and both the hand and foot ties slid off.

"Come on!" Lluck threw Longwing's arm over his shoulder.

"We've got to get out of here," Jilly urged. "Now, while they're still distracted!"

"No problem," Lluck smiled. "It'll be a piece of cake with my powers back."

A strange man in a pale purple get-up jumped into the midst of the Erlking's nearby flunkies, shouting, "There's no need to fear, the Phantom Phennel is here!" He brandished an odd-looking gun and started shooting some kind of liquid in every direction.

"Oh no, not him!" Lluck said.

"Wait, you know him?"

"Oh yeah. Oh shite."

* * *

Qwyrk and Holly edged their way to the top of the hill, crouched down, and peeked over. Sure enough, the grotesque gathering was going on strong, though Qwyrk was thankful she didn't see Jilly or Star Tao; she hoped they were in the shadows behind the now-empty poles, but she tried not to think about it. The Erlking read aloud from a book held in his right hand, while his left gestured, drawing what looked like symbols in the air. His guttural speech was too muffled for her to understand the words, but the language was probably something unintelligible, anyway: Atlantean or Gothic or drunken sod, or some such.

"I don't see Lluck anywhere," Holly fretted.

"Hey, it's all right," Qwyrk put a hand on her shoulder. "We're going to save him, we're going to stop this."

"I swear if he lays one finger on my son, I'll destroy him!"

"And I'll enjoy watching you do it."

"What should we do?"

"I want to get a sense of what's going on first, look for a weak point where we could strike, where they wouldn't expect an attack. Right now, we have the element of surprise on our side, so if we can use stealth to our advantage..."

At that moment they saw an odd fellow in a lavender purple, tight-fitting costume with a green cape and a poorly-fitting mask run into the middle of the proceedings, shout something, and start shooting what looked like a water pistol at every creature near to him.

"Well," Qwyrk winced. "So much for that idea."

* * *

"Come on, damn you, you surly, toad-bellied, egg-spawn!"

Blip trudged across the frozen landscape of the Moors, step by step, little by little, dragging his less-than-enthusiastic steed, who stopped all too often to sample the local vegetative delicacies along the way, icy and crunchy though they were.

"We don't have time for this! We must leap into the fray! The battle is at hand! There's glory to be won! Stop denying me my chance at grandeur, you errant alligator!"

Snickerwocky showed no compulsion to hasten her pace despite his urgings, and seemed quite content to amble here, meander there, waddle up, and toddle down, wherever her fancy took her.

Blip resorted to stomping up and down, but she continued to traipse about as she pleased.

"Fine, have it your way, you miserable, useless flap-dragon." He threw down the reins. "Stay out here and freeze if you like, I'm off to battle."

Snickerwocky looked at him as if in curiosity for a moment, before resuming her chewing and seeking out other tasty frozen treats.

"The indignities we men of war must endure! Caesar never suffered such opprobrium! Bah, I'll find glory on my own, then you'll be sorry, you cast-off crocodilian creature!"

He stormed off and swung his cane sword about in front of him, cutting through the air with whooshing sounds and stomping over the icy ground with his fancy Regency war-boots, determined to win the triumph and fame he deserved.

✳   ✳   ✳

"Hullo, ladies. Out for a wee bit of a night-time stroll are we?"

Qwyrk and Holly turned around to see a mini-flock of large, horrid monstrosities. Five, to be exact. They were unsettlingly large and muscled creatures with beady eyes, lower lip tusks protruding upwards, and big, knobby turned-up noses. Each was adorned in dirty scraps for clothing and armor, and carried an assortment of ugly-looking, rusty, hand-made weapons. They loomed over Qwyrk and Holly at a height of eight feet or more.

"Hobgoblins?" Holly asked.

"Truth be told, they're more properly ogres, I reckon," Qwyrk answered.

"Oh, my mistake."

"No worries, really. Big, dumb, and stupid; it's easy to confuse them."

"See," the largest ogre said, "I'm thinkin' the boss would like to know what you're all doin' up here, 'cause it probably ain't nothin' he would approve of. And if he don't approve of it, it don't happen. Not on *my* watch."

"I can assure you, he most certainly wouldn't approve," Holly said, standing up to face them. Qwyrk stood beside her, fists clenched and more than ready to administer a proper pummeling.

"Why look at that, it's a Yakshi," the same ogre said. "You're a long way from home, sweetheart. Whatcha doin' all the way up in the chilly Kingdom of Northumbria, eh? Tryin' out some of the local curries? Or maybe workin' on your tan?" A chorus of chuckles babbled and bubbled up from the others.

"Actually, 'sweetheart,' I'm just getting ready to kick your contemptible arse," Holly answered, a menacing smile forming on her face.

Qwyrk beamed with admiration, and maybe just a little libidinousness.

"Go on then, Fae girl, give it your best shot, let's see..."

Before he finished the sentence, Holly had flung her stick (not even opened), scoring a direct hit on his forehead. The elegant weapon clattered to the ground and bounced back to her feet, where she knelt to retrieve it.

The ogre's eyes crossed as he wavered, stumbled, and fell

forward, flat on his lumpy face. He was out cold, to the utter astonishment of his mates.

"Well that was... brilliant," Qwyrk muttered in shock.

"Right then," Holly said. "Who's next?"

The remaining muster of ogres hesitated.

"She um, she just got lucky, lads, that's all," one in the back said, as if trying to convince himself.

"Well then," another answered. "If you're so brave, why don't you take her out?"

"Lads," Qwyrk announced, trying to get their attention.

"I think she's got special magical powers; the mysteries of the East, and all that," a third chimed in.

"Um, hello?" Qwyrk said. She looked at Holly, who just shook her head.

"What's so mysterious about the East?" the first one asked.

"Don't know, I think it's out by Hull somewhere, some spooky stuff out that way."

"Um, we're standing right here, remember?" Qwyrk said.

"Get out, you pissy-arsed plank! There ain't nothing spooky out there!"

"Boys?" Holly tried, to no avail.

"Oh yeah? Last summer, I was near the coast up Scarborough way, and this crazy old lady in a blue shirt and a cowboy hat could actually see me. Don't know why. She screamed her bloody head off and scared the living shite out of me! It were awful, it were!"

"Are you actually kidding me?" Qwyrk said. Holly glanced at her in confusion. "Long story," Qwyrk clarified. "Right, then, that's about enough of this!"

Qwyrk strode up to the nearest ogre and laid a devastating

punch across his face, sending him sprawling backward into the others. "Now that I have your attention."

To Qwyrk's surprise, the other ogres recovered quicker than they should have been able to (that damned Erlking magic!), and though she ducked under the swing of a battered old sword from the nearest one, she fell flat on her bum and slid several feet on the slick ground, wounding her pride, if nothing else. Certainly, looking like a klutz in front of Holly after her marvelous martial display was not on. So Qwyrk rolled to one side, stood up in a flash, and kicked out at the next available ogre, connecting with his knee cap, and eliciting a howl as he stumbled back and fell to the ground, clutching his broken leg and whimpering with all the conviction of a football player faking it in writhing time.

But as she stepped back and drew some satisfaction from her somewhat cheap shot, she almost didn't hear the whoosh bearing down on her.

"Qwyrk! Look out!" Holly ran and slammed into her, knocking her down so that they both just missed the swing of a giant ogre axe. That was the good news. Unfortunately for them, they landed at the edge of the dark side of the hilltop, and with the icy ground beneath them giving way, there was nothing to slow them down as they skidded, rolled, and tumbled over the side together, plunging into darkness.

CHAPTER NINETEEN

Carl fired more "shots" out of his gun, but they were nothing more than rotten veggie juice splashing potential opponents randomly; in fact, a couple of targets seemed to enjoy it. But the majority of the gaggle of astonished creatures surrounding him just stared in confusion. To make matters worse, he glanced over to the wooden poles and saw that Lluck and his fellow captive were no longer there.

"Um, all right, I might have miscalculated a bit here."

One smaller goblinoid creature in a tattered jerkin took a few steps toward him. "Uh, are you like a jester, or somethin'? Are we like, supposed to be laughin' right now? 'Cause, to be honest, I didn't really get the joke."

Come on Carl, be strong, you can do this! "I am a righter of wrongs and a defender of justice, foul one! I stand against evil, in all of its foul forms."

The goblinoid stared at him, looked back at his mates, and back at Carl.

"Heh. Heh heh. Hmphphwaaahaha!"

The Unseelies in the vicinity burst into similar raucous laughter.

"He he heeee!" The little creature doubled over before lifting himself back up. "Now *that* was funny, mate! Ya got another one?"

"I wasn't joking, criminal!" Carl answered. "I'm here to put an end to your nefarious deeds!"

"Bwahahaha! Stop, yer killin' me!" The creature fell to the ground in another fit, while the others also chuckled and giggled hysterically, slapping their knees, slapping each other on the backs, elbowing one another roughly, sending their cohorts tumbling to the ground.

"Oh bollocks. Right. Enough!" Carl yelled, but he couldn't be heard over the rising drone of incessant mirth spreading out even to those who hadn't heard him. He put his gun back in its holster and folded his arms. "Look, I'm giving you all one last chance..."

The merriment was interrupted by the arrival of the large figure in the long grey robe, his face hidden under a massive cowl, floating just above the ground. His creatures made room for him and fell silent, kneeling and groveling as he passed by.

"You are intriguing," he said to Carl in a deep voice with a slight Germanic accent.

"I am?" Carl shrank back, trying not to look terrified.

"Indeed. There is something about you, something unique? You are mortal, but somehow touched by magic."

"Oh, I'm no one special. Just a citizen trying to make a difference."

"Your scent is... hmm."

"What? What are you talking about? And where's the boy? The one who was over there?"

"Of course," the figure said. "You, little man, little pathetic fleshling, have every reason to be here, of course you would try to free him. But if you are here, is *she*, as well?"

"She? Who?"

"Bind him," the menacing figure said, waving a clawed hand, "and bring back the boy. He won't have gone far."

Several minions set upon Carl and tied his hands tight with a ratty old rope. He struggled and cursed, but as they marched him toward the center of the gathering he couldn't free himself.

"The blood of two will prove better than the blood of one, and if the third is here, as well, my victory is assured!"

* * *

"Ow!"

"Gah!"

"Ouch!"

"Dammit"

"Watch out!"

"Oof!"

Roll! Crash! Thump! Splat!

Qwyrk and Holly tumbled down the side of the hill and landed in a small crevice between the two rises. Holly fell on her back and Qwyrk promptly landed on her stomach right on top of her, finding herself very up-close and face-to-face.

"Um, hi," Qwyrk said after the dust (or rather, the ice) had settled, looking down on the Fae woman she so admired lying underneath her.

"Hello," Holly replied with a smile.

"So, that was a bit of a tumble." Qwyrk looked to where they'd plummeted from. "Are you all right?"

"I think so," Holly said. "You?"

"Fine, yeah. You broke *my* fall this time; sorry about that."

"Not at all."

"And thanks, for saving me, I mean."

"Happy to do so. It was a very nasty-looking axe."

"So, I suppose we should get out of here; there's still a battle going on up there and all that."

"A good idea. We haven't won yet."

"True. Though those stupid sods are probably fighting each other by now. Not that this isn't rather nice and all."

"I've been in worse situations."

"Yeah, me too! Excuse me." Qwyrk put her hands on the ground and pushed herself up into a sitting position, straddling Holly.

"Um, sorry," she said. "Bit cramped down here."

"It is quite the squeeze."

"Yeah, it's not like we fell into a field, or something, that would be a lot easier."

"It would."

"I mean, then we wouldn't be crammed in here, me sitting on you, you being sat on by me, probably wondering why I'm sitting on you."

"That's true, but maybe you'd be sitting on me, regardless."

"That's the funny thing, isn't it? I might have landed on top of you, anyway."

"Or me on you?"

"Yeah, that would have been a laugh, wouldn't it? Who would have landed on whom? I guess we'll never know, unless we tumble down a hill into a field together some time. Not that I *want* to do that with you; but not that I *don't* want to, either. I mean, if you *like* tumbling down hills into fields, then that's a perfectly good thing to do."

"It sounds enchanting. Perhaps some other time, but we definitely do need to get out of here, which means you need to stand up." Holly raised herself up, resting on her elbows.

"Sorry! There's that whole ritual thing happening up there and here I am, sitting on you and babbling on about tumbling into fields."

"I wouldn't call it babbling; it's more like musing."

"Musing! Yeah. Musing about what would happen if..."

"Qwyrk, you're still sitting on me."

"Right! Sorry! I'll just get up, then."

"That's for the best. I mean: battle, evil monsters, the end of the world, saving my son; that last one, especially?"

"Absolutely! Couldn't agree more!" Qwyrk stood and reached down with a hand to help Holly up.

"Right! Brilliant! Come on then, let's go save your son! And the world!"

"So, how do we get out of here?" Holly asked, looking up.

"Hm. I don't want to risk teleporting into the middle of that lot, if they're still up there. Hang on. No, for real, hang on." Qwyrk slipped her arms around Holly's waist and pulled her close. Holly put her arms around Qwyrk's neck and shoulders in a tight embrace and they were face-to face once again. Qwyrk's stomach butterflies came on with the force of a minor hurricane.

"Why, Ms. Qwyrk." Holly smiled with a raised eyebrow. "You *are* rather forward. But please, feel free to rescue me any time."

Qwyrk swallowed hard and let out an appallingly embarrassing giggle that she was sure was the most appallingly embarrassing giggle in the history of appallingly embarrassing giggles, but somehow she forced herself to think about the task at hand. Crouching slightly, she jumped and they propelled through the air, right back to the top of the hill, landing with one gentle motion, quite in contrast to the undignified thud of a few moments ago. The muster of ogres was gone, at least.

From that vantage point, they could see what has happening. It wasn't good.

* * *

"Damn it! We've got to help him!" Lluck whispered as he and Jilly hovered in the shadows, just beyond the light of the magical flames. Longwing stirred, but Lluck still had to hold him up.

"Who *is* that?" Jilly whispered, annoyed that their escape was so rudely interrupted.

"He's this odd bloke who took me in a couple of days ago, let me stay with him in Leeds. He's a strange one, thinks he's some kind of superhero, but he's all right. I don't know why he's here or how he even found out about this, but I can't let them kill him. And that big prat..."

"The Erlking?"

"Yeah, whatever. He's already noticed we're gone."

"Let's get back to Qwyrk. She'll know what to do."

"She's cocked it up pretty bad, so far."

"Only because you didn't listen to her, you nitwit!"

"Whatever," he sneered.

"Anyway, don't you want to meet your mum?"

"Of course I do, but we can't just leave Carl out there. They'll murder him!"

"Let's just find Qwyrk, all right? She'll know how to save him!"

"Sorry young one. The only people that you're gonna be saving, er, I mean, are gonna be saving you are, well, uh, no one's gonna be saving you, actually!"

Jilly and Lluck turned around to see two chickens with antlers glaring at them with malice.

"And just what are you supposed to be?" Jilly asked, failing to be surprised by anything she saw anymore.

"Elwetritschen!" one announced with obvious pride.

"What now?" she said, shaking her head.

"Elwetritschen, fearsome avian attendants of the Wild Hunt, heralds of his Dark Majesty, callers at dusk of the impending doom!"

"You're chickens, with fuzzy little deer antlers."

"Yeah, all right, but you have to admit, we're jolly well frightful!"

"Um, not really, no."

"Oh, come on, weren't you a bit startled? Unnerved? Unsettled? Just a little?"

"Actually, you're making me a bit hungry, mate," Lluck said. Jilly stifled a laugh. Vegetarian or not, that *was* funny.

"Look, we're not going to argue about this," the bird-creature started.

"Well, you do look rather tasty sometimes," his companion said.

"What?"

"I'm just sayin'. If we were trapped on a deserted island, I wouldn't hesitate to eat ya, that's all."

"Oh, thank you very much, you knob!"

"Stop your whining! It's a compliment! You'd be proper delicious!"

Jilly motioned with her head to Lluck to sneak off, while these quarreling *galli domestici* were distracted.

"I reckon you taste more like venison, anyway!"

"I taste like chicken, thank you very much!"

"Oh yeah? How do you know?"

"I just do!"

Jilly, Lluck, and Longwing were almost out of earshot when she heard the fluttering of wings, and saw one of the beasts come crashing down in front of her. It wobbled on its chicken feet for a moment, and then stood up to its full height... of almost eighteen inches.

"Where d'ya think yer goin', then?"

"Are you really going to stop us?" Jilly asked, incredulous.

"Quite possibly." The creature opened its beak and revealed a rather shocking row of razor-sharp teeth. "Now, then, shall we proceed to see the master?"

"Bollocks," Jilly said, looking at Lluck, who shook his head in disgust.

Longwing raised his head up and looked around. "W-where are we?"

"We've just been taken prisoner by a couple of talking chickens, mate," Lluck said. "And that's not even the strangest thing that's happened tonight."

* * *

Qwyrk and Holly looked out over the assembled oddities, leading a man in a lavender costume with a purple cape to the center of the gathering. A good number of the night beasties seemed to be laughing at him.

"Wait, who is that?" Qwyrk said.

Holly squinted. "No, it can't be!"

Qwyrk was confused. "Can't be what?"

Holly took a few steps forward, unleashing her staff.

"Holly?"

"Oh no, no!" Holly whispered.

"What is it? What's wrong?'

Holly looked back at Qwyrk in horror and then turned and pointed. Qwyrk came up beside her and looked to where she directed. Jilly, Lluck, and the third captive were also being shoved through the Unseelie mob by... chickens? They were led to the same place as the fellow in purple, a cleared space where the Erlking waited. "We can't wait, Qwyrk. He's going to do it, he's going to kill Lluck!"

"We don't have much of a plan for this one," Qwyrk said, looking at her as if to apologize.

Holly took her hand. "Remember what I said. If there's anyone I'd want here, it's you."

Qwyrk gave Holly's hand a squeeze. "Well then, let's go kick some arse, shall we?"

They set off together down the side of the hill, not bothering to try to hide. Run-of-the-mill goblins were stationed as guards, now preoccupied with the proceedings. Holly conked one on his helmet, sending him collapsing to the ground in a heap, while at the same time Qwyrk grabbed the other by his tattered chainmail and tossed him back up the hill behind her. Holly swatted one of the floating eyeballs with her stick and sent it flying into the darkness (good riddance, really!).

On they strode, growing more determined with each step. Soon, they reached the bottom, still unnoticed. All the various and sundry beasties seemed more concerned with whatever their master was doing than with looking behind them, which wasn't the smartest of ideas. For them, at least.

"This could be fun," Qwyrk said, as she pummeled the nearest troll with three successive punches to the head. He fell back with a thud to the iced earth and didn't move again.

"Not a bad night out, really," Holly answered, as she tripped a hobgoblin and whacked him on the side of the head as he went down.

"I mean, I do expect to encounter a few difficulties." Qwyrk kicked a kobold in the privates and as he doubled over, she picked him up and threw him off into the darkness.

"I would expect so." Holly imitated Qwyrk's attack by bringing her staff up between the legs of an approaching wirry-cow, who went wide-eyed, whimpered, and fell over. "But nothing we can't handle, I should think."

Several Darkfae now turned to see the commotion behind them.

"Ah, crap," Qwyrk said in a nonchalant tone. "I think we've made them mad."

Holly swung her staff, leaving a trail of sparks in the air and causing several of their enemies to pause and back up. "I'd be rather disappointed if they weren't. What say you, darling, shall we make them really angry?"

Qwyrk smiled. "Let's crack on!"

* * *

Jilly, Lluck, and Longwing trudged through the assembled mass of snickering and jeering unsavories. Some commotion seemed to be happening on the far side of the clearing, but Jilly couldn't see what it was. In a moment, they stood before the floating figure in grey, his face ever hidden under his hood. A hobgoblin held a sword to the throat of the purple-costumed man, now on his knees and looking quite irritated.

"I know who you are!" Jilly said in defiance.

"Good!" the Erlking answered. "I have no desire to keep myself a secret. But I also know who you are. Due to unfortunate circumstances, I could not take you with me when we became acquainted at your ancestor's cave. But how gracious of you to deliver yourself to me now, daughter of the witching!"

"Ooh, I like that! Is that my title?"

"What?"

"'Jillian Joanne Pleeth, Daughter of the Witching.' That sounds brilliant!"

"You... you are missing the point here."

"Oh, I know the point, all right. I'm not aiding you. I helped take down de Soulis last summer, by the way!"

Lluck look at her in confusion, but she ignored him.

"I don't need you to aid me," the Erlking taunted. "I just need your magic, a magic that I can draw out of you, just as I can pluck out the good fortune of our mutual friend there." He gestured toward Lluck and then turned toward Longwing. "As for you, little traitor, I will just pluck out your miserable life."

Longwing spat at him. The Erlking chuckled.

"We have friends," Jilly announced. "Quite a few of them are already surrounding this place, and more are on the way." *Wow, I'm a bad liar!*

"Good, that is good. The more blood I spill, the more efficacious the ritual will be. Invite them in. Bring them all here! Let me welcome these wondrous protagonists."

Jilly held her tongue for a minute. *Think, Jilly, think!* "No, thanks, I'll just let them stop by in their own time." *Well, that was pathetic!*

"A pity you'll be dead before they arrive, then."

Jilly panicked. She reached into her coat, feeling for the book still tucked into an inside pocket. She hoped the Erlking didn't notice.

"You know," Longwing said, sounding weak and in pain, "I'm really tired of your shite, Greylocke. You promise, you boast, you threaten, but in the end, you're just a pathetic wanker with nothing going for you outside of all the crap lies you tell."

"Brave words when I hold your sister's life in my hands," the Erlking taunted.

"Actually, you don't. See, I think it's all just a part of your stupid attempt to be scary. Truth is, my sister could rip any one of your little minions here to shreds and laugh about it. You haven't gone after her and you never will. You're bluffing, you big, dim saddo!"

Jilly was surprised that the Erlking didn't answer, which gave her hope. She felt the book again, then patted her trouser pocket.

"Since you seem eager to invite death, perhaps I should start with this one," The Erlking pointed to Carl, and the hobgoblin at his side moved his sword closer to Carl's throat.

"No!" Lluck yelled.

"Ah," the Erlking responded. "So, you care for this pathetic weakling, then, this would-be hero? Tell me, what interest is he to you?"

"He's just a good bloke, all right? He wants to do the right thing, to help people, and that's brilliant, something a scumbag like you wouldn't get if it bit you on the arse!"

"Would it interest you to know," the Erlking paused, presumably for dramatic effect, "that he is more than that to you?"

"What are you talking about?" Lluck scrunched up his face in confusion.

"Hmm. Tell him, little man. It seems you have not, yet. So please, do it now."

"Carl?" Lluck asked.

Jilly glanced back and forth between them, having no idea what was happening.

"I'm... I'm your dad, Lluck." Carl lowered his head, looking ashamed.

"What? No, no! That's not possible. It can't, you can't..." He stared at the ground, eyes darting from place to place, as if trying to process it all. He seemed completely lost, floored, and Jilly could only feel pity for both him and his father.

"It's true," Carl said. "I wasn't keeping it from you, I swear. I didn't even know you existed, and I really only put it together after you were kidnapped. Call it parent's intuition or something. Plus, you do look a bit like me, and you definitely look like your mum."

"Where is she?"

"No idea. I haven't seen her since the night we... you know." He blushed.

"Heh," the Erlking chuckled. "I was just going to kill you, Carl, is it? But this has become so much more enjoyable. Perhaps, father dear, I will let you witness your son's death first, before you join him."

Carl snapped his head around in anger to look at his captor, his exposed neck dangerously close to the hobgoblin's blade. "Just try it, you vile sack of sh..."

"My lord!" a nefarious nixie called out, as he ran into the gathering, out of breath. "We're under attack! Two girls at the perimeter. Just slid down that there hill and piled into us, and they're provin' way more difficult to dispatch than we'd like!"

Jilly pumped one fist behind her back.

"I already know they are here, you servile maggot," the Erlking replied without the slightest hint of surprise. "I have allowed them to be. Why don't we invite them to come and join us in this little chat?"

Jilly's heart sank.

* * *

Qwyrk kicked kobolds, Holly hit hobgoblins, but both beat bugbears. More monstrous minions attempted to take them down, and even Qwyrk had to admit to that the effort was getting a bit tedious, if not tiring. She forced her attention back to whatever beastie tried to best her at any given moment, and not get distracted by Holly's grace, strength, and kick-arsery. Still, they made their way through the initial cohort of creeps, but something happened they didn't expect: their enemies seemed to call a unilateral cease-fire, er, cease-fight, something.

Said minions parted into two groups, and formed a path that led straight to someone in the distance. A large figure in a grey robe, floating just above the earth held out his clawed hands in a gesture of welcome.

Qwyrk and Holly looked at each other with trepidation.

"Well, I guess this is it," Qwyrk said.

Holly exhaled a sharp, misty breath into the cold air and glanced at Qwyrk with what looked like genuine fear.

"Come on," Qwyrk tried to be reassuring. "We're in this together. We'll figure something out along the way."

* * *

"This does appear to be a bit more than we bargained for, Mr. Dill."

"I agree, Mr. Chives. However, I recommend we wait a short while longer before taking action. Our client seems quite capable of taking care of herself, and we shouldn't interfere except in the most dire of circumstances. We are but investigators, after all."

"That we are, Mr. Dill; that we are."

* * *

The sniveling, sniggering, gibbering, nattering hordes of Unseelies and unseemlies held their ground, hissing and whispering, growling and taunting, but none dared to get in the way of Holly or Qwyrk—much less challenge them—as they proceeded down that grim gauntlet. Qwyrk had the thought of making a joke about an especially appalling wedding march, but thought better of it.

"I had hoped that something like this might happen," the Erlking announced as they made their way into the clearing, "even if I did sow the seeds of schism between you."

Just give me an opening, you idiot, Qwyrk thought, sizing up her robed and cowled opponent.

"I mean," the Erlking said as he reached up and pulled back his hood, revealing Greylocke's head and face, looking too small for his over-sized body, "you were so appallingly stupid to fall for that ruse." His voice changed into the English of his human role and he looked at Qwyrk. "Seriously, did you *really* think that I was some helpless human victim of hers, who hired a bunch of occult flunkies to find out all about you? It was a piss-poor lie, to be honest, but I thought, why not try? It might be amusing. And it was! My magic tricked you right from the start."

"Oh, I had doubts about it all along, you wanker," Qwyrk said. "But yeah, you worked your little spell well enough. How'd you manage to pull off seeming human, by the way?"

"Ha! A trade secret. A proper trickster never tells."

"Shame. I guess I'll have to beat it out of you."

"Qwyrk!" Jilly shouted. "Be careful. He's way more powerful than he seems."

"Heh. She's right, you know," he taunted. "But I suppose this little human face does look a bit foolish and non-threatening. Fair enough, that's kind of the point. Let me slip into something more comfortable."

He shook his head back and forth and it began to change, to morph, to grow. His skin turned grey, his hair fell away, his ears and nose grew decidedly more pointed, and his eyes shifted to a glowing yellow. "What do you think?" he asked in his own voice. "Better?"

"Not even close." Qwyrk rolled her eyes. "I mean, come on, at least Greylocke's kind of a fit, mature gentleman, but you..."

Holly said nothing. She seemed to be trying to calm herself, to keep from lashing out in rage. Qwyrk tried to telegraph to her: *not yet!*

"Ah well," the Erlking said with a shrug, "your opinion matters little. What we are here for, of course, is me! Tonight, the process is completed; tomorrow, my reign begins."

"Yeah, yeah, blah, blah, blah," Qwyrk mocked. "I swear you dark lords are all really just the same bloke who somehow keeps coming back for more punishment. Remind me, what was your name again?"

"Oh, you will remember after tonight, if I let you live. I will be more than a legend!"

"In your own mind, maybe. Which incidentally, sounds like a pretty cuckoo place, to be honest."

"Hm. I've changed my... abnormal mind; how about we start the sacrifices with this one?" He lifted Carl up by the cape. Carl tried to free himself, but the Erlking's grip was clearly too strong.

"No! Dad!" Lluck yelled, struggling to free himself from his hobgoblin captor, to no avail.

"Dad?" Holly whispered in horror. "Oh no, he knows!" She raised her staff, but Qwyrk caught her arm. "Not yet," she whispered.

"I'll be the one who decides that, thank you," Holly snapped, shaking her arm free, to Qwyrk's astonishment and immediate regret.

"I'm sorry..."

Holly strode toward the Erlking. "Let him go, now!"

The Erlking smiled and dropped Carl, who landed and rolled for several feet. After a moment of fiddling and fumbling, he stood up again.

Holly continued on, but the Erlking held up his hand. "Stop!"

As he spoke, he had already floated over to Lluck. He grabbed him with the same ease as he had Carl, drawing him near and bringing a clawed hand up to his chest. "Take another step, Yakshi, and you'll watch your son die even sooner than you had feared."

"Son?" Carl looked at her in astonishment. "No, is it?"

Lluck flicked his hands, perhaps to change his fortune, but it didn't work. He glanced over at Holly. "Mum?" Holly's eyes were wide with fear, but she didn't move.

Qwyrk froze. For once, she had no idea what to do. "Damn it!" she whispered, ranging over options, plans, and tactics, none of which seemed even a little bit useful right now.

* * *

"There is a preferred order to this ritual," the Erlking announced, holding Lluck close. "But that can change, if necessary. All that really matters is that I feed on this boy." He glanced at Jilly.

"And since she, the daughter of the witching, is here as well, their magics will be mine. As full preparations have already been made, all the rest is merely theater. But I do like a good spectacle, as you can imagine."

An assortment of minions laughed.

"Now then," he continued.

"Oh, now then, now then," Longwing interrupted.

Jilly tensed up, fearing the worst.

"You know," Longwing went on, "I've heard just about enough of your bollocks to last a lifetime." He elbowed his goblin guard in the face and stepped forward with his arms open wide. Jilly was suitably impressed. She was even more impressed when he jumped into the air and flew at the Erlking, landing a punch to the creature's face that made him drop Lluck. Longwing flew just out of reach and darted down to strike again. The Erlking swore and grasped at the air while his minions growled and snorted.

Qwyrk made fists as her eyes began to glow red. Jilly knew that look: Qwyrk wanted to rush at the Erlking to help finish the job. Jilly glanced over at Holly, but of course, Holly seemed preoccupied with keeping an eye on Lluck.

"Longwing, be careful, mate!" Lluck shouted as he scrambled away, only to be met with more guards who grabbed hold of him. Holly gasped and started toward him.

Jilly pulled herself free of her hobgoblin, reached into her coat, and pulled out her book. She opened it and starting riffling through the pages, locating the spell that had stopped these things before. She found it and looked up in triumph, only to see the Erlking grab hold of Longwing's coat as he attempted another assault. In a swift and terrifying move, he slammed Longwing down onto the ground and towered over him in an instant. Without hesitation, without taunts, without mercy, he drove his talons into the young man's chest.

Longwing's eyes went wide and blood spurted from his wounds.

"No!" Lluck and Jilly screamed almost in unison. She was at once sick, weak, and almost buckled over. She nearly lost her grip on her book, and all thoughts of working magic fell away.

* * *

Qwyrk stood stunned for a moment. But only for a moment. Anger welled up inside her, a rage that wasn't going to be sated until this monster was taken down. As the Erlking stood up, the lad's blood on his claws, he smiled and laughed, and his expression invited a challenge to Qwyrk, one she wasn't going to shy away from.

Before anyone else could react, she jumped for him. He ducked and avoided her first swing, though she caught him with her second punch, a blow to the midsection that made him gasp and float back a few feet.

"Now that I have your attention, you bastard," she threatened through clenched teeth, "I'm going to pound you so far into the ground, it'll take an archeology excavation to find you, you sick, utter wanker!"

The Erlking threw his arms out wide, and an inky darkness emerged from between his hands. It grew and rushed at Qwyrk before she could react.

Damn it, he did it again!

She recoiled as the black mist surrounded and enveloped her, entering her nostrils and making her choke with its noxious, burning fumes. She could feel the magic draining out of her, even as she tried to resist. She heard Holly shout her name, but she seemed to be far away, almost under water. As the mist cleared, she was dazed, nauseated, and weak. She stumbled a little and struggled to keep her balance.

"Now, little Shadow, shall we end this?" His minions cackled and gibbered as he raised a fist that glowed with the same energy the goblins had used in Jilly's backyard.

The Erlking rushed at her and backhanded her across the face, sending her crashing backwards to the frozen ground, rolling over and over. Pain surged in her forehead, and she could feel the warm wetness of her blood oozing from the head wound and from her nose. Weak and dizzy, she gasped and struggled to sit up. She heard taunts and laughter all around her.

"Qwyrk!" Holly screamed, running to her and kneeling down. She cradled Qwyrk in her arms, stroking her head. Qwyrk treasured her gentle touch, even in this humiliating, quite possibly final, defeat.

"How does it feel to be like them? Weak, mortal, afraid?" the Erlking mocked. "Without your powers, you are nothing before me. I could crush you. I could snap you in two."

"Yeah, yeah," Qwyrk said, her breathing labored and her chest hurting. "You all sound the same. Seriously, do you morons get your dialogue written by the same hacks? It really might be time to switch it up a bit."

"Your defiance in defeat is amusing, even admirable, but it will not save you."

For once, Qwyrk feared he was telling the truth.

* * *

"If you touch her again, I'll kill you!" Holly threatened, anger consuming her.

"Ah, my dear little Vishala," he taunted. "So fierce, so strong, so precious, so beautiful. When first I saw you, all those centuries ago, I knew you were special. I'm glad nothing has changed."

"What? What are you talking about?"

"Your mother never told you, did she? Once, in my wanderings across this vast world, I came to your lands. I beheld the magnificent Yakshi, though you were the one who captivated me the most. A sweet thing, barely more than a child, but you were not like the others. You shimmered with magic, with fortune, with potential power. I saw that a union between us would produce a brood of amazing power, able to bend destiny to our will. And so, rather than simply steal you away, I decided to be honorable, from one Fae to another. I offered your father a chance to give you to me willingly."

"What?" Holly gasped.

"He refused, despite my repeated offers, so I gutted him. I killed him with my war spear. He had his chance, but he made the wrong choice."

"No! You bastard!" Holly sobbed. She had a sickening realization that he spoke the truth.

"A weakling's death for a superfluous Fae with no strength, no vision. He could not comprehend the greatness I beheld."

Holly cried and held Qwyrk closer. A wave of volatile emotions crashed over her, and she didn't know what to do. Qwyrk reached up and touched one of her arms, as if trying to offer some comfort, despite her semi-dazed state. Holly could hold on to her, at least.

"But before I could claim you," the Erlking continued, "your mother fled, taking you far away and into lands unknown, where she was able to keep you hidden for centuries. I had given up on finding you, until I received word of a boy with the potential for powers of luck and good chance. I sought him out, and sure enough, I learned that he was yours, but that he was the son of some stupid human of no value at all, the imbecile in the ridiculous costume over there. So I watched, and I waited for the child's powers to grow, until it was time, until now.

He held out his clawed hands, palms facing up and shrugged.

"The boy is of no use to me as an heir, you see, but he still holds your remarkable power in his blood, now that he has come of age. And so, when I complete this ritual, and dig out and devour his heart, I will gain his gift to enhance fortune; not all of his gift, but enough. In my human form, I will be unchallenged. I will amass wealth beyond all imagining and make whole nations do my bidding. And in my true form, I can roam this Earth and harvest souls as I like, until all bow to me."

"You're as bloody insane as you are full of yourself!" Qwyrk blurted out, wincing. Holly wanted to comfort her, but she couldn't even help herself. The horror of it all threatened to overwhelm her.

"Perhaps, but it is I who hold the upper hand, not you, Shadow, who I have made so weak, so mortal. It is a pity," he said, looking back to Holly. "I am curious to know what our offspring would have been like. Perhaps we will yet have a chance, little Vishala?"

"I would die before I would defile myself with your touch!" Holly spat, tightening her hold on Qwyrk.

"Yes, I can see that now," he said, looking back and forth between them. "So be it, you may perish together in each other's arms. A romantic demise, if you will. Juliet and Juliet, a modern tragedy."

"I'm sorry," Qwyrk said, tears streaming down her face. "I'm so sorry, Holly. I should have done more. I should have..."

"Shhhhh," Holly whispered and kissed her head. "No, darling.

You tried. We tried." Her own tears watered her vision, and she knew that everything was about to end. They'd failed.

* * *

Jilly watched her beloved Qwyrk battered to the ground by this monster and saw the Erlking's guards holding Lluck so close that they could end his life at any moment. She fought back tears, fought back her fear. There was no one else to help; Longwing was dead, Qwyrk was hurt, badly, and Holly held her but wouldn't dare move with her son in such peril. Jilly had no time to work a spell.

But there was something else, something that just might work. She reached into her pocket. Something else, indeed.

* * *

"Now," the Erlking taunted as he approached Qwyrk and Holly, both hands glowing with unearthly energy. "Let us finish this."

"Qwyrk!"

Qwyrk looked over to her left, and to her horror, saw Jilly break free of her captor and rush toward her, now not more than twenty feet away. But Jilly didn't look afraid; she was smiling, confident, brave, even as the clueless kobold chased after her.

"Here, catch!"

She tossed something at Qwyrk, who reached up on instinct to grab it out of the air. It was the amulet. The birthday present. The faulty magical item that had filled Jilly with rage.

"Put it on, now!" Jilly insisted. "Just do it!"

As if sensing she was on to something, Holly let go of Qwyrk and stepped back. Qwyrk heeded Jilly's plea and slipped the cord over her neck. At once, an amazing power surged through her, like an electric shock. The pain vanished, her head cleared, and she sprang to her feet. It was incredible; she'd never experienced anything like it. In a few moments, she was strong again, stronger than ever. Magic poured through her, connecting her with the arcane forces all around them. Her skin tingled and almost glowed. Jilly was right; whatever the amulet did, it made her more powerful in the moment. She felt almost invincible.

She looked over to Jilly, who was grinning ear-to-ear, and then to Holly, who seemed more shocked than anything else. Finally, she looked back to her foe. The Erlking had stopped and appeared confused, while his minions shrank back in fear, much as they had when Jilly confronted them at Granny's cave. Even Jilly's captor hesitated from grabbing her again.

"I don't really know what just happened," Qwyrk said to him, her eyes glowing red, "but I'm going to kick your sorry bum from here to Bavaria and back, you half-arsed Rumpelstiltskin! Holly, darling, would you care to join me?"

Holly said nothing, but the determination on her tear-stained face told Qwyrk everything she needed to know. She already had her Silambam staff in hand and was swinging it about her, leaving trails of sparks and lights in the air as the Darkfae nearest her cowed to avoid being hit.

"Right, this is going to hurt," Qwyrk announced. "A lot!"

"What are you waiting for, you pathetic swine?" the Erlking bellowed at his hapless minions. "Assail them, rend them with your claws, scatter their remains to the elder winds!"

"See?" Qwyrk said. "I was expecting you to say something like 'seize them' or some other clichéd bollocks, and there you go, being all clever and almost-poetic and messing up my hopes. I give you some props for originality, though. I can honestly say I've never heard that one before. Problem is, it's not really very windy tonight, so it might get a bit messy if you're just flinging bits about."

Holly charged past her and, swinging her staff, ended up in front of a particularly nasty looking line of guard-trolls who'd moved in front of the Erlking. She proceeded to take out three of them with one swipe, knocking them down like a row of revolting bowling pins. She gutted a fourth in the stomach with the end of her stick, making him double over and fall to his knees. She ducked to avoid the rusty sword swung by a fifth, tripped him, and as he fell, clocked him on the back of his lumpy head, so that his fall to the ground was quick and merciless. She swung her staff a few more times before coming to a stop, stepping up onto the unconscious body of one of her foes; the remaining guards shrank back and came no closer. The whole thing had barely taken ten seconds. She looked seriously pissed off and not even out of breath.

Qwyrk stared at her with an open mouth. "Good Goddess, that was hot!"

* * *

"I do believe, Mr. Dill, that as the rather vulgar saying goes, the shite has hit the proverbial fan."

"I do believe you are correct, Mr. Chives."

"Shall we, then?"

"After you, Mr. Dill."

"You are ever the gentleman, Mr. Chives. Ever the gentleman, indeed."

CHAPTER TWENTY

The shite had truly hit the fan.

CHAPTER TWENTY-ONE

Qwyrk lost sight of Jilly and Lluck in the chaos. She tried to find them, but more and more beasties of all kinds crowded in to protect their master. All she could do was hope her friends were resourceful enough to get out of harm's way. Holly held her own and thumped a good number of monstrosities, but many of them quite rudely didn't stay down after they'd been thumped, which meant even more effort on her part.

Qwyrk landed several good punches across the one-eyed visages of a squad of cyclops, sending them sprawling in a big mythological heap. Her power seemed to increase with each blow; it was fantastic, intoxicating, and she reveled in it. She didn't want it to end. She looked around and saw that the Erlking had retreated behind a sizable legion of lackeys of all kinds, drawing symbols of light in the air.

"That's not good," she said, steeling herself to wade through that gaggle of gruesomeness and put an end to whatever he had planned.

Before she could, Holly finished off a particularly grumpy minotaur with a blow to the head. He reeled backwards, crashing into a harpy, knocking both of them out cold. Apparently, she and Holly were currently enmeshed in the Greek mythology cadre of the minions.

"As long as a damned herd of centaurs doesn't show up—Holly!" she called out.

Holly looked over to her. Qwyrk motioned in the direction of the Erlking and his eldritch hand-waving. She nodded and charged toward their mutual foe. Qwyrk dodged a bipedal polecat's pole axe and kicked it, catching its bipedal feet and sending it back-peddling and caterwauling through the air.

"Everything going all right?" she asked Holly as they joined up again.

"Smashing! And you?"

"Damned good at the moment, I have to say!"

"I've lost sight of Lluck," Holly said.

"He's with Jilly. I think they'll be all right." Qwyrk had to say it out loud to convince herself. "But we can stop this now."

"He's just over there," Holly motioned to the Erlking. "Shall we?"

"Oh, we shall. We shall indeed. Come on!"

In that moment, she heard hooves, and a herd of centaurs bore down on them, a host of smaller Unseelies shrieking and jumping out of their way, and a few of the less fortunate being trampled under their hooves.

"You've got to be kidding me!" Qwyrk stopped and turned to Holly.

"I don't think we can fight all of them." Holly scanned the oncoming onslaught.

"You're right, but we've got to try to stop them or they'll finish us."

They glanced at each other, nodded, and assumed fighting stances side-by-side, knowing this was a very bad idea. Possibly a fatal one. As the creatures drew nearer, Qwyrk tensed, hoping against hope that her enhanced power would be enough. It would be enough. It had to be.

"Get out of here," she blurted out to Holly. "I can take them."

"What? Are you mad?"

"Go and find Lluck, he needs you."

Thundering hooves thundered.

"You just said he'd be fine with Jilly!"

"But I don't know that for sure!"

Stampeding hooves stampeded.

"I'm not leaving you!"

"Holly…"

It was too late. The creatures were almost upon them, weapons of all kinds drawn and ready to cut them down.

A blast of fire roared across the centaurs' front line from the darkness of the right-hand side, setting the first rank aflame and causing them to roar, rear up, and veer off. But the second line crashed into them as they did, making a noisy horrible mess of tangled limbs, both humanoid and equine.

"Huzzah!" a voice called out from the dark, and in a moment, Snickerwocky trotted into view, Blip astride her, bedecked in Roman helmet and breastplate, Regency riding boots, and sword cane drawn. The Komodo dragon stopped in front of the remaining centaurs, who had pulled up short and now backed up, making panicked conferrals with each other in their ancient tongue.

"My dear war beast," Blip said with an air of casualness. "Would you be so kind as to show these miscreants the proverbial door?"

Snickerwocky belched, inhaled, and as the centaurs cried out in alarm, she let out another burst of flame right at them. They howled, they screamed, they turned and bolted, trying to put out the many fires that burned their horses' arses. As the dust settled, they'd fled, down to the last beast.

Blip adjusted himself in his saddle, his smug grin as widely smug as could be. Qwyrk groaned. She knew what was coming.

"You're very welcome, by the way," he said.

"Yeah, all right, thanks," Qwyrk said, annoyed and a bit humiliated. "But where the hell have you been?"

"Bah, it simply took a bit of time for her to be prepared to charge into battle." He patted the lizard on the back. "Once fully nourished, she was ready to go!"

"That was rather remarkable, I must say," Holly said in astonishment.

"Thank you, my dear." He tipped his helmet to her. "Now then, where next? I yearn for battle, and the pride of a glorious offensive!"

A loud noise behind them drew their attention, and they turned to see a fully-armed horde of hobgoblins, trolls, wyverns, and other creatures lumbering straight toward them.

"When I said a 'glorious offensive,'" Blip grimaced, "I meant something like Agincourt, not Thermopylae, thank you very much."

* * *

Jilly grabbed Lluck and dodged the exploding chaos all around them as Unseelies scrambled to attack Holly and Qwyrk, while others strived to get their master to safety.

"We can't leave Longwing behind!" Lluck yelled.

"He's dead, Lluck," Jilly cried. "I'm so sorry, but we have to get out of here. We'll come back for him if we can."

"Where's Carl? Where's my dad?"

"I'm here, son." Carl lurched toward them, ripping off his cape and tossing it aside. "Come on, we've got to move!"

They bounded past, ducked under, and jumped over various beasties that seemed less interested in them now than in piling on to Qwyrk and Holly. As they stumbled away from the mêlée, they paused to catch their breath and look back at the mayhem.

"I've got to help them," Jilly said, leafing through her book. "I stopped these things before, back at the cave. I can do it again."

"But there's so many," Carl said.

"I know, and they'll kill Qwyrk and Holly if we don't stop them, no matter how powerful Qwyrk is with that amulet. I have to try."

"Wait," Lluck said. "I think I'm better now, but something feels different. Before, when we were tied to those poles, they were magic, right? Blocking my powers."

"What do you mean?" Jilly asked.

"The Erlking did that when he was holding me captive, and then again, when I was up close with him."

"Your point?"

"Well, you undid the spell on the poles, but my power shorted out again when I got near him. Now, I'm far enough away from him, and I don't think he can get at me from a distance without help. "

"Okay, so?"

"So, dummy! If you cast a spell again from that book of yours with my powers helping you out, it should have a bigger effect, right?"

"Do you think you can power up my gun again?" Carl asked.

Lluck shrugged. "Worth a shot, so to speak."

Jilly sighed. "Fine, let me start on a spell and then see if you can 'luck' us and try to make it stronger. But we've got to hurry.

Our ladies won't last long against all those creeps. The Erlking's regrouping, and then he'll come after us again."

"Let's get on with it!" Lluck said.

* * *

Qwyrk and Holly drew in closer to each other, neither of them especially keen to snuggle up next to a fire-breathing Komodo dragon, useful though she was. The creatures all around them had indeed regrouped and began to advance, looking more and more confident because of their sheer numbers.

The amulet's magic surged through Qwyrk. She felt powerful, a conduit for something far greater than her, but even she knew it might not be enough against these odds.

"Remind me again," she said to Holly. "What the bloody hell were we thinking, charging down here with no backup, no army, and no plan?"

"We were thinking we were going to save my son and stop that wretched creature from taking over the world," Holly answered. "And that's still the plan, right?"

Qwyrk frowned. "I want it to be, but even I have to be realistic."

"Nonsense, my dears!" Blip said, astride his combustible beast. "With my gallant steed at our side, our victory is all but assured."

An arrow soared by his head. He ducked down, clutching at his helmet as a chorus of laughs erupted from the presumed source of the shot. "Damnation! That was unfair! Just what are these louts playing at?"

"They're not playing, Blip," Qwyrk said. "That's the problem. They fully intend to kill us."

The horde hoarded itself around them on three sides, all growls and giggles, snarls and sneers, weapons drawn, knocked, raised, and poised. And then they charged. They ran, limped, ambled, hopped, and bounded over the frozen ground. A few slipped and fell in the most spectacular of ways, only to be trampled by their fellows to a multitude of grunts and swear words. They waved weapons and misfired missiles at the trio as they closed in.

"Brace yourselves," Qwyrk warned.

But just like the centaur skirmish, the front line of would-be attackers was mowed down, though not by dragon fire. Indeed, Snickerwocky had found another clump of frozen but tasty something-or-others, and seemed preoccupied with it. No, this time it was a succession of laser beams, straight out of a sci-fi film and shot from two vintage pistols held by two odd-looking fellows wearing black trench coats, bowler hats, and sunglasses, despite the lateness of the hour.

"Top of the evening to you, ma'am," one of them tipped his hat to Holly. "We're not normally in the habit of interfering in such matters. However," he said as he shot another laser burst from his gun, mowing down a gaggle of goblins, "given that you are our trusted client, and a well-paying one at that, it seemed prudent to intervene to sway the odds in your favor, if possible. Also..." He reached into his pocket, fished out something and lobbed it at her; she caught it with one hand. It was a thin gold ring with an emerald set into it. "I believe that belongs to you, ma'am? We couldn't reach you earlier, for which we profoundly apologize, but having found it out here, we now know the reason why."

"You're geniuses! Thank you!" Holly laughed.

"Excuse me," Qwyrk interrupted, glaring at the two men. "Who are you?"

"Dill and Chives? My detectives? And the ring I tried to tell you about?"

"Oh right! Brilliant. Nice guns, those!"

The second of the two tipped his hat to Qwyrk before firing at a duo of wyverns descending on them with ill intent. The creatures crashed into each other and then down to the ground, taking out a squad of Korrigan who didn't even see them coming.

Unfortunately, more of every kind of creature (except orcs) appeared, answering the Erlking's summons, arriving from other nefarious planes of existence, which was all rather inconvenient. Dill, Chives, Qwyrk, Holly, and Blip—still trying to get his mount to show any interest in the commotion—despite their formidable abilities, soon found themselves hemmed in on all sides, lasers, a martial arts staff, a sword cane, and magically-enhanced fists not-withstanding. The creatures howled and yelped, gnashing their teeth and hurling insults.

"Not so tough now, are ya, you tasty white meats?" one troll bellowed.

"Hey, I resent that!" Holly said.

"Ooh, look lads, that one's got a mouth! I bet she's really exotic-tasting!"

"Great," Qwyrk said. "A troll who trolls."

"Just so you know," Holly smiled a thoroughly insincere smile. "I'm going to knock those crooked teeth of yours down your throat. I'll bet they'll taste really exotic, too!" She whipped her staff around a few times in front of her dim-witted tormentor, who stepped back. But others took his place and closed in.

"The reserves in our weapons are beginning to run low, Mr. Chives."

"Would you say that this appears to be the proverbial sticky wicket, Mr. Dill?"

"The stickiest of said wickets, Mr. Chives." He turned to Holly. "Our apologies, ma'am. We may ultimately not be as useful or effective in this endeavor as we had hoped."

"No worries, gentlemen. At this point, every little bit helps."

The Unseelies and assorted no-goods swarmed around them, prepared to strike.

"This is probably going to hurt us more than it is them," Qwyrk said.

They waited, tense and fearful.

And then they heard it. At first, it was faint, but it grew louder and louder. A fanfare that sounded like... a kazoo? Actually several kazoos. Qwyrk and her companions looked to the direction of the sound, a low hill opposite the ridge they'd hidden behind earlier. And there they appeared. The tiny herald and several more like him emerged from the darkness, playing their wretched little tune through their noses, over and over. And dozens, scores, hundreds of others swarmed over the ridge: Nighttime Nasties of all shapes and sizes, though mostly diminutive, but armed to the teeth and looking right pissed off.

Bogtrotter stood tall among them, a smug grin on his face. And flanking him on either side—Qwyrk squinted to be sure—were Silktassel and Sneezewort, armed with spiked clubs and blending in with the rest of the motley assortment.

"You bastards!" Qwyrk laughed out loud. "Come on, then, let's knock these wankers down to size and finish this!"

Bogtrotter nodded and the Nasties descended down the slope en masse in a cacophony of screams, shouts, and kazoo noises, their sharp weapons and testy temperaments more than making up for what they lacked in physical stature. Like a swarm of bees, they overran the Darkfae and assorted other villainous sycophants, with Silktassel and Sneezewort bringing up the rear and finishing off the ones still standing; there was much shouting and bellowing. Bogtrotter waved his hands, and above the horde, bags of badly-packed rubbish materialized out of thin air and promptly burst, spilling their revolting contents all over the Erlking's finest warriors.

Qwyrk laughed as she joined the fray, gleefully punching, kicking, head-butting, and anything else she could think of in her enhanced state, while trying to avoid the raining rubbish. She barely noticed what her friends were doing, but she was quite sure they were enjoying this as much as she was.

With the advent of their new allies, they started to beat back their attackers with some ease, as the unconscious bodies of their enemies piled up in droves. Those that didn't get beaten to a pulp hastened to retreat, aware that they were now on the losing side.

And Qwyrk reveled in her newfound invincibility, craving more and more of its exhilarating power. As she pounded goblins, hobgoblins, trolls, Korrigan, fanged eyeballs (oh come on!), and a half-dozen other foes, she noticed that in the distance, the Erlking had not yet fled. Instead, he seemed to be determined to hold his ground, and that filled her with worry.

※　※　※

"We have to move fast," Jilly said. "He's up to something, and even if Qwyrk knocks down his minions, he's going to strike at her and Holly."

"Well, hurry up, then!" Lluck insisted, prompting an annoyed glance from Jilly as she focused on the sigil. "Here!" He flicked his hands at her again.

"Look, this worked before, so with luck—no pun intended—I can do it again and turn all these scary monsters into scared little tossers."

She focused on the shape, trying to draw the energy from it and direct it toward her book, her hand, something. But try as she might, nothing happened.

"Damn it!" she swore after trying multiple times, "it's not working!"

"Why not?" Lluck asked.

"How should I know? If I knew, I'd do the exact opposite and make it work, wouldn't I?"

"Yeah, well, those things are gonna notice us soon, so you'd better figure it out, that's all."

"Oh, thanks for the pep talk."

"Sorry," Carl interjected, "I don't mean to interrupt, but what exactly are you trying to do?"

"She's like a wizard or something, apparently." Lluck rolled his eyes.

"No way! For real?" Carl said. "Like Merlin, or Gan—"

"No, no!" Jilly cut him off. "I'm a witch, I think. I'm descended from Granny Boatford, the sixteenth-century mystic from Knettles, who's still alive, by the way."

"How's that even possible?" Lluck crossed his arms.

"Long story," she answered. "Look, just keep your eyes open while I figure this out. If any of those things get too near, deal with it."

"How, exactly?"

"I don't know, just 'luck' your way out of it."

"Oh, just 'luck' my way out of it. Why didn't I think of that?"

"Look, I don't care. Just keep an eye out, all right?"

"Do what you have to," Carl said as they turned to face the peril, "and we'll keep them at bay. Damn it, I really need a theme song!"

* * *

Carl pulled out his gun and looked at his son. "Can you do your stuff again, for real?"

"I can try."

"Good, 'luck' my gun and see what happens."

Lluck flicked his hands at the gun. Carl held it up and pulled the trigger... and a thin squizzle of rotted veggie juice trickled from it.

"Sorry mate, uh... Dad," Lluck said. "Maybe I'm not working right after all. I couldn't help Jilly, either."

"Well, it was worth a shot, eh?"

A growling, screaming goblin, carrying a rusty old axe and running toward them snapped their attention away from each other. He seemed to be in a very bad mood. Lluck looked back to see Jilly staring intently at her book, ignoring everything around her.

"We have to do something!" Lluck yelled. "Now!"

Carl held up his gun in desperation and pulled the trigger... Squizzle.

"Damn it!" he said. "Oh, sorry son."

"No worries, I say a lot worse all the time."

"You do?"

"Dad, focus! Try again!"

The goblin was ten feet away. Squizzle.

Lluck flicked his hands again.

Five feet away.

Squizzle.

One more flick.

The goblin raised his axe.

A plume of gas shot forth from the gun, enveloping and over-powering their foe. He dropped his weapon, fell to his knees, and choked and wheezed as foul-smelling vapors rendered him completely useless.

Carl turned to Lluck and grinned. "See? What did I tell you? Nothing to worry about! Now, let's go get some more, shall we?"

* * *

Jilly was vaguely aware of a goblin retching in the near distance, but she was too preoccupied to take much notice. "Come on, you stupid turnip! This can't be that hard. Think! Focus! Do something!"

As she held her hand over the sigil in question, she began to sense some warmth and a bit of tingling in her palm. "Yes, that's it! Come on. Work!"

And it fizzled out again.

"Gah! What do I have to do?" She heard a second something-or-other go down, apparently another victim of Carl's noxious veggie gas. She held her hand over the symbol and tried again. This time, it began to glow, and she felt the energy surging off the page and into her hand.

Another beastie inhaled the mists of vegetative doom, coughing and sputtering. Carl did a backflip and landed in front of a goblin, throwing a punch that sent him sprawling.

"Maybe I'm going about this wrong," Jilly said. "Maybe I don't need to take them all down; I just need to get to him. If he falls, they all do, right?"

She placed her hand on the page and closed her eyes.

"Just think about the Erlking," she told herself. "Forget about the others."

"Jilly!"

She opened her eyes to see Lluck facing her. In the distance, Carl was mowing down Unseelies left and right with noxious veggie gas on the one hand and feats of derring-do on the other, and clearly having the time of his life doing it.

"It's back! It's working again! Try now!" He flicked his hands at her before turning his attention to more incoming imps.

She closed her eyes again. Heat ran up her hand from the symbol, sending a primal power surging through her body and out through her free hand. She thought of nothing except the monstrous master in the distance, the one who had tried to kill them all. She focused every bit of her attention on bringing him down.

Her eyes sprang open as a brilliant light burst from her hand, lighting up the battleground. A beam of energy shot straight toward the Erlking. She focused, directing every bit of her power towards him.

* * *

Qwyrk and the others watched as enchanted light surged from Jilly's hand, hitting the Erlking and the beasties nearest him hardest. He writhed and contorted in its embrace, and while his remaining minions fell to the ground or fled, their master seemed trapped in its enchanted luminance. He looked shocked, lost, and even afraid.

"Got you, you bastard!" Qwyrk pumped her fist.

"Qwyrk?" Holly gave her a worried glance.

"I've got this."

She pushed her way through the ranks, swatting and thumping, beating and bumping, tossing them aside with an ease that surprised even her. She broke through the last few of the freaky flunkies and there he was, his face contorted in anger and fear. He was alone, empty and useless, his magic spent, caught in Jilly's light.

"Well, look at that," she taunted, "most of your precious fellow wild hunters have decided to bugger off, and you have no power left. How does it feel to be the weakling, now, eh? This is over, you twat. You're finished!"

Before he could even respond, she leaped at him and unleashed her full fury.

"I..." Punch!

"Have had..." Smack!

"Just about..." Whap!

"Enough..." Pound!

"Of your crap!" Stomp!

Hit after hit connected with devastating effect. She held nothing back and savored every second of it.

The Erlking collapsed.

He sprawled, groaning beneath her, black blood staining his visage. She gripped his cowl and paused for a moment to take a breath.

It was over. He was beaten.

But she didn't want to stop. Rage surged through her, sending her into as close to drunken madness as she'd ever experienced. Raw anger fed her, provoked her, and strengthened her. She became an avenging goddess in her own right, and now this hideous creature would pay.

"I'm going to rip your miserable head off of your pathetic body and stomp it into the ground!" she yelled, grabbing him in a headlock. She laughed at how weak and pitiful he now seemed. "Who's the master now, you arsehat?" She raised her hand to deliver a killing blow.

"Qwyrk!" Jilly screamed. "Stop! Please!"

Qwyrk looked up from her rage to see Jilly running toward her. Qwyrk's eyes glowed red hot, and her vision blurred, cloudy at the edges. She looked back down at this monster, broken and beaten. She smiled and tightened her grip a little more, ready to twist his head in whatever direction it would go.

"I'm begging you! Don't do this!" Jilly cried. "It's the amulet, it's too much, just like it was for me. It saved you, but now you have to take it off. Please, save yourself by getting rid of it."

"Stay back, Jilly!" Qwyrk threatened, her heart pounding and her head aching. "This murderous bastard is going to pay for what he's done."

"And he will, I promise, but this isn't the way to do it. It's not who you are."

"You don't know me, you don't know anything about me." She pulled her grip even tighter, choking her fallen foe.

"That's not true! I know that I love you like a sister, and the real Qwyrk, the one I love, wouldn't become a murderer just to get revenge."

"It's not revenge, Jilly. It's justice!"

"Qwyrk?"

Qwyrk looked to her left to see Holly, holding out her hand. "It's me, darling. It's Holly, I'm here. Can you see me? Can you take my hand? Jilly doesn't want you to do this, and neither do I. Killing him won't bring my father back. I want justice, too, but we have to do it the right way. Let him go, take off the amulet. Come back to us... come back to *me*." She held her shaking hand out closer.

Qwyrk looked at Holly for a moment, her face like a calming stream in the heat of Qwyrk's rage.

"Holly?"

Holly smiled. "Take it off. And take my hand, please?"

With that calm came a cooling sensation, then regret and remorse, and Qwyrk's eyes filled with tears. She grabbed hold of the cord and yanked it off her neck, letting it fall to the frozen ground. She reached out to Holly's hand and took it, and in an instant, the world returned to her. Her grip on the Erlking eased, and he groaned as he thudded to the earth. Qwyrk dragged herself to her feet, threw her arms around Holly, and cried.

"I'm sorry. I'm so sorry."

"It's all right, darling, it's all right." Holly held Qwyrk as she sobbed. After some time, they parted and Qwyrk gazed at her through tear-blurred eyes, trying to smile, but not really succeeding.

"Sentimental weaklings!" the Erlking growled, pulling himself up. "Your mercy and forgiveness will be your undoing."

"Oh, shut the hell up!" Jilly stepped up, kicked him in the face, and sent him sprawling to the ground again.

"Nice one, Jilly!" Qwyrk beamed with teary pride.

"So, what are we to do with him?" Holly asked.

"That is for me to undertake!" a woman's voice boomed in the distance.

They looked over to see—yes—Star Tao striding toward them, eyes glowing, and a determined expression on his face. "Stand away from him. He is my father, and I will see justice done unto him!" The voice—deep, powerful, and commanding—emanated from his mouth.

"What?" Qwyrk, Holly, and Jilly said at the same time.

"Wait, the Erlking already has kids?" Jilly asked. "That's just wrong."

"I suppose when he couldn't claim me, he found someone else to bear him a child," Holly grimaced. "How revolting."

"Begone, Elvermø!" the Erlking coughed. "I do not know how you are here, in the body of that imbecile, but you will not have victory over me this night!"

"The choice has already been made, father dear," Elvermø answered from Star Tao's body. "You will join us beyond this Middle Earth, where you can no longer harm its peoples."

Star Tao extended a hand, which began to glow, and came closer.

"Stay back, daughter! I will not warn you again." He pointed a threatening claw at his offspring.

"Your warning has no authority over me," he answered in her voice. "It is I who now decides your fate."

"This is about the time you wanted a pet basilisk and I said 'no,' isn't it? You've never forgiven me for that. Insolent daughter!"

"Excuse me, um, hang on a second," Qwyrk interrupted, looking at Star Tao. "With all due respect, and honestly, and I don't even really know who I'm addressing. Really creepy hearing your voice come out of his mouth, by the way—yeah never going to get used to that—but we have our own quarrel with this idiot, who's basically been trying to kill us all for days, so..."

"That surprises me not," Elvermø answered. "But believe me, he will receive true justice in our realm, and this Earth will never hear of him again."

"Yeah, well, you're asking us to take a lot on trust, here," Qwyrk said. "How do we know you won't just free him as soon as you're out of sight?"

"I am the elf daughter, my word is my bond," she replied.

"Wait, you're an elf? Oh, fabulous!" Qwyrk rolled her eyes.

"And what is your issue with us?"

"You know? Just this once? Nothing, absolutely nothing at all. At this point, an eternity among silliness might be the best thing for him, actually. Carry on!"

Star Tao walked toward the Erlking, who edged away from the daughter he clearly feared, though all could see that he was too weak to flee. His remaining minions cowered and whimpered; none dared to defend him.

Star Tao reached for him with a glowing palm. "Come father, the time is at hand. Your reign of evil and fear in this world is at an end."

"Stay away from me!" he yelled. "Get back!"

But Star Tao touched the Erlking's head. The light from his hand expanded to envelop the Erlking until it was blinding, forcing Qwyrk and the others to shield their eyes. The Erlking screamed and faded into the light. Then the light itself dimmed into nothing. As it left Star Tao, he stumbled forward and he fell unconscious on his face. Jilly ran to him and tried to bring him around.

Where the Erlking had been, there was nothing but melted ice and steam.

The few remaining Darkfae gawked in wide-eyed terror, scrambled to their feet, and bolted away into the night. The Nasties cheered as they watched them flee. Bogtrotter nodded his bovine head, and whole companies of his minions set off in pursuit. "Let 'em have a bit of fun," he said, with a smile.

※ ※ ※

"So, you lot decided to come out and fight, after all," Qwyrk said, wandering over to him as his union members chased off the last of their enemies.

"Yeah, well," Bogtrotter answered, "this Erlking was a pillock and was gettin' in the way of us Nasties conductin' our business."

"Or maybe it was just the right thing to do," she said.

"Now don't be goin' around and sayin' things like that. We got a reputation to uphold, after all."

"My lips are sealed," she said with a—for once—genuine smile.

"See to it you keep it that way." He turned to leave. "And next time, I definitely want to see the dance."

"Deal! And thank you."

He flashed a toothy smile, nodded, and trotted off.

"Remind me to be there for that," Holly said.

"What? Bollocks, you weren't supposed to hear that!"

"Too late!" She laughed. Her expression turned more serious as she looked out over the battlefield, littered with bodies. Qwyrk followed her gaze to where Lluck and Carl were, already making their way toward her.

Qwyrk put a hand on her shoulder. "Go to them."

Holly placed her hand over Qwyrk's, squeezed it, and nodded.

"By the way," Qwyrk said. "I know it's 'Silambam.' I was just winding you up."

"I thought so." Holly said with a wink. And then she turned to set off.

⁕   ⁕   ⁕

"Lluck?" Holly stumbled over rough terrain, icy patches, and various fallen and unconscious Unseelies.

"Mum?"

"Lluck!" She picked up her pace into a full run. A moment later, she stood in front of him at last, but hesitant and not sure what to do.

"Mum, I, I..." Tears flooded his eyes, and it was all Holly needed to know. She wrapped her arms around him and held him tight, her own tears flowing. He returned her embrace and they hugged, holding on to each other for dear life.

"Oh, Lluck, my darling boy! I'm so sorry, I'm so, so sorry. I never should have left you alone all those years ago, I never should have..." She laid her cheek on his head and cried some more.

"It's all right mum," he cried. "It's all right."

"No, no, it's not," she sobbed, stroking his hair. "This is all my fault. You almost died because of me, because I wasn't there. Please forgive me, please..."

"I do, I do, mum! You didn't know this would happen. You couldn't have known! I know why you left me behind, I get it, all that magic and shite. I understand."

She took a step back to look at him, sniffing and wiping her eyes, before running a hand though his unkempt hair. "Look at you, just look at you! All strong, magical, powerful. I couldn't be more proud. My beautiful son."

"Um, hi."

She turned to see the man in purple, his costume ripped, the remains of his cape in tatters, his mask fallen off. He smiled a little and looked back and forth between them.

"Mum, this is..." Lluck started.

"I know," she smiled. "I remember."

He took one step forward. "I'm, uh, I'm Carl."

"I'm Holly," she sniffed with a smile.

"Brilliant," he said. "Nice to meet you, uh, again, sort of."

She let out a tearful laugh and beckoned him closer. "Oh, come here. Just come here!"

"Mum, dad, you're both here. I can't believe it!" Lluck sniffed.

Carl stepped in to embrace them both, as he began to sniffle. They all broke down and cried, holding each other tight, sobbing, laughing, crying again. Holly gave in to wave after turbulent wave of the emotions washing over her: happiness, regret, sadness, relief, and joy, all jumbled together in one amazing, lovely, terrible, magnificent mess. It was the best night of her life.

* * *

From some distance away, Qwyrk watched them and wrestled with her own happy and sad feelings. A moment later, Jilly was at her side, throwing both arms around her.

"Hey, big sis!" Jilly hugged her tight. "Guess what? I can see you now! Must have been that magic I worked before. Tipped me over into your world for good, I reckon!"

Qwyrk didn't answer right away, and Jilly looked at her a moment later. "Are you all right?"

"Sorry, that's great news. Look at them, Jilly. They're so happy. Things could've easily gone wrong, badly wrong, but there they are. Somehow, through all of it, they're reunited, or united for the first time, whatever. They're a family, they need each other."

"Yes, but Holly needs you, too!"

Qwyrk looked down at her and smiled, though it was a fake smile, and shook her head. "No, she doesn't. Come on, it's obvious. She needs to be with her son, and maybe, I don't know, maybe she wants to see if there's something there with Carl, too. It makes sense. I understand."

"I kind of doubt that."

"Well, at the risk of sounding condescending, you're young, and these things are just complicated sometimes. Happily-ever-after isn't really a thing, sorry to say. At least not for me."

"You're right, that was pretty condescending, to be honest. And why are you selling yourself short for like the millionth time? She wants to chat with you, right? In private?"

"I guess." Qwyrk fidgeted.

"Then have the chat! What have you got to lose?"

"Oh, my pride, my self-esteem, my optimism, the comfy fantasy about us that I've built up in my head. Other than all that, not much."

Jilly squeezed her again. "Oh my poor, beautiful friend. Will you just let things be and get out of your own way? I'm going to drag her over here in a minute and make you two talk if you keep up with this nonsense!"

"No need," Qwyrk said, her voice shaking. "Here she comes."

Holly had stepped back from her group hug. She kissed Lluck on the head, patted Carl on the back, and said something to both of them. They turned to walk together, arm-in-arm, toward the road. Holly and was now striding back over.

"Well," Jilly grinned. "I'm actually very busy and have to go see, um, someone about, um, something for very busy reasons. 'Cause, we're really busy and all. Bye for now!" With that, she ran off before Qwyrk could say anything else.

Qwyrk turned back to see Holly sporting a big smile and now hastening toward her. She opened her arms and ran up to Qwyrk, throwing said arms around her neck and fairly smushing Qwyrk in a huge hug as she laughed. Qwyrk was so astonished she didn't quite know how to respond, but she wrapped her arms around Holly's waist again and held her close, something she was getting very used to doing. A little too much, actually. The scents of rose and amber filled her nose again, and she almost swooned.

"We did it!" Holly fairly shouted out with glee.

"We sure as hell did! Did it, we did! It, that is. It was done by we, us, I mean."

Holly stepped back and looked at her, but kept her arms draped around Qwyrk's neck and shoulders. Her smile was like sunlight breaking through the clouds after a heavy rain. Or a single rose blooming on a spring morning. Or Blip and Star Tao buggering off somewhere and never coming back.

"Oh, Qwyrk, I can't thank you enough. I'll never be able to thank you enough!"

"Well... that's probably not true!" Qwyrk answered, shaking her head, her voice wavering and her mind reeling. "I'm just glad we stopped it all in time. Could've been a right mess, otherwise."

"It could have, but it wasn't, and you're a big part of why it wasn't."

"Yeah, um, look, I'm sorry about before, trying to hold you back. It wasn't my place to tell you what to do."

"Not at all, you were just worried. And I was wrong to be so sharp with you. But I was in a bad way and I snapped. I apologize."

"No, it's fine, really. And thank you for talking me down from killing the Erlking. 'Rage Qwyrk' isn't a good look on me, and I would've regretted it if I'd done something awful. You were amazing with that."

"No more than you. I just appealed to the remarkable woman I knew was still in there."

"Um," Qwyrk faltered, "well, it *was* a team effort."

"True, and you and I make a rather marvelous team!"

"We do?"

"I think so!" Holly beamed.

"Brilliant, lovely. Um, so..."

"So?" She raised her eyebrows.

"Yeah, so. You um, you probably have family things you want to do, right?"

"Yes, yes, of course. I'm riding back with Dill and Chives to Carl's house in Leeds, so I can catch up with both of them. I have a lot of time to make up for."

"Yeah, that makes sense." Qwyrk's heart sank. "So, um, I suppose I'll see you around some time, then?"

"Well, I should hope so!" Holly furrowed her brow. "We still have a chat to have, don't we?"

"Do we? Uh, yeah, right, we do! But, Lluck, I mean... Carl? Aren't you, I mean, are, um, you and him, you know?" Her stomach was in knots and she was terrified of what Holly might say next.

Holly looked almost sad for a moment. "Oh? Oh, Qwyrk!" She reached up and ran her fingers through Qwyrk's short hair, every now and then caressing her pointed ear tip. Qwyrk thought she might pass out right there.

"No, no," Holly said. "I love Lluck, and I'm going to be a part of his life from now on, no matter what, and of course, I also want to get to know Carl better. Even if he is a bit odd," she chuckled. "But he's also kind, loyal, brave... a good man. He'll be a wonderful father. But..."

"But?"

"But he's not…"

"Not what?" Qwyrk could hardly breathe and her heart thumped.

Holly's voice shook. "He's not you."

Qwyrk swallowed hard and flashed a nervous smile. Holly responded in kind with a nervous chuckle. They edged closer to each other. Holly parted her lips a little, and tilted her head to one side. Closer, closer. Their noses were almost touching. They both closed their eyes.

Oh, Goddess, Qwyrk's mind raced, *this is really happening!*

"All right, Qwyrk?"

"Oh, bloody hell!" Qwyrk jerked her head around to see Star Tao standing right behind her, hands in pockets and a cheeky grin on his face. She was ready to punch him and had to control the urge. Like, *really* control it. "What?"

"Yeah, sorry to bother you, right," he continued, "but the Divine Lord Blippingstone says he really needs to talk with you as soon as possible. Reconnoitering, or wrapping up, or post-battle strategic notes and debriefings, or some such. More than my mortal mind can comprehend, no doubt."

No doubt, Qwyrk almost growled. "Fine! Tell him I'll be along in a few minutes."

"Shall do, cheers!" Star Tao waved and wandered off.

She turned back to Holly, who was smirking her Holly smirk. "Is it always like this?" she smirked smirkingly.

"Sorry! Yes, unfortunately. Most often, they do my head in. I have to keep reminding myself that they're good folks and actually *have* made a difference. But sometimes, I just want to smack the lot of them, except Jilly, of course."

"She's a remarkable young lady."

"She is. And she's only going to get more amazing as she gets older, kind of like your boy."

"Speaking of which, I should probably get back to him," Holly pointed towards Lluck and Carl.

"Right, yes! Of course!"

"So, that chat?"

"Um, tomorrow?"

Holly nodded. "As I said, I suspect I'll be up till all hours, but maybe early afternoon, say one o'clock? At the inn? Fewer distractions that way."

"Sounds brilliant! One it is."

"Right then."

"Right!"

"I'm going."

"Good! I mean, not good that you're going, but good that we've got a plan."

"We do."

"Indeed, we do."

"Good night, then, and thank you again, ever so much." Holly stepped back, gave her a lingering glance, smiled, and turned away.

Qwyrk thought she was ready to let her go, to stand back and allow her to disappear into the night without another word. But she couldn't, not this time.

"Oh, sod it!" Instead, she reached out to Holly and, touching her shoulder, turned her to face her again. She took hold of Holly's coat lapel and, pulling her close, planted a kiss on her lips. Not a long kiss, mind you, but more than a quick peck, and certainly enough to say what she needed to say without actually saying it. It was lovely, perfect, everything she could have hoped for. But short, far too short, even if it was also just right.

As they parted, Holly looked astonished, but delighted. "You *are* forward, Ms. Qwyrk." She flashed a warm smile. "Though, the offer to save me at any time still stands, however you'd like."

"Brilliant! I'll keep that in mind, then! Getting into trouble of all kinds is a specialty of mine! Um, I mean, you know what I mean."

"I'm sure I don't." Holly grinned with mischief, turned away, and strolled back toward her son and Carl, without another word.

Qwyrk stood there, staring after her, still not sure what had just happened, and contemplating either doing cartwheels or just fainting.

"All right?" Star Tao was behind her again.

She sighed, and turned to face him. "What now?"

He smiled knowingly. What on Earth was he about to say? She cringed.

"I just want to let you know, I get it now."

"You... get it."

"Yeah, it all makes sense."

"Well, that's good, I guess. Um, what makes sense, exactly?"

"You know."

"Nnnno, not really."

"Come on, I mean, I see it. You fancy the ladies, right? That's brilliant. That's groovy. I'm absolutely down with that. And she's quite the looker, I must say. It totally explains why you weren't keen on me when we first met last summer. I understand now, and I want you to know I'm fine with it!"

She stared at him blankly for a moment, or three, or seven. "Yeah... all right, we'll just go with that, then."

"No worries, cheers!"

And off he wandered again.

Qwyrk would normally be exasperated, but for once, just this once, she found him—all of them in fact—endearing. She smiled as she wandered across the almost-sacrifice site and watched Holly and the others get into Dill and Chive's car and drive away.

"I'm sure I don't," she repeated with a silly grin, in imitation of Holly's gorgeously posh accent. "Oh... I'm sure you do!"

CHAPTER TWENTY-TWO

"All things considered, it could have been a far worse evening, Mr. Dill." The unusual duo returned to their car.

"I concur, Mr. Chives. Though the outcome was uncertain, and the methods used were unorthodox, in the end, a desirable conclusion was nevertheless achieved."

"Though, things did look a bit dire for a while, Mr. Dill."

"They did, indeed, Mr. Chives."

"Happily, our client has been reunited with her son and the lad's father. I've informed them that we will provide transportation back to his home, and they seem amenable to that suggestion. In fact, here come the man and his son now."

"A generous offer, Mr. Chives. Should we consult in any way with the others? The Shadow and her cadre?"

"I think that falls outside of the purview of this investigation, Mr. Dill. Though Ms. Qwyrk and her unusual colleagues do seem to have a knack for getting themselves into the middle of absurd and apocalyptic supernatural crises, so it might behoove us to watch them from afar for a while."

"Are you suggesting that something is afoot, Mr. Chives?"

"Not necessarily, Mr. Dill, but an increase in such events could foreshadow a bigger happening, so forewarned is forearmed, as the saying goes."

"I concur, Mr. Chives. I propose that we put Qwyrk and her companions on our watch list and return to them as needed."

"An excellent suggestion, Mr. Dill, an excellent suggestion, indeed."

*　*　*

Jilly hurried over to Lluck and Carl as they made their way towards the car.

"Hi," she said.

"All right?" Lluck answered.

"Um, Carl, could I speak to Lluck for a moment?" Jilly asked. "Alone?"

"Sure, of course." He turned to Lluck, "I'll see you at the car, son." Lluck nodded.

"I'm so sorry again about your friend," Jilly said. "I promise Qwyrk will take care of him, and bring his body back to her world."

"He wasn't really my friend," Lluck said. "I mean, he's the one that kidnapped me, for freak's sake. But he tried to do the right thing in the end, and it got him killed. It's weird; I've never seen anyone die before."

"I have," Jilly said as she put a hand on his arm. "It's horrid, and it never gets easier. But if you want to talk about it, I'm here for a listen, seriously. It might be good for me, too. I've seen some completely mad things since last June, and it would be nice to have someone to talk to who's more, I don't know, like me?"

"Yeah, I might well take you up on that. How do I get in touch with you?"

Jilly searched her pockets. "I don't have a pen on me, sorry. But tell your mum and she'll take care of it."

"Yeah, she'll probably get in touch with Qwyrk, or something."

"I have no doubt about that." Jilly teased.

"What?"

"Nothing. But you *do* know your mum really fancies Qwyrk, right?"

"Hadn't thought about it, to be honest." He happened to glance over at Qwyrk and Holly. "But yeah, they do seem to be quite keen on each other, now that you mention it. That's all right, I suppose. But I do kinda wish..." He looked down.

"What?"

"Well, that she and Carl and I could be like a family, you know?"

"You *are* a family now, no matter where she is, or who she's with. She loves you so much, and she's not letting you go again."

"I guess."

"And with Qwyrk in the picture, you've also got me, Blip, and all us crazy magic folks for an extended family!"

"Yeah, cheers for ruining the moment."

"Oh, you're funny!"

"I think so." He flashed a smug expression.

"Go on, give us a hug then." She threw her arms around him before he could deflect, but he embraced her awkwardly. She found she rather liked it.

"Um, I should go to my dad," he said.

"Yeah, off with you. And get in touch, really. This stuff's a bit overwhelming, and I can help."

"I will, I promise, when things get a bit more settled. Cheers, then, bye!"

They waved at each other and he turned and hurried off.

"He seems like a good lad," Star Tao said, coming up and putting an arm around her.

"Yeah, he's had a hell of a week! Kind of like ours last summer. I'll try to help him out a bit, and maybe he can help me, too. I've got this whole witch thing to figure out."

"Yeah, that's brilliant! I'll be havin' you teach one of me workshops, some day!"

Jilly gazed up at the stars, her mind reeling with all the possibilities of where her new magical life might lead. "I think I'd like that very much."

* * *

As she made sure none of the Erlking's minions remained (and avoided Blip's reconnoitering), Qwyrk spied her former goblin nemeses hiding in the shadows. She figured that acknowledging them was the right thing to do, so she wandered over to them, trying to be as non-threatening as possible.

"Hi. Um, it was good of you to help out," she said. "I mean, I'm not sure exactly why you came back, but thanks." She looked at Silktassel, "And your head's looking a lot better, by the way. Hooray for that?"

"Yeah well," Sneezewort responded, "we felt a bit bad about it, what with you helpin' us out and all, so it was the least we could do."

"So," she said, "since you bailed on the Erlking, what now?"

"I always fancied opening up a nice lit'le tea and coffee shop." Sneezewort mimed sipping tea, pinky extended, of course.

"Tea and coffee shop?" Qwyrk furrowed her brow.

"Yeah, I gotta nose for smells, ya know? Real good at discernin' fine aromas. I'd have a good go at sourcin' out lovely coffees and dainty teas like Earl Greys, and maybe some of the flowery ones. That'd be real nice."

"Um, you are the same goblin that was going to bite my head off the other night, right?"

"Yeah, again, sorry about that. That was the Erlking's doin'. I was gettin' drunk on his power and stuff. No hard feelings, eh?" He held out his lumpy hand. Qwyrk stared at him.

"Um, right. Anyway, so where exactly are you going to do this, um, tea shop?"

"Well, that's the thing; don't know yet. I figure I'd have to cater to both mortals and magics, you know? Just to encourage the biggest possible number of customers. Maybe have coffee and cakes on one side of the menu and things like peach pit tea and raw blood sausage on the other. I mean, folks could order whatever they like from either side, of course. No judgements."

"Oh, I do love a good raw blood sausage!" Silktassel interjected. "Especially with a side of sautéed mealworms with garlic!"

"See, that's what I'm thinking!" Sneezewort slapped Silktassel on the shoulder.

"Well, that all sounds... lovely?" Qwyrk forced down some mild revulsion. "I'm sure you'll make a good go at it. Just promise me you'll both leave the boy alone in the future, all right? I don't want to have to bust your heads again."

"Not a problem," Silktassel said with confidence. "We were only doing the Erlking's bidding because he looked like he was on the winnin' side. Now, we are happy to bugger off as far away from you as possible."

Sneezewort nodded. "Yeah, I always thought he was a right twat, anyway. I don't care what the lucky boy does; I got me business to plan."

"Right," Qwyrk said, looking back and forth between them with disbelief. "Have fun with all that!"

* * *

Everything had been set to right, all the flames had been extinguished, and all the remaining Unseelies had been thumped or chased off back to their own dimensions. True to her word, Qwyrk gently laid Longwing's body down on the ground in front of them, ready to take him and the rest of the Farce Force back to her world, Blip's beast included.

"It's so sad," Jilly said. "He seemed like a good bloke, just lost his way a bit."

Qwyrk nodded. "That's what happens when angry, bitter old folks taint the young with their poison to get what they want."

"Yeah," Jilly answered. "He threatened Longwing's sister, too, but at some point, Longwing figured out it was all a bluff, or that she was too strong for him to hurt her."

"Who is the sister, if I may ask?" Blip said.

Qwyrk shook her head. "No idea, but it sounds like she's someone we should find. I don't know if she and Longwing were in touch, but she deserves to know what happened to him, at least."

"And if she's in trouble, we can help her," Jilly offered.

Qwyrk smiled and put a hand on her shoulder. "Always thinking of others, aren't you?"

"I kind of picked that up from someone." Jilly put her own hand on Qwyrk's.

"We'll see that he's given a proper funeral," Qwyrk said, "and try to find any family or friends he may have had. Come on, then."

Qwyrk waved her hand, and they disappeared from this world.

* * *

After leaving Longwing and Snickerwocky with Qwyzz (along with that troublesome amulet; the gargoyles were quite fascinated with the dragon, it must be said), she winked the Farce Force back to Jilly's home in Knettles, fortunately before Jilly's parents had returned from yet another of their interminable evening gatherings. Qwyrk again pitied Jilly, but it did make their comings and goings at all hours so much easier.

"So," she turned to Star Tao, "who exactly did you channel back there? The Erlking called her his daughter?"

"Yeah," Star Tao answered, "as far as I can tell, he's got a whole elvish family somewhere else who were right annoyed with him. I think I must have channeled another of them when I was here."

"Yeah, that was scary," Jilly said.

"Sorry about that! But none of them could really get over here to do anything or stop him, or they'd have done it already. Maybe they got stuck in another dimension a long time ago, or something. Anyway, she came through loud and clear; must have been all that magic he was usin'. She used my form to work her own mojo, I guess, and that was that. Don't think we'll be seein' him again any time soon."

"I still don't know how you do it," Qwyrk said, shaking her head. "But thanks, honestly. It saved us a lot of trouble."

"No worries. Happy to help." He swayed back and forth with a big smile as if dancing to a space rock tune. "Right, this has been groovy, as always, but I really should head on out and back over to Manchester. Freedom's, I mean, Qwypp's bound to be worried, and she's probably gonna be right mad that we didn't bring her along."

"Well, give her my best," Qwyrk said, "and maybe don't tell her all the details? Problem solved!"

"You know she'll find out sooner or later," Jilly said.

"Yeah, you're right. Maybe just tell her it all happened too fast? That's actually mostly true," Qwyrk offered. "And tell her to get in touch with me, already! We haven't chatted in ages!"

"Shall do, and no worries, I'll come up with something to explain it all. Thanks again, everyone!" Star Tao gave Jilly a hug, Qwyrk a handshake (which Qwyrk suspected had something to do with his new-found "knowledge" about her), and bowed deeply at Blip. "Farewell, my lord. Until our next encounter."

"I look forward to it, young man! Keep spreading my good news in those workshop affairs of yours."

"I shall, oh lord." He nodded, and then let himself out the front door with a final wave.

"Well, I know you two don't sleep," Jilly said with a yawn, "but I am knackered! Magic really takes it out of you. I'm going to have a bath and go to bed. Mum and dad will be home soon, so you might want to dash off, too."

"Good night, dear one," Blip said, giving her another of his usual, awkward hugs. "I am going to attend to my steed and will speak with you anon. Cheerio!" He walked into a nearby wall and vanished.

"So, what are you going to do with this new-found magic of yours, which was amazing tonight, by the way? I suspect you passed your first test with ease." Qwyrk wrapped a proud arm around Jilly's shoulder.

"I'll check in with Granny tomorrow and find out; I'm sure she'll want to know everything."

"Well, *I'm* sure it's the start of an amazing adventure, and you'll have to tell me all about it. I want to know what you actually did at the cave and out on the Moors. That was seriously impressive."

"Heh! You and me both. I'll let you know when I do. But what about you, then? Any big plans in your near future?" Jilly winked.

Qwyrk's cheeks flushed. "Well, I *might* just be meeting up with someone at some place about something tomorrow." She tried to suppress a smile, but couldn't.

Jilly giggled and squeezed her hand. "Good night, then. Sweet dreams, or whatever it is you do when you're not awake. You really don't sleep, do you?"

"Not really," Qwyrk said. "But after the last few days, maybe tonight, I'll try to."

* * *

Sure enough, the next afternoon (but having not slept, because it still wasn't necessary), Qwyrk found herself, yet again, at the inn on the country lane north of Leeds.

"I'm getting too familiar with this place," she said. "I'm going to scare the daylights out of someone."

She slipped in the back door and left an apologetic letter and a £20 note on a small table for the lock she'd angrily broken. She made her way up the stairs as quietly as possible, and walked down the hall to Holly's room; the green door was ajar.

"Holly?" She pushed it open and peered inside. The room was

empty. She felt a twinge of disappointment. There was no sign that Holly had ever been there.

"This is odd."

She looked around a bit more: under the bed, in the closet, but every trace of her charming new friend was gone.

Feeling a bit rejected, she turned to leave.

But she saw a note on the back of the door. Well, it wasn't really attached to the door; it floated right next to it.

She swiped it from the air with giddy excitement and began to read:

Dearest Qwyrk:

Hoping you find this in time, as I didn't have another way of contacting you. Foolishly, I forgot about setting that up with you in all the commotion of the last few days.

I'm still with Lluck and Carl at Carl's home today. Things ran late, so I dashed here and then back over there. There are some more things we needed to talk about, so I've left this Fae-gram.

But if you, Jilly, and Blip can manage it, I'd love to see you all afterward. Perhaps at Nicewood Park in Leeds, on the west side, near the forest? Should be good for hiding from too many curious human eyes! Say, 3:00pm, sun or snow? And perhaps we can go for a wander and have that chat we've been meaning to have as well?

Missing you until then.

~ H xoxo

Qwyrk clutched the note to her chest, then read it again. And a third time. She let out a little laugh, tucked the treasured missive into her jacket pocket, and bounded out of the inn, as light as a feather. Now to fetch Jilly and Blip, and maybe have a rendezvous with destiny, or something like that.

*　*　*

Holly and Carl stepped out of his house and paused at the front door. A light snow fell over them.

"Thank you again," she said. "I'm tired but blissful at having spent the night catching up with you both."

"No, thank you. It was better than I could've hoped."

"So, do you think he'll be able to stay with you?" she asked.

"Well, the solicitor I chatted to on the phone earlier while you were sleeping on the couch said I'll need to take a paternity test, and there's some other legal matters to sort out, but yeah, once that's done, if he wants to come here and live with me—which he does—he should be able to. I'll make appointments to set it all in motion as soon as possible. I think I've got a good case. I'm a respectable business owner, thank you very much. And the authorities don't need to know about my, um, nighttime activities. Plus, I think his foster family would be happy to be rid of him, honestly."

"I'm so glad he can live with you. All I've ever wanted for him was a good, happy home. Some place where he could feel safe, and loved."

"And he will, I promise. But, what about you? You could live here too, if you wanted. We could be a family. I'm sure he'd love to have you around. And I know I would."

Holly knew her sadness showed on her face. "I can't stay here with you, Carl, even if I wanted to. If I'm not connected to a forest, I grow weak; I could even die. And you two can't come and live with me; you'd go mad from the magic in my realm. Our worlds are just too different; mortals and Fae can't mingle for long. That's just the way it's always been."

She gave him a caring smile.

"We had a lovely night together all those years ago when I needed someone, but it can never be more than that, I'm afraid. Beyond all that, I love Lluck and I love you, too, but I'm not *in love* with you, and I couldn't live a lie. It wouldn't be fair to either of us."

Carl frowned and nodded. "No, it's all right. I understand. I figured you've already got someone, anyway."

"Maybe? I'm not sure yet. Honestly, I don't know. But I'd like to find out."

"Well, whoever it is, they're very lucky, and I wish you nothing but happiness."

Holly rested a hand on his cheek. "You already have the best part of me here, with you. And I'll be back, often. I want to train him, help him learn how to use his powers properly, and I could teach you some Silambam."

"What, that fancy martial arts thing you do with the stick?"

She nodded.

"Oh, that would be brilliant!"

"You'll need some combat skills if you're going to go out risking your life helping people at night."

"I'm down for that, thank you! You're the best, Holly; it's an honor to know you."

"The honor is mine. We made something beautiful together, and I think one day, he's going to help both of our worlds."

"He's a special lad, all right. I never thought I could be this proud of something I've done."

Holly smiled. "I should go. I have to meet our other friends and thank them, too."

"Ah, well, give them my best."

"Of course."

She hugged him, gave him a quick kiss on the lips, and then stepped down to the snowy pavement. She walked to the car where Dill and Chives waited.

"Gentlemen! I trust that payment has been made to your satisfaction?"

"It has, indeed ma'am," Chives replied. "It has been our pleasure doing business with you. Please do not hesitate to call on us again, should the need arise and you find yourself in another supernatural predicament."

"I certainly will! Might I trouble you for a stopover in Nicewood Park for a bit before you drop me off? Our other friends are waiting there, and I'd like to thank them, as well."

"It would be our pleasure ma'am; anything to accommodate a well-paying client."

* * *

Soon after, an unusual meeting of unusual beings convened in Nicewood Park. They met near the edge of a forest, well away from prying mortal eyes. A bit of blue sky peeked through the clouds as Qwyrk, Jilly, and Blip conversed with Holly. Dill and Chives chatted by their car in the distance, probably about their next case, which no doubt involved misplaced mummies, vanishing vampires, or edgy eldritch grimoires.

"So, according to the news, Mr. Greylocke is taking an 'indefinite leave of absence' from his company. Yeah, I'll bet he is!" Jilly laughed.

"He will not be missed," Blip declared. "Deceptive scoundrel!"

"I still can't believe we did it!" Holly said, beaming.

"We all did," Jilly responded. "You were amazing, Holly!" She flashed a quick, knowing look at Qwyrk, who steadfastly ignored her.

"Oh," Holly answered sounding a bit embarrassed, "it's just what my mother taught me; she gets the credit. But in any case, I can't thank you enough."

"It was our pleasure," Qwyrk smiled, her voice faltering a little. "Really, I'm just glad we were able to get to him in time—and save the world again, too. I mean that was a nice bonus, all things considered."

Holly laughed. "It certainly was. You helped me save my son's life. I'll always be grateful to all of you." Her eyes never left Qwyrk's.

Qwyrk swallowed hard and tried to ignore a wash of nerves. She seemed to be doing that a lot lately. "Gratitude is... nice."

Jilly flashed an exaggerated smile at Holly. "Um, Holly, can you excuse us for just a minute?"

"Of course. I'm sure Mr. Blippingstone will be delighted to keep me entertained."

"Well, I am rather known for my enthralling and illuminating discourse, as you're no doubt well aware," Blip announced proudly. "Come, my dear, I shall regale you with a stirring discussion of the Hegelian dialectic as it pertains to the early decades of German Romanticism, a very apropos topic considering what we've all just been through, I daresay!"

Qwyrk was not in the slightest pleased to leave them alone

together. "If he screws this up for me, I'll kill him. I mean, really kill him."

Jilly took her aside. Or rather, she grabbed her arm and pulled her into the tree cover, out of earshot.

"So, you're going to talk to her, right? You promised!"

"Yeah, yeah, I will. I'll do it. I'm just working myself up to it, you know?"

"Qwyrk..."

"All right! Just, at least let me get ready."

"You've had ages to get ready; you're doing this, today, now!"

Qwyrk exhaled and paced back and forth. Looking over, she saw that Blip was already expounding, gesticulating, and blathering, and Holly, bless her, was at least feigning interest.

"I don't believe you." Jilly threw up her hands. "You helped take down William de Soulis, Redcap, and the Erlking, and stopped the end of the world—twice—and now you're scared of going and talking to her? What's there to be afraid of? She obviously adores you! Go. Now! Before I drag you back over to her and supervise the whole thing myself! Do something daring, something romantic."

Qwyrk fidgeted; her heart raced. She looked over again at Holly, in that long purple coat, that voluminous grey scarf bundled around her neck, and her loose raven-black mane sprinkled here and there with little snowflakes. Damn it. Holly gave her a quick glance and smiled. The butterflies in Qwyrk's stomach felt more like pterodactyls.

"Bollocks. Bollicky, bollicking, bollocked, bollocks! Right, fine, you win. To hell with it; I'm doing this. Um, Holly!" She strode back toward her. Jilly grinned and clapped her hands a little, but Qwyrk ignored her.

"Yes?" Holly turned.

"Can I, um, talk to you for a bit?" Qwyrk worried that she looked far too eager. Blip seemed miffed to have been interrupted, but she ignored him, too. "Can we, maybe, you know, go for a walk and have that chat before you head out?"

Holly gave her a warm smile. "Of course, I'd be delighted. Do excuse me, Mr. Blippingstone. Shall we continue this anon?"

Blip scowled and mumbled, "Some other time, then."

Qwyrk somehow kept her wits. *Don't cock this up, you pillock!* They strolled away from the others.

"So, there's something we were going to talk about, if I recall," Holly said, as she took Qwyrk's arm and they walked off alone.

"Yeah, about that. I was, I was thinking, because, heh, I do that sometimes," Qwyrk started and stuttered. "There's this brilliant out-crop at Sutton Bank in the Moors overlooking the countryside. It's really pretty at this time of year, all covered in snow, and I was just, well, wondering, if you'd, you know, like to, maybe, I don't know, go see it with me and watch the sunrise some morning? I mean, obviously when it's not snowing, otherwise, there wouldn't be any sunrise to see and that would just be stupid, but maybe sometime while it's still winter, because you know, it, it snows in winter and wouldn't really work so well in, I don't know, say, July—but it's real nice then and that's good, too—but snow, snow's only around when it's cold, so we'd need to go there before it melts, whenever that hap-pens, which I suppose is when it warms up, probably." *Oh Goddess, just kill me now!*

Holly stifled a giggle. "Are you asking me out on a date?"

"No! I mean, maybe? I mean, I don't know. Do you, do you want it to be date?"

"I think it sounds lovely."

Qwyrk almost gasped in relief. "Great! Okay, right, um, I mean it's cold up there—obviously with the snow and all—but I could bring a wool wrap or something and we could, well, wrap it around ourselves and maybe you could drink something to keep you warm? A bottle of single malt scotch or something."

Holly laughed. "That may not be the best idea. I mean, look what happened the last time I had a whole bottle to myself!"

Qwyrk waved her hands. "No, no, I didn't mean it that way! I was just thinking about how I could warm you up." *Please just let the earth open up and swallow me...*

Holly looked down with an embarrassed smile.

"So, um, great!" Qwyrk offered after a moment of awkward silence. "We'll make a plan, and do it! Go sit and take it all in, sometime soon? Yeah, while there's snow, but sun, too. You know, sun-snow, snowy sun, snowy snow, something. Um, anyway." She stopped walking. "How do I get in touch with you? Do you have like a faerie mobile or something? I don't really use Earth technologies all that much, myself. Jilly's the computer whiz."

Holly held up her hands, palms facing each other, and a green light swirled between them. A slender gold ring set with a little green stone appeared in her lower palm.

"Give me your hand."

Qwyrk held out her right hand, hoping it wasn't shaking too much. Holly slipped the band onto her ring finger, and it fit perfectly. Holly's hands were inviting; Qwyrk didn't want her to let go.

"Use this. I gave one of these to Lluck as well. All you have to do is look at it, think about me, say my name, and I'll hear. If I'm able, I'll contact you back right away. I mean, unless I'm having a bath, or something."

Qwyrk's mind wandered off for a moment. "Um, great,

fantastic, thanks! So, I'll be thinking about you soon, probably all night, *to*night, 1 mean... you know what 1 mean! I'll be touching myself—BE IN TOUCH—um, bollocks. I'll contact you tonight. We'll set up a day this week, hopefully a really cold day with snowy snow and sunny sun, and nothing melting, yeah?" *I'm such a prat!*

Holly laughed, and Qwyrk thought she seemed a bit flustered. *Well that makes two of us.*

"Sounds lovely. Bye for now, then?" Holly said. She kissed Qwyrk's cheek and cast her a lingering gaze before turning away.

Qwyrk nodded and just stood there, poised precariously somewhere between wanting to dance with joy and needing to throw up.

"Coffee," Holly said after a few paces.

"What?"

Holly looked back at her. "Bring coffee. You know, for 'warming me up'? That will be lovely."

"Oh, right! Of course. I'll do that. Probably without the scotch, though."

"That would be for the best. Bye for now, then." Holly gave her a wink and a wave, and then turned around. She also waved at Jilly and Blip before walking back to where Dill and Chives stood waiting. She chatted with them for a moment, and Qwyrk watched as they all got in the car and drove off.

Somehow, Qwyrk managed to trudge back to her friends without falling over multiple times. And sure enough, Jilly stood with her arms folded and a wide, silly grin beaming across her face.

"What?" Qwyrk asked in annoyance, but also wanting to burst into song.

"You asked her out on a date, didn't you? And I'm guessing she said 'yes.' And you *know* I'm never going to stop teasing you about this!"

"Oh, please! We're just going to have a friendly morning get-to-gether over coffee, you know, watching a country sunrise, huddled together under a shawl... oh, all right, it's a date!"

Jilly giggled and bounced with joy.

"Look, it's not that big of a deal, yeah? We're just going to spend some time together, see if we get on, see how it goes."

"Qwyrk has a cru-ush! Holly has a cru-ush!"

"Oh, shut up!"

"Qwyrk and Holly, sitting in a tree, K-I-S-S-..."

"Look, I'm warning you!"

"Ahem." Blip came striding up. "If you're quite done with court-ship overtures to your comely dowsabel, may we leave now? As fond as I am of the winter months, it's getting a bit unpleasant out among the elements, and somewhere warmer would be of benefit to my increasingly chilled extremities."

"You're right, Blip." Qwyrk was actually relieved for his inter-ruption. "We should go back to Jilly's. You two could do with being somewhere warm."

"Splendid idea. A fine aged brandy and Bach's *Musical Offering* would be most welcome at the moment."

"Still," Qwyrk said, "it would be a shame not to take in some of this lovely snow-covered countryside on our way back, don't you think?"

"What are you talking about?" Blip answered with alarm.

"I mean, look at all this gorgeous fresh snow. It'll look even nicer outside the city, especially if we can see it from above."

"Now just a damned minute, girl! You're not suggesting what I think you're..."

"Come on!" Qwyrk wrapped her left arm around Jilly's waist.

"Are you going to do what I hope you're going to?" Jilly giggled.

"Damn you, Qwyrk," Blip swore. "I will not be a part of this! I will not..."

But Qwyrk scooped him up and slung him over her right shoulder.

"Merciful melodic merfolk, woman, put me down at once!" He beat on her back with his fists, but to no avail.

"Oh Blip, where's your sense of fun?" Qwyrk teased.

"In the pit of my stomach, where it won't stay for very long if you do what you're about to do!"

"Too bad, mate. I'm in a lovely mood and I want to jump for joy! Literally. Several times, actually. All the way back to Knettles, in fact!"

"Put me down at once! Put me... aaahhhghghGHGHGH!"

Qwyrk had already bounded into the sky, with Jilly squealing in delight and Blip shrieking in terror; both sounds were music to her ears. As she flew through the cold air, the lovely wintry landscape of Yorkshire spread out below them, she laughed out loud.

ACKNOWLEDGEMENTS

This second trip into the strange and silly world of Qwyrk and her friends has proved to be even more fun to write than the first book. As with *Qwyrk*, there were once more several good people behind the scenes who made the writing process enjoyable. Thanks again to my agent Maryann Karinch, for believing in this odd series and wanting to share it with the world, and thanks to Armin Lear for providing a home for it. There's more to come!

Special thanks to my wonderful partner, Abigail Keyes, for enduring these stories as I dramatically read them out to her, audio book style. And thanks for her amazing editing skills. Once again, she's taken my draft (first, second, third, you name it) and turned it into something special that I'm proud of.

Thanks to my readers: Heidi Waterman, Samara Metzler, Laura Tempest Zakroff, and Donna Manalo, for feedback that helped make the book so much better. Each of them offered suggestions that greatly improved the story as a whole. Also, special thanks to Laura Tempest Zakroff, for introducing me to the delightful Lady Quintessa Apple Fairybottom!

Finally, thanks again to Freya, for continuing inspiration and insight.

Coming Soon!

CHANTZ

It's like Qwyrk can never get a break. Spring is springing, but she's stuck breaking up drunken faerie fights as Beltane approaches. She really wants to take things to the next level with her possibly-probably-girlfriend Holly, but keeps coming down with a chronic case of the chickens. And now, her best human friend, Jilly Pleeth, has had a rather odd encounter while at a concert featuring her favorite new band, the Mystic Wedding Weasels. Jilly is struck (quite literally) by their enigmatic Irish singer's voice; there's something downright magical about it, and her.

It turns out that there may be more to said singer—who performs under the stage name "Chantz"—than meets the eye, or ear. Our friends soon discover that something has attached itself to the young lady. If this entity gets what it wants, things could become very bad, very soon.

Meanwhile, Qwyrk's romantic preoccupation lands her in trouble with the council she reports to... well, more trouble than she's usually in. And behind everything, there seems to lurk a new menace, perhaps the most dangerous one of all. The conspiracy that Qwyrk has feared since last summer may be unfolding at last.

Chantz is the third in a series of four novels about the comic misadventures of a group of misfits at the edge of normal reality in modern northern England, a world of shadows, Nighttime Nasties, eldritch screaming horrors, appalling neo-Shakespearean sonnets, undead corvids, an abundance of sarcasm, and bloody hell... Qwyrk is *not* an elf, all right? They're just silly!

AUTHOR BIO

Tim Rayborn is an internationally acclaimed musician. He plays dozens of unusual instruments that quite a few people of have never heard of and often can't pronounce, including medieval instrument reconstructions and folk instruments from Northern Europe, the Balkans, and the Middle East.

He has appeared on over forty recordings, and his musical wanderings and tours have taken him across the US, all over Europe, to Canada and Australia, and to such romantic locations as Marrakech,

Istanbul, Renaissance chateaux, medieval churches, and high school gymnasiums.

On the writing side of things, Tim lived in England for nearly seven years and has a PhD from the University of Leeds, which he likes to pretend means that he knows what he's talking about. He has written a large number of books and magazine articles about music, the arts, history, the strange and bizarre, and general knowledge, and undoubtedly will write more (whether anyone wants him to or not).

He currently lives and writes amid many books, antique musical reproduction devices (i.e., CDs), and instruments, as well as with a sometimes-demanding cat. He is rather enthusiastic about good wines, smoky single-malt Scotch, and cooking excellent food.

timrayborn.com
timrayborn.bandcamp.com
twitter.com/Tim_Rayborn
facebook.com/TimRaybornMusicandWriting

www.ingramcontent.com/pod-product-compliance
Lightning Source LLC
Chambersburg PA
CBHW030550020726
47494CB00005B/1555